Praise f

'A MUST READ in my book!!'

'Utterly perfect . . . A timeslip tale that
leaves you wanting more . . . I loved it'

'I may have shed a tear or two! . . .
A definite emotional rollercoaster of a read
that will make you both cry and smile'

'Oh my goodness . . . The pages turned
increasingly quickly as my desperation to find
out what happened steadily grew and grew'

'Very special . . . I loved every minute of it'

'Brilliant . . . Very highly recommended!!'

'Touched my heart! A real page turner . . .
The perfect read for cosying up. I can't recommend
this gorgeous book enough'

KATHLEEN MCGURL lives in Christchurch with her husband. She has two sons who have both now left home. She always wanted to write, and for many years was waiting until she had the time. Eventually, she came to the bitter realisation that no one would pay her for a year off work to write a book, so she sat down and started to write one anyway. Since then, she has published several novels with HQ and self-published another. She has also sold dozens of short stories to women's magazines, and written three How To books for writers. After a long career in the IT industry, she became a full-time writer in 2019. When she's not writing, she's often out running, slowly.

Also by Kathleen McGurl

The Emerald Comb
The Pearl Locket
The Daughters of Red Hill Hall
The Girl from Ballymor
The Drowned Village
The Forgotten Secret
The Stationmaster's Daughter
The Secret of the Château
The Forgotten Gift
The Lost Sister
The Girl from Bletchley Park
The Storm Girl

The Girl with
the Emerald Flag

KATHLEEN MCGURL

ONE PLACE. MANY STORIES

HQ
An imprint of HarperCollins*Publishers* Ltd
1 London Bridge Street
London SE1 9GF

www.harpercollins.co.uk

HarperCollins*Publishers*
Macken House, 39/40 Mayor Street Upper,
Dublin 1 D01 C9W8
Ireland

This paperback edition 2023

1

First published in Great Britain by
HQ, an imprint of HarperCollins*Publishers* Ltd 2022

Copyright © Kathleen McGurl 2022

Kathleen McGurl asserts the moral right to be
identified as the author of this work.
A catalogue record for this book is
available from the British Library.

ISBN: 9780008480905

MIX
Paper | Supporting
responsible forestry
FSC™ C007454

This book is produced from independently certified FSC™ paper
to ensure responsible forest management.

For more information visit: www.harpercollins.co.uk/green

Printed and bound in the UK using 100% Renewable Electricity
by CPI Group (UK) Ltd, Croydon, CR0 4YY

For Jo, Lu and Ali
my friends for so very many years

All changed, changed utterly:
A terrible beauty is born.

— *W.B. Yeats, 'Easter 1916'*

Prologue – May 1916

She wondered if she'd simply dreamt it all, for a sweet, brief moment that morning when she woke at dawn. Perhaps none of it had really happened: last night in the prison chapel, the few days in a cell with other women, and even the week before that, the week of rebellion. Was any of it real?

In her hand she was clutching a handkerchief. She brought it to her face, wondering if it held any scent of either of them. But there was nothing. The initials, GG and JP, were embroidered in a corner, entwined in a loving knot. It had been dropped and forgotten, last night in the chapel, and she'd picked it up. Holding it now gave Gráinne a little comfort – it was a tiny reminder that things had once been normal, handkerchiefs had been embroidered and given as gifts, and maybe those days might come again, in time.

She thought about her friend Grace who'd embroidered the handkerchief, and Joseph to whom it had been given, and wondered what they were doing now, what they were thinking, how they were dealing with the horrors of this day that had barely even begun.

And as she had that thought, shots rang out in the prison yard, as Gráinne had known they would. A volley of shots, fired all at once, on a command given by some unknown officer. A volley of shots that ended the life of someone Gráinne had fought alongside. She crossed herself and muttered a prayer for the soul of whoever it was, bringing the handkerchief close to her face once more.

Was it all worth it? Had any of it been worth it? They had not succeeded, not the way she'd hoped they would. It had all ended in less than a week, with loss of life, and now . . . these terrible dawn executions. The rebellion had ripped the city apart, it had torn families and loved ones apart. Grace and Joseph, herself and Emmett. They'd fought for what they believed in, fought for the greater good, but for themselves as individuals it had been little more than a tragic disaster.

She'd never forget a minute of it, she knew. She was so young still, but for as long as she lived, she knew this last week or two would shape her life for ever.

Chapter 1 – February 1998

Nicky didn't really have a lot of choice. Mum was coming today, whether Nicky liked it or not. And if she didn't go to meet her mum in the campus café as arranged, Mum would come up to Nicky's accommodation and bang on the door demanding to be let in. It would be *so* embarrassing. Why couldn't she just leave her alone? Nicky was 19. She was an *adult*, for goodness' sake. She'd left home, gone to university, and was making her own way in the world now. She didn't need her parents on her back the whole time.

But her mum didn't seem able to accept that.

Nicky pulled on her battered leather jacket. It had been a present from Conor, her boyfriend from back home, who was now at a different university. Even though the jacket was second-hand, it would have cost him a fortune and she'd appreciated the thought he had put into choosing it. It was exactly her taste and she loved it. She stuffed her purse into her pocket. Mum would no doubt ask why she didn't use a handbag like other women and would then ask if she'd like one for her next birthday, and Nicky would say no. They'd had that whole conversation several times. Why couldn't Mum see that pockets were easier to use. Simpler.

She sighed, closed the window of her study bedroom, hung up the towel that she'd dropped on the floor after her morning shower, and left the room, locking it behind her. She checked the clock in the shared kitchen area – ten minutes until she was due to meet Mum. Long enough to walk through the campus to the café and be there on time.

Although she'd rather be late. Just a couple of minutes late – long enough for Mum to start looking at her watch and sighing, not so long to risk Mum leaving the café and walking up to Nicky's student flat.

She dawdled, checking the time once more on the campus bookshop clock as she passed it. 'Why don't you wear a watch?' Mum had asked her so many times with a sigh, but Nicky didn't like watches. They were a tool of the Establishment, designed to keep you in line, on time, doing what you were supposed to, when you were supposed to. She used to wear a watch, back when she'd lived at home, but not since starting university.

At five past, the perfect five minutes late, she entered the café. Mum was already there, as Nicky had hoped she'd be, seated at a table that had a view across the courtyard from which Nicky approached. She tapped her watch as Nicky entered.

'Nearly six minutes late. And you only have to walk across campus. Me, I had a two-hour drive to get here. Honestly, sometimes I think you do it on purpose.'

'Hi Mum. Sorry.' Nicky wasn't sorry, but she said what her mum expected to hear, as she leaned over and kissed her cheek. 'Shall I order? What do you want?'

'A daughter who's on time and asks how my journey was. Failing that, tea and a scone with butter. They were nice here the last time.'

Nicky nodded and went to order at the counter. Yeah, the last time. Last term, only four weeks after Nicky had started at the university. No one else had termly visits from their mum. Just her. Mum taking up her precious free time, getting in the way, when all Nicky wanted to do was get on with being a student, living her own independent life. Was that so much to expect?

Her coursemate, Sabina, had said she'd love to have her parents visit. 'They sound so supportive,' she'd said, when Nicky had complained about this visit from Mum. 'You're lucky.'

Not lucky, Nicky thought. Stifled. Suffocated. Smothered.

She ordered the tea and scone for Mum and a hot Ribena for herself, ('It'll rot your teeth, all that sugary nonsense,' she heard her mother's voice say in her head) but no cake. She paid, but only so that her mother couldn't use that as ammunition against her ('You just take, take, take, Nicola. Time you learned to give a little back.')

'Still drinking the sugary nonsense?' Mum said, right on cue, as she returned to the table with the tray.

'Yep.' Nicky took a sip, scalding her mouth on the far-too-hot liquid but refusing to even flinch.

'Well. I had to leave at eight this morning, so I was caught up in all the rush-hour traffic. Especially around Chichester. Such a nightmare. And then an accident near Worthing. It took ages to get through. I'm parked up in the top car park, where your dad and I parked last time. Seems to be the best place.' Mum smiled, too brightly. 'Anyway. Tell me what you've been up to. You hardly ever phone us. We feel like we know nothing about your life here.'

'I phone every week.' Nicky rolled her eyes. Or almost every week. What more did Mum want? *Daily* calls? There were a few students who phoned home daily. Some had mobile phones, paid for by their parents, to do so, but Nicky didn't have one. She had to queue to use the payphone in the lobby, which was shared by several flats. She always made sure she had only a couple of 10p pieces so the calls didn't need to go on for too long.

'A five-minute call once a week, and even then, you forget some weeks. Just doesn't feel like enough, Nicola. Even your dad was saying he'd like to hear from you more often.' Mum was fishing in her bag for something. For a horrible moment Nicky thought she was looking for a tissue, that she was going to embarrass her by weeping and wailing here in the café. But Mum pulled out a green piece of plastic and handed it over. 'There. A phone card. You said the phone in your flat accepts them. It's a five-pound one, so that'll keep us going with nice long chats for a few weeks.'

Nicky stared at it. If she accepted the card, it would be a point to Mum. But on the other hand, it would be easier and would save her money. She could use it to call Conor as well.

'Well? Are you going to take it?' Mum flapped it in the air in front of her.

'Yeah, er, thanks.' Nicky tucked it into her back pocket.

'Don't lose it now, it's worth five pounds. I wish you'd use a handbag. They make life so much simpler. Well. Have you heard from Conor lately?' Mum's expression had turned to one of smugness. She, too, was aware that she'd scored a small point here.

'He wrote me a letter. He's visiting next weekend.'

'Oh, that's nice.' Mum's face softened and she tilted her head on one side. 'I am pleased you two are still managing to stay together. It's not easy with you being at different universities, and him so busy with that charity he works for as well. But he's good for you. Dad and I were saying that, just the other day, how good he is for you. Honestly, without Conor's influence lately I dread to think . . .' She broke off, finally noticing that Nicky was glaring at her.

6

'*Good* for me? What do you mean? Why do I need someone who's *good* for me? Am I that bad?' Nicky's tone was deliberately mocking. Again, this wasn't the first time she'd heard this from Mum. She'd been going out with Conor since they were sixteen – over three years now. He was steady and dependable, of course Mum loved him. Steady, dependable, ever so nice, and if she was being honest with herself, ever so slightly boring. Conor was the kind of boy who would always toe the line, do what was expected of him, do whatever his parents asked him. Sometimes she wondered if he even had a mind of his own. He was, she was beginning to think, just a bit too *conventional*. She wished he could be a bit more rebellious. Like she was.

She did love him, she thought she always would love him, but these days she was beginning to wish she was free of him, free to make the most of student life while she had the chance.

'Well, you can be that bad,' Mum said, but she was smiling now, recognising they'd been round this loop a few times. She took a bite from her scone, and Nicky watched in silence as she ate it and then dabbed at her lips with a napkin, leaving a smudge of pink lipstick behind. 'Sometimes I think you and I are just not quite on the same wavelength, you know. Anyway, let's not fight. How's the studying going?'

'Yeah, it's all good,' Nicky said. She didn't want a fight either, but sometimes Mum's comments provoked her into starting one. She was right, at least, about them not being on the same wavelength. Not the same planet, either.

'Finished that essay?' Mum asked.

'What essay?'

'Oh, the one you were working on the last time I asked you about your coursework. Something to do with . . . what was it . . . conflict in India, partition, Britain's role creating the problems in Kashmir, something like that?'

7

'Oh, that one. Yeah, finished that.'

'Did you get a good mark for it?'

Nicky snorted. 'It's not like that here, Mum. It's not primary school. You don't get ticks, or A-pluses, or whatever. You get feedback.'

'So did you get good feedback on it, then?'

'It was OK.' Actually, it hadn't been. She'd received a lot of criticism of it from her tutor. She was only in the first year of her course on modern history, and although the tutors said the first year was all about bringing everyone up to the same level, she'd been told that essay was not up to the standard required. She was slipping behind and was going to need to work harder. Research more, read more, think in more depth about the issues she was writing about. Apparently, it was no longer enough to know *what* happened; she needed to explain *why* it had happened, and what the knock-on effects were. What had led up to the events she was writing about? How did they occur? And what changed as a result? And then, if possible, what could we learn from studying it today?

'Well, good.' Mum seemed disappointed with her answer. She'd wanted to hear that Nicky had been singled out as best in the class, no doubt, the way she had been back in GCSE days. It had been easy then. Learn the facts and regurgitate them, come top of the class, get given a wodge of money from Mum and Dad as a reward. But she'd been sixteen then, young and immature. She was older now, a university student. The work was much harder, but the life was so much more fun – being free to go out and have fun with no one asking where you were going or who you were seeing and telling you what time to be home by.

'And what's your next project?' Mum was asking. You had to hand it to her – she did seem genuinely interested in the course.

'Rebellion. We've got to pick some sort of uprising and research it. They want us to use the internet as well as books for this project.'

'What event are you going to write about?'

Nicky shrugged. 'Haven't the first idea at the moment. But I've got ages to do it in. Might look at women's suffrage, that sort of thing.' Women as rebels – that interested her more than anything else. Women she could relate to, who kicked back against the Establishment, women who changed the world.

'Ha – rebellion's a good subject for you, isn't it? You've always thought of yourself as a bit of a rebel. I remember all those petitions you organised at school against having to wear a uniform. You were always kicking back against authority. You should find this project easy to do.'

Nicky felt her hackles rising as Mum belittled the things she'd felt so strongly about at school. She hadn't objected to wearing a uniform. It was the school's attempts to insist that everyone bought identical black trousers from an expensive uniform shop, rather than being allowed to choose cheap ones from Asda. Nicky's petition had forced the school to rethink. She'd done it for the sake of poorer families who'd have struggled to afford the dearer uniform.

'Yeah, well, at least I fight for what I believe in, rather than just put up with stuff I'm not happy about.' Nicky stared at the window. There was a sticker on it asking customers not to open it. She leaned over and undid the catch, pushing the window open.

Mum sighed. 'Always the rebel, Nicola, aren't you?'

'You know nothing about being a rebel, Mum.'

'Oh, you'd be surprised, my girl.'

They fell into an awkward silence for a few minutes. Nicky came up with a dozen retorts but all would have ended up with them arguing, and she had a whole day of being with Mum to get through. It wasn't worth it.

9

At last Mum broke the silence. 'So, how do you use the internet?' Computers were really not her thing.

This was a safer subject. 'There's a room of computers in our department. You can book them for an hour at a time and go online, search for whatever it is you're interested in.'

'And what happens – does it print out stuff for you?'

'No. You read documents on the screen, or maybe find a reference to a book that looks helpful, which, hopefully, the library will have. It's about finding ideas and connections that haven't already been written about in textbooks, then following them up.'

'Hmm. Original research.'

'Yeah. That's what my tutor called it.'

Mum nodded, looking pleased with herself. Then she leaned forward, an excited gleam in her eye. 'Ooh, I've had an idea. Something you could write about, some research you could do.'

Nicky forced herself to try to look interested. Her instinct was to retort once more that she was no longer in primary school and parents weren't expected to help with homework. But she was short on ideas so thought she might as well listen. 'Yeah?'

'Your great-grandmother.'

'Supergran?' Nicky used the old name she'd used since she was tiny for her great-grandmother Gráinne.

'Yes. It's a shame you didn't come to her 100th birthday celebration last month. You could have spoken to her then.'

Nicky felt a pang of guilt that she'd missed the celebration. But she hadn't wanted to leave Brighton. 'Spoken to her about what?'

'Ireland. The Easter Rising, in 1916. She played a part in that, you know. I don't know all the details, but she was certainly involved.'

'Bloody Ireland. I don't want to write about Ireland, Mum. There must be something more interesting.' Nicky had never paid much attention to her Irish ancestry. She'd lived all her life in England, as had her mother.

'But this would be original research! Get Gráinne's story, what she did, what she thought of it all, written up. I bet there'll be something there you can use. She was in the . . . what was it called? The Cumann Ban, something like that. No, Cumann na mBan – that's it. Women's council, it meant. Like a women's wing of the Irish Republican Army.'

'Now you want me to write about a terrorist organisation?'

'One man's terrorist is another man's freedom fighter, remember. Back then, in 1916, they were heroes. And it's so *topical*, Nicola. What with the IRA ceasefire last summer, and the chance of a long-term peace agreement on the cards! Your great-grandmother was right there at the start of it all, and you could be telling her story now, when it's looking as though there might soon be a huge step forward in the peace process at last. If you wanted to focus on women in rebellions, she's a perfect subject.' Mum leaned back in her chair, looking thoughtful, while Nicky took in what she'd suggested. 'Also, I suppose I'm being a bit selfish here. Gráinne's 100. She's still so with it, her mind's as sharp as ever, but she's not going to be around for very much longer. I can't help but think it'd be wonderful to have her story written up. I know she'd be happy to tell it.'

'So why don't you do it? You ask her, you write it down.'

Mum shook her head. 'Ah, I'm no writer, Nicola. I can't string a sentence together. Not the way you can. And I'm no student of history.' She put her palms flat on the table as though she'd made a decision. 'Look, you missed her 100th birthday. I know you had things to do here, and we all accepted that. Anyway, there were so many people there you'd barely have been able to talk to her. But she asked

11

after you – I think you were always a bit of a favourite.' She chuckled. 'To think she had six children, seventeen grand-children and God knows how many great-grandchildren but she always remembers your name and which university you're at and what you're studying. She's remarkable. We should capture her story before it's too late.'

'Why me? Of all those relatives? Why should I be the one to do it?'

'Because you're the history student in need of a topic to write about on the subject of rebellion! And she was a rebel whose story hasn't ever been fully told, as far as I'm aware! Not to mention you see yourself as a bit of a rebel too.' Mum laughed, and Nicky couldn't help but join in a little.

'Yeah, well, maybe. Let me think about it, yeah? She still lives in the same house in Dublin, right? How would I get the story out of her – over the phone?'

Mum shook her head. 'You should visit. Go there for a weekend. You can fly from Gatwick to Dublin for next to nothing if you go with Ryanair. I might even help pay for your flights if you're lucky. Great-Gran lives in Malahide – that's not far from the airport. You can get a bus from the airport to the end of her road, or even a taxi wouldn't be too expensive. It's only a ten-minute journey.'

'Would I stay with Supergran?'

'Yes, I would think so. You remember from last year; she's got plenty of space. She's so fiercely independent, she refuses to go into an old people's home.'

'Wouldn't I have to, like, be her carer if I stay there?' Nicky grimaced at the thought.

'You might have to help a bit, but not much,' Mum replied. 'They'd do it all – Jimmy and Eileen and Mary and the rest of them. Quite a few of my cousins and aunts and uncles live in Malahide or north Dublin, another one in Howth, and they all chip in to help. They have a rota going these days. It was so nice seeing them all together back in January at the birthday celebrations. You'd be able to spend the time sitting with her, listening to her story. And visiting Dublin. You could see the places where it all happened.' Mum grinned. 'Oh if it was me as the history student, I'd be on this like a shot.'

Nicky was torn. She had to admit it was actually a good idea. But that would be handing Mum a barrelful of points for nothing. 'Yeah, well, let me think about it, as I said.'

'You do that.' Mum shrugged. 'You know, if I'd given this idea to any other student, I reckon they'd have said, "Wow, thanks, what a fabulous idea!". But you, all I get is a "Yeah, well". You can be so ungrateful, Nicola. It's time you grew up a bit and recognised when people are just trying to help you. You don't need to act the grumpy teenager for ever, you know?'

And you don't need to act the controlling mother for ever, Nicky wanted to yell back at her, but stopped herself. Instead, she just smiled tightly. 'Have you finished your tea? We can head into Brighton now. That's what you wanted to do today, isn't it? A spot of shopping?'

'Yes, of course, just let me go and pay for this.' Mum began rummaging in her bag for her purse.

'No need. I already paid,' Nicky said, and was satisfied to see a look of disbelief and astonishment cross her mother's face. Point scored.

Chapter 2 – August 1915

It was a warm day at the start of August. Gráinne tugged at the collar of her dress, trying to allow some cooler air in under her clothing. She was standing among a huge crowd of people that thronged the streets of Dublin, who were all there for the funeral of the old Fenian, Jeremiah O'Donovan Rossa. His body had been brought back from New York where he'd died at the grand old age of 83, and was to be buried today in Glasnevin Cemetery, on the northern edge of the city.

But first the coffin, carried in a hearse pulled by four black horses, was to be paraded through the streets of Dublin so that everyone might turn out to pay their respects. Gráinne had found a spot to stand about halfway along the advertised route. The crowd was three or four deep on both pavements, but a tall man standing on the kerbside spotted Gráinne behind him and ushered her forward. 'There, little miss. Now you can see, so you can.'

She smiled and thanked him, though inwardly felt her blood pressure rise at being called 'little miss'. She was 17. She was a woman, and a proud Irishwoman at that! A member of the Cumann na mBan, campaigning for Irish freedom from British oppression, just as the great man being buried today had done.

Nevertheless, she took the tall man's place at the kerbside, grateful that she would indeed now have a good view when the hearse went past. She pushed a strand of hair beneath the straw hat she'd put on to keep the sun off. The man who'd given way to her was standing a little too close for comfort behind her, but she could not move forward without stepping off the kerb. She would have to put up with feeling the additional heat of his body too close to her. On her right was another man, his head bare and bowed, his cap held over his heart as though already paying his respects even though the funeral cortege was nowhere to be seen yet. On her left, a woman with three small children was trying to keep them under control, but the youngest was grizzling in the heat of the day. 'Ssh now, Jimmy. 'Tis a big day, one you'll remember. Now stop your mizzling and keep a look out for the big black horses.'

'It's too hot for them, poor loves,' Gráinne said to her, sympathetically.

The woman nodded. ''Tis that and all, but I had to come, and I'd no one to leave them with. My man's away at the war, so he is.'

'My brother is too,' Gráinne replied. She didn't like to think too hard about what Sean might be doing, over there at the Western Front. There were newspaper reports every day of the fierce battles taking place in trenches . . . and her dear Sean, an Irishman, was over there fighting the English war, like so many of his countrymen.

'Look, so, isn't that him coming now?' The woman pointed along the road. All heads in the crowd had turned that way, and yes, Gráinne could see that she was right. The procession was on its way.

The hearse, pulled by four magnificent black horses with plumes on their heads, was in the lead. Behind it, a couple of motorcars carried some men in the uniform of the Irish Volunteers. And then regiments of Volunteers, some of them bearing rifles, marched two by two along the street. Were those rifles the very ones Gráinne herself had helped to land the previous year, at Howth? Very likely, she thought.

The crowd was still and silent as the procession passed. Men removed their hats and women dabbed at their eyes with handkerchiefs. The only sounds were the occasional snorts of the horses, the motorcars and marching feet.

At the back of the procession, members of the crowd shuffled solemnly along behind. It seemed almost everyone wanted to go to the cemetery, to hear the speeches and see the coffin of the great man finally laid to rest. Gráinne made a snap decision. She too would follow the cortege. There'd been rumours that Pádraig Pearse himself would speak. He was the founder of St Enda's school at which her father taught – a school dedicated to Irish culture, Irish ways and the Irish language. After centuries in which the British had tried to suppress Irish culture, it was now making a comeback, thanks to Republicans like Pearse. Her father was the mathematics teacher at St Enda's, and had spoken highly of Pearse on many occasions. 'A future leader of our country, I'd say,' he'd told her, nodding with pride, 'when we're finally free to govern ourselves.'

Freedom. That was what it was all about. English land-owners had taken everything, worked Irish peasants to death during the Great Famine, made Irish Catholics second-class citizens in their own country. It was time it all changed.

Gráinne stepped off the kerb and joined the funeral followers, walking side by side with men in the uniform of the Volunteers, women with Cumann na mBan armbands, and members of the general public. Everyone had their heads held high and proud. O'Donovan Rossa had led a good, long life. This was not a sad occasion but one in which to remember him and all he had done to promote Irish independence.

Slowly the procession made its way northward, out of the city centre to Glasnevin Cemetery. A few peeled away as they got closer. It was going to be too crowded to see or hear much, but Gráinne wanted to stay, regardless. As they made their way along the paths among the graves, she did her best to jostle through the crowd, squeezing through gaps, dodging around groups of people who were trying to stay together, moving closer to the front.

'Gráinne MacDowd? Is that yourself?' A familiar voice called her, and she stopped, staring about her to see where the voice was coming from.

She spotted him, standing at the edge of the crowd. 'Emmett O'Sheridan! It's a long time since I saw you, all right!'

'Come over here,' he beckoned, and nodded over his shoulder. She could see what he was suggesting. Rather than follow the huge crowd there was another way, cutting between some tall memorials. It might be possible to get nearer the grave, where Rossa's coffin was now being reverently unloaded and draped with the green flag of the Irish Republicans.

She hurried over to him, and he caught hold of her hand and pulled her across the grass, between a couple of sarcophagi and around a tall stone cross, until they emerged behind the grave. There were still too many people in front of her for Gráinne to see much but at least here she'd have a chance of hearing the speeches.

The priest was talking, saying prayers for the departed, and Gráinne and Emmett fell silent along with everyone else. She was only half listening. It was Pearse she wanted to hear, not the priest. Beside her, Emmett stood tall and broad-shouldered. He'd been her brother's schoolfriend. She hadn't seen him for a few years, certainly not since Sean had left to join the British army the previous year. She'd always liked Emmett but knew that he saw her only as his friend's annoying little sister, always trying to cut in on their boys' games. 'Go and play with your dolls, Grá,' he'd told her more than once, laughing. He and Sean had been busy making fishing rods and were planning to see what they could catch in the Liffey. She'd been pushed away then, by both boys, though Sean had apologised later in the day.

'Here's Pearse now, getting ready to speak,' Emmett whispered in her ear, and Gráinne stood on tiptoes trying to get a glimpse of him, but to no avail.

She could hear him, however, and she listened carefully as he gave a stirring speech, referring to Rossa as 'this unrepentant Fenian', and calling on all Volunteers present to stand together for the 'achievement of the freedom of Ireland'.

The listening crowd was absolutely silent as Pádraig Pearse reached the conclusion of his speech, with words that Gráinne knew then that she would never forget, words she instinctively knew would echo down the ages inspiring all those that loved Ireland.

'Life springs from death; and from the graves of patriot men and women spring living nations. The Defenders of this Realm have worked well in secret and in the open. They think that they have pacified Ireland. They think that they have purchased half of us and intimidated the other half. They think they have foreseen everything, they think they have provided against everything; but the fools, the fools, the fools! They have left us our Fenian dead, and while Ireland holds these graves, Ireland unfree shall never be at peace.'

Gráinne let out a little gasp at these closing words. She couldn't help herself, but she was not alone. Emmett had too, and as she looked up at him, she saw that his eyes brimmed with tears.

'It is a call to arms, Grá,' he said quietly. 'A call to arms, and not the call your brother answered.'

She nodded, too overcome by emotion from Pearse's words to speak. She wished Sean had not joined the British army. But he'd been convinced it was the right thing to do, along with so many others. She stood quietly while O'Donovan Rossa's coffin was lowered into the grave and a volley of three shots fired over it, and cast her mind back to events almost a year earlier, the year in which everything began to change.

War had broken out in Europe. The Home Rule bill, that had seemed so close to passing through Parliament in faraway London, had been shelved for the duration. Irish national- ists were understandably frustrated. They'd been so close to achieving self-governance via the political route, but the war had scuppered that for now. In September, John Redmond, who had founded the Irish Volunteers, of which Sean was a member, had urged his Volunteers to enlist in the British Army. Sean had listened, and had signed up.

He'd come to visit her in her lodgings in the centre of Dublin, where she was a shop assistant in the grand depart- ment store of Clerys on Sackville Street, right opposite the General Post Office. She lived in a staff dormitory on the upper floors, but there was also a staff refectory where she could buy him a cup of tea.

He'd come to say goodbye, and explain his actions. 'If we help the British now in their hour of need, they'll remember this and thank us when the war is done, and Ireland will be rewarded with Home Rule.'

Gráinne sighed. 'They won't. They'll promise lots and deliver nothing, Sean,' she replied. 'Just as they have so many other times. Didn't you ever listen when Dad talked to us about our history? They'll use you up and spit you out, that's if you even survive! Don't do this, Sean. Fight for Ireland, not for England.'

'But there's no fight here, is there? There's only talk, so. There's nothing more. This is a route to Irish independence, and it's a route that will work. We can see the way ahead. John Redmond says so, and what better politician do we have than him?'

'There are others who say differently.' Gráinne had joined the Cumann na mBan at the age of fifteen, and had already proved her worth with the other women. She listened carefully to all the chatter, especially that of the older women and the members of the Irish Volunteers who sometimes came to their meetings. 'There's talk the Volunteers will split. That those who don't want to enlist will stay here, and when the time comes, they'll fight for Ireland.'

'But that's my point, Gráinne!' Sean ran his hands through his hair in frustration. 'When the time comes – when will that be? Who's going to pick the fight?'

'I've heard that . . .' Gráinne stopped, and bit her lip. Should she tell him? It had been an overheard conversation, between an important member of the Volunteers and a senior Cumann na mBan woman.

'You've heard? Come on, Gráinne. I'm your brother, and a patriot, and you can tell me.'

She nodded. Of course she could tell him. Even though he'd just signed up to join the British army, he was an Irishman first and foremost. 'I've heard people say that England's difficulty is Ireland's opportunity. That while England is distracted with this war, it's the perfect time.'

'Perfect time for what?'

'For a revolution.' There. She'd said it. The word was out, hanging in the air between them. The word that promised so much, the word that might bring freedom and self-governance to their oppressed land.

But, to her dismay, Sean merely threw back his head and laughed. He had a loud, merry laugh that usually she could not but help join in with. But not today. Today she scowled at him, her arms folded across her chest.

'Ah, my lovely, sweet sister. The Irish have tried it all before, rebel, rise up and break free. Sure, didn't Wolfe Tone try in 1798 with his United Irishmen? And then the Young Irelanders in 1848? Every generation they try, and every generation they fail. But now we have the possibility of Home Rule – wasn't it agreed by Parliament, and on the point of implementation when this damned war broke out? We'll get it, just as soon as we've seen off the Kaiser's armies. We'll help defeat the Germans and then we'll have our Home Rule, and Ireland will be as good as independent from Britain. You'll see. This is the way to go. There's no appetite for a fight here on home soil, unless it's to defend against the Kaiser.'

'I think you're wrong.' It was all she could say to him. He was convinced he was right, and she'd always agreed with him and trusted his judgement in the past. At four years her senior, he'd always been the person she'd looked up to. But not this time.

Sean shrugged. 'Well, we'll see, won't we? Time will prove who's right and who's not.' But he grinned as he said it, and winked, and she knew he was convinced that he was right and she was just being that irritating little sister again, the one who tried to cut in on his games with his friend Emmett, the one who didn't really understand anything.

Sean had left within a day or two of that argument, sailing over to England to start his training. And the Volunteers had indeed split. Most had followed Redmond, leaving only a few thousand left in the Irish Volunteers, under their new leader Eóin MacNeill. Gráinne had accompanied Sean to the docks on the day he sailed, and hugged him farewell with tears in her eyes. 'Stay safe,' she'd urged him, 'and come back to us soon. Ireland needs you. I need you.'

'I'll be grand, Gráinne. Don't fret.' He'd kissed her forehead and strode up the gangway onto the ferry, waving over his shoulder at her and at his country.

'Will we go, now? Emmett said, bringing her with a jolt back to the present, back to the funeral. Around them people were beginning to move away, to return to their homes and their lives. 'Will we get ourselves a cup of tea somewhere we can catch up?'

She smiled at him and nodded. 'I'd like that.'

Emmett held out his arm and she took it, and they walked together back through the cemetery towards the city, until they found a suitable café. Emmett pulled out a chair for her to sit down, at a table by a window. 'I'm perfectly capable of seating myself, Emmett,' she said, and he grinned.

'Of course. I forgot how independent you can be. Sorry, Grá.' He sat back as she ordered tea for two from the waitress. 'But you'll let me treat you to this? Please?'

'I suppose so.' Inwardly she was pleased. Money was a little tight. Her job at Clerys was a good one, but she was saving every penny she could so that she would be able to move out of the staff dormitories and into her own private flat. Emmett worked as a solicitor's clerk, and she guessed his wages would be substantially more than hers.

'Have you seen or heard from Sean, since he signed up?' Emmett asked, once their tea had arrived.

Gráinne stirred a sugar lump into her tea. 'He came home on leave after his initial training, and stayed with Dad. That was around December last year. But we haven't seen him since. He writes, though. It sounds as though he spends most of his time digging trenches.'

'Has he been involved in any battles?'

'The letters are censored. So we're not sure, but I think he's seen some fighting at Ypres.' There'd been reports that gas attacks had been used in the battles at Ypres. Gráinne shuddered at the thought of Sean being caught up in that.

Emmett reached across the table and took her hand. 'Let's hope he's able to stay out of the worst of it.'

She sniffed and nodded. 'I wish to God he hadn't gone. It's *their* war – the British and the Germans and the Serbians and the Austrians and all those others. It's nothing to do with Ireland, sure it's not. We have our own battles to fight here. I told him this, when he came to tell me he'd signed up. But he was so certain this was the right thing to do.'

'As Redmond said.'

'Yes, fight for the British so that they reward us when it's all over. Emmett, do you think that will happen?'

'I'm sceptical, Grá. I'd like to think so – I'd like to think that the sacrifices our Irish boys are making over there will not be for nothing. But I'm not so sure.' He stared down at his cup of tea then looked up, directly at her. 'I have joined the Irish Volunteers. And the Brotherhood as well, Grá. When the moment comes, I'll be fighting for Ireland.'

She gasped. The Irish Republican Brotherhood was the most militant and the most secretive of the various organisations that had sprung up in recent years. Although, she reminded herself, the IRB was hardly new. It had been around for fifty years or more, arising from the ashes of past failed rebellions and committed to making Ireland an independent republic. 'As will I, Emmett. I'm in the Cumann na mBan.'

'I know you are.' He smiled. 'You women do a wonderful job. I was at an event last week where the Countess Markiewicz herself gave a speech. She was very inspiring. She thinks that women could not only work as nurses and messengers in a future rebellion, but could also possibly bear arms themselves. I don't know if that's right . . .'

Gráinne glared at him until he backtracked a little.

'I mean, I'm sure some could, and will. But we should not expect them all to.'

'We should not force anyone to fight who doesn't want to. Man or woman.' Gráinne spoke firmly. She'd also heard the Countess speak on this topic, and it was because of Markiewicz's words that she herself had joined the Cumann na mBan. The Countess, or Madame as she liked to be called, was one of the Anglo-Irish aristocracy. She'd married a Polish Count, but for many years had lived apart from him and had thrown herself into the Republican cause. Gráinne knew that the Countess had joined the Irish Citizen Army, a socialist group fighting for workers' rights, as it was the only one of the rebel organisations that treated women as equal to men. If there was ever to be an Irish republic, Gráinne fervently hoped it would be one that respected women, that treated women as equal citizens, allowing them to vote and take an active part in politics and government.

'Of course not.' Emmett smiled at her and once more took her hand. 'But I think the fight will be coming sooner rather than later. Before the end of the war in Europe, that's for certain.'

'Have you heard anything definite?'

Emmett shook his head. 'No. I'm not senior enough to know. But there're talks, always talks. Often at the Countess's house in Rathmines. I'd like so much to be a part of all that, to be there when the big decisions are made, wouldn't you?'

'Yes, I certainly would,' Gráinne replied. She could think of nothing she'd like more than to be at the heart of it all, whatever happened.

Chapter 3 – March 1998

It had been an OK day with Mum in the end, Nicky had to admit. After sniping at each other in the café they'd both called a ceasefire while they shopped. They'd managed to steer conversations away from the usual flashpoints, though they'd come dangerously close a few times. Nicky had allowed her mother to buy her a pair of jeans and a couple of T-shirts for the summer. Mum had wanted to buy her a floral blouse and a floaty cotton skirt, until Nicky had fixed her with a look and said, 'Really? Have you ever seen me in that kind of outfit?' For a moment it had looked as though the war would restart but then Mum had burst out laughing, agreed she had not, and headed towards a rail of black and khaki T-shirts that she no doubt hated but Nicky loved.

They'd ended the day having a late lunch in a vegetarian restaurant that Nicky had chosen, mainly because on her parents' last visit they'd gone to a steakhouse, and Nicky had ended up eating only salad. Knowing Mum was a dedicated meat-eater, this was payback time. But Mum had happily agreed with the suggestion, announced she enjoyed her spring vegetable quiche with couscous salad, and had paid the bill.

'This has been a nice day, Nicola,' Mum said as they walked to the station to take the train back to the university campus. 'We've proved we can do it when we try, haven't we?'

'I guess so.' Nicky lifted the bags of shopping she was carrying. 'And thanks for these.'

Mum waved her hand dismissively. 'No problem. Nice to buy you a few things even if they're not my taste. And God knows you need more clothes that aren't ripped.'

Nicky looked down at her favourite faded black jeans that had tears across both knees. 'I like torn stuff, actually.'

'Hmm. Well don't tear the new jeans on purpose, eh? Let them wear out naturally.' They'd reached the station, and as the train pulled in Mum gave her a spontaneous hug. 'It's been a great day, love. I'm looking forward to Easter now.'

'Easter? Why, what's happening then?' The hug was kind of nice, but Nicky extricated herself before it went on for too long.

'It'll be the next time I see you, of course! When you come home for the Easter break!'

Nicky shook her head. 'I hadn't planned to come home then. I was going to stay here. I'll be home in the summer though, unless I get a summer job in Brighton.'

'Not come home at Easter? But what will you do here?'

'Get ahead on that project I need to do. Go out with friends. Live my life.' Nicky was annoyed now. She'd left home, but Mum seemed to think she should go back every chance she had.

'Oh love. You were only home for three days at Christmas. You missed your great-grandmother's 100th. And now you're saying you won't be home at Easter? But you must come for the long weekend, if nothing else. Everyone else you were at school with who's gone to university will be home. Conor's coming home then, so his mother tells me. Surely you'll want to see him?'

26

Nicky shrugged. 'Well, maybe I'll come just for that weekend. Definitely not for the full three-week break. My life's here now.'

'Oh. Well, that'll be better than nothing. Perhaps you'll change your mind.'

'Why would I? Stop trying to tell me how to live my life, Mum.'

Mum sighed. 'Your problem, Nicola, is not with me. It's with yourself. You've a lot of growing up to do, but you just don't seem to realise it.'

That was it. The flashpoint they'd avoided up till now. Nicky couldn't hold back any longer. 'You say I need to grow up. I say you need to let me be my own person, Mum. You laugh at me for being what you call "a bit of a rebel".' She made speech marks in the air around that phrase. 'It really pisses me off, you know, when you try to take over and tell me what to do. I don't need it and I don't want it.' She knew that last part would hurt Mum but she just didn't care.

The train arrived then, and they got on. They sat in silence for the short journey up to the station nearest the campus.

'You should cut through that way to the car park,' Nicky said, pointing to a path leading behind a couple of buildings. 'It's quicker. I'm going this way, so . . . goodbye.' She stood waiting to submit to a hug and a kiss, get it over with quickly.

'Oh. All right then.' Mum took a deep breath. 'Be a rebel by all means, Nicola. Just make sure that what you are rebelling against, and fighting for, is worthwhile.'

There was no hug or kiss. Mum just lifted a hand in a half-wave, and set off at a brisk walk in the direction of the car park.

Nicky let out a huge sigh of relief as she watched her walk away. Yes, she loved her mother. You were supposed to, weren't you? But did you have to *like* her? Even if she was controlling and bossy and didn't seem to want to accept her daughter had grown up and had her own life now?

Conor was due to visit Nicky the weekend after Mum's visit. But on the Wednesday before his visit, a letter from him arrived. Neither of them had mobile phones, so they'd always had to communicate by letter since they'd started at university. Conor's letter made Nicky sigh. He worked a couple of evenings a week for a charity that put together packages of medicines and health-related supplies to send to conflict zones, or areas ravaged by famine, around the world. He'd been asked to work on a Saturday as there were a number of key personnel off sick. *You know how strongly I feel about doing my bit in practical terms to make the world a better place,* he'd written. *I know I was supposed to visit you this weekend. How about I come next weekend instead? As far as I remember, you said you were free then. Hate letting you down like this but I also don't want to let the charity down. Hope you understand.*

The charity ranked above her then, in his priorities. Nicky did understand how important it was to him. He'd often talked about how he wanted to make a real difference to the world. But this change of plan meant she was now at a loose end at the weekend. An odd mix of emotions surged through her. There was disappointment that another week would go by before she saw him again, but it was tinged with excitement that she was free to go out with her coursemates, have a few drinks and maybe go clubbing with them, pretending for a couple of days that she was unattached. She'd been with Conor for so long that sometimes she found herself resenting him a little. Having him always there in the background of her life while she was at university sometimes felt stifling and restricting.

* * *

Nicky had known Conor for ever. That's how it often felt. Their parents were friends – they'd met years ago as guests at a wedding, hit it off and swapped contact details. Then they'd met up once or twice every month for a meal out, or a dinner party at one or the other's house, or just to have a few drinks together. When Nicky had been small, usually she'd have been left with a babysitter but sometimes she went along too, and would play in the garden with Conor while the grown-ups chatted. He'd always been a part of her life.

Then, when they were 15, Conor's family had moved house, and he'd joined Nicky's school. They were at that awkward age, when childhood friendships were no longer cool, and they'd spent the first couple of terms barely acknowledging each other in the playground. Until they both went on a school trip, where they stayed in a youth hostel in Snowdonia. One day the class walked halfway up Snowdon, searching for the source of a river. They followed it from a tarn down to the valley, taking measurements of width and flow, while the teachers pointed out how it had shaped the landscape. Partway through the day, Nicky and Conor found themselves walking side by side, hanging back a little from the rest of the kids.

'It's nice, being at the same school as you,' Conor said. 'Like having family there. But not family, if you know what I mean.'

'Yeah. I kind of like having you around too,' she said, and surprised herself to find that she meant it. 'You staying on for A levels?'

'Yes. You?'

'Yes.'

He grinned, and Nicky was struck by how good-looking he was. Growing up seeing him regularly she realised she hadn't really noticed before. But yes, he was, now she came to think of it. Sandy haired, freckled, with even white teeth.

Broad shoulders that gave an air of strength to him. As though he was someone who could be depended upon.

'We'll still see each other in sixth form, then,' he said. 'Maybe we could . . . I dunno . . . see each other a bit more anyway? Like, out of school, and not just with the parents? If you want to . . .'

'Are you asking me out?' The words slipped out before Nicky had a chance to think about what she was saying. But this was Conor, whom she'd always felt so comfortable with. She didn't have to try, didn't have to pretend to be anyone she wasn't around him. He knew her so well that he'd see straight through any pretence. So being upfront and asking him a direct question was actually the best thing to do, she decided.

'Yeah, Nicky. I am.' He stopped walking and caught hold of her hand. 'So, what's your answer?' He was looking at her with hope.

'Well . . .' she began, while a million thoughts rushed around her head. She'd known him so long – would it be like dating a brother? What would their parents say? It would be so embarrassing telling them. Would it be better just to remain friends? And then her instincts took over, and her heart rather than her head took control. 'Well, why not?' She smiled and he pulled her close and kissed her. Just a quick kiss, for they were halfway up a mountain with their school class complete with teachers just a little further along the path. It wouldn't do for them to be spotted.

They broke apart as though having the same thought. 'We'd better catch up, or they'll be wondering what we've got up to,' Nicky said.

'They'll start all sorts of gossip about us,' Conor added, as they began walking quickly up the path to catch up with the group.

'And they'd be right!' Nicky dissolved into fits of giggles and Conor joined in.

They tried to hide their new relationship, but that lasted all of about half a day before friends started asking if they'd got together, and telling them they made a perfect couple and what had taken them so long?

From then on, they'd been pretty much inseparable through the rest of their school and sixth form years. Their relationship had matured as they did. There'd been times when Nicky had wished they hadn't met until they were older, perhaps in their mid-20s, and their relationship could have progressed quickly to marriage and lifelong commitment. But as Conor said when she voiced this, you couldn't change the past, and they were lucky that they *had* met. It was up to them what they made of their relationship.

'Whether it's for ever or whether it comes to a natural end some day, whatever happens Nicky, I'll always be glad to have known you and to have spent this time together,' he'd said on more than one occasion.

She'd kissed him, loving him all the more for his wisdom, his pragmatism and his ability to accept willingly whatever happened. She was the one who constantly fretted about the future, rather than living in the moment.

The weekend without Conor turned out to be a fabulous one. Together with a couple of people from her course, who were fast becoming her best friends, Nicky went paintballing on Saturday and out for a pizza followed by the pub with Sabina and Jez that night.

'I bet you're looking forward to seeing Conor next weekend,' Sabina said, as they downed the third of several pints. 'He's gorgeous. And he adores you.'

Nicky shrugged. 'He does, and yes, he's lovely, but . . .'

'But what?'

'I don't know. It's just kind of . . . restrictive, having a boyfriend like him.'

Jez laughed. 'Ah, she wants her freedom as well as her fella. Cake and eat it, eh?'

'She doesn't know what's good for her,' Sabina said, and although her tone was jokey there was an underlying seriousness to her words. 'Like when she moans about her mum being too involved with her life. She bought you a pile of clothes last week, didn't she? My mum wouldn't so much as buy me a pair of knickers, honestly. You're so lucky, Nicky, and you don't even know it.'

'Lucky with my mates, at least,' Nicky said, raising her glass to the pair of them.

On Sunday she went into Brighton and walked on her own along the promenade. It was a blustery day with occasional rain showers and a wind that whipped the sea into a froth and sent her hair flying wildly around her face. The kind of day that made you feel alive. As she walked, enjoying the solitude, she thought long and hard about her relationship with Conor and . . . she hardly dared voice it even in her head . . . whether it was still what she wanted.

And then, a week later, it was time for Conor's rescheduled visit. Nicky was nervous about it. She'd made a decision, and it was not going to be easy to follow through on it. But she'd convinced herself it was the right thing to do.

She had spent the week psyching herself up for what needed to happen. Immersing herself in student life – both the studying and partying – and making the most of having a new life away from the small, sleepy town where she'd grown up. This was what it was all about. New friends, new surroundings, new opportunities.

Conor arrived at lunchtime on Saturday, and walked up to her student flat from the station. As she opened the door to him, he kissed her and dumped a small rucksack on the floor. 'God it's good to be here again! Rubbish train journey today. Had to change twice and get a bus for part of it. So sorry for letting you down last weekend. Anyway, I'm here now, and we can relax and have fun for a couple of days.'

'Mmm. Sure. Can I make you some lunch? Cheese on toast?'

'Fab, yes please. I'm starving. Was up at stupid o'clock to try to maximise time with you.' He grinned at her – that broad, genuine smile he'd always had. She still loved that smile. She still loved Conor – she thought she always would, no matter what.

'Right then, I'll go and make it.' She went to the kitchen she shared with nine other students, unlocked her cupboard and put a couple of slices of bread in the toaster. She had an opened packet of cheese in the fridge, which, thankfully, no one else had stolen. She cut some slices and put them on the toast under the grill. Conor had followed her in, and perched on the counter as she worked.

'So, how've you been? You had your mum here a couple of weeks ago, didn't you? How was that?'

Nicky rolled her eyes. 'Oh, same as ever. She's so controlling, and she belittles me every chance she gets.'

'I like her. She's always been generous to me.'

'Yeah, well, she bought me some clothes but I'd rather she just kept away.'

'I guess it's hard on parents to let their kids spread their wings. She'll get there, Nick. Just give her time. Nice of her to buy you stuff.'

Nicky shrugged. 'Yeah, I suppose.' Sabina had said the same thing. She handed Conor a plate of food and a cup of tea. 'There you go.'

She watched him eat in silence. How was she going to tell him? Maybe she should have gone to his university

33

this weekend, and told him there. Then she'd have been in control of when she left. This was going to be so difficult.

'You all right, Nick? You seem quiet today?' Conor went to wash his plate and put it on the draining board. 'And you've had nothing to eat.'

'I'm not hungry. I'm all right. Although I . . . need to talk to you.'

'Ooh er, sounds ominous!' Conor gave a little laugh. 'Shall we go back to your room then?'

It was as good a place as any, and she might as well get this over with now. She nodded and led the way.

'So what you're saying is, "it's not you, it's me", is that it?' Conor's expression was one of disbelief mixed with misery. He was sitting on her bed, leaning forward, his elbows on his knees. She was perched on her desk opposite, barely able to look at him.

'It's just . . . better for both of us. We should make the most of our student days. Get fully involved, meet new people, do new stuff. I just think that's kind of hard to do when you have a partner in another university and all your weekends are used up seeing them.'

'I'm taking too much of your time. Should we . . . I don't know . . . limit ourselves to once a month?' He raised his head to gaze at her, and she was heartbroken to see the glimmer of hope in his eyes; that maybe reducing how often they saw each other would mean they could carry on as a couple.

She shook her head. 'No, I think . . . a clean break. We stay friends, and who knows, after we've graduated . . . but for now . . . I guess . . .'

'You want your freedom.' He finished the sentence for her. 'Have you met someone else?'

'No. It's not that. I told you there is no one else. But I want to be free in case . . .'

34

'In case you do find someone better.' He sighed, and in that sigh was the recognition and acceptance, she hoped, that what they'd had over the last three years had run its course. They'd grown up and grown apart. Well, she had, at least.

'I'm not looking for anyone, Conor. I doubt I could find someone "better" than you. You're a gorgeous bloke. Kind, funny, good-looking. I still love you. I just want a bit of space, I suppose. I don't want the . . . responsibility of having a boyfriend who's halfway up the country. You always said, we'd enjoy it while it lasted but would accept it was over if either of us wanted to end it.' She put a hand on his shoulder and gave it a perfunctory rub. 'You'll find someone else in no time, I reckon.'

'I don't want anyone else. I love you, Nick. Always have and always will. But if I can't change your mind now . . . I guess I have to accept it. If this is really what you want. And yes, I would like to stay in touch, remain friends if we can.' He stood up and slipped on his jacket. 'I'll go, then. Sooner you can start your new, unrestricted life the better, I suppose.' There was a tinge of bitterness in his voice that he was trying to hide. But he couldn't hide it from her. She knew him too well, she always had.

Nicky couldn't think how to answer him. It was sad, but it was right. For her, at least. 'Shall I walk with you to the station?'

'No. I'd rather walk on my own.' He picked up his rucksack.

'I'll see you out.' She opened the door to her room and led the way to the flat's front door.

'See you at Easter, maybe? As friends?'

'I'm not planning on coming home much, if at all. Actually, I think I'm going to Dublin, to see my great-grandmother.'

'Oh. Well, bye then. Let me know if . . . you change your mind at all. And enjoy Dublin.'

With that he was gone, and Nicky was free. Her life was ahead of her, full of promise and opportunity. But for now, she felt strangely deflated. The look in Conor's eyes when she'd ended it had almost stopped her in her tracks, but she'd made her decision, so she'd pressed on.

And now she had another completely free weekend. There was a grunge band playing in the student union bar that evening. She'd go to it. Conor wouldn't have wanted to – it wasn't his type of music. Wasn't hers either, really, but it was an opportunity, so she'd go. Sabina and Jez had said they were going. And meanwhile, she'd better get in touch with Supergran, arrange to go over to Dublin sometime soon, and book some flights. Now that she'd told Conor she was going she might as well. She had no other ideas for her rebellion project, after all.

Chapter 4 – Autumn 1915

There was a Cumann na mBan meeting during the week after O'Donovan Rossa's funeral. It was held at Liberty Hall, as so many meetings had been. Gráinne went along, excited to see her Republican friends again, looking forward to hearing what they thought of Pádraig Pearse's words at the funeral.

After the main business of the meeting was over, the Countess Markiewicz approached Gráinne who was sitting at the side of the hall. 'Gráinne MacDowd, isn't it? I remember you from last year, when we landed those guns at Howth. You did a fine job that day, organising those boys from the Fianna Éireann.'

Gráinne jumped to her feet. 'Yes, Madame. That was a frightening moment, when we thought the military were going to seize all the guns we'd landed.' Gráinne recalled being terrified the whole mission would be a disaster, and worse, that some of them might be arrested or hurt. But she'd managed to get the boys to hide the guns in a nearby Christian Brothers community, and in the end only a few rifles were seized with over 1600 spirited away, later distributed among regiments of Irish Volunteers.

'It was a huge success,' the Countess said now. 'And in no small way thanks to you. I think we will be able to make good use of your quick thinking and leadership ability. Tell me, where do you work?'

'At Clerys department store, Madame,' Gráinne replied.

'Hmm. Do you know where I live? Surrey House in Rathmines? Would you be able to pay me a visit on your next day off?'

'That would be Sunday. Yes, Madame, I know where it is and I can come. But why?' Gráinne was proud to have been singled out by the Countess, who was the head of the Cumann na mBan, but was at a loss as to what the Countess wanted from her.

The Countess smiled. 'I have a proposition for you, but it is best discussed at my house rather than here. Come around midday.' She patted Gráinne's shoulder and moved away to talk to another woman.

Gráinne took care to look her best on Sunday, dressing in a clean and simple grey skirt and blouse, with a dark green jacket. She pinned up her hair and added a narrow-brimmed hat and flat-heeled boots and her Cumann na mBan armband. It was an outfit that was comfortable and allowed her to move easily – unlike the hobble skirts that were so fashionable now, in which women could not take long strides. She had no idea what the Countess might ask her to do, so had tried to be ready for anything. More gun-running? A recruitment drive? Helping train the younger Fianna boys? Though what she'd be able to train them in she couldn't imagine.

She took a tram across the city to Rathmines and walked the last section to Leinster Road. Surrey House was situated on a corner. It was a tall, gabled building, joined to its neighbour, looking like any other red-brick, middle-class house in the area. The only thing setting it apart from the others was the fact it was very clearly being watched, by a man Gráinne assumed was a plain-clothes policeman. He was leaning against a lamppost opposite, a cigarette dangling from the corner of his mouth. Judging by the several butts on the ground at his feet, he'd been there for some time. He stared hard at Gráinne as she walked up to the front door, and she noticed him write something in a notebook. So now she was known to the authorities. But she hadn't done anything wrong, so she held her head high and rang the doorbell.

It was opened by a lad of about 14 years, who was dressed in Fianna Éireann uniform. 'Are you wanting Madame?' he asked.

'Yes please.'

He nodded towards a door that led off the hall, closed the front door behind Gráinne, and ran off towards the back of the house. Gráinne went into the room he'd indicated. It was a sitting room, stuffed with an assortment of chairs of all shapes and sizes. There were several people there, men and women, some in uniform, some not. Another boy in Fianna uniform was collecting up some empty teacups on a tray. They rattled as he stumbled across the room, and without thinking Gráinne stepped forward. 'Here, let me take that,' she said, and the boy gratefully let her take the tray from him. 'Now show me where the kitchen is.'

He led the way back to the hallway and along a passage to the back of the house, where another boy was washing-up. Gráinne put the tray on a table that took up the centre of the room.

'Thank you. A little thing, but exactly the kind of initiative I need.' Madame Markiewicz had followed them into the kitchen. 'Now come and meet everyone, Gráinne. Then I'll find a quiet spot, if such a thing exists in this house, and I'll tell you my proposal.'

Gráinne followed her back to the sitting room where she was introduced to various people. She had heard of a few of them but not all, and she took great care to commit their names and faces to memory. James Connolly, the founder and head of the Irish Citizen Army, was there, a man in his forties with receding hair and an impressive moustache. He seemed to be a great friend of Madame Markiewicz, referring to her as Constance. Joseph Plunkett, a young fellow who was wearing bright scarves and several items of jewellery, rings and bangles. He smiled kindly at Gráinne. 'Pleased to meet you. And this is my fiancée, Grace Gifford.' Gráinne shook the hand of a pretty young woman who was sat beside Plunkett.

A small dog, a Cocker Spaniel, was curled up on the Countess's chair. 'And that is my dear Poppet,' the Countess told Gráinne, as she scratched behind its ears.

With the introductions done and a fresh round of tea distributed, which Gráinne helped make, the Countess nodded at Gráinne and gestured to another door from the hallway. It led to a small office. There were a couple of men in there having a heated discussion, but at the Countess's arrival they jumped up and left the room. 'We'll go elsewhere, Constance,' one said. 'It's all yours.'

'Thank you. Now Gráinne, please take a seat. As you can see, this is a busy house. Sometimes it can be hard to stay in control.'

'Madame, I think there's a man outside watching who comes and goes.' It seemed right to warn the Countess of this, but to Gráinne's astonishment the other woman just laughed.

'Yes, of course. He, or one of his colleagues, is there most days. Noting all my visitors, writing things in books. They don't see anything of any importance, however. If we want to do anything secret, we do it at night when they've gone.

They only keep watch during daylight hours. But thank you for the warning. It shows you are thinking along the right lines. Now then, here's my proposition for you. I have seen that you are a competent young woman who sees a job that needs doing and just gets on and does it. The abilities you showed organising the landing of those guns last year was admirable. What I need is someone to help me here. Someone who can take on any task from providing refreshments for my many visitors to organising the Fianna in teams to do leaflet drops. Someone I can trust with anything. Someone who's bright and clever, who could also help create and print those leaflets.' She smiled at Gráinne's frown. 'Oh yes, I have a small printing press in the basement here. You could help run that too. What do you say?'

'Madame I . . . I have a job—' Gráinne began, then mentally kicked herself for sounding as though she wasn't interested. 'I mean . . . I don't have a lot of free time, but I'm very happy to come here when I can to help.'

'I was wondering,' the Countess continued, 'whether you might like to change your job. You could work here. I will pay you a salary equal to whatever Clerys pays, and, of course, there is board and lodging here too. I have an attic room you can use. I need a right-hand woman. Someone to take on some of the work I would normally do myself, but there's simply too much to be done right now.' She leaned forward in her chair, elbows on the desk. 'It's a big commitment, you understand. It puts you at the heart of our endeavours. You will need to exercise discretion, for you will hear and see things in this house that you must not tell to another soul.' The Countess looked directly at Gráinne, her expression deathly serious, her gaze intense and questioning. 'And if you choose to take this on, there may come a time when you are asked to do something that puts you in danger. Of arrest, injury, even death. We don't know what the future holds for our cause, but we do know that, at some point, things will become dangerous. If you agree to come here to work for me, you need to be fully aware of what you are getting into.'

Gráinne blinked and coughed before she was able to answer. Of all the scenarios that had run through her head of why the Countess wanted her to come today, she had not expected this. She was excited but also awed by the prospect. Could she do this? Could she really take this job on? The Countess seemed to think so. 'Madame, I am honoured that you should ask me to do this. And yes, I would like to do it. I believe passionately that Ireland should be free and self-governing, and I am prepared to fight towards that aim.'

The Countess smiled and nodded. 'That is precisely how I feel too. And all those others you have met today in the front room. Well now, if you are sure you want to do this, let me show you the bedroom that will be yours, and the printing press. You will need to work your notice period at Clerys of course, but then I will be very happy to have you here as soon as possible. Come, I will give you a tour of the house.'

Gráinne followed the Countess around the house. There was a dining room set up as a meeting room, the kitchen she'd already seen, a well-stocked pantry, a room originally intended as a breakfast room that overlooked the garden, which was currently in use as another meeting and planning room. In the garden, a group of Fianna lads were cleaning some rifles. 'Be careful, boys,' the Countess told them. 'Make sure they are unloaded. We don't want anyone accidentally firing one again.'

'Madame? Did that happen? Was anyone hurt?'

'No one was hurt. The boy fired into the air. The only problem was that some neighbours complained, and we were raided by the police. Thankfully, we'd removed all the guns by then. We don't store weapons here as a rule. Just a few that are in need of attention.'

'Where's the main store, Madame?'

The Countess regarded her quietly for a moment. 'You'll find out, in time.'

Upstairs was the Countess's bedroom, a bathroom and three other bedrooms which each had more than one bed in. 'We have a lot of people staying overnight. Sometimes meetings go on late, other times Fianna lads stay here. And, occasionally, there are people in need of shelter. I don't turn anyone away if they are Irish and proud of it.'

In the attic were two further rooms tucked into the eaves. Both were originally intended for servants, but they were cosy and pleasantly furnished, and definitely a step-up from the shared dormitory Gráinne had been sleeping in at Clerys.

'This room is yours,' the Countess said, showing her a room with a view over the garden. It contained a small bed with a neat green bedspread, a washstand, a chest of drawers, a bentwood chair and a hand-knotted rug in shades of green and gold.

'It's beautiful,' Gráinne said.

'So will you take the job?'

'Of course I will. I can start in a week.'

The Countess smiled and shook Gráinne's hand. 'That's perfect, and it's all settled, then. Bring your things next week. Oh, and I must show you the printing press.'

They went downstairs, and from a door in the kitchen a further set of steps led to the basement. It was lit only by gas lamps. A small hand-operated printing press sat on a table. Beside it was a pile of blank paper and a tub of ink. 'It's a cumbersome process, but with a team of boys we are able to produce simple leaflets and fliers here, to help get our message across. There is a bigger and better one, used to print newspapers, housed elsewhere.'

'At Liberty Hall?' Gráinne knew that Connolly's Irish Citizen Army used Liberty Hall as its headquarters, and papers such as *The Irish Worker* and *The Workers' Republic* were produced there. Every now and again such papers were banned by the British government, but as soon as one was shut down another would spring up to take its place.

'Yes, that's right. Good – you've kept your eyes and ears open since joining the Cumann na mBan. Well now, I will show you how this works, for we have a poster prepared of which we want to print a hundred copies. I'll send a couple of boys down here to help with the printing, and the Fianna will then distribute them around the city overnight.'

Gráinne couldn't believe her luck, that already she was being asked to do something useful and exciting. Already she was at the very heart of the simmering revolution, just as she'd always hoped she would be. An image of Emmett flickered through her mind, and she found herself hoping she'd see him again soon and tell him about her new job. Although, of course, she couldn't tell him everything about it.

She watched carefully as the Countess showed her how to work the printing press. Partway through, Grace Gifford came down to join them. 'Can I help at all?' she asked, and the Countess nodded.

'If I can leave you two girls to it, that would be most helpful.'

Gráinne nodded – she'd got the hang of the press now, and liked the idea of being able to get to know Grace a little. It was good to have someone nearer her own age around the house.

'You're going to be a frequent visitor, are you?' Grace asked, when they were alone.

'I'm going to be moving in,' Gráinne replied. 'To help out around the house.'

'Oh, that's marvellous! It'll be nice to have someone younger here. Sometimes the place is full of crusty old men. I swear some of them are old enough to have fought in the 1798 rebellion.' Grace laughed and Gráinne joined in.

'I only saw young boys of about 14 when I arrived, spilling cups of tea everywhere.'

'Yes, that's the choice. Old men or young lads. Apart from Joseph, of course, but he's spoken for.' Grace smiled wistfully as she thought of her fiancé.

'Have you been engaged long?' Gráinne asked, as she took another stack of printed leaflets from the press.

'A while, but no date set. We've known each other since we were children, so. He's always been the only one for me.'

'Childhood sweethearts! Oh, that's so romantic!'

'Ah, sure it will be if I can ever pin him down,' Grace said. 'And you, do you have a young man?'

An image of Emmett crossed Gráinne's mind, for some strange reason. 'No, I don't.'

'But you're thinking of someone!' Grace nudged Gráinne playfully with her elbow. 'I can tell!'

Gráinne blushed. 'He's . . . just a friend of my brother. I saw him again last week.'

'Friends of brothers are perfect, as we already know they're the right sort.' Grace smiled. 'I hope it works out for you. And I'm glad you're going to be here. I suppose we should get on with this job now.'

They worked well together, and Gráinne couldn't help but think she'd landed on her feet. A new job, a new friend, and the chance to be at the heart of the Republican movement. What more could she want?

Gráinne handed in her notice at Clerys the next day. She only had to work a week more in the shop, but the days seemed to drag now that she had something new, exciting and, above all, worthwhile ahead of her. Working in a shop was all very well but working for the Countess, in a house that was becoming one of the nerve centres for the Republican movement, felt so much more important a job. And Grace – she'd only met her once but already thought of her as a better friend than any of the other girls she'd known at Clerys. She wrote to her father to tell him the news and had a quick reply from him, wishing her all the best and stating that he was proud of her.

Halfway through the week she had a visitor. Emmett was waiting for her when she finished work. She smiled in greeting, pleased to see him.

'I thought, if you like, we could go out for dinner somewhere? My treat.' He blushed as he asked her, and she had the impression he'd possibly rehearsed the question a few times in advance.

'I would like that very much. I have nothing on tonight, but I'll be needing to change my clothes first.' She gestured at her shop assistant's uniform. 'Will you wait outside?'

'I will, of course.'

She hurried up to her dormitory, washed and changed into her best dress and smart shoes. She added a daub of lipstick too, but then rubbed it off, thinking it made her look too superficial. She didn't want someone who liked her only for her looks. It was important to her that anyone she stepped out with should like her for her mind, her politics, her intelligence. It was too soon to say whether Emmett was such a man, but she found herself hoping he was.

He smiled broadly at her when she came back down. 'You look beautiful,' he said, and offered her his arm. She took it, and they walked round to Sackville Street and down it towards the river. 'I thought we might go over to the south side, and have dinner at the Shelbourne Hotel? We could take a little stroll around St Stephen's Green first, while it's still light, and then go in for dinner.'

'The Shelbourne? Isn't that rather . . . expensive?'

'Ah, you're worth it, Grá,' he replied. 'Sure and what's the point of earning money if I can't spend it having a lovely evening out with a wonderful girl?'

'I won't be able to treat you to anything as extravagant in return,' she warned him, but he shook his head.

'That doesn't matter. Come on, let's go out and enjoy ourselves.'

It was a warm evening, and strolling around St Stephen's Green while the sun dipped down behind the buildings was very pleasant. The flowerbeds were full of dahlias and roses, and the paths amongst them were well tended. There were plenty of people out, enjoying the mild early autumn.

In the Shelbourne, a group of British army officers and their wives sat at a table not far from Gráinne and Emmett. Gráinne glanced over at them in dismay. She did not want to be reminded of the war this evening. It made her think of Sean, and of the fact that if, or when, a rebellion came in Ireland, it was officers such as those who would be leading the fight against the Volunteers. That was a sobering thought.

Emmett had noticed them too. 'One day,' he whispered to her, 'they will be the enemy. But until then, let's ignore them. Right then, what will you have?'

Gráinne smiled and perused the menu. Steak, mutton stew, braised beef, even lobster were present. Such wonderful food – a different league to what she was used to having at the Clerys staff refectory. She chose her meal then picked up the glass of wine Emmett had poured her and sat back to savour it, determined to enjoy every minute of this wonderful evening.

Chapter 5 – March 1998

It was all very well being free to do what she liked now that she wasn't tied to Conor, but the band playing in the student union were rubbish. Nicky's friends from her course – Sabina and Jez – left after the first set, apologising to her, but saying they couldn't stomach any more of it. By then Nicky had already drunk several cans of lager, enough to deaden the pain of losing Conor. Even though it had been her who finished it, it somehow still felt like a loss. Sabina had been horrified when she told her: 'But he was gorgeous. You're mad. I hope you don't regret your decision.'

Nicky had shrugged, not wanting to talk about it or even think about it anymore. When her friends left, she decided to stay for the second set. Might as well – there was nothing else to do.

She was standing near the bar nursing her latest can of lager and scanning the crowd for any other faces she recognised, when a tall student with a shock of black hair and wearing an expensive-looking black leather jacket came to stand beside her.

'Hi. Enjoying the band?'

'Not really,' she said, then bit her lip. What if he was a friend of one of the band members? She should have pretended to like them, at least a little.

He laughed. 'Well, you're honest, aren't you? You're right though, they're crap. And they're about to start up again. Drink up – let's go somewhere else where we can talk.'

He spoke in the tone of someone who was used to being obeyed. Without really thinking about it, she downed her drink and followed him out of the bar. It was a miserable, wet evening with a persistent drizzle, and she was glad of her own leather jacket. The one Conor had bought her, she realised. It would always remind her of him. Perhaps she'd need to get herself a different one.

'We could go to the East Slope bar, or into town if you prefer?'

'East Slope's good,' she replied. 'It's cheap.' Not that he looked the type to care if beer was a few pence more a pint. He had the kind of voice that suggested a private education and comfortably off parents in a large detached house with a Mercedes in the garage.

'East Slope it is, then. Sebastian Price-Warner. But call me Seb. And you are?'

'Nicky Waters.' She shook the hand he'd held out to her and smiled at him. He had a long, straight nose and well-defined lips. *Very* nice looking, she thought.

'Nicky. Pleased to meet you.' He returned her smile, and it felt as though he'd bestowed her with a gift of sunshine and gold.

The East Slope bar was full of its usual throng of students who lived on campus. Seb bought them each a bottle of Becks and led her away to a table tucked in a corner, where there were some spare stools. 'Mind if we sit here?' he said to the couple who were already using that table. Not waiting for an answer, he pulled the stools out and beckoned Nicky to sit on one. She smiled a thank you to the couple and took her seat.

'So what are you studying?' he asked her, as he pulled a packet of cigarettes out of his pocket and offered one to Nicky.

She shook her head. 'No thanks. Modern history. And you?'

'Life, and how to live it.' He lit a cigarette for himself and blew smoke towards the ceiling.

She was about to make some sort of comment when he grinned. 'Well, officially I'm studying philosophy with cognitive science, which seemed like a good idea when I picked it at random out of the prospectus. But really, I'm just here to have a good time. To enjoy life while I'm young, among other young people. To drink, get high, get laid, go on a few protest marches – have the full university experience, you know?'

She nodded, feeling excited. It was like a sign – on the very day she'd cut her ties with Conor, she'd met this boy who had exactly the same ideas as her regarding what university life should be all about. Trying different things, kicking back against authority a little, experiencing freedom from parental constraints. 'I do know. I mean, we get these three years, three years in which we don't have to go out and earn money, in which we're surrounded by interesting, intelligent people. Away from the control of parents. Got to make the most of it!'

'Absolutely, and just do the minimum work required to not get kicked out. I scraped through the first year exams but they've let me stay.' He took a swig of his beer. 'Anyway, we're not here to talk about our courses. Tell me about you, Nicky. What gets you excited, eh? What floats your boat, tickles your fancy, turns you on?'

She gave what she hoped was an enigmatic smile. 'Rebellion.'

He grinned again and regarded her thoughtfully as he took a long drag on his cigarette. 'A rebel, eh? And an attractive one. Just my type.'

'Are you a rebel?' she asked, hoping she sounded flirtatious.

'Oh yes, sweetie. You'd better believe it.' He looked at her sideways as he exhaled smoke. 'I fight the Establishment, at every opportunity. Somebody has to, eh?'

Nicky picked up her beer and drank, hoping to hide her sudden feeling of confusion. She'd told Conor only hours earlier that she didn't want anyone else. But this guy Seb – with his black hair falling over one eye, his intense gaze, his charm and cultured manners – oh she wanted him all right. She'd never thought she'd be the type to sleep with a boy on a first date, and to be honest Conor was the only person she'd ever slept with, but she made the decision then and there that she'd sleep with Seb, if he wanted her.

Nicky ended up bringing Seb back to her room that night. He produced a half-bottle of vodka from a pocket and they sat up for a while drinking it, although Nicky was well aware she'd already drunk too much. They sat side by side on her bed, talking of many things, and she tried to cement them in her brain so that she'd remember it all when sober.

'So, what kind of a rebel are you, then?' she asked, remembering their conversation in the bar.

'The kind that sticks up for the rights of the people against those who make the rules. The kind that fights against those who'd have us cowed and submissive.' Seb leaned forward as though warming to his topic. 'You know that guy Swampy, yeah? The one who leads protests against road building?'

Nicky nodded. She remembered seeing news items the previous year when Swampy and his pals had lived in tunnels they'd dug beneath the route of a planned new road in Devon. They'd managed to delay works while the police and courts battled to try to evict them. And back in 1996, Swampy had been part of the protests against the Newbury bypass, living in a tree to stop it being cut down. Nicky had admired his spirit and dedication to his cause, especially since her parents had done nothing but tut and talk about how Swampy was simply wasting taxpayers' money. Even Conor had commented that Swampy was an irresponsible idiot and that there were better ways of putting his point across.

'Yeah, him. Well, I sort of know him, you know? The Newbury bypass runs near my parents' place. I went out to those woods when he was up in a tree.'

'You joined the protest?'

'Yeah.' Seb looked pleased with himself, smiling proudly at her.

'Tell me more! Did you live in a tree? Which camp were you part of?'

'I was all over. Moved around, you know? It was a big thing. We stopped the road building for ages. Nearly succeeded stopping it for good.'

'It was awful the way they cut down all those ancient woodlands. I mean I know we need decent roads, but . . .'

'They tell us we need roads, as they want us all driving along them like sheep. All part of the plan to control us, Nicky. Don't let them in here, whatever you do.' Seb tapped gently on the side of her head, then let his fingers trail down her cheek to her jaw. She gave a little gasp, and he smiled at her, staring right into her soul as though he could read her every thought.

And then he cupped his hand around the back of her head, and pulled her towards him, his lips seeking hers. She closed her eyes and kissed him back, feeling her body respond even though her brain felt a little foggy from the vodka.

After that, things moved inexorably forward, and she was soon in bed with him. A part of her brain felt as though she was cheating on Conor but she pushed that thought down. She and Conor had broken up, freeing each other to do exactly this, if they wanted. She hadn't met Seb until after she'd split up with Conor, so there was no reason why she should feel guilty. And yet, she did, a little.

Seb was an adventurous lover, encouraging her to try different things, to push the boundaries. Sex with Conor had been loving and safe, giving her a feeling of closeness and belonging. With Seb it was exciting, exhilarating and just a little bit scary, as though she was taking risks, doing something dangerous. This, she thought, was what had been missing from her life.

Afterwards, he'd checked the time on his expensive-looking watch (why a rebel like Seb felt the need to be governed by time she didn't know) and had groaned to see that it was past three o'clock in the morning.

'Early meeting with my tutor tomorrow. Got to go, babe. They'll kick me out if I don't make that meeting.'

'You can stay here?' Nicky said, sleepily. She wanted nothing more than to fall asleep in his arms.

But Seb had shaken his head. 'No. Need a change of clothes. And to pick up my notes so I can be prepared. It's too late for trains so I'll have to take a taxi back to my flat. Sorry, babe. Been a good evening.'

'I'll see you again?'

He grinned as he pulled on his clothes. 'You certainly will. *Adios, mon amie.*'

She laughed at the mix of languages and sat up to kiss him goodbye. It was only after he'd left that she realised she had no means of contacting him. No phone number, no address (apart from knowing he didn't live on campus). She only knew his name and the subject he was studying. So at least she could put a note in the relevant pigeonhole at university, if she didn't catch up with him some other way.

A few days passed with no sign of Seb. Nicky could not stop herself thinking about him. A small part of her, that she was suppressing, felt dirty at having got drunk and slept with him within hours of meeting him, but the larger part was excited at her newfound freedom and glad that already she had made the most of it.

Still, the fact remained that he had not contacted her again. He knew her flat and room number; he could have come round to see her or pushed a note under her door. He hadn't been back to either the student union bar or the East Slope bar – she'd checked both each night.

Should she, or should she not, write a note for him and put it in the pigeonhole in his faculty? Would that look too pushy?

Maybe he had a mobile phone. If he had, he hadn't told her or given her a number. But would she have the nerve to ring it even if he had?

The only thing that progressed over those few days was that she made a decision regarding her rebellion project. She would hold her nose and follow Mum's advice, and write about the 1916 Easter Rising in Dublin. She'd tell her great-grandmother's story, focusing on the role of women during the rebellion. Nicky knew she needed to do well with this project, to get herself back on track on her course. And although she hated to admit it, her mother's idea intrigued her.

She took the train into Brighton one afternoon and called at a travel agent's to check out flights to Dublin. Thankfully, a Ryanair flight from Gatwick was pretty cheap. If she made the right noises to Mum, no doubt Mum would pay for it anyway. She'd offered to help. But it would be a point to her, that Nicky didn't want to give away.

Next job was to call Supergran and make sure it was convenient for her to visit. There were daily flights, but it would be best for her to go over a weekend. She had no lectures on Friday afternoons or Mondays so it was possible to take three days. There was a phone box near the station, so she headed there and made the phone call, using the phone card Mum had given her.

'Hi, Supergran. It's me, Nicky. Karen's daughter, in England.'

'Nicky! Lovely to hear from you, so it is. Your mum said you might call. You're wanting to visit me, is it, to ask about 1916? Such a very long time ago that was!' Her voice was bright and clear, with only a little wavering to hint at her age.

'Yes, that's right,' Nicky replied, feeling simultaneously pleased that her great-grandmother had had a head's-up about her call and annoyed that Mum had interfered, as she so often did. What if Nicky had come up with a different idea for her project and had decided not to go to Dublin after all?

'That's marvellous! I'll be delighted to have you to stay! And very happy to talk about that time. It was so long ago, and there's not many nowadays that want to hear an old woman's story.' She sighed, and Nicky imagined her shaking her head a little. 'Now don't be worrying you'll need to be looking after me at all. I've a whole network of people coming in to see to me every day and they'll keep coming. You know your mum's cousins Caitlín and Diarmuid, and then there's my daughter Eileen, that's your mum's aunt, and then Jimmy helps now and again when Eileen can't come.'

Nicky's head was spinning with all the names. She remembered her mum talking about these people but wasn't sure if she'd ever met them all. The Irish lot were, in her mind, not much more than a jumble of names of great-aunts and uncles and cousins of her mother, whom she may or may not have met when she was a child. 'I can help too, Supergran. I mean I can cook for you, and do the shopping . . .' If she had to, she supposed she could. Though she'd draw the line at personal care, helping the old lady get dressed or into bed.

'That's kind of you but sure we have everything worked out. A system, like, and it's probably easier to stick to it. Now then, when are you thinking of coming?'

'A week on Friday, if that's convenient? I'd stay till Monday.'

'Any time's convenient, Nicky. I don't go out much these days. Just let me know what flight you're on and I'll ask Jimmy to meet you at the airport. He won't mind. You remember Jimmy? Eileen's lad. He's out of work at the moment, so he is, so he'll not mind running up to the airport to fetch you.'

'Oh, that would be great,' Nicky said. She vaguely remembered meeting her mum's cousin Jimmy a few times. A big fellow in his late thirties with a loud voice. She remembered liking him; he seemed a bit of a rebel, like her. There'd been a family occasion – a wedding – where he'd been the only one of the men not wearing a suit. Instead, he'd worn a pair of jeans and a loud Hawaiian shirt. She hadn't liked his dress sense but she had liked that little hint of a rebellious nature. He'd bought her a pint, even though she'd been underage. Mum had been horrified, until Jimmy pointed out with a chuckle that it was only a shandy.

'Well look, so, I'll give you his number. Can you write it down? Then you can ring him and tell him when your flight gets in. He lives only a rabbit's skip from the airport, so you can call him when you land and he'll come for you.'

Nicky fumbled in her pockets for a pen and scrap of paper to write the number down, thanked her great-grandmother and ended the call, feeling pleased with herself. A few minutes later she was back at the travel agent's to book the flights. There was some useful background reading she could do before going to Dublin, which would help her make the most of her time with Supergran, asking her about her activities during the 1916 Rising.

Booking the flight felt like a good day's work, and she hadn't even had to set foot in a lecture theatre or the library. Nicky headed back to the station grinning happily. Maybe she would go to the library now and search out some books for background reading.

There were fifteen minutes to wait until the next train up to the university campus at Falmer. Time to give her mother a quick ring. Mum would score a point for Nicky having taken up her suggestion for the project, but on the other hand, she might also offer to pay the travel expenses, which Nicky had just written a cheque for. It would be good to have that reimbursed as soon as possible.

She used her phone card once again, and dialled her home number. 'Hey Mum, it's me. Only got a minute but—'

'You've broken off with Conor! His mother let me know. The poor boy's devastated. I can't believe it. Neither can your dad. What are you thinking?'

'Er, Mum . . . that's not what I called about—'

'Well, it might not be but it's an important thing to talk about! Why, Nicky? That poor, lovely boy!'

'Mum, I had my reasons. It's not really any of your business.'

'You've met another boy? That's it, isn't it?'

Nicky began to protest when she spotted a familiar figure striding across the station concourse in her direction. Seb was grinning as he approached, then he stood leaning against the wall just a little way off, arms folded, cigarette dangling from his lip, waiting for her to finish the call. He was near enough to hear anything she said, so how could she now say that no, she hadn't met anyone else?

'Mum, I'm not talking about that right now, OK? I'm at the station, there's a queue for the phone. I was just phoning because I've booked flights to go to see Supergran next Friday and you said you might pay.'

'Oh, you're calling because you want money. And that poor lad with his heart broken. Well, I promised so I'll transfer some money into your account, but really, Nicola, you need to have a good hard think about what you've done. It might not be too late, Conor's mum said he'd have you back like a shot and well I do think—'

'Ah, sorry Mum, there's the pips, got to go,' Nicky cut in.

'Are you not using the phone card I gave you?'

'Bye Mum, I'll ring again on—' And with that, Nicky hung up as though the call had been cut off. She retrieved her phone card, which still had over four pounds on it, and tucked it back into her purse.

'Naughty, naughty!' Seb shook his head and tutted. 'Telling porkies to get off the phone with your mum, were you?'

'She'd talk for ever if I let her,' Nicky said. She felt a rising tide of excitement at seeing him again. His eyes were as blue as ever, his hair still black, flopping over one eye. The ever-present cigarette at the corner of his mouth made him look like a cool Chicago gangster.

'You heading into town?' Seb asked.

'Yeah.' Nicky suppressed a smile, trying to play it cool. Well, she had been heading back to campus to start work on her project, but if there was a chance of spending time with Seb, that was a much better use of the afternoon.

'Fancy a stroll along the pier? Get some chips and a beer?'

'Yeah, why not?'

She walked with him back out of the station and down the road towards the promenade and the Palace Pier. She loved this part of Brighton, especially out of season when there were no tourists and it belonged to the locals and the students. It was a blustery day and the wind was whipping up white-tipped waves that crashed onto the shingle beach, rolling the stones up and back musically. The salt tang in the air heightened her senses . . . or was it Seb's closeness that was making her tingle all over? She still could not believe that she'd slept with this gorgeous boy just a few days ago, and that he seemed to like her and want to spend more time with her. He was chatting as they walked, about the music he liked and the bands he'd seen playing at the university or at the Brighton Centre. Nicky hadn't heard of many of them but she nodded knowingly and just hoped he wouldn't think her uncool if she admitted that Backstreet Boys and Aerosmith were her current favourites.

'So, your mum,' he said, looking sideways at her as they made their way along the pier, past the amusement arcades and candyfloss stalls. 'I couldn't help but hear something about you booking flights and she's paying. Where are you off to? Anywhere nice?'

'To Dublin. I just booked the tickets today.'

'Cool city! Friend of mine went to his brother's stag weekend there. Said there were some great pubs in Temple Bar. You going there?'

'Um, not sure. I'll be touring round a bit, I think. Research, for a project I'm doing.'

'Research? Like, work? *University* stuff?'

'Yeah. Actually, I'm really excited about it. I've got to write about a rebellion, and find a new angle, and it turns out my great-grandmother, who's 100 but still got all her marbles, played a part in the 1916 Easter Rising, and so I'm going to look at the women's roles in that. Too much of history is written by men. And Supergran – uh, that's my great-grandmother – lives just outside Dublin, so I'm off to stay with her and hear her story . . .' Nicky broke off as she realised that Seb was looking at her indulgently, the way he might look at an overexcited child.

'Aw, it's sweet that you're so thrilled about it all. A visit to Granny, eh? God, I'd hate to have to stay with mine to do a project. The old dear's batty as hell.'

'Great-grandmother.'

'Whatever. Old people are all the same. Spend all their time dissing the young. I got no time for them. They've had their day, fucked things up, and now they should leave the world to us young ones. Well, shall we get some chips? We can sit on a bench that's out of the wind, eh?' Seb didn't wait for a reply but strode over to a kiosk on the pier selling food and ordered for both of them. They chose a bench in a sheltered spot overlooking the beach and he handed over a paper carton of chips, then produced a couple of cans of beer from his pockets.

'Were you carrying those beers round with you all day?' Nicky asked.

'Yeah, on the off-chance I might meet someone to drink them with,' he replied, flashing her a grin and a wink. Did he mean he'd been hoping to bump into her, or would he have shared them with anyone? Nicky had no idea. *Just live in the moment and stop overanalysing everything*, she told herself, as she opened her can and clinked it against his.

'Well, cheers, then.'

'Yeah, cheers. Oi, get off, you bugger!' A huge seagull had swooped down and snatched a chip right out of Seb's hand. Nicky couldn't help but chuckle, but a moment later she too was having to battle to save her chips from a gull. Laughing, they ran together into one of the buildings on the pier to take cover from the predatory birds.

When they'd finished eating, Seb pulled out a packet of cigarettes to light up.

'Not sure you're allowed to smoke here,' Nicky said, pointing at a prominent 'no smoking' sign on the wall.

'Ah, who cares? Thought you were a rebel like me!' Seb lit his cigarette anyway.

'It's not good for you . . .' Nicky began, then stopped herself. She was sounding like her own mother. What business was it of hers whether Seb smoked or not?

'So they say. But it's all a conspiracy, isn't it? Telling us we can't smoke is just part of the nanny state trying to control us. I smoke to assert my independence. Speaking of which, did you hear they've banned smoking from the union bar on campus as of next week? Bloody cheek, that is.'

'I did hear. Apparently, some girl had a bad asthma attack there as it was so smoky and ended up in hospital, so now they want to give asthmatic students somewhere safe to go.'

'By banning the smokers. What happened to our civil rights?' Seb looked really cross about it.

'You can still go if you don't smoke. Or smoke in other bars?'

'But I want to smoke in *that* bar. And I used to be able to – met you there, didn't I? Now they've taken that right from me. They've discriminated against smokers. I'm not happy about it, Nicky.'

Privately, Nicky thought that it was a good thing there was now a safe bar for asthmatics to go to, or anyone else who didn't want to be surrounded by a fug of cigarette smoke while they drank. But she decided it was best to keep that opinion to herself, and just enjoy the day with Seb.

Chapter 6 – Autumn 1915

On the walk home from the Shelbourne, once they were far enough away that there could be no danger of being overheard by the army officers, Gráinne told Emmett about her new job. 'I don't entirely know what I'll be doing,' she said, which was more or less the truth. 'I'll be helping out around the house but also doing jobs for the Countess, things she hasn't time to do herself.'

Emmett stopped walking and pulled her round to face him. 'Gráinne, that's . . . that's wonderful. I know how strongly you feel about the Republican movement, and it's so good that you will be able to play an active role in it. More active, I mean, than you already were. But . . . is it safe? You said you thought a detective was watching the house. I would hate you to get in any kind of trouble. I feel . . . responsible for you, in a way.'

'Responsible? Why?'

He put his hands on her shoulders. 'You are only seventeen. Your brother was my best friend at school. Your father is a man I look up to and respect. I feel I should . . . look after you.'

She stepped away, scowling at him. 'I don't want to be looked after, Emmett. I want to play my part, and this is my chance to do that. And I'm almost eighteen.' Her birthday was a few months away still, but even so.

'Then let me support you while you play your part. Maybe as a team we can fight for Ireland together.'

'Now that, I'd like.'

He held out his arms and she stepped forward and into them. He held her close and she wrapped her arms around him, enjoying the feel of his strong, tall body next to hers. She thought about what he had said. Yes, it might be dangerous. Her name and face would become known to the authorities – the Countess herself had warned of this. If there was trouble, she'd be caught up in it, one way or another. But she knew she could not just sit back and let others fight for Ireland's future. She had to play her part, do what she could to help. If she was to hold her head up high for the rest of her life, she had to know she'd done everything in her power to help the Republican cause. She owed it to those past generations, her own ancestors who'd died during the Great Famine. To those who'd had their land taken by the English. To all those who'd had their culture, their language, their rights suppressed for centuries.

There were another three working days at Clerys and then, at last, it was the end of her notice period. Gráinne had already packed her belongings into her bag, so as soon as the shop closed on that Saturday afternoon she said goodbye to her colleagues, went up to the dormitory for the last time to collect her bag, and then made her way to Surrey House by tram and foot, as before.

The Countess was expecting her, and the house was a little quieter than it had been on Gráinne's previous visit. There were no Fianna boys loitering around, and only a couple of Irish Citizen Army men in the dining room, their heads bent over a ledger filled with numbers. She was disappointed to see that Grace wasn't there today, and wondered how often she would be a visitor. The Countess herself had opened the door to her, giving a cheery wave to the man who was sitting on a garden wall opposite, watching all comings and goings. He half lifted a hand in reply, then clearly thought better of it and turned the gesture into a scratch of his head. 'Ah, the poor fellow,' Countess Markiewicz said with a chuckle. 'It must be a tedious job. There's nothing he can report on, but he has to sit there and watch in any case. He'll be gone in an hour when it gets dark. Now then, Gráinne, you remember where your room is? Take your things up there, freshen up, then come down for a bite to eat. It's only bread and ham, but there's plenty of it.'

Gráinne did as she'd been asked. Someone, presumably the Countess, had put a small vase of Michaelmas daisies in her room, and there was a fresh ewer of water, a bar of soap and a towel on the washstand. Poppet the dog was curled up on the bed. 'Hello, boy. This is my room now, but I don't mind sharing,' she told the animal. Poppet wagged his tail and licked Gráinne's hand in welcome. She smiled. She was going to like living here, she was sure of it.

Later that evening, after she'd eaten and after dark, a group of Fianna lads came to the back door of the house. Gráinne helped the Countess hand them bundles of fliers that urged people to join the Irish Citizen Army and fight for the rights of ordinary Irish workers. 'James Connolly's words,' the Countess told her. 'Each time we distribute a pile of these, we get a few more recruits. It's about spreading the word and making people realise there's another way. Ireland doesn't have to be Britain's lapdog any longer.'

A second batch of leaflets read: *No conscription for Ireland. Let English men fight English wars*, and Gráinne was once more reminded of Sean, fighting that very same English war.

But he was fighting it because he believed that was the best way to achieve Irish Home Rule.

The boys were sent out to different parts of the city, to pin the fliers onto lampposts and park railings, or paste them onto gable ends of buildings. Anywhere they'd be seen. 'Don't get caught putting them up now, lads,' the Countess warned.

'Ah, we know what to do, Madame,' an older boy said, and the Countess smiled and ruffled his hair.

'Of course you do, Michael. You've done this many times. But I still have to warn you, you know I do.'

'Worse than my mam,' Michael muttered but he was grinning broadly.

The boys didn't return that night. The Countess explained they normally went straight home after distributing the leaflets and only returned if they had any news to report.

Gráinne settled in quickly to life at Surrey House. She was kept busy from morning to night, partly as a maid of all work, partly as a cook and partly as the Countess's personal assistant. She liked working directly with the Countess best – helping write and edit fliers, operating the printing press, organising the Fianna boys. She was also, on occasion, allowed to stay in the dining room when Connolly, Plunkett and others were there discussing strategy. Sometimes she'd be asked to leave, or the meeting would fall silent when she entered with refreshments, but on other occasions the Countess would nod to her to take a seat at the table, and perhaps write some notes of what was said. This was her favourite task. This was when she felt most involved.

A couple of weeks after moving in, the doorbell rang while Gráinne was busy in the kitchen preparing a pot of stew. They had a full house that evening, with every bed taken.

The Countess was sheltering a couple of women who'd been beaten by their husbands; one had brought young children with her. And there were some Volunteers up from Cork to discuss potential cooperation with Connolly's Irish Citizen Army. Gráinne took off her apron and hurried to answer the door.

'Emmett! What are you doing here?' He was standing, cap in hand, on the doorstep.

'Grá! Come to see how you're getting on, so I have. Is this a bad time? Are you busy?'

She laughed as she ushered him inside and closed the door. 'Sure aren't I always busy? Come on through to the kitchen. I'm making a pot of stew. There'll be enough for you, though the good Lord knows where you'll sit. We've a full house tonight.'

'I can see that!' Emmett had glanced through open doors as he followed her to the kitchen at the back of the house. There were people everywhere. The Countess looked up from a paper she was reading to see who'd arrived.

'Madame, this is Emmett O'Sheridan. He's a family friend, and a patriot.'

'Then he's very welcome here.' The Countess shook Emmett's hand, and he looked pleased but flustered to meet her.

'Thank you, Countess. I won't stop Gráinne getting on with her work. In fact, I'll help her in any way I can.'

'How good are you at peeling potatoes?' Gráinne asked him, arching her eyebrow.

The Countess laughed. 'A man who can peel a potato is a man for the future, I'd say. Excuse me, we have a meeting that's about to start. Tea for seven in fifteen minutes, Gráinne, if you would?'

'Of course, Madame.' Gráinne nodded, and went back to the kitchen with Emmett on her heels.

'So hand me the potatoes and a knife and I'll do that while you make the tea, eh? Wonder what their meeting's about?'

'Mr Connolly's here, and Mr Plunkett, and some others.' She stepped forward to whisper in Emmett's ear. 'I think they will soon be making a decision.'

'About what? Whether to stage a rebellion?' He picked up a potato and began peeling.

'Not whether. When.' She gazed at him meaningfully. 'Surely the Brotherhood's been talking along the same lines too?'

'I'm sure the top tier has. But I'm too lowly to hear anything yet. Good to hear things are moving along. One spud done, about fifty to go, eh?'

She laughed. 'Not quite, but all those in that sack please.'

A short while later, Gráinne had prepared a tray with cups, a tea pot, milk jug and sugar bowl. 'I'll take this through now, Emmett. You keep on peeling.'

'Yes, ma'am.' He gave a mock salute and she laughed again. It had been enjoyable working alongside him in the kitchen. She found herself hoping there would be many more such occasions.

In the dining room, the Countess, Connolly, Plunkett, and three other men were sitting at the table with various papers strewn across it. In a corner sat Joseph Plunkett's fiancée, Grace, who was not involved in the discussions but was sitting quietly embroidering something on the corner of a handkerchief. Gráinne was delighted to see her again, and flashed her a broad smile as she entered with the tray.

Grace leapt up. 'Let me clear a space for that,' she said, pushing some papers together. One looked like a map, but not of Ireland. It was of Germany, Gráinne thought, but she said nothing.

'So you'll go then, Joseph?' Connolly was saying. 'See what help you can rustle up for us? Arms, men, supplies, anything. In return we provide a distraction and divert British troops over here.'

'I'll go. I'll see what can be done.'

'Arms are the priority,' Connolly added.

'Joseph, will you be safe?' Grace was looking at her fiancé with concern.

'I'll endeavour to keep myself safe so I can return to you, my love,' he replied, in a tone that warned her not to argue the point. 'We must all take some risk and make sacrifices, if we're to succeed.' Grace nodded and passed round the cups of tea Gráinne had poured out. Gráinne managed to throw her a sympathetic smile. Whatever it was Plunkett was being asked to do, it was clear Grace wasn't too happy about it. But Gráinne knew all too well that you could not stop a nationalist, whether man or woman, from following their beliefs and doing all that was in their power to help the cause. Wasn't she doing that herself?

She returned to the kitchen with the tray and empty tea pot. Emmett had just finished peeling the potatoes. 'Thank you for that. It's been a big help. Now, what did you come here for today? Wasn't just to peel some spuds, was it?'

'Just to see you,' he said, and there was a hint of a blush on his cheeks as he spoke. 'To see how the job's going, to check you're well and happy. I was curious too, I suppose.'

She smiled. 'Well now you've seen me, met the Countess and checked out the house where it all happens. You'll have been noted down in a detective's notebook too, you know. A fellow stands opposite and writes down all the comings and goings. Come after dark if you don't want to be added to the list.'

'I'll ... I'll do that.' Emmett frowned, then suddenly grabbed Gráinne's hands and pulled her close. 'Grá, it's all very real, isn't it?'

'It is in this house, sure. They're planning something now, in the dining room. I think someone's being sent to Germany, to try to get hold of some guns.'

Emmett nodded. 'I suppose the Germans think helping us will hinder the British war effort. I don't care whether they're right or not, but if we can get some arms out of it, that's a good thing. It'll be a step closer, Grá.'

She nodded, her expression serious. Step by step it seemed that Ireland was inching towards a rebellion.

By mid-December the atmosphere in Surrey House was warming up, as though the route to a rebellion was becoming ever clearer and closer. Grace was a frequent visitor to Surrey House even while Joseph Plunkett was away on his mission to Germany. She would come to the kitchen and spend a while with Gráinne, helping out with meal preparation. She seemed to want to confide her worries about her fiancé's safety. 'I think about him all the time,' she said while they prepared a vast pan of soup for the many visitors one day. 'I wonder where in Germany he is, who he is seeing, whether they will help or consider him some kind of threat.' She stifled a small sob. 'And Gráinne, I wonder if he'll ever come back. What if it all goes wrong, somehow?'

Gráinne put down the wooden spoon she was holding and gave her friend a hug. 'It won't go wrong. Joseph's a clever man – he'll know the right things to say and do to ensure he gets what he's been sent there for. Don't worry.'

'I try not to. It helps, you know, coming here and talking to you.'

'Anything I can do, I will, Grace.' Gráinne wondered how she would feel if someone she loved was putting himself at risk for Ireland. Sean was, of course, but he was her brother. That was a different kind of love to what Grace felt for Plunkett.

It crossed her mind that one day it might be Emmett putting himself at risk in the fight for independence. She was growing ever fonder of her brother's friend, who visited Surrey House most weeks now. Occasionally, he'd take her out – a stroll around the city, a drink in a pub, or a lunch out. She enjoyed those occasions but was careful not to read too much into his attentions. She was still, she was sure, just his friend's little sister as far as he was concerned.

One day later in December, there was a long meeting held at Liberty Hall. The Countess asked Gráinne to go along with her, and provide some refreshments from the hall's kitchen. James Connolly was there, and Eóin MacNeill of the Irish Volunteers and Pádraig Pearse, and several other people Gráinne recognised as being important among the Republican movement. After serving tea to them, she was leaving the room when the Countess called her back. 'Stay a moment, Gráinne. You should hear what is being said today. This affects you as much as anyone.' She glanced at Connolly who nodded, as though giving her permission.

Gráinne perched on a chair in a corner, and listened to the rest of the discussion. It seemed they had come to a definite decision that there would be a rebellion in Dublin and throughout the country, at some point in the following year. 'I have had word from Joseph Plunkett that Germany will help us with a supply of arms. 1916 will be our year,' Connolly said, 'when we will rise up and finally throw off the shackles of British rule.'

'Autumn will be the best time,' MacNeill put in, but Connolly shook his head.

'No, sooner than that. Spring. We must do this, and do it decisively. No agency less powerful than the red tide of war on Irish soil will ever be able to enable the Irish race to recover its self-respect.'

These were stirring words and Gráinne felt a shiver run down her spine. The 'red tide of war' was coming, and within only a few months! This was good – for the future of Ireland, but what would it mean for her, Emmett, Grace? For the ordinary people caught up in it all, trying to live their lives around it?

Chapter 7 – March 1998

Nicky saw Seb a couple more times before her trip to Dublin. Seb owned a mobile phone, and had given her his number. Now she could ring him anytime from a pay phone. They had a lunch on campus and another afternoon out in Brighton.

'He's definitely pretty fit,' was Sabina's verdict after she'd seen Nicky with Seb on campus. 'Though I'm still not sure I'd have swapped Conor for him.'

'I met Seb *after* ending things with Conor,' Nicky told her, not for the first time.

She also spent an evening with Seb in a Brighton pub; afterwards they went back to Seb's room in a house in Kemptown that he rented with two other students. As they went into his bedroom, Seb grabbed a sheet of paper from his windowsill. 'Hey, babe, sign a petition for me?'

'Sure,' Nicky replied. 'What's it for?'

'Legalising cannabis.' He passed her the paper and a well-chewed biro.

'Legalising it?' Nicky's eyes widened. 'Surely there's no chance of that happening?'

'There should be. It's great, cannabis. Not just to smoke, like, but as a medicine. Helps with all sorts, you know?

Epilepsy, chronic pain, all sorts. It's criminal that it's not already legal, I reckon.' He laughed at his own joke.

'Well, I suppose . . .' She took the pen and scrawled her name at the bottom of the sheet.

'Cheers. Nanny state again, stopping people's freedom, and in this case, stopping them from using a drug that can help so many. So signing this is doing some real good, right? Besides,' he grinned slyly at her, 'I quite fancy a spliff before bed. I'd have one now only I ain't got none at the moment.'

Nicky shrugged, hoping it looked as though she was vaguely disappointed. Actually, she was relieved. She wasn't sure whether she wanted to get into that world or not, and she knew Seb would have easily persuaded her to try a puff of a joint. She'd prefer to have the chance to think about it in advance and make a positive decision, rather than feel pressured into it, on the spot.

'Yeah, shame. Another time, eh, babe?'

She smiled in response, and he lit up a cigarette instead.

Nicky spent the night at Seb's, but had to leave early in the morning to make her nine o'clock lecture. 'Aw, don't go. Skip it, stay with me,' Seb wheedled as she got dressed.

She was tempted, but the subject of the lecture interested her and she wanted to attend. Besides, she knew she needed to step up her work to ensure she wasn't thrown off the course at the end of the academic year. 'No, Seb. I've got to go. See you later, eh? I'll be getting lunch in the Falmer House café, if you want to meet me there?' They did a good range of vegetarian options and it was one of her favourites.

'Yeah, maybe,' he said, sounding sleepy, then rolled over away from her.

She leaned over to kiss him goodbye. 'I'm off to Dublin tomorrow. Won't be back until Monday afternoon. I'll come round then, shall I?'

'Monday? Yeah. No, wait.' Seb suddenly sat up in bed. 'Got something in mind starting this weekend. A protest, you know? Shame you won't be here for the start but you can join me when you get back, yeah?'

'A protest!' Nicky felt a pang of regret that she wouldn't be there for it. 'What protest?'

Seb tapped the side of his nose. 'Ah well, you'll find out, eh? Ring me from Dublin. Once we're all set up, I'll tell you about it. It's big. Something I'll be remembered for. Smokey, they'll call me. The new Swampy.' He laughed loudly at his own joke, and reached for his packet of cigarettes.

The next day Nicky took an afternoon train to Gatwick for her flight, and arrived in good time for a browse around the airport bookshop. It was the first time she'd been on a plane by herself. All previous flights had been with her parents for holidays or visits to Irish relatives. She'd flown to Dublin several times before so she felt she knew this trip well, and, indeed, it all went smoothly and before long she was in the arrivals hall at Dublin, calling cousin Jimmy on a pay phone as Supergran had suggested.

He sounded as though he'd been expecting her call. 'I'll be there in under ten minutes, Nicola. Go to the departures level where there's a drop-off zone. It's easier to pick you up there, saves me having to pay to park. It's a big old red Galaxy I'm driving. You can't miss it.'

She did as he'd instructed and sure enough, within ten minutes, a Ford Galaxy in a deep red colour pulled up. She hopped in quickly. 'Thanks for doing this, Jimmy! Much appreciated.'

'Sure, it's no problem,' he said with a grin, and she was reminded how much she'd liked him when she'd met him before. He navigated his way out of the airport. 'Now then,

Gráinne says you're working on some sort of project about the Easter Rising, is that right now?'

'Yes. I'm studying modern history and we've to write about a rebellion, finding a new angle. I thought I'd write about the part women played.'

'Ah. You'll be wanting to write about the Countess Markiewicz, then. Ask Gráinne about her. She knew her well back in those days, I believe.'

'I will, thanks.' Nicky had come across the name in the brief reading she'd done so far. If her great-grandmother had known the Countess, well she must have been right at the heart of the rebellion. Nicky felt a surge of excitement at the thought. Mum's idea for this project had been a good one, not that she was ever going to tell her that. Jez had chosen something to do with India's battle for independence, and Sabina was somehow making a rebellion project out of the 'Summer of Love'. Both sounded interesting, but Nicky thought her own project, especially with the first-hand story she hoped to hear from her great-grandmother, was the best of the three ideas.

The journey was a short one from the airport to Malahide. Jimmy drove round a loop of the small town to point out to Nicky where the station was. 'You can get trains into Dublin – Connolly station – from there. You'll be wanting to take a look at the GPO, I'm thinking. General Post Office, I mean. Give me a call if you need a tour guide, but I'll understand if you'd rather go by yourself.'

And then he headed along a coast road a short way before turning into a housing estate and stopping outside a bungalow that Nicky recognised from previous visits. 'Here you are, so. Give my love to Gráinne and I'm sure I'll see you again before you go back.'

'Thanks so much, Jimmy.' Nicky retrieved her rucksack from the back seat and waved at him as he drove off, then turned to face Supergran's house. There was a small front garden either side of the path that led to the front door. Daffodils and forsythia were in full bloom, their yellow flowers brightening up what was otherwise a dull grey day. Nicky smiled to see them, then walked up the path and rang the doorbell.

She half expected another cousin or great-aunt to answer the door but it was Gráinne herself who opened it.

'Nicky, it's you! Oh, come on in. Delighted to have you here, so I am!' The old lady seemed even smaller than Nicky remembered. Tiny and birdlike, but with bright blue eyes that sparkled in her lined face. Her hair was a cloud of white. She wore a pink housecoat over a tweed skirt and cream jumper, but as Nicky followed her into the house she unbuttoned it and took it off. 'Look at me, still in my overalls! I was doing a spot of dusting in your room. Making it all nice for you.'

'Ah, there was no need for that,' Nicky replied. She leaned over to kiss her great-grandmother who responded with a surprisingly strong hug for someone who looked so frail.

'Now, you'll have a cup of tea.' It was a statement not a question, and Gráinne went straight to the kitchen to put the kettle on. Nicky was delighted to see she hadn't changed a bit since she'd last seen her.

'I will, thanks.' Nicky put her rucksack down beside a sofa and followed Gráinne to the kitchen. On the wall was a framed poster, headed *POBLACHT NA H ÉIREANN – THE PROVISIONAL GOVERNMENT OF THE IRISH REPUBLIC TO THE PEOPLE OF IRELAND*. Nicky went closer to read it.

'Ah, that's a copy of the Proclamation of the Republic. Your grandfather Michael bought that for me, on the fiftieth anniversary of the Rising. He had it framed and all. You know, I was there when it was read aloud for the first time.' The old lady's eyes became clouded as she stared wistfully out of the window. 'And it wasn't Pádraig Pearse who read it out first, despite what you'll read in your history books. Oh no.' She smiled, looking pleased with herself, and set to work to make the tea.

There was a story there, Nicky thought, making a mental note to ask her more about it later on. For now, she needed to put her bag in her bedroom, take off her shoes and use the bathroom.

As if reading her mind, Supergran turned to her. 'Your room is the one on the left along the passage there. Bathroom's opposite, you'll remember. Away with you now, sort yourself out, then come and join me in the sitting room for our tea. Caitlín will be along soon with some dinner for us. 'Tis her turn tonight.'

Caitlín arrived later, armed with tupperware containers of vegetables, already peeled and chopped, and a couple of salmon fillets. 'Your mum said you're vegetarian but eat fish,' she said to Nicky. 'Hope this is all right.'

'Perfect. Can I help?'

'No, you just sit there. Quicker if I do it all myself, I find.'

Caitlín, who Nicky wasn't sure she'd ever met before, didn't seem to want to chat. Nicky left her to the cooking and soon she and Supergran were sitting down to a meal of stir-fried vegetables with salmon. Caitlín had dished it up and then left, after Nicky assured her she'd do the washing-up.

'They have a rota, see,' Supergran said after she'd left, 'and sometimes that one doesn't want to be on it. But her mum, my Eileen, says she has to, as she only lives down the road from me and has no children at home anymore. They're all off studying, like you. One's in Belfast, one's in France somewhere and the other's at Trinity College and lives in the city. They'd be your second cousins, I suppose.'

One day, Nicky thought, she should draw up her family tree. At least the part of it that descended from Gráinne. Then maybe she could get all these great-aunts and second cousins straight in her mind. Mum would know them all, of course. It was the kind of thing you could rely on Mum for. Maybe that was a good reason to get the detail from Supergran, to avoid having to sit down and go through it with Mum.

Later, once they'd eaten and the washing-up was done, Nicky fetched her notebook and a pen and sat down with her great-grandmother to start asking her about her part in the Easter Rising. But the old lady looked tired, and she kept glancing at her watch before Nicky managed to get started with the questions. She closed her notebook and smiled. 'It's a bit late to get started, I think. How about we wait until the morning?'

Her great-grandmother looked relieved. 'I'm better in the morning. Thank you. Eileen will be here shortly to help me get into bed. I've told her I can manage by myself but she won't have it, you know.'

The following morning, Nicky got up when she heard a key being turned in the front door. It was Eileen again, come to help get her mother out of bed.

'I could have done it,' Nicky said, out of a sense of duty. 'You didn't need to come.'

'Ah sure, it's no bother, I come every day. Mum likes things done in a particular way. She wouldn't be wanting someone she doesn't know as well, someone as young as you and no offence, to be sorting her out of a morning. She'll be up and about shortly, and after a nice cup of tea she'll be all yours. And if you're wanting a lift to the station or anything, you're to ask Jimmy. He won't mind a bit, sure he won't.' Eileen, a grey-haired seventy-something with her mother's blue eyes smiled kindly at Nicky.

'Thanks, Great-aunt Eileen. I can't believe how kind everyone is here.'

'We look after our family. Now. I must be getting on.' She bustled along to her great-grandmother's room.

Nicky got herself washed and dressed, and then went to make a pot of tea and find some breakfast. It wasn't long before Eileen left and Supergran joined her.

'Well, come on, shall we get started?' Supergran said as they finished their second cups of tea. 'I've been longing to tell the whole story. Fetch your notebook and let's get a shift on.'

Nicky did so and rejoined Gráinne at the kitchen table.

'It all started, so, with the funeral of O'Donovan Rossa. I was there, and I heard Pádraig Pearse speak at the graveside, and stirring words they were too. My brother Sean had joined the British army, to fight against the Germans in France. There were those who thought that was the best way to an independent Ireland, you see. Help the British with their war and afterwards be rewarded by being made a free state.' She sighed. 'And there were those who didn't see it that way at all. England's difficulty is Ireland's opportunity, they'd say. Emmett was one of these. He'd been a friend of my brother, and at the O'Donovan Rossa funeral, we met up by chance and from then on we became close.'

'I don't think I knew you had a brother, Supergran,' Nicky said, gently. 'What happened to Sean?'

'Ah, there's a mystery. I don't know, tell the truth. He . . . disappeared.' Her great-grandmother looked sad as she gazed out of the window. 'I saw him last not long before the Easter Rising. He might have gone back to France and died there, or he might have gone into hiding and . . . just vanished. I looked for him, after it all. We all did, but we couldn't find him or any word of him, and then there was the War of Independence and then the Civil War . . . oh Ireland was such a mess for many years. I wasn't the only one to lose someone. I just had to consider myself lucky to have Emmett, and my father.'

'What was your brother's name?' Nicky asked.

'Sean MacDowd.' Supergran sighed as she answered. Nicky had the impression she'd really looked up to her brother. It must have been hard never knowing what had happened to him. She made a note of his name. Maybe, somehow, she'd be able to find out.

'Anyway, so, I was already a member of the Cumann na mBan. The Women's Council, that is. We were doing what we could to help the men. Back at the start, it was about the revival of all things Irish – the language, the Gaelic games, our culture.' She sighed. 'Ah I wish I'd learned to speak Irish properly. I only ever learned a few words, *Go raibh maith agat* and the like.'

Nicky smiled. Even she knew the term for 'thank you' in Irish. 'And it was through the Cumann na mBan that you got to know the Countess Markiewicz. Jimmy said I should ask you about her. I read a bit about her in a book.'

'She was Anglo-Irish aristocracy. Married a Polish Count, which is where her title came from. She was a playwright and then a suffragette for a while, and then she got involved with the Cause, as we called it. She was a great friend of James Connolly.'

'One of the leaders of the Rising,' Nicky said, trying to show she'd already done a bit of research.

'Yes. He'd founded the Irish Citizen Army and that allowed women to join, whereas the Irish Republican Brotherhood didn't. Connolly was a frequent visitor to the Countess's home in Rathmines.'

'Rathmines?'

'South Dublin.' Gráinne smiled. 'She asked me to go and work there, living in an attic room. That's how I got so deeply involved.'

'Living with Countess Markiewicz? Actually in her house?' Nicky was amazed to hear how close her great-grandmother had been to the heart of the rebellion.

Gráinne nodded. 'Yes, I was a kind of maid and what you might call right-hand woman to her. Some of the decisions relating to the Rising were made at that house. I'd bring them refreshments as they sat around the dining table with their plans and notes and maps.'

'That sounds very exciting, being so close to it all.'

'It was, yes, but also rather frightening. I knew, see, that if or when the Rising actually happened, people would get hurt. People I'd come to care about. Emmett, see, was in the Irish Republican Brotherhood. The Countess had a gun and had sworn to fire it when the Rising began. And then there were people like Grace Gifford and her fiancé Joseph Plunkett. He was in the IRB and a leading figure in the Rising. Grace was a lovely person. She became a friend to me when she visited. She'd help me in the kitchen.'

Nicky scribbled down all the names. More people to look up. 'Can we go back a step, Supergran? What was the context – why was it so important to you and so many others, that you were prepared to fight for Irish independence? Did everyone feel that way?'

'Ah, not everyone, no. There were plenty who didn't like what we were doing, even though we were doing it for them. For all the Irish people. You see it was—' Gráinne broke off and stared into space, as though working out the best way to explain it '—as though Irish Catholics were second-class citizens in their own country. Oppressed for years. Now don't take offence, you being more English than Irish, but we'd been treated badly, so we had. Things needed to change. And they believed, those at the top, that bloodshed was the only way to bring that change about.'

Chapter 8 – Christmas 1915

It was possible to send letters to soldiers fighting on the Western Front, though Gráinne had no idea how the letters reached the addressees. Nevertheless, she'd been writing regularly to Sean, hoping her missives might cheer him up a little, remind him of life that went on outside the trenches, and give him something to think about that might help keep him going. She'd received a handful of letters back from him.

It was time to write him a Christmas letter. Christmas the previous year had brought reports of a one-day ceasefire, of German and British troops meeting in no-man's-land and shaking hands, showing each other family photographs, even playing football. With the increased intensity of fighting during 1915, Gráinne suspected nothing like that would happen this year, though she prayed the soldiers would at least get one day of peace, one day of safety.

She wanted, in her Christmas letter, to provide some clues as to what was going on in Ireland. But she knew she'd have to be very careful. Letters to and from troops were opened and read, and censored in case they fell into enemy hands. But, in this case, the enemy were the censors themselves. She would have to be careful not to give away anything not widely known.

Dear Sean, she wrote,

I hope this Christmas brings with it a few moments of peace for you and your fellow soldiers in the trenches. I think of you every day and pray every night that God will bring you home safe, having done your part for Britain. Ireland too needs you, as I know you are aware. Conflict is all around us and coming closer by the day. I find myself looking forward to the spring time, but not without fear of what it might bring to our beloved country as we remember how our Lord sacrificed himself for us upon the cross. I hope the war in Europe might turn a corner by then as well, though from what I read in the papers this seems unlikely. Please God you are able to stay safe, warm and as comfortable as it is possible to be in those cold dark trenches. I enclose some socks and chocolate for you – little things but they're what has been suggested are the most useful gifts. Dad sends his love; I am sure he will write to you too. And your old friend Emmett is here in Dublin. He and I have met up a number of times. We find we have a lot in common, not least our views on Ireland's politics, and our desire for a future in which we are all free from all our enemies and oppressors. He sends his regards as well. Stay safe, dear brother, and come home to us soon. May 1916 be a good year for all of us, and for our country.

With fondest love, Gráinne

There. She hoped that Sean would be able to read between the lines, and guess that she was hinting a rebellion may happen as soon as spring. She could not put anything more concrete than that. Indeed, she didn't know anything more definite than that. If only he could come home on leave and they could meet and discuss events! She'd added her new address to the top of the letter but there was no reason that

Sean would know it was a meeting place for the Republican movement. She packed up a parcel of the socks she'd knitted and some bars of chocolate, added the letter on the top and took it immediately to the General Post Office on Sackville Street. She had some time to spare afterwards and spent it wandering around Clerys opposite, remembering the previous year when she'd been working there on the run up to Christmas, saying hello to a few members of staff she knew from her time there. She missed the camaraderie of the women's dormitory, but not the work. What she was doing now was so much more important.

For Christmas Day itself, Gráinne had agreed to stay at Surrey House and help cook for the several guests the Countess was due to be hosting. In lieu of this, she was granted a full day off two days before, to go to visit her father. He was a mathematics teacher at St Enda's school, situated on the southern edges of Dublin. The school had been founded by Pádraig Pearse to promote all things Irish: the language, sports and culture that were part of the country's heritage. Many lessons were taught in Irish. It was a more subtle form of rebellion against the British, a reclamation of Ireland's individuality.

Gráinne had a small gift of some jars of preserves she'd made in the kitchens at Surrey House and a knitted scarf to take to her father. She also wanted to talk to him about Ireland's future, Ireland's politics. Her father was a patriot and a Republican too.

She arrived at the school in the late morning. Her father lived in a few rooms at the school, and helped supervise the boarders. At this time, so close to Christmas, the school was almost empty. Only a few boys were staying there over the festive period, and there were no lessons scheduled until after New Year. She walked in through the grand entrance and, as always on visits here, cast her eyes up towards a fresco of the legendary Irish hero Cúchulainn and the school motto, in Irish, beside it. She translated it and spoke the words out loud: '*I care not if my life has been only the span of a night and a day if my deeds be spoken about by the men of Ireland.*'

'Stirring stuff, eh, Gráinne?' Her father was coming down the stairs to meet her. His rooms overlooked the front of the school so he must have seen her approaching.

'Hello Dad,' she said, giving him a kiss. 'Yes, strong words.' And in a similar vein, she thought, to what she'd heard Connolly say just a week or two earlier.

'Well, that's Pádraig Pearse for you.' Dad laughed, hugging her. 'He's all about putting Ireland first and oneself second. Come on up and we'll have some tea and a bite to eat, eh?'

'Thank you.' She followed him up to his little apartment in the attics of the building where he made the tea while she browsed his impressive collection of books. 'Have you heard from Sean?' she asked him, as he handed her a cup of tea.

'Just a couple of letters spattered with mud from the Front,' he replied. 'He seems to have kept himself out of trouble so far. Pray God that continues.'

'Yes, indeed. I wonder will he be able to come home on leave anytime soon? I miss him so much. There is so much I want to talk to him about, that cannot be put in a letter.'

'About life with the Countess? About those secret meetings held in her house?' Dad smiled at her.

She nodded. 'Yes, about that. And about Emmett – remember his old school friend? I bumped into him in the city centre – actually at O'Donovan Rossa's funeral. Since then . . . I've seen him once or twice more, and he always asks after Sean.' She felt heat rise to her face as she spoke of Emmett.

'Ah.' Dad nodded knowingly, a small smile playing at the corner of his mouth. 'Emmett O'Sheridan's not just Sean's friend now, is he? He's yours too. Your young man?'

She looked away. 'N-nothing like that, Dad. Just friends, united by our political beliefs.'

'Hmm. He's a good man. You could do a lot worse.' Dad leaned across to her and took her hand, squeezing it. 'Just be careful, both of you, in what you get caught up in. It's a worthwhile and noble cause, but a dangerous one, and you two are young with your lives ahead of you.'

Gráinne stared at him. He was right, she supposed. It could end up becoming dangerous. So far it was all about plans and leaflets, and bringing in guns for some far-off future rebellion, but that future was coming closer and when it came, those guns might be put to deadly use. If so, of course the other side would be firing back and lives might be lost. But Emmett? Would he get caught up in it all? Her stomach gave a lurch. She hoped not, she fervently hoped he'd stay safe. 'I'll pass on your message to him, Dad. And for myself, I'll only be on the sidelines, being a woman.'

Dad shook his head. 'There are peaceful ways to achieve what we want. By talks, by waiting until this war in Europe is over and letting the Home Rule bill make its way through Parliament. We can get what we want by politics, not by war. I've said as much, or at least hinted of it, to Pearse and others, but they say no, that we need bloodshed.' He slammed a hand down on his desk, making Gráinne jump. 'As if there isn't enough bloodshed going on already, over in those damned trenches! My boy . . . my Sean . . .'

'We can only pray for Sean,' Gráinne said.

'Yes, we can only pray. He joined the army because he thought a swift war, helping Britain, would in the long run help Ireland. And now we're a year and a half into the war and there's no sign of it ending anytime soon. Yet, still,

Pearse wants more bloodshed, here on Irish soil! I think he's wrong, Gráinne.'

She thought otherwise, but did not like to argue with her father. She made a non-committal sound and let him continue speaking.

'This school, this promotion of the Irish culture and language – this is right. I fervently believe in it. Pearse did a good thing here, setting up the school, so he did. But if he pushes on with these thoughts of violent rebellion, it could be the end of it all. It'll fail, like all the other rebellions in the past, and the British will clamp down again, stop the Home Rule bill for good, and close down this school. And we'll have to wait another generation before we can try again.' Dad looked agitated as he spoke, and Gráinne stood to wrap her arms around him.

'But what if it doesn't fail, Dad? What if Pearse is right, and the time is right, and we succeed?' She spoke quietly. She wanted her father to believe in this, with all his heart, the way she did.

'Hmm.' Dad looked as though he was going to say something more, but had decided against it. He held her for a moment, and then gently pushed her away, back to her seat.

He changed the subject, and began telling her anecdotes about the boys he taught and the escapades they'd got up to. 'Ireland will be a fine place when the likes of them are running it,' he said with a chuckle, and she smiled, wondering if there ever could be a time when her country was run by its own people from its own capital.

Christmas at Surrey House was a riotous affair, with everyone who was living there chipping in to help produce a meal, sitting round the table for hours drinking beer and discussing politics, with the volume going up and up as more bottles of beer were consumed. Gráinne spent most of the time serving people and clearing up, but managed to join in with the festivities too. The Countess had a female visitor – a friend from Scotland named Margaret Skinnider. She was a studious-looking woman with a soft face and round spectacles. She looked more like a school teacher than a revolutionary and when Gráinne told the Countess this on St Stephen's Day in response to being asked what she thought of Miss Skinnider, the Countess threw back her head and laughed. 'Why, that's exactly what she is, when she's not fighting for Ireland! We all have multiple identities, don't we? You a sister, daughter, shop assistant and revolutionary. Me a mother, wife, Countess and revolutionary. Margaret a school teacher, crack shot with a rifle, and revolutionary. And . . .' the Countess looked sideways at Gráinne as if weighing up whether to tell her something or not. She leaned in close and whispered. 'Margaret brought some interesting items over from Glasgow. Hidden in her skirt, and in her hat of all places! We are going into the Wicklow Hills tomorrow to test them out.'

'Madame, that is good she was able to bring the items. What are they?' Gráinne asked, surprised but pleased to have been entrusted with this information.

'Detonators!' The Countess grinned as Gráinne gasped. 'Oh, don't worry. We won't blow anything up – not tomorrow, anyway. We'll just test out the detonator itself, find out how they work and how to use them. I don't feel I can quite trust this task to the Fianna boys. Better that we women do it.'

The following day, Gráinne helped load up a motorcar borrowed from James Connolly with bags of equipment, a flask of tea and a basket of scones. The Countess laughed when she saw the basket. 'Oh, my dear Gráinne, thank you so much for that. We are not going on a picnic; this is a rather more serious excursion. But I am sure Margaret and I will be able to make good use of the tea and scones.'

'We certainly will, Constance,' Miss Skinnider said. 'Wasn't it Napoleon who said that an army marches on its stomach? In just the same way, it's important that we are able to feed our Volunteers, both now during the preparation period and even more so when the Rising actually takes place.'

She spoke like a school teacher, Gráinne thought. The Countess brought out a tarpaulin from the house, and instructed her to tie it down over the bags of equipment. 'We don't want any nosey police or military asking what's in those bags,' she said, as she pushed a couple of rifles underneath as well. 'And we can also practise our rifle shooting, eh Margaret? She's an excellent shot you know, Gráinne.'

'All those years in the rifle club in Glasgow,' Miss Skinnider said with a smile.

Gráinne had never handled a gun in her life. A thought occurred to her, and she was unable to stop herself from voicing it immediately. 'Madame, when the Rising comes, will women be expected to . . . bear arms? To shoot people?'

The Countess and Miss Skinnider glanced at each other, and then the Countess nodded at Miss Skinnider as if to say, go ahead and answer Gráinne.

The school teacher smiled kindly at her. 'Only those who want to. No one will be forced to do anything they are not comfortable with. Some of our male commanders think that women should not carry arms, but Connolly says women are to be the equal of men in the new Irish Republic. If we are equal, then we have as much right as the men to bear arms and fight, to put ourselves on the front line. But only if we choose to do so.'

'And . . . will you?' Gráinne could imagine the Scottish woman as a strict school teacher, standing no nonsense from her pupils. But women, bearing arms, shooting in a revolutionary war? She tried to imagine herself with a rifle, pointing it at someone, firing it with the intent to kill. She couldn't imagine it at all.

'I will, yes. I will do everything I can for this cause, and I am a good shot, as the Countess said.' Miss Skinnider fixed Gráinne with a piercing gaze, looking fierce and proud.

With the motorcar loaded up, Gráinne was dismissed to continue her chores inside the house, while the other two women headed off to the Wicklow mountains to test their equipment. Gráinne felt a mixture of relief and disappointment that she had not been asked to go along. Disappointment not to be included in what could be an exciting activity, but relief not to be putting herself in danger, not today at least.

The Countess and Margaret Skinnider returned after dark on St Stephen's Day, flushed with excitement after a successful day. 'Detonators worked a dream,' the Countess whispered to Gráinne.

Gráinne had spent the day preparing a meal. There was to be a gathering that evening for several of the key members of the Irish Citizen Army and Irish Volunteers. She'd spent the day mostly in the kitchen, preparing vegetables and a mutton stew, a bread-and-butter pudding and a leek and potato soup. Three courses were far more than they usually managed, but it was still Christmas as the Countess had said, and as the year drew to an end, there was a feeling among all the Surrey House crowd that 1916 would be a momentous year for Ireland, a year that would change the course of history.

Everyone began arriving after dark, and gathered in the sitting room where Gráinne handed round glasses of sherry provided by Connolly. Gráinne was pleased to see Grace there, along with her fiancé Joseph Plunkett who'd returned from his trip to Germany.

'Gráinne, it's good to see you again,' Grace said. 'Now, is there anything I can do to help? I hear Constance and Margaret were off blowing things up today, leaving you to do all the cooking. Do you need an extra pair of hands?'

'Thank you, Grace. I have done everything . . . I think . . . oh, except for setting the table!'

'Ah, well I am good at that, so I am,' Grace said with a laugh, and the two of them went through to the dining room to begin setting out cutlery, glasses and plates. 'Actually, Gráinne, I'm glad to have you alone for a moment. There's something I wanted to tell you.'

Gráinne put down the glasses she was holding and looked at her friend. Grace was smiling, so Gráinne smiled too. It must be good news coming. 'What is it?'

'Joseph and I have set a date for our wedding. I'd like you to be there, if you are able. We're going to marry on Easter Sunday.'

'Oh, that's wonderful news, Grace! What a lovely holy day to get married. Of course I will be there, if the Countess can spare me.'

'Oh, she'll be there too, I hope! I want everyone to come. I'm so happy, Gráinne. We've been engaged a while as you know, but we've not been able to set a date until now. It's less than four months away, can you believe it?'

'Four months! 1916's going to be such a good year for you!' Gráinne stepped forward and hugged Grace tightly.

Grace's eyes were shining brightly. 'A good year for all of us, I hope. For all the people of Ireland. And yes, for Joseph and me especially.'

Gráinne couldn't help but wonder if it would be a good year for herself and Emmett too. A year in which, she hoped, they'd become closer. She imagined herself in Grace's position, with a ring on her finger and a date set for their wedding, a future mapped out. It was early days for her and Emmett – they hadn't been childhood sweethearts like Grace and Joseph – but she was hopeful and increasingly certain that he was the one for her.

Chapter 9 – March 1998

Nicky listened enraptured as her great-grandmother told her about events in the year before the Rising, and how membership of the Irish Volunteers had increased. She heard about the guns smuggled into Howth that were then hidden and used in the Rising. She loved hearing about Margaret Skinnider's visit, bringing detonators, which she and the Countess tested in the Wicklow hills. Supergran's narrative brought it all to life, and she could imagine the women finding a quiet spot away from farms and roads, laying a fuse and testing a detonator.

And then Gráinne had talked about Joseph Plunkett and his childhood sweetheart Grace Gifford, and how they'd set a date to marry on Easter Sunday, 1916.

'Plunkett was right at the heart of the plans,' Gráinne said. 'He was thought to be a great strategist. You wouldn't think it to look at him. He'd spent time in Algiers and had a penchant for wearing lots of scarves and bracelets.' She sighed and shook her head sadly. 'He was a good man. He didn't deserve what happened to him. And poor Grace, that lovely, gentle woman.'

'What happened?'

But the old lady shook her head again. 'We'd be getting ahead of ourselves. Anyway, look, I have a box somewhere, with some newspaper cuttings and the like, that I kept back then. About the Rising, and the events before and after it. If you can get it down for me – it's in the loft and Eileen says I'm never to go up there – you can look through and see if there's anything in it that helps you.'

The cuttings were in a shoebox, tucked in a corner of the attic along with boxes of old school books and suitcases of clothes. 'Eileen says I should throw all that other stuff away, but I can't bring myself to do it,' Supergran said, as Nicky climbed down the ladder with the shoebox. 'I tell her she can get Jimmy to do it after I'm gone.'

'Don't throw it away if you don't want to,' Nicky agreed, as she pushed the loft ladder back up and closed the hatch. 'Now then, another cup of tea while I look through these?'

'Not for me, Nicky. I'm away to sit on the sofa now. Perhaps I'll have a little nap.' The old lady smiled. 'It's quite tiring, all this remembering and talking.'

'Of course. No problem. I'll go out this afternoon and let you have some peace.'

'Call Jimmy. Get him to take you to Glasnevin and Howth – the places I've been talking about.'

'Good idea.' Nicky went to the telephone in the hallway and phoned Jimmy who seemed delighted at the prospect of being a tour guide for the afternoon. Then after checking Supergran was comfortable and settled on the sofa, she went back to the kitchen table and began leafing through the clippings in the shoebox.

She read through each one, making notes. She paid especial attention to any that mentioned women or any of the events Supergran had mentioned. Some clippings were from papers such as *The Workers' Republic* which had been published by the Irish Citizen Army. There were some wonderful pieces by James Connolly that would have stirred up nationalist sentiment in anyone who read them. And to think her great-grandmother had known Connolly personally!

As well as the clippings, there was an old watch inside the box. A dainty silver lady's watch in a brown case.

And at the bottom of the box, folded inside a battered old brown envelope, was something else. Nicky extracted it carefully and unfolded it; it was a handkerchief, stained yellow with age. In one corner the initials JP and GG were embroidered entwined together. Nicky frowned as she looked at it. JP and GG? Joseph Plunkett and Grace Gifford? How had Supergran come by this? She made a mental note to ask her about it, when she'd woken from her nap.

When Nicky had finished reading through the clippings and taking notes, she had time to spare before Jimmy was due to pick her up. Gráinne was still asleep. She decided to phone Seb, to let him know she'd arrived safely and was getting on well with her research. Not that he'd be interested in the project, she knew, but she wanted to talk to him anyway. Perhaps he'd tell her something more about this protest he was planning. Her head was full of images of Connolly and Plunkett and the Countess sitting around the Countess's dining table planning the rebellion. She found herself picturing Seb in a similar meeting with other student rebels, heads bent together over maps and notes, planning their action. Was it more road-building they were trying to stop? Or a protest against student tuition fees? Or something else entirely?

She went to the hallway and dialled Seb's mobile number, hoping it wouldn't be costing Supergran too much. When he answered it, she had the impression he was still in bed. He sounded sleepy, as though he'd just woken up.

'Hey, it's me. Just wanted to let you know I got to Dublin OK, and I'm with my great-grandmother. She's got so much to tell me about the Easter Rising. I'm so glad I came.'

'Yeah, babe, that's good then,' Seb replied, and she heard him yawn. 'I'm stocking up on sleep. Not going to get much over the next few days, once my protest gets going.'

'Where will you be?'

'On campus, babe. Not too far from your accommodation. You'll be able to visit me, and the others. Bring us supplies, raise awareness, that kind of thing. You cool with that?'

'Sure, but what is the protest about?'

'Ah, wait and see, babe.'

She couldn't see him, but she could picture him tapping the side of his nose as he said that. She wished he'd confide in her and tell her the details. Perhaps she might have some helpful suggestions for him. But then she thought about what Gráinne had told her about how the Irish Republican Brotherhood had been organised, with each member only knowing the names and faces of those in the same cell, and each cell commander only knowing a few others at their level. Secrecy had been the name of the game back then, and it made sense for Seb to work in the same way now. She'd know soon enough, once the protest was underway, what it was all about. For now, she just had to trust Seb. Whatever it was, she was sure it would be worthwhile, an attempt to make the world a better place, as all decent protests should be.

'All right, will do. I'm back on Monday evening. I'll ring you then, yeah?'

'You do that. It'll all have kicked off by then. Gonna change the world, we are. Make it a better, fairer place. Wish me luck, eh?'

'Good luck, Seb. I'd better go.'

'Cheers then. Bye.'

Nicky hung up, smiling. It had been good to hear his voice. He was clearly very enthused by this latest protest, whatever it was. 'Change the world' might be a stretch, but getting his voice heard, the voice of the ordinary people – that's how Ireland had achieved independence, in the end. Ordinary people, fighting for what they believed in.

And one of those people had been her own great-grandmother.

Jimmy arrived after lunch, making the bungalow feel suddenly small with his larger-than-life presence. Nicky smiled to see how Gráinne lit up when he was there. She had the feeling he was one of her favourite grandchildren.

He towered over the old lady to kiss her hello. 'Grandma! You're looking as sprightly as ever. Now, I'm going to take this young colleen away for a bit. Give you a rest, hey? What time do you want her back?'

'Oh, anytime, as long as it's in time for our tea,' Supergran said.

Jimmy smacked his forehead. 'And it's me cooking your tea tonight anyway, isn't it? How about I pick us up some fish and chips for the three of us for our tea?'

'Ooh, what a treat!' Supergran actually clapped her hands together.

'Good for me too,' Nicky said.

'Let's get going then.' Jimmy ushered her out to his car. 'Right then. A tour of the area. Portmarnock beach and Howth, I thought?'

'Can we also go to Glasnevin Cemetery?' she asked as she climbed into the Galaxy.

'A cemetery? What are you wanting to go there for, Nicky?'

'Supergran was talking about it. Gráinne, I mean.' Nicky blushed. 'I've called her Supergran since I was very little. She was there, in 1915, when O'Donovan Rossa was buried.'

'Ah, the fools, the fools . . .' Jimmy said, with a grin.

'I'm sorry?' Nicky was confused.

'Something Pádraig Pearse said at O'Donovan Rossa's graveside. Right then, we'll go to Glasnevin first, then loop round to Howth and finally Portmarnock. Got plenty of time, so we have.'

They chatted companionably as Jimmy navigated the streets of north Dublin towards the cemetery. It covered a huge area, and a visitor centre at the entrance provided maps detailing where prominent people had been buried. 'Ah, there's Éamon de Valera's grave,' said Jimmy, pointing to a marker on the map.

'Who?' Nicky asked, wondering if she should know the name.

'You've not heard of him? He was . . . oh, what wasn't he? Major figure in the War of Independence. Taoiseach – that's the Irish prime minister – for far too long. President. Founder of the Fianna Fáil party.'

'They teach nothing of Irish history in British schools, Jimmy,' Nicky said. 'Despite the fact our two countries have such an entangled history. Did de Valera have anything to do with the Easter Rising?'

Jimmy nodded. 'Yes, he was a commander. Only escaped execution because he'd been born in the US, and executing him could have caused an international incident. But look, there's O'Donovan Rossa. We'll see his resting place first, shall we?'

Jimmy led the way through the maze of neatly tended paths between rows of graves, some with ornate statues and others with simple headstones. At last, they found the one they wanted, and as Nicky stood contemplating the renovated grave – an angled slab with an engraving of a phoenix rising from ashes, surrounded by neat gravel – she tried to imagine the scene in 1915. The crowds of people her great-grandmother had described, the stirring words of Pádraig Pearse that inspired so many to join the Republican cause. She leaned over to read the inscription at the bottom of the grave. '"The fools, the fools, the fools, they have left us our Fenian dead, and while Ireland holds these graves, Ireland unfree shall never be at peace." Is that from Pearse's speech?'

'Sure it is.' Jimmy was grinning. 'We'll make a Republican of you yet, young Nicky.'

They wandered around the cemetery a little longer, with Jimmy pointing out several other prominent Irish rebels and politicians. All were men. Nicky had a thought. 'What about the Countess Markiewicz? Is she buried here too?'

Jimmy frowned. 'Not sure.' He consulted the leaflet he'd picked up. 'Ah, she is, so. Let's find her.'

Her grave turned out to be marked only by a simple stone at the edge of a path. No stirring words or phoenix engravings for the Countess. Nicky felt strangely sorry to see this. It was certainly time that the women of Ireland were commemorated for their part in the Rising.

They left the cemetery after seeing the graves of several other prominent republicans. Nicky made a few notes about each. And then Jimmy drove out to the coast, to Howth. Nicky had spotted the small lump of land jutting out into the sea from her aeroplane as it began its descent to Dublin. Jimmy parked at a small harbour, beside a row of small shops and cafés. They had a cup of tea and a sandwich in one of the cafés.

'Not sure this place has much to do with the Rising,' Jimmy said. 'I could be wrong though. I paid very little attention at school.' He laughed. 'Probably why I've no job now.'

'Supergran said she helped land a shipment of guns here, in 1915.' Nicky gazed around, trying to imagine the teams of Cumann na mBan women and Fianna Éireann boys forming human chains to offload the weapons from a boat.

'Brought from Germany? They did supply the rebellion, I think.'

Nicky nodded. 'Yes, I think so.' She was a bit unclear on it all. Maybe she should draw up a timeline to help get all the facts she knew about in order.

'Well, now we can walk up over the hill, or go on to Portmarnock and take a walk on the beach there. Or leave Portmarnock until tomorrow. It's only down the road from Gráinne's house anyway.'

'Walk here now, and Portmarnock tomorrow, if the weather's fine?' Nicky suggested.

'Sure, we can do that.' Jimmy paid for the teas and sandwiches and they set off, walking up a path that climbed the hill, flanked on either side by gorse and bracken. The gorse was in full flower and its vanilla scent hung in the air. At the top there was a trig point and the view, overlooking the Liffey estuary with huge expanses of beach on both sides and the Irish sea, was incredible.

'That island there – that's called Ireland's Eye,' Jimmy said, pointing. 'It's a bird sanctuary. And that beach is Dollymount Strand. You can drive right onto the beach there. Sometimes the tide comes in fast and catches motorists out and they lose their car, the eejits.'

'It's a lovely part of the world,' Nicky said, gazing around at the open ocean on one side and the outskirts of Dublin city on the other. Up there, high on the hill, it felt as though she was on the top of the world. As though she could see for miles – across the city, over the sea, to the past where Irish rebels landed guns and plotted rebellion . . . and into her own future. A future with Seb? It was early days, but she felt as though he could be a kindred spirit . . . a rebel, someone who was trying to change the world to make it a better place.

'Penny for your thoughts? You look to be away with the fairies,' Jimmy said. He'd come to stand beside her, looking out over the scene below.

'Ah, just thinking about my project,' Nicky replied.

'Must be good to be so fired up by your course,' Jimmy said. 'Wish I'd gone to university and studied something I liked so much. I was always the little rebel at school. Did everything I could to avoid doing any actual work. Had to retake my Leaving Cert three times, and by then all my friends had been to university and left, so there seemed no point going. They probably wouldn't have taken me anyway. I ended up working for an uncle in his garage, then when that business folded and my uncle moved to the States, I worked in Dunnes Stores for a few years. Then they reorganised their staffing structure and I was left on the scrapheap. Since then, I've just been doing odd bits of work, here and there, you know? Not good at sticking at things, sure I'm not.' He shrugged, sadly.

'I bet you are. Just haven't found the right thing,' Nicky said. He was a nice bloke, this cousin. He deserved better from life.

Jimmy smiled at her. 'Thanks, cousin Nicky. I guess I like having my time to myself too much. Not good at answering to a boss, sure I'm not. So, shall we get back to Gráinne then? We need to pick up some fish and chips. Then tomorrow, I can collect you around the same time, when Gráinne will be wanting her nap.'

'Yes, thanks. Today's been lovely. Thank you so much.'

'Ah you're welcome. Been nice having something to do, someone to show around. I like driving my car here and there, with a purpose to it.'

It was later that evening, after they'd eaten fish and chips and Jimmy had left, that Nicky remembered she'd wanted to ask Supergran about the embroidered handkerchief. She brought the shoebox into the sitting room, where they'd been sitting and chatting over yet another cup of tea.

'There's something in here I wanted to ask you about,' Nicky said, as she sorted through the contents of the box, searching for the brown envelope.

'Oh, yes? Did you find those bits and pieces interesting? I never really knew why I kept everything for so long, I suppose it was because I'd been a part of it all, and having the newspaper clippings made it seem real, so it did.'

'Of course. I can understand that. Ah, here it is.' Nicky pulled out the brown envelope and took the handkerchief out of it. She passed it over to her great-grandmother. 'Those initials – JP and GG – who are they? You talked about your friend Grace engaged to Joseph Plunkett. Is it them?'

Supergran was holding the handkerchief and staring at it, as though she'd never seen it before. Or hadn't seen it for a very long time. 'I was after wondering where this had got to,' she whispered. She held it close to her face, as though breathing in any scent it might still have.

'Whose is it, Supergran?' Nicky prompted.

The old lady shook her head. 'I shouldn't have it. I should have given it back. I don't know why I never did. Oh, to think of that turning up again, all these years later!'

To Nicky's horror there were tears rolling down her great-grandmother's cheeks. She quickly moved over to sit beside her, and wrapped her arms around her. 'Don't get upset, Supergran. I'll put it away again. No need to think about it now.' She gently took the handkerchief and tucked it back into its envelope, then passed her a tissue.

'Don't mind me,' Gráinne said, with a weak smile. 'Just a silly old lady getting sentimental. I'll tell you about that handkerchief some day, but not now. I'm tired.'

Right on cue, Nicky heard the front door opening and Eileen was letting herself in, come to help get Supergran into bed. Nicky was happy to go to her room, write some more notes, think about everything she'd seen and learnt that day and wonder what was the story behind the handkerchief?

Chapter 10 – Jan/Feb 1916

It was the middle of January and the weather had been unrelentingly grey and damp for weeks. That kind of weather got into everyone's soul, Gráinne thought, and dragged them down. Gone were the lively days of Christmas, the camaraderie over food as revolutions were planned. Gone were the joyous occasions celebrating successful testing of detonators and dates for weddings being set. Now life seemed dreary; Gráinne's work was almost entirely that of a housekeeper – cooking and cleaning – and there were fewer guests.

The only bright spot, for Gráinne at least, had been her 18th birthday. She'd been about to get up early as usual, to make everyone's breakfast, when the Countess tapped on the door of her room and entered bearing a tray. On it was tea, toast, a plate of eggs and black pudding, a card and a small package wrapped in brown paper.

'Happy birthday, Gráinne my dear! Breakfast in bed for you today.'

'Thank you, Madame! What a treat!'

The Countess smiled. 'You deserve it. You work so hard. Now, open your present.'

Gráinne unwrapped the parcel carefully. Inside was a small jewellery box, and inside that a wristwatch on a narrow brown leather strap.

'It's not new I'm afraid, it's an old one of mine, but I noticed you didn't have one and I thought you could make use of it,' explained the Countess.

'It's perfect,' Gráinne said, as she strapped it onto her wrist. It had a small silver face with delicate hands in black. It was the first one she'd owned. 'Thank you so much.'

'It'll help you get to the rebellion on time, when it comes,' the Countess said with a small laugh.

'Nothing would keep me away,' she replied.

She'd had an afternoon off, and had gone out with Emmett who'd given her a gift of a green silk scarf. 'It's the colour of Ireland,' he told her. 'I hope you like it.'

'I love it,' she'd said, wrapping it around her neck and kissing him on the cheek in thanks.

Other than that, January had been a dull, slow month. Even James Connolly, who was usually at Surrey House most days, hadn't been seen for days. The Countess seemed distracted, wandering from room to room as though looking for something to do.

'I don't even know where he is,' the Countess confided in Gráinne, one wet afternoon. Gráinne was dusting the dining room, stacking papers, polishing the table beneath and then carefully replacing the papers exactly as they had been.

'Sorry, Madame, who do you mean?'

'Mr Connolly. He's disappeared. He didn't say he was going anywhere, and he's not anywhere he's usually found. It's strange. I'm a little bit worried, to tell the truth.'

'Ah, I'm sure he'll be back soon. Probably with new plans for the Rising.' Gráinne tried to reassure her mistress, then wondered if she'd overstepped the mark a little. Who was she to comment on whether Connolly would return with or without plans?

'I'm sure you're right.' The Countess gave her a small smile. 'I'm probably worrying for nothing. Well, life goes on whether he's here or not. We have a Cumann na mBan meeting tomorrow evening, in Liberty Hall, do we not?'

'Yes, Madame. I have printed off those leaflets you asked for, and they are on the sideboard there ready to take along.'

'Thank you. You've proved yourself to be a wonderful worker, Gráinne. I'm truly grateful.'

Gráinne felt herself blushing. 'It's nothing, Madame. I enjoy the job.'

The following day, in the early afternoon, James Connolly returned to Surrey House. He looked tired and dishevelled, as though he'd slept in his clothes for several days. Or perhaps not slept at all, Gráinne thought. He was hungry too, and Gráinne was dispatched to the kitchen to rustle up a meal for him, while the relieved Countess led him through to the sitting room to rest, and to tell her where he had been.

Despite his fatigue, there was a glint of excitement in his eye, Gráinne thought, when she brought him a tray of soup, bread and cold meat. He held the tray on his lap and tucked into it immediately, thanking her through a mouthful of bread. 'I needed this, thank you, Gráinne. It's been a tough few days.'

'You were with the Brotherhood this whole time?' the Countess asked him, as Gráinne was leaving the room.

'Yes, with Pádraig Pearse and others. And we have agreed a date for the Rising.' Gráinne heard his reply as she closed the door behind her. She suppressed a gasp. A date agreed! And by the sound of things, an agreement reached between all Republican groups. She was pleased. The only way they could make a difference would be if they fought together – the IRB, the Irish Citizen Army and the Volunteers, together of course with the Cumann na mBan and the Fianna.

She shouldn't do it, she knew, but she couldn't help herself. She stayed there, just outside the door, where she could hear what was being said inside. It wasn't as though she was any risk – she was as dedicated to the Cause as anyone – and it surely wouldn't be long until the news was out. But when she heard the date agreed, her stomach lurched. Why then? Why had they decided on Easter Sunday, of all days? Grace and Joseph's wedding day. Poor Grace – her wedding would have to be moved to a different date. And yet, when would she hear of this? Gráinne wouldn't be able to tell her. Surely Connolly would tell Joseph of it soon, and he would tell Grace. And how would Grace feel? She would have to put her country ahead of herself.

Gráinne made her way back to the kitchen, still pondering what she'd heard. Wondering too, in Grace's position, how would she herself feel? It wasn't about their own little lives. It was a bigger thing than any of them, and the only way it would work was if they all put the Cause first and their own personal lives second. Would she be able to do that, when the time came?

Three days later it was clear that Joseph Plunkett knew of the date, and had told Grace. She came to visit one afternoon with reddened eyes, clutching a sodden handkerchief. Gráinne opened the door to her and ushered her straight through to the kitchen. 'I'll put the kettle on, and you'll have a cup of tea,' she told her friend.

'You know, don't you?' Grace said as she sat down heavily at the kitchen table.

'I'm guessing you and Joseph are having to postpone your wedding,' Gráinne said quietly.

Grace nodded, and a tear ran down her cheek. 'Why did they have to pick that day, of all the days? We've been engaged for so long. We should have been married long ago but we were waiting for the time to be right. And Easter Sunday this year felt right! And they've stolen that from us.' She shook her head. 'I know, I know, the Cause is the most important thing. But—'

Gráinne sat beside her and wrapped her arms around her friend. 'The Cause is important, but so are you, Grace. I fear there is nothing to be done about this – Joseph will want to play his part in whatever happens. But we can hope that the Rising goes well and will be over before very long, and you and Joseph will be able to marry in a free Ireland.'

Grace smiled weakly at her. 'Yes, and that would be worth delaying for.' She squeezed Gráinne's arm. 'You've cheered me up a little. Thank you. I knew I could rely on you.'

'You're welcome. I only wish I could do more for you.'

'Ah, all we women can do is support our men, through this turbulent time. Now, about that tea you offered? I'll make it shall I?'

'We'll do it together.' Gráinne smiled, happy to have helped her friend. Nobody ever said revolution would be easy, and she supposed they would all have to make sacrifices sooner or later.

Gráinne had arranged to spend her next day off with Emmett. It was proving increasingly difficult to find time to be together these days, and with the actual date of the Rising planned that would surely only get worse. Yet she wanted to see him, to discuss the latest happenings with him and find out what the mood was in the Irish Volunteers.

Thankfully it was not raining when her day off finally came around, although there was a chill wind blowing. Gráinne dressed warmly, as they had decided to take a trip out to Portmarnock to stroll along the beach there. It was an outing probably better taken on a calm summer's day, but as Emmett had said, they should take every opportunity possible to have fun and enjoy themselves, for who knew what was around the corner? With the war in Europe raging on, and war in Ireland looking increasingly likely sooner or later, chances to take trips like this would only become more and more scarce.

They met up outside Liberty Hall. A new banner had been erected over the entrance. '*We serve neither King nor Kaiser, but Ireland,*' Gráinne read aloud.

Emmett grinned. 'Eight little words but they sum up the policy of all revolutionaries perfectly.'

He was right. If only Sean could see what was happening in Dublin now! He was still over in France, serving the King. But if he knew, if he saw how things were changing, how plans were being made, would he perhaps join them, and serve Ireland first? She hoped so. He was her much-loved brother, and she had to believe his politics were the same as hers. She simply had to, even though their father disagreed. This was *their* time, their generation's chance to fight for what they believed in.

'Shall we go, so?' Emmett broke into her thoughts and reached for her hand. A train and then a bus journey took them to Portmarnock, where they walked along the road that led around the coast and then down onto the beach. The tide was out revealing a huge expanse of flat sand. Out to sea in one direction was Lambay Island, its castle just visible. In the other direction was Ireland's Eye, the island tucked in beside the headland of Howth and home to thousands of birds. They stood for a while gazing out at it, while the wind whipped up the surface of the water into white-tipped waves that chased each other up the beach towards them.

'Beautiful, isn't it?' Emmett said, and Gráinne nodded.

'I think I love it more on a winter's day than in the summer. We have the whole beach to ourselves, look!' She threw her arms out wide and spun around. Usually in the summer, there'd be families picnicking on the sand, children and dogs running wild, couples strolling arm in arm. But today there were just the two of them, beneath a pale blue sky with small clouds scudding over.

'Yes, just you and me.' But Emmett wasn't looking at the beach, she realised, but at her. He had an odd, half-smile on his face as he watched her spinning around, arms outstretched, and she stopped, embarrassed. Had she made a fool of herself? A strand of hair had plastered itself across her face, and she pushed it away. As she did so, he took a step forward and caught hold of her, pulling her towards him. 'Gráinne.' Just one word, her name, but in it she heard so much more. She heard an echo of her own feelings towards him, feelings she had not wanted to acknowledge in case their relationship came to nothing, in case to him she was still nothing more than his friend's annoying younger sister.

She smiled up at him and he must have recognised that she felt the same way, for he pulled her closer still, dipped his head to hers. Her mouth found his and they kissed, long and deep. Gráinne felt a warmth surge through her despite the chill of the day, a wonderful warmth that spread into every corner of her body. In his arms she felt as though she'd found a home, a place of calm, a safe harbour in this turbulent world. She never wanted to leave.

But he ended the kiss and separated from her, pulling her across the sand, laughing. Too late she realised the reason – a wave had rolled further up the beach and was lapping at their boots. She felt the icy-cold water seep through to her toes and squealed as she ran with him up the beach. Once they were out of danger, she fell into his arms again.

'Now, where were we?' he whispered, and they kissed once more. All thoughts of rebellion, of rising against British rule, of guns stored in basements and printing of seditious material fell away and there were only the two of them in the world, only this moment and this man, and she knew that her future was with him, whatever happened to her country.

Chapter 11 – March 1998

The next day was Nicky's last in Dublin, and she was due to travel home on an evening flight. As on Saturday, she spent the morning chatting with Supergran, hearing all about the run-up to the Easter Rising, the Cumann na mBan meetings she'd attended, the Volunteers' manoeuvres on St Patrick's Day in 1916 and other plans. Nicky jotted down pages and pages of notes. By lunchtime Gráinne was tired.

'We haven't yet got to Easter week,' Nicky said. 'Shall we continue this afternoon?'

'Ah, my sweet colleen, I think we will have to continue this by phone. Or perhaps you'll be able to come to stay again in a week or two? I will pay your airfare. I've loved having you here, Nicky. But I've underestimated how long I can talk to you at any one time.'

Nicky was disappointed. She'd hoped to get enough material in this visit to write up her project. But Supergran had been so closely involved she had more to say than Nicky had expected. The main events of Easter week, 1916, she'd be able to glean from textbooks but the setting, the atmosphere, and the actions of ordinary people like her great-grandmother were not written up anywhere. She'd definitely have to come back. Phone calls would cost a fortune and would not be the same. She hadn't even had a chance to go into the city centre and tour the key places involved in the Rising. She smiled. 'Yes, I'd love to come back again. Actually, I don't have to complete this project until the middle of May. So how about I come back over Easter? That would mean I could stay longer.'

'Sure and wouldn't that be perfect?' Gráinne smiled, obviously delighted by the idea. 'It'll be grand to have company again over that period. And so fitting for you to be here at Easter too.'

Mum wouldn't think so, Nicky thought. She'd no doubt be disappointed Nicky wasn't going home over the Easter break, but she wouldn't be able to complain if the reason was because she was getting on with her project – the one Mum herself had suggested. And it wasn't as though Nicky had actually promised to go home. Mum had just assumed she would. Yes, it was a perfect solution. 'Fantastic. I'd love to come. Thank you so much.'

Jimmy arrived, as promised, after lunch, to take her out to Portmarnock beach while Supergran had her afternoon nap. As Nicky climbed into his Ford Galaxy, she had an idea. A bit of a brainwave, she thought, though she wasn't quite sure how to broach the subject with him.

It was a short distance through Malahide to the coast road, and along to Portmarnock. Jimmy found a parking spot and they left the car to walk along the beach. It was very different to the steeply shelving shingle of Brighton beach that Nicky was used to. With the tide out, there was a huge expanse of sand stretching for miles. They walked to the water's edge, with Nicky picking up occasional seashells that caught her eye.

'It feels as though you could paddle across to Wales, when the tide is this far out,' she commented, and Jimmy laughed.

'I wouldn't try it if I were you. But yes, the sea goes out a long way on this coast. Did you get much more from Gráinne this morning? You're off back to England this evening, aren't you?'

'I did, yes, and I am. But I'm going to have to come back over in a couple of weeks. She has so many stories to tell and she gets tired quickly.' Nicky smiled. 'I want to do a good job on this project.'

'I envy you doing something you are so interested in. What job do you think you'll do when you finish university?'

Nicky shrugged. She'd never given it much thought. To date, life had been school, sixth form college, university. Study, study, study, while trying to have a life of her own around it all. She'd never really thought beyond it, and she still had over two years left. 'I don't know, Jimmy. Teach, maybe? I could do a post-grad teaching course. I'll wait and see how I feel when I graduate. I want to travel a bit before settling down to a career, anyway.' And maybe take part in a few protests along with Seb, see if they could make the world a better place. She didn't feel as though she wanted to say this to Jimmy though. He might laugh, or say something to put her off, or question her about exactly how she wanted to change the world, which was something she did not feel she had an answer to.

'Travel's a good idea, while you're young. Wish I'd had the money to do it. Sure and it's a bit late for me now,' Jimmy said, kicking up a mound of sand with his foot.

'Never too late. And doesn't need to cost much if you do it on the cheap.'

'I've not a penny to my name, so I haven't,' Jimmy said. 'I need to find a job soon.'

Here was her opening. 'I had a thought about that, last night,' Nicky said, tentatively.

'About a job for me? Typing up your thesis or something like that?'

She laughed. 'No, I was thinking about you having that big car, and living so near the airport . . . have you thought about signing up with a minicab company? You obviously like driving people around, and you might as well make money from it!'

'Ah, my car's old and scruffy,' Jimmy said. 'People want something smarter from a taxi.'

'If you gave it a thorough clean inside it'd be fine. And there aren't that many seven-seaters around. I reckon there could be quite a demand for large taxis going to and from the airport.'

'Hmm. It's worth looking at, sure. I'll investigate. Thank you, young cousin.'

Nicky smiled with satisfaction. She'd passed her idea on. She had no clue how difficult it would be for Jimmy to set himself up as a minicab driver, or whether he'd ever considered it before. But she could imagine the job might suit him well.

They strolled along the beach chatting about various topics, from the relative prices of beer in England and Ireland, to the ongoing peace talks aimed at ending the Troubles. There'd been a ceasefire since the previous summer, and peace talks between Unionists and Republicans had begun. Jimmy was hopeful it would lead to a lasting agreement. 'It's been more than seventy-five years since the treaty was signed and Ireland was partitioned,' he said, 'and there's been violence on and off ever since. It's about time it all came to an end, and sure aren't I feeling more hopeful now than at any time in my life before.' He turned and grinned at her. 'If they reach an agreement, wouldn't that make a fabulous end to your project – it would bring it right up to date.'

'It would.' Nicky made a mental note to check up on current affairs. Her head was usually so deeply buried in history she forgot to check the news.

There were dark clouds coming over, and Jimmy glanced up at them. 'I'm thinking we should be heading back to the car, before that lot reaches us,' he said.

Nicky nodded. 'Time to get back to Supergran and say goodbye, anyway.'

They just made it back to the car before the first spots of rain began to fall. 'Irish weather,' Jimmy commented. 'You know what they say: if you don't like the weather in Ireland, wait five minutes and it'll change. We had the best of the day anyway.'

Back at Gráinne's, Nicky packed her bag and said goodbye to her great-grandmother over yet another cup of tea.

'Sure and won't you be back again in no time?' Supergran said with a smile. 'As soon as you have your ticket booked, telephone me and let me know. Jimmy'll pick you up at the airport again, won't you, Jimmy?'

'Of course. Delighted to.'

It was an uneventful early evening flight back to Gatwick followed by a train to Brighton and then the short journey up to the campus. Nicky dumped her bag in her room and went straight to the pay phone to call Seb. She'd missed him so much. His protest would have started, and she was keen to find out what it was all about.

There was a queue at the pay phone – it was Sunday evening and many students chose that time to call their parents. Nicky fidgeted as she waited, drumming her fingers on the wall and shifting from foot to foot. What was Seb doing? She'd promised she'd phone him as soon as she got back. He'd be expecting her call. She needed her own mobile phone, she decided. Maybe she could get a cheap pay-as-you-go one. Or ask Mum for one for her next birthday. But then Mum would be able to call her anytime she wanted. It'd be good to have a phone, but the downside would be losing the control she had regarding when she phoned home.

At last it was her turn, and she dialled Seb's number. He answered within a few rings.

'Hey, Seb, it's me. I got back from Dublin. Where are you?' There was a loud hubbub in the background. People talking and laughing, someone singing, *We shall not, we shall not be moved.* It was clear the protest was definitely underway and well supported.

'Hi Nicky! Glad you're back. Come and join us! We moved in around midday and we're not moving. Actually, bring me a sandwich, yeah? I didn't bring enough food and they've turned the gas and electric off so we can't cook anything here.'

'Sure, will do. But where are you?'

'Student union bar.'

'Right. A sit-in?'

'Yeah, a sit-in. Got about twenty here. Real party atmosphere, babe. It's going well.'

'I'll come and join you, if you'll let me in. What's the protest about?'

'Our rights, Nicky. Protesting against the curtailment of our rights. What better thing to protest against?'

'But what, exactly?' She was trying to work out why they'd chosen a sit-in in the student union bar of all places. Seb sounded elated and excited and it was rubbing off on her. He was right – protesting about losing your rights was definitely worthwhile.

'Come and see. Gotta go, babe. Come round to the kitchen entrance, yeah? We'll let you in. Password is Benson. Got that?'

'Benson?'

'Yeah. Don't talk to any press or police. Not yet. We gotta bed this in first, then we'll work on getting publicity tomorrow. See you soon.'

He hung up before Nicky had a chance to ask if she needed to bring anything else. He'd asked for a sandwich. She went to the kitchen she shared with nine other students and checked the contents of her cupboard. Half a loaf of bread; out of date but with no visible mould. Half a jar of jam. She had some cheese in the fridge, she thought, but when she checked it had gone. Someone else had probably used it. Jam sandwiches it was, then. She made as many as she could, wrapped them in foil and put them in a carrier bag along with a packet of biscuits and a bag of crisps. She wondered about making up a flask of drink of some sort, tea perhaps, or coffee, but then remembered the sit-in was in a bar. They'd have enough drink. Probably too much.

She went back to her room and looked around, trying to decide if she should take anything else. Was she going to join the sit-in overnight? Should she take some clean underwear? Her sleeping bag? She decided against it. She'd go there with the food, find out what was going on, and then come back for anything else that was needed. Maybe her job would be as a runner, fetching and carrying, taking messages, rather than actually joining the sit-in. She would be on the edge, rather than in the thick of it. Nicky couldn't decide whether that would be more or less fulfilling. Well, soon enough she'd find out.

She locked her room, stuffed her key into her jeans pocket and set off to the union bar at the other end of campus, with the carrier bag of food swinging at her side. Halfway there she realised she'd only catered for Seb. Was she supposed to be providing sandwiches for everyone? There was a small supermarket on campus, but it would be closed at this time on a Sunday evening. What she had in the carrier bag would have to do.

At the student union building, there was a handful of people outside the front entrance to the bar. Most looked like students, though there was one older man who Nicky thought might be the manager of the union bar. He was talking loudly on a mobile phone, sounding cross. As she watched him, he paced around, waving his arm. 'I can't get in. Just a bunch of students, smoking. Probably best to leave them be for tonight. They'll soon get bored. If they've damaged anything they'll pay. Yes, we'll probably open up tomorrow, if it's not in too bad a state in there.' With that he walked away, brushing off a student brandishing a notepad who tried to talk to him.

Nicky went around to the back entrance of the bar, as she'd been told. Again, there were a couple of students hanging around, all of them smoking. She walked past them and tried the door, which was locked. She banged on it.

'Trying to get in, love?' one of the smoking students said.

'Yes, got some food for one of them.' She held up the carrier bag.

The student banged loudly on the door. 'Someone wanting to come in, guys,' he yelled.

'Password?' came a call from the other side of the door.

'Um, I was told to say Benson?' Nicky said, feeling faintly ridiculous.

The door was unlocked and Nicky ushered in. She followed the student – a scruffy chap in ripped jeans with unwashed hair – through the bar's kitchen area and into the main room. It was dark – the only light came from a few candles and a couple of torches. The bar itself was brighter, lit by external streetlamps that shone through the front windows. There was a pall of cigarette smoke over everything.

She scanned the room for Seb and spotted him, sitting at a table with a few others. All were smoking. She made her way over.

'Hey, Seb. Brought you something to eat. Not much, but all I had, and the campus shop is closed . . .'

'Babe!' He stood up and kissed her. 'You made it. That's fantastic! We need a non-smoker here, to show that what we're doing is supported by everyone.'

She smiled, and was on the point of asking once more what the protest was about, but stopped herself. It would look bad on him if his girlfriend wasn't sure what was going on. 'Well, here I am.' She handed him the carrier bag which he took without a word and began rummaging through. A moment later he was munching on the jam sandwiches.

'Cheers for this,' he said, waving one around. A lit cigarette was still lodged between his fingers.

Nicky looked around the room and realised that everyone was smoking. Every table had an overflowing ashtray on it. A pile of packets of cigarettes was on the bar beside a handful of lighters, and the protesters every now and again were helping themselves to yet another smoke. Was this it, then? The big protest? She remembered Seb had been outraged that smoking had been banned in this bar, after an asthmatic student had a bad reaction. He'd gone on about how it infringed on his liberties, and smokers should be allowed to smoke anywhere.

She moved to a quiet corner and gestured for him to come over to her. She needed to hear it from him.

'So, you're protesting against the smoking ban, right?'

'Too right, babe! People have smoked where they like in this country for thousands of years. Just because some asthmatic had a coughing fit, doesn't mean the rights of all smokers should be stamped on.'

'Um, about 500 years,' Nicky said quietly, trying to remember when tobacco had first been introduced to Europe from America.

'What? Whatever. You're with us, yeah? I know it's like one bar in one university, but it's the principle of the thing. They can just have a no-smoking corner or something, if

120

it's that important. Like the no-smoking carriages in trains and that. Got to fight for our rights – otherwise it's like the thin end of the wedge, yeah? We give in here, and before we know it smoking'll be banned in all bars on campus, all pubs in Brighton, all public transport. Then they'll say we can't even smoke in our own homes. It's a curtailment of our rights. Need to nip this in the bud, here and now, is what I think. Got to fight for our freedom.'

He took a drag of his cigarette and coughed. Nicky was trying to decide how to respond. She had sympathy with what he was trying to do – so often rights were eroded bit by bit, so people barely noticed each incremental change, and by the time they did it was too late and things had gone too far. But this – this was about health. That student had been hospitalised after a major asthma attack, which was thought to have been brought on or exacerbated by her being in a very smoky atmosphere. Surely she and others like her had the right to go to a bar and drink safely? There were other bars, or perhaps smokers could go outside to smoke . . .

'So what I want you to do, babe, and by the way, cheers for the food, is to get in contact with the local press. The *Evening Argus*, the *Falmer* magazine, any others you can think of. And then the nationals. Get phone numbers of journalists, and give them my number. They'll want to cover this. Look, we got twenty students here, and we ain't moving, not till the smoking ban's been lifted. They're good people. They've all promised they won't touch the booze or damage anything. We're not doing this to nick stuff – we got principles, yeah?'

He took a drag of his cigarette. 'This'll be huge. This'll stop the trend towards banning smoking, when they see that smokers ain't gonna take it lying down. You'll do that for me?' He stepped towards her and cupped her face in his hand, then leaned over to kiss her.

It wasn't the best kiss she'd ever had. He'd been smoking so much, it was all she could taste. And he had to break away to cough again.

'I will, Seb. But you know . . . this chain smoking isn't doing you any good. I mean you can have your protest without having to ruin your own health in the process, can't you?'

He stared at her. 'My choice, babe. That's what it's all about.'

'Well, I suppose for the greater good we all have to make personal sacrifices.' She hoped he wouldn't notice the hint of sarcasm that had crept into her tone of voice.

'Sod that. It's all about freedom, innit?'

'Whose, Seb?' It was on the tip of her tongue to ask about the asthmatic student's freedom to visit a bar without endangering her health but she held back.

'Mine, babe.' He grinned at her. 'I'll cut back on smoking once this protest is over.' He dropped his cigarette butt on the floor and ground it under his heel, then walked away from her to the stash on the bar and lit up another.

She shrugged. His choice, as he'd said, and she respected that. Maybe, after the sit-in had ended, she'd find a way to gently broach the topic again. She'd prefer him to give up altogether. There was nothing sexy about those coughing fits.

Well, she'd promised to help, and he'd given her a job to do. It was a better one than spending the night locked in the bar in that smoky atmosphere. She went out the same way she'd entered, and headed to the library. She could use one of the bank of computers there to look up contact details for newspapers. Hopefully all of them, in this day and age, would have a website.

Chapter 12 – March 1916

The house was as empty as it ever was, with only the Countess doing some paperwork in the dining room, and Gráinne taking the opportunity to give the kitchen a thorough clean. It was just after dark and the ever-present policeman opposite had checked his watch, written one last note in his little book, and left. Within minutes the doorbell rang.

Gráinne sighed – there'd been no let-up in the number of visitors lately, and keeping them supplied with cups of tea and meals was a full-time job. She'd been looking forward to a quiet evening. Get the kitchen done, have a soak in the bathtub, and an early night with a book – that had been her plan. She sighed, pasted a smile on her face and opened the door.

'Emmett!' And now the smile was genuine. 'What a surprise! What brings you here? 'Tis only Emmett,' she said to the Countess who'd put her head out to see who'd arrived.

'Ah, Emmett. Well, I expect he's here to see you and not me, so I can get on with my paperwork,' the Countess said.

'Will you be wanting another cup of tea, Madame?'

'No, no. I'm grand as I am.' The Countess went back to her work, closing the door.

'Anyone else here?' Emmett asked.

'No, it's quiet tonight.' She led him through to the kitchen.

'Good.' He sat at the table. 'I was hoping we'd get a few moments alone. It's going to be harder and harder for us to find time for each other. I want, I hope, that we will have a future together, Gráinne . . .'

'Oh, so do I!' She couldn't help herself from interrupting him then.

He smiled and took her hands across the table. 'I was going to say, but for now we must put our relationship on hold. Put our country and our beliefs first. I know you feel the same. It's hard, but it is what we must do.'

'I know,' she whispered.

'But Gráinne, our day will come, be sure of that, my love.' With that he pulled her towards him, and they kissed. There was longing in his kiss, passion and romance, and also determination. He was right. There was so much at stake now. If they could snatch a few moments here and there they would, but they couldn't count on it. Ireland first. Emmett and Gráinne second.

There was a march planned for St Patrick's Day, through the city. The Cumann na mBan were to take part, along with the Irish Volunteers led by Eóin MacNeill. If all Volunteers turned up, there could be thousands of them. Gráinne was excited to be taking part in manoeuvres. Emmett had taken part in many, mostly at night, but this was to be in daylight, across the city, with similar marches planned in other cities. An enormous thing to be part of!

St Patrick's Day dawned bright and clear. Gráinne was up early, dressed in her grey skirt and jacket with her Cumann na mBan sash and armband, then went to the kitchen to make tea and prepare breakfast for the household. The Countess came to help, and together they produced a mountain of fried bacon and eggs for the numerous people who'd spent the night at Surrey House, ahead of the big day.

Breakfast was a lively affair with everyone talking noisily about what the day might bring. Gráinne cleared up afterwards, roping in a Fianna Éireann lad who looked to be at a loose end to help with the washing-up.

They left the house shortly after, taking with them piles of leaflets advertising the Cumann na mBan. Each Cumann na mBan member would carry a stack to hand out to any curious women they passed on the march. First stop was a local church for a St Patrick's Day service. After the service, the Cumann na mBan march began, from in front of the church heading northwards, in towards the city centre. All over Dublin similar marches were happening, Gráinne knew, starting from various churches and aiming to congregate at College Green in front of Trinity College, along with the Irish Volunteers and Irish Citizen Army. Emmett had said he would meet her there, but if there were thousands of people on the marches, she didn't see how this would work out. Their fall-back plan was to meet in St Stephen's Green after the manoeuvres were over.

As the women marched two by two along the streets, there was a palpable air of excitement. Onlookers stared at them curiously, and every now and again a woman broke ranks to hand out a leaflet or two. The Countess was at the head of the parade, dressed in uniform and carrying a rifle. Gráinne marched beside a young Cumann na mBan girl she hadn't met before, who looked a little nervous at the proceedings.

'It's exciting, isn't it?' Gráinne said to the other girl, hoping to help her relax a little. 'I'm Gráinne, by the way.'

'I'm Sarah. Yes, it's exciting, but I'm fearing there might be trouble. What if we're stopped by the police?'

'I don't think we will be. Why would they stop us? It's just a peaceful march, isn't it?'

Sarah nodded but said nothing more.

As they came closer to the city centre they joined up with the Irish Volunteers, as planned. Eóin MacNeill was to inspect his troops at College Green and on the southern quays of the Liffey. The Volunteers also had leaflets and pamphlets to hand out, and Gráinne managed to get herself a copy of each. One was entitled *Twenty Plain Facts for Irishmen*. She glanced through it as she marched. 'It is the duty of every Irishman who desires for his country her natural right of freedom, and for himself the natural right of a freeman, to be an Irish Volunteer,' she read aloud.

'What about Irishwomen?' Sarah asked.

'Indeed. We have a duty as well, even if the Irish Volunteers don't say so. Thankfully, the Irish Citizen Army allows women to join, so I understand.'

They were almost at College Green, and there were men and women everywhere. The Volunteers, Gráinne noted, were carrying rifles as Emmett had said they would. Not all of them, but perhaps every second man had a rifle. They looked to be the same ones Gráinne had helped bring in at Howth. That day seemed so long ago now.

As they approached College Green, the crowd of Volunteers was so huge it took up the full width of the road. Dame Street was the same. Traffic was stopped on those streets and all side streets, and even the trams were unable to run in that area. 'Well, we've stopped the traffic, so we'll make headlines in the papers tomorrow,' Gráinne said to Sarah. That was good for publicity. The people of Dublin needed to see that the Republican forces were strong, that they meant business, and that they were fighting for the good of the country.

On a corner, a group of women wearing shawls stood watching. Gráinne broke ranks to approach them, thinking to hand them a couple of leaflets but as she approached one woman spat at her. 'Get away from me. Real Irishmen are fighting for their country in the trenches, with neither bed nor bolster. My Jimmy's out there. Your lot are just play-acting here and stopping us getting about the city on our holiday. Shame on you all!'

There was nothing Gráinne could think of to say to this. She wiped the spit off her jacket and stepped back into line alongside Sarah.

'See, that's what I'm afraid of. They don't all think the way we do, do they?' Sarah looked a little tearful at the reaction of the women.

'No, they don't,' Gráinne replied. 'But they will, when we gain independence from Britain. For then, their men will come home from the war in Europe, and that is what they want. They want the same as us, even if they don't think our way is the best way of going about it. We're fighting for them.'

'Even though they don't want us to?'

'They don't understand.' It was hard to put into words how she felt, Gráinne thought. She'd had the same worries as Sarah, but the Countess and other senior Cumann na mBan members had helped her work through them. Now, like those women on the corner, she wanted the men of Ireland home and safe, among them her brother Sean. But the way to do that, the way to secure the best future for her country, was to fight for it.

'I thought there'd be cheering crowds lining the streets,' Sarah said.

Gráinne had not expected there would be, but had to admit in her heart she had hoped for it. Instead, she felt as though Dubliners simply weren't interested in them. A few onlookers had taken her leaflets, glanced at them with raised eyebrows and then dropped them on the pavements.

Others had shaken their heads when she tried to pass them one. At least only that one woman had spat at her.

The Volunteers were lining up now, blocking the entrance to Trinity College. One motorcar made its way through and pulled up outside the Bank of Ireland. Gráinne saw that it was Mr MacNeill's car. He climbed out and walked slowly along the ranks of men, who stood to attention. He spoke a few words to some of them. The point, Gráinne realised, was to look like a proper army, sending a message to onlookers that they would be able to defend the nation. There was no need for British troops on Irish soil.

She estimated there were perhaps two thousand Volunteers on the streets. A fraction of the total number of Volunteers but not a bad showing, and there had been similar marches planned for Cork and Limerick. Gráinne kept her eyes peeled for glimpses of Emmett but had no luck spotting him.

After an hour or so, MacNeill dismissed his troops, and the Countess did the same for the Cumann na mBan. Gradually, people began to disperse, and traffic once more flowed through the streets. It had been a peaceful march, but whether it had achieved much remained to be seen. Gráinne made her way to St Stephen's Green and entered the park, wandering over to a bench beside a flowerbed that was filled with daffodils and crocuses. She sat down there to wait for Emmett.

He arrived ten minutes later, wearing the dark green uniform of the Irish Volunteers. He sat beside her and flung his arms around her, kissing her solidly. 'What a show we put on! A decent turnout. Now they'll see we mean business. And oh, Gráinne, how good it was to march while carrying an actual rifle. We've had to hand them back in but it's good to see there's a decent number of them around.'

'There'll be more, soon. I believe a shipment is on its way from Germany. Remember when Joseph Plunkett was sent over to negotiate a deal back in December? Well, it paid off.' She'd glanced around before saying this, to check there was no one who might overhear.

Emmett raised his eyebrows. 'That's good to hear. Dare I ask if you know when?'

'Easter.'

'So soon! The revolution will not be long after that, I'd say.'

She nodded. 'I think you are right.' She wished she could tell him, but dared not.

The St Patrick's Day parades had been a success. James Connolly praised those who'd participated in them, writing in his paper, *The Workers' Republic*, a few days later: '*Despite all the treasons of all the traitors, Ireland still remains as pure in heart as ever, and although Empires fall and tyrannies perish, we will rise again.*'

Gráinne read these words out to Emmett as the two of them enjoyed a half-day off, sitting in the spring sunshine in St Stephen's Green.

'We will rise again!' he repeated, grinning at her.

She smiled. 'Yes, we shall. What I don't understand though, Emmett, is why we were allowed to march? Why did the authorities not break it up and send us home? They could have . . . they could have confiscated all the weapons, maybe even arrested some of the Volunteers. Yet they left us to it.'

Emmett shrugged. 'If they had taken action against us, that might alienate the Irish population, and gain us more support. That's the last thing they want to do. They need the Irish people to continue supporting the war in Europe – they need Irish soldiers to fight for them.' He thought for a moment before continuing. 'As for confiscating arms, well I think if they took arms from the Irish

Volunteers, they'd have to treat the Ulster Volunteers, and even Redmond's National Volunteers, the same way. And those groups are the ones supplying most of the Irish soldiers. So, I think they didn't dare do anything but let us get on with it, as long as it remained peaceful.'

That made sense, Gráinne thought. And it worked in their favour. If any hearts at all had been won, if any more support for the Cause had been generated, then it had been a worthwhile day.

About a week later, Gráinne was shopping with the Countess, stocking up supplies for the endless stream of visitors to Surrey House. They were on Liffey Street, going in and out of various shops, placing orders and bringing smaller items away with them in a bag that Gráinne had slung over her shoulder. As they left a grocer's shop, a young lad whom Gráinne vaguely recognised as being a member of the Fianna came charging up to them, out of breath.

'Madame, Madame! So glad I've found you. It's the police, they're at Liberty Hall! They're going to raid it, and Connolly said to tell you and any other patriots I find. The police will find the guns and arrest Mr Connolly!'

'Ssh, lad. Don't be shouting about our arsenal,' whispered the Countess to him, and the boy blushed and looked about. Thankfully, there was no one close enough to have heard. 'Gráinne, I must hurry over to Liberty Hall. Take this shopping home, alert anyone who comes to Surrey House, and stay there awaiting orders.'

Gráinne nodded, and the Countess set off at a jog along with the Fianna boy, towards Liberty Hall. It was only a couple of blocks from where they'd been shopping and Gráinne wondered about following them, but she'd been given her orders. She hurried down the street, across the river via the Ha'penny Bridge, and caught a

130

tram to Rathmines and so back to Surrey House. The news had reached there, and more alarmingly, an order from Connolly mobilising the Irish Citizen Army had also been received. As Gráinne put away food in the kitchen, a stream of men ran through the house, grabbing the few weapons that had been stored in the basement, and then ran off in the direction of Liberty Hall.

'It's too soon,' Gráinne muttered to herself. 'We're not ready. This shouldn't be happening now.' Her instinct was to go to Liberty Hall, find the Countess and see for herself what was happening, but she'd been told to stay at Surrey House, so that is what she did. She set up a little command centre in the dining room, to receive and pass on any instructions or information that came her way. She began noting down times and events in a notebook, so that she'd be able to report accurately on all that had occurred there. Was that the right thing? She had no idea, but it felt like the sensible and useful thing to do.

It was early evening before things calmed down. The Countess returned; Connolly was with her. Both were flushed with excitement but also looked worried. 'That could have been a disaster,' Connolly said. 'We'll guard Liberty Hall day and night from now on. We can't risk a real raid.'

'Madame, what happened?' Gráinne asked. She was sitting at the dining room table, her Command Post as she was privately calling it. The other two came in and sat with her.

'Ah, the police were after the latest copy of *The Irish Worker*. It wasn't a raid at all.'

'Even so, it was a good practice. I was pleased to see so many men mobilised so quickly, despite having had no notice.' Connolly nodded with satisfaction.

'Some went from here, with weapons,' Gráinne said, and passed over her notebook.

Connolly scanned it quickly and looked pleased. 'Good

work. Useful to see who responded and what they did. Thank you.'

Gráinne smiled, delighted with his praise.

'One result of today is that I have had an idea.' Connolly leaned across the table. 'Gráinne, can you print up a poster downstairs, that says, *Attack on Howth tomorrow. Citizen Army, regiments 45–60 to assemble here at midday.*'

'Attack on Howth tomorrow?' Gráinne was stunned. Such short notice, and why Howth? She looked at the Countess to gauge her reaction, but to her astonishment, Madame Markiewicz was smiling broadly.

'And another poster, that says, *Dublin Castle to be attacked at midnight.*'

'And one saying, *All regiments of the Citizen Army to report to Trinity College for immediate attack on all military garrisons,*' the Countess added, with a snort of laughter.

'What?' Gráinne could not stop herself from gasping. 'Why alert the authorities to these attacks by putting up posters?'

'You've heard the tale of the boy who cried wolf?' Connolly asked her. 'He pretended there was a wolf so many times that the villagers grew complacent. Then, when there really was a wolf, they all ignored his cries for help.'

Gráinne frowned, trying to understand. 'You mean, the authorities will work out that the posters are meaningless, and then when the real call to arms comes, they'll ignore it?'

'Exactly that, my dear. They'll think we're deluded and harmless, and that might just buy us some time when the real thing comes.'

Gráinne smiled now. A clever plan. She noted down the wording of posters they'd suggested and promised to get them printed off as soon as she could. There'd be a new one posted up every week outside Liberty Hall.

* * *

From then on, as Connolly had said, Liberty Hall was given a permanent guard. The Countess herself took turns at the sentry post, standing guard, rifle in hand, for hours at a time. And the posters had the desired effect. 'The Citizen Army showing off again,' Gráinne heard a woman say in the greengrocer's. 'It'll come to nothing. It's all just a fantasy.' She smiled to herself but said nothing. They'd find out soon enough. She just hoped that when the time came, the people of Dublin would be on their side.

Chapter 13 – March 1998

By the time Nicky had found contact details for reporters at a couple of local newspapers, it was very late, she was starving hungry, and she had a feeling no one would be present at the newspaper offices anyway. She jotted down the names and phone numbers she'd found and left the library. She could call them first thing in the morning. Her first lecture was at ten o'clock so there'd be time. If Seb was disappointed not to have reporters there that night, well, it was too bad. He could have tipped them off himself before it all started, or asked someone else to do the job sooner. She'd had a busy weekend, a long journey home and now it was time to look after herself.

She headed back to her student flat, running over in her mind what food there was that she could have. No bread – she'd used that for Seb's jam sandwiches. Nothing fresh, as she'd used it all before going to Ireland. Hopefully some tins that she'd be able to use, and maybe something in the freezer.

Dinner ended up being a piece of frozen fish in bread-crumbs with a tin of baked beans. She felt better after eating, but it was by now nearly midnight, and she needed to be up early.

*　*　*

The following morning, after a cup of black tea (no milk, no chance to buy any yet), armed with her phone card that was running short on funds, and as many 10p pieces as she could find, she went to the pay phone. Her first call was to the *Evening Argus* news desk. She had high hopes for the *Argus* – if they ran the story, it'd be in the afternoon edition. Any other paper wouldn't have the story in print until the next morning. She felt strangely nervous dialling the number, and before her call was answered she hung up. She should speak to Seb first, she realised. She should find out how they'd got on overnight and check everything was OK before talking to a reporter. She decided to call him – it was quicker than going all the way through campus to the bar.

'Hey, Seb? How's it going? Just about to talk to the *Evening Argus* and I thought I'd find out how things are with you first. Did you get much sleep?'

'Hey, babe. Yeah, slept a bit. Uncomfortable, but OK.' She could hear a few voices behind him, but it all sounded quieter than it had the previous day. Maybe most of the protesters were still asleep.

'Good. So, anything you especially want me to say to the reporter?'

'Just get them here to take photos and do interviews and stuff, yeah? Thought they might turn up last night, and put the story in this morning's papers. Hey, maybe they did. Can you have a look, and get me any papers that are covering it?'

'Sure, will do. Right, well, I'll call the *Argus* now. They'll print the story in today's paper, I'm sure.'

There was the sound of Seb yawning. 'Cheers, babe. I'm going to try to get a bit more sleep before it all kicks off. See you later – bring some food around lunchtime, yeah?'

'Sure.' She hung up, took a deep breath, and redialled the number for the *Argus's* news desk. A bored-sounding reporter answered quickly.

'Hi. Um, I'm a student at the university, and I wanted to let you know there's a sit-in being staged. Wondered if you'd send a reporter to cover it?'

'Sit-in?'

'Yes. A group of students, like maybe twenty or so, have occupied the student union bar. They've been there all night, and they're not moving until their demands are met. Is that something your paper would be interested in?'

'Maybe . . .' There was the sound of scribbling. Nicky was pleased to hear he was taking notes. 'So, what are they protesting about?'

'Removal of their rights,' Nicky replied. She didn't want to admit that it was all down to a ban on smoking in one bar. If she could only get a reporter there, she was sure Seb would get some coverage.

'Where's this at?'

'Student union bar, on campus. Let me give you the number of the guy who's organised it. He's there now. He's got a mobile.' She reeled off Seb's number, which the reporter read back to her.

'OK, got that,' he said. 'And you are?'

'Got to go, my phone card's running out,' Nicky said quickly, then hung up. She frowned. Why had she done that? Why hadn't she given her name? She hadn't consciously decided to distance herself from the protest, but now it seemed like a good idea. She'd kept her promise to Seb, and it had sounded like the *Argus* would send a reporter.

She had less luck with the other paper she called. She was passed from one person to another, and then put on hold. After a couple of minutes of listening to tinny music, her phone card really did run out and she was cut off.

And then there was the campus news-sheet to try, though surely whoever ran that would already know about the protest, given that its office was immediately above the student union bar. Nicky glanced at a clock on the wall. It was about time she headed to her lecture. She'd shop for food, take it to Seb, and call in at the campus paper's offices at lunchtime, when she had a gap between lectures.

Later that day, she managed to pick up a loaf of bread and some ham and cheese, as well as a few packets of biscuits and crisps. Seb could make his own sandwiches, as he liked them, she thought. She put everything in a carrier bag and set off down to the student union bar. She was expecting to see crowds down there, reporters and cameramen, perhaps even a film crew if word had got out by other means. Surely, she wasn't the only person alerting the press? Seb had his own phone and could be calling people on that.

But there were only a pair of security guards, who were standing looking bored by the front entrance. They stared at Nicky as she walked past them and round to the back as before. Another security guard stood there.

'Um, am I allowed to pass some food inside, to my boyfriend?' she asked.

He just shrugged. 'Sure. We're not stopping anyone going in or out. Just keeping an eye on things, in case there's any trouble. Not expecting this to last much longer, miss.'

'OK, thanks, well I might go in and talk to him, but then I'll need to come back out.'

'Sure.'

He pushed open the door, which was no longer locked, and ushered her inside. This time there was no one asking her for a password. There were fewer people in the bar than yesterday, but the atmosphere was as smoky as ever and there was an increasing amount of rubbish on the floor and the tables. Seb was sitting at a table on his phone, talking loudly and gesticulating wildly.

'This is big, yeah, and we're not moving until the ban's been lifted. Doesn't matter if it's days or weeks – we're set up here and we're staying. Send a camera crew round, yeah? The security guys say they'll let reporters in, no problem.' He spotted Nicky and waved at her, then gave an exaggerated eyeroll. 'Yeah, we're serious. It's important. It's like, if we let them erode our rights a little bit, they'll then take more and more. Before you know it, there'll be no smoking allowed anywhere, and that's discriminatory, right? Not allowing smokers into places non-smokers can go. We're putting a stop to it, starting here and now. Yeah, you can quote me. Get up here and report on it, yeah?'

The conversation ended shortly after, and Nicky had the impression it hadn't gone entirely the way Seb had wanted. 'Who was that you were talking to?' Some of the other protesters gathered round to hear what Seb had to report.

'*Evening Argus*. Said you'd tipped them off. Wanted to hear what was going on directly from me. I told them, but they said they probably won't send anyone here today. Said they might "in a day or two", he made quote marks in the air with his fingers, 'if the protest is still ongoing. 'Course it bloody will be! I mean, it'd be nice if we could have got what we wanted quickly and then we could all go home and have a shower. But if it takes a week, then it takes a week, yeah? We're here for the long haul.'

There were a few 'yeahs' and 'too rights' at that, but the protesters didn't seem as enthusiastic as they had been the day before.

'Good they called you about it anyway,' Nicky said to Seb. 'And here, I brought you a pile of food, should last you a little while.'

'Great, thanks.' He took the bag from her and put it in a corner on top of his jacket without looking in it. And, she noted, he didn't offer to pay her for it. It was as though he expected her to support him through this protest, financially as well as practically. She decided not to say anything for now, but if it went on a long time, she was going to have to ask him to pay for his food. Her own finances were a little precarious this late into the term.

'So have any other reporters been here?'

'Just the campus ones, took a few pics, got some quotes from me and a couple of others. Not enough though, is it, to get it in the poxy little campus newsletter. I want national coverage of this! Well, if it takes a few more days, then that's what we have to do.'

'Have some people left?' Nicky glanced around, assessing numbers.

Seb pulled a face. 'One or two, yeah. Felt their studies were more important. And one got a call from his daddy telling him there'd be no allowance next term if he didn't get out of here quick. Fucking loser, that one. Rest of us are sound, though, and we'll stay.'

Nicky pulled out a chair and sat down with him. 'Want me to stay too?'

'Only if you want to, babe.' Seb lit another cigarette. 'Not going to ask you to, as you're not a smoker, and anyway, you're more use bringing me food and stuff. Hey, if I give you my key, can you go to my flat and pick up a few clean clothes? I'm beginning to stink.'

'Not that I've noticed,' she said with a smile. 'But yes, will do. I can probably go this evening and get them.'

'Cheers.' Seb lapsed into a brooding silence. Nicky covered his hand with hers and gave it a squeeze. He believed in this, he believed what he was doing was right and necessary. She got that, she really did. The constant chipping away of rights and freedoms had to be stopped.

'I'll pick up the *Argus* this afternoon for you,' she said. 'They might have decided to cover it even without coming here.'

That seemed to lift his mood a little. Nicky checked the clock on the wall. 'Got to go now, Seb. I'll be back here later this evening with your clothes.'

'Yeah, and pick me up a pizza, will you? There's a place at the end of my street. I don't care if it's cold by the time you get it back here. Meat feast would be great.' He smiled and she was reminded of why she'd fallen for him. Those looks, those deep brown eyes and that floppy hair. He was, she told herself, better looking and a hundred times more interesting than Conor had been. Seb was a rebel – that was what she had wanted in a boyfriend, wasn't it?

'OK, sure. I'll be off then.' She kissed him and left the building.

'Any sign of them giving up and going home yet?' the security guard asked as she left. He seemed to be finding it all a bit of a joke.

'No, they're in it for the long haul,' Nicky replied.

'Yeah, well, we'll see,' the guard answered. 'Kids, play-acting. They should bring back National Service for these lads. That'd help them see what's what.'

Nicky had no answer. She left the guard to his grumbling and went on her way.

Nicky found it hard to concentrate during her afternoon seminar. Her mind was running over what Seb had said and what he was doing. She had to keep telling herself he was fighting for what he believed in, and that was something she could only support. Freedom of speech, the right to fight for your beliefs – that was sacrosanct, wasn't it?

When her seminar was over, she decided to go straight to Seb's flat and pick up his clothes. She could get herself a pizza for her dinner as well as buying the one for him; if they weren't too expensive. And she'd need to go via a cashpoint. She was down to her last fiver.

It took her forty minutes to get to his flat. She bought a copy of the *Evening Argus* at the station on her way, but didn't immediately open it. It felt strange letting herself into his flat. It wasn't as though they'd been together very long. Thankfully, none of his flatmates seemed to be in. She went into his bedroom and scanned around, looking for a bag to pack some clothes in. If it had been Conor's room, she realised, she'd have known exactly what to pick up for him. She knew his favourite T-shirts, the fact that he hated going a day without cleaning his teeth, the way he was happy to wear clothes more than once if they showed no obvious dirt and passed the sniff test. 'No sense killing the planet by doing more laundry than is necessary,' he used to say, as he declared a T-shirt fit for a third day's wear.

Seb's clothes seemed to be mostly on the floor, and many looked rumpled as though they needed washing. She found a tatty rucksack shoved inside a wardrobe, and in a chest of drawers there were some obviously clean underwear, socks and T-shirts. She hadn't seen those T-shirts before but they were neatly folded and looked as though they'd been ironed. Everything on the floor appeared dirty. She packed as many clean items as she could find, then searched for toiletries. Presumably the protesters were washing in the bar's loos. There was a deodorant on top of the chest of drawers, and in the bathroom a toothbrush and toothpaste she thought she'd seen him use when she'd stayed over. He certainly needed to clean his teeth, after all that smoking, she thought!

And then she left to call at the pizza takeaway. She chose a vegetarian one for herself, and was horrified to find the meat feast was the dearest one on the menu. But she'd promised, so she had to buy it. Time, Nicky thought, to start totting up what he owed her.

She took her own pizza to a bench on the prom to eat, and watched the sun turning the sky red and then purple as it sank below the western horizon. There was a little wind whipping up the edge of the sea into gentle waves that sucked and pulled at the pebbles. How she loved that sound! So had Conor, she remembered, when he'd first come to visit her in Brighton. 'It's the constancy I love,' he'd said, 'the way the waves just keep on coming, one after the other, rolling the stones over and over, smoothing them into perfect round pebbles over centuries. Millennia, even.' He'd picked up a pinkish pebble that had a streak of white quartz running through it. 'How pretty is that? And it is just one of thousands of millions of stones on this beach.'

'So beautiful, but so insignificant,' she'd said. 'Just like each of us. We're just pebbles on a beach.'

He'd turned to her. 'No, we're not insignificant. We, each of us, can make a difference. We can make the world a better place, if we want to.'

She'd smiled and taken the stone from him. She smiled again now, realising that she still had it, sitting on a shelf in her student bedroom. It was only a stone, but somehow, she didn't want to throw it out.

She finished eating her pizza, threw its box into a bin on the prom, and set off back to the campus. Seb's pizza would be completely cold by the time she got there but he'd said that didn't matter, and there wasn't anything she could do about it anyway.

At the union bar, things were much as before. Still no power, still a couple of security chaps guarding the entrances, and no sign of the media frenzy that Seb had hoped for. Inside was a different story. The protesters had decided to hell with their vow of not taking anything from the bar. They'd raided the stock of bottles of beer, and by the looks of things, had been partying since she'd last visited.

Two protesters were involved in a drinking game at one table, while another group were sitting around a table laughing loudly at each other's jokes. The table was crammed with empty bottles and there were more on the floor around them. Another protester looked as though he was sleeping off a heavy session, his head slumped over his chest and a line of dribble running down his chin.

Seb was sitting on his own in a corner, with a single beer in front of him. 'Hey,' Nicky said, as she approached him and passed over the pizza and bag of clothes. 'Got what you wanted. Pizza's cold.'

'Cheers, thanks,' he said, and immediately opened the pizza and tucked into a slice. 'Christ, I was starving.'

'Did you eat all the stuff I brought you earlier?' Nicky glanced around but could see no sign of it.

'The bread and ham and all that? Yeah, the lads ate it,' Seb replied, through a mouthful of meat feast.

'It was meant for you, Seb. I'm not providing food for everyone here. Can't afford to.' Nicky felt aggrieved that he'd passed the food on. Why couldn't the other protesters get their own friends to support them? 'And I see the rule about not drinking the bar's stock isn't in place anymore.'

Seb shrugged. 'Yeah, well, we've been here two days now, and the lads were thirsty. Not much I could do to stop them. Anyway, this is what happens in a protest, babe. You start with rules, yeah, but then you have to be flexible and let things change as you go on.'

'Don't you worry that you'll all be in trouble when this ends? They'll look at the mess, and the amount of drink that's been taken, and sue you for it.'

Seb shrugged again and took another enormous bite of the pizza. It was a while before he could answer. 'Nah, they won't. If they do, my parents'll bail me out, I reckon. Don't be worrying about it, babe, yeah? Did you get me a paper?'

Nicky pulled the *Evening Argus* out of the bag of clothes she'd brought him. Together they scanned through the paper, looking for a mention of the protest. 'Doesn't look like you're in here,' Nicky said, as they reached the last few pages that contained local sporting results and small ads.

'Fuck 'em,' Seb said, throwing down the pizza crust he'd been eating. 'We go to all this trouble, and for what? Nothing. And look at this shower, just getting themselves off their heads. Fuckers.'

'Seb, should you leave? Walk out of here, leave the others to it? You're not drunk, they can't blame the mess and thefts on you.' As she spoke, he began shaking his head decisively.

'No. What do you take me for? I set this thing up, and I ain't gonna drop them in it, when we've come this far. Shame they've drunk so much, but we're here, and I'm staying, till the end.'

They fell silent then, and Seb leafed through the paper. One article caught his attention and he stabbed a finger at it. 'Look, they've started building this Millennium Dome thing, in London. Waste of public money that will be.'

'Good to celebrate the millennium, though, don't you think? I quite like the idea.'

'Just another year. Doesn't mean anything. And this millennium bug thing they're going on about? That's all just a means of controlling us, yeah? There's no such thing. All these scare stories that appliances will stop working after the millennium – that's just the manufacturers trying to sell us new shit. And they say aeroplanes will stop flying – that's just to keep us in our place. Make us worried about nothing, then when it doesn't happen, we all say how brilliant the government is for stopping it. That's how it works, babe. Don't fall for it, yeah?'

Nicky blinked. She'd never really thought about it much. She'd just assumed that some computer software would need updating or replacing to cope, and that the IT industry would get on and do it, so in the end there'd be minimal problems. She had never thought that maybe the whole thing was a hoax, if that was what he was saying.

'They'll fix it, though, won't they? The IT people. They'll sort it out so nothing goes wrong.'

'Nothing to sort out, babe. It's all just bollocks. Believe me.' He tapped the side of his nose. 'I know this stuff. I know what's real and what's not. I know what we got to take a stand against, when we need to stop the government. Like now, here. They're trying to stop us smoking, but it's got to be people's own choice, yeah? Not the fucking nanny state.' He pulled a cigarette out of his pocket and lit up.

Nicky left soon after, and breathed in the fresh evening air outside with relief.

Chapter 14 – April 1916

The weeks flew by, and suddenly it was the week before Easter, and yet there was still so much to do, so much to plan. The Countess had put together a Citizen Army uniform for herself – a dark green woollen blouse with brass buttons, black stockings and boots, and a pair of green knee breeches that could be concealed under a skirt. 'So I can convert from woman to soldier at a moment's notice,' she said to Gráinne. James Connolly had appointed the Countess as his 'ghost'; she'd been informed of all the plans, so that if anything untoward happened to him she'd be able to step in and take over. 'And you, Gráinne, are my right-hand woman. I won't tell you everything, but I will inform you of everything you need to know in order to fully play your part in it all.'

And so Gráinne was informed when a notice was put in the daily papers, advertising that all Volunteers should report for 'manoeuvres' on Easter Sunday. The Irish Citizen Army was also alerted, and the Countess confirmed that the IRB had been told too. 'All working together,' she said. 'We're making a real stand. We'll fly the flag of free Ireland over Dublin from Sunday. Oh!' The Countess clapped a hand over her mouth.

'What is it, Madame?' Gráinne asked, fearful that there was some terrible flaw in the plan and that it could not go ahead after all.

'A flag! We must have a flag to fly! I am not sure Connolly, or anyone else for that matter, has thought of it! Come with me, Gráinne. It's not too late.' She ran up the stairs, Gráinne following, and into her bedroom. An emerald green bedspread was on the bed, and she tugged it off and ran through to another room that was being decorated. There she grabbed a pot of gold paint and a brush. 'Downstairs!'

Gráinne clattered down the stairs after her, and watched with astonishment as the Countess spread the bedcover over the grand piano in the front room. She sketched out a design on a piece of paper, then used the gold paint to replicate that on the bedspread – the words 'Irish Republic' in large letters. James Connolly came in when it was part done and nodded with approval.

'We'll fly that from the headquarters,' he said. Poppet had come running in with him, and seeing the bedspread hanging over the edge of the piano, he jumped up and down, trying to grab one of the tassels that decorated the ends. He got hold of one and pulled.

'Oh no, the dog!' Gráinne leapt forward to stop him while the Countess held on to the bedspread. There was a ripping sound, and Gráinne wondered what they would use for a flag instead, if this was ruined. But, thankfully, Poppet had only managed to tear off a tassel and a small piece.

'It's salvageable,' the Countess said. 'Gráinne, could you shut Poppet in another room while I finish this? She looked stressed. There was so much to be done, so much at stake, and the last thing they needed was a small dog ruining the first flag of the free Irish Republic.

Gráinne picked up Poppet and carried him out to the kitchen. She gave him a few tidbits to eat and then pushed him out into the garden and closed the door. The little dog looked back at her mournfully, as though he'd expected Gráinne to go out to play with him. But some things were more important than a dog's playtime. She went back to the front room where the Countess was putting the finishing touches to the flag.

'There. When the paint's dry, Gráinne, would you sew some tabs to it, so we can attach ropes to hoist it?' Gráinne nodded, delighted to be able to play a part in making the flag.

'Thank you. I should let you know too, that I will be moving out of here tomorrow. I'm going to stay in a flat nearer the centre of town, on Henry Street, so that I am close by and on hand when the Rising starts. So, you'll be in charge here. Poppet, however, is to be looked after by a neighbour. We'll have enough to think about without worrying who's going to feed or walk him.'

'All right, so,' Gráinne agreed, feeling a surge of excitement. After so long preparing for this, now it was almost upon them.

That evening, while Connolly was still at Surrey House, there were several other visitors. The Countess had asked key members of the Cumann na mBan to call. Among them were Margaret Skinnider and a nurse named Elizabeth O'Farrell whom Gráinne had met before. The Countess introduced each of them to James Connolly. 'Remember their faces, James. These women you can trust with anything. And the same goes for Gráinne, but of course, you are already familiar with her.'

Gráinne was proud to be included in the set of women Connolly could trust. The women didn't stay long but Connolly had noted their names and the roles they'd been assigned for the Rising. One was to be the chief medical officer, another would manage a field kitchen. Gráinne and others were to be couriers, carrying messages, food and ammunition between rebel outposts.

'And what do we have lined up for you?' Connolly asked Margaret Skinnider.

'Well, as she's a crack shot with a rifle, that's how we should employ her,' the Countess cut in. 'She'll be with me.'

'Looking forward to it,' Margaret said, grimly.

The following day a letter arrived for Gráinne, from her father. In it was some exciting news, to say that he'd had word Sean was coming home on leave. He was due to arrive in Dublin that very day. Gráinne had not had a letter from Sean for some time, but the Surrey House household had long suspected that police might be intercepting and reading their mail.

'Sean's coming home!' she said to herself, repeatedly. But what dreadful timing! Any other week and she'd have been able to take time off to see him. But now – with the Rising only days away and the Countess having left her in charge of Surrey House – how could she get away? Perhaps she could send Emmett to meet him, with a message. She could not bring Sean here to Surrey House. Even though he was her brother, he was a soldier in the British army. He'd be in his uniform. She could not put him in that terrible position of knowing something that he might feel he should report. His loyalties were split already, and it would not be her place to make that worse.

She sat down to write a note to Emmett. Perhaps she could send a Fianna boy to his workplace with the news. She had barely set pen to paper when the doorbell rang, and she hurried to open it. To her surprise Emmett was standing on the doorstep, a letter in his hand.

'Gráinne, have you heard? Sean's coming back to Dublin today!'

'I heard from my father; I was just about to send you a note to see if you could meet him. Come on in.' She took him through to the kitchen where she'd been peeling potatoes ready for the evening meal, though how many would be there she had no idea.

'I thought we could go together? His ferry should get into Dublin Port around midday.'

'I'm not sure . . . I've been left in charge here. The Countess has moved to Henry Street.'

'Ready for Sunday?'

She nodded. 'I'm not sure I can leave.'

'How about I stay here a while, you go and meet Sean. I suppose he'll go to stay with your father. You need to see him first and it'll be easier to catch him off the boat than go to St Enda's, especially this week.'

'You're right. But will you manage?'

'I can answer the door and take messages. I can also peel those spuds.' He smiled at her, and cupped her face in his hands. 'I'll cope.' He kissed her, and she wrapped her arms around him and wished they could just stay in that moment for ever. There was so much going on, and all she really wanted was to be with Emmett. But that would have to wait.

'Thank you. I'll go now. It'll take me a while to get to the port and I don't want to miss him.' She took off her apron and handed it to Emmett who put it on with a laugh. And then she grabbed her coat and left the house, taking trams and buses and reaching the port area just in time to see the ferry from Holyhead docking. She stood with a crowd of others, mostly women, who all appeared to be straining to catch a glimpse of their loved ones. As the passengers disembarked, it seemed that around half were soldiers home on leave. A few limped off the boat, or had bandaged heads. With all the excitement of the upcoming

Rising, she'd almost forgotten about the other war, the big one that was engulfing all of Europe. The war Sean had been away fighting in.

And then she spotted him. To her relief he did not appear to be injured, though he was thinner than when she'd last seen him. He shuffled down the gangplank carrying a kit bag, and headed towards the bus stop.

'Sean! Sean, it's me!' She ran over to him and caught his arm.

'Gráinne! How wonderful!' He pulled her into a tight hug. 'I wondered if anyone would be here to meet me. I suppose Dad's teaching today, and Emmett's working. And you – I thought you'd be busy working too?'

'I am, but well . . . long story. I managed to get away for a couple of hours. It's so wonderful to see you! Come on, let's find a café in town and catch up, before you head out to Dad's place.'

'I'm not going to Dad's,' he said, as he gently extricated himself from her embrace.

'What? Where are you going to stay?'

He swallowed, and then turned to her. 'I don't know. But I can't go back to the war, Grá. I'll have a cup of tea with you, and then I'll be gone. Don't worry about me.'

'But . . . have you left the army?'

He shook his head. 'We can't leave, unless we're injured. Or dead. I'm not going back to risk either.'

They were at the bus stop and boarded a bus to go back into the city centre. They did not speak during the journey, and Sean kept his head turned away from her, gazing out of the window as though drinking in the sights of Dublin that he'd been deprived of for so long. They alighted near Liberty Hall where Sean noticed the banner over the door. He gave a hollow laugh but made no comment. Gráinne led him to a café she knew, where she ordered tea and sandwiches.

'Eat these. You look like you need to put a bit of flesh on those bones.' When the waitress had left, she leaned towards him. 'So tell me, what are your plans?'

'Just . . . to not go back. I'm going to disappear, until it's all over. If I'm caught, I'd be court-martialled. But I can't go back.' He shook his head, and there was a note of despair in his voice. 'I can't do it anymore, Grá.'

She caught his hand in hers. 'I understand. I've been thinking about you, in those awful trenches . . .' She sighed, and considered whether it was safe to tell him anything about the plans for the Rising. If Ireland was free, then Irishmen would no longer be obliged to fight for Britain. Men like Sean could come home without any fear of reprimand. Perhaps there was hope for him, in what they were doing. 'Listen, I can't say much, but you should know, that there are plans. Soon, very soon, if things go well, Ireland will be free. And that means you'd be free as well.'

'I guessed something was being planned. I read between the lines in your letters.' He gave a small smile.

Gráinne leaned towards him. 'How long is your leave, officially?'

'I'm supposed to be on the boat on Monday.'

'Easter Monday?'

He nodded. 'But I won't be on it.' His jaw was set firm and she could see he'd made up his mind. She wouldn't try to talk him out of it though. It was his decision, entirely his. But she was worried – if he was court-martialled for desertion, what was the penalty? She dared not ask him. She did not want to hear the answer.

'I'll find you somewhere to stay. Maybe if you agree to help . . . with anything that happens . . .'

But he shook his head. 'If you're asking me to pick up arms against other men, for any cause, I-I don't think I can. I'm finished with that. I've . . . blown men's heads off with grenades. Looked them in the eye as I shot them. Run them through with a bayonet. Dodged a thousand bullets myself. I can do no more.' He squeezed her hand. 'I'm sorry, Gráinne. I know you believe in it and all, but . . . you haven't seen the horror of war like I have. I can't do it anymore. It's not in me. Not even for Ireland.'

'Will you see Emmett, before you . . . leave Dublin?' He didn't know about her relationship with his old friend. She had not written about it in her letters to him, only that she'd seen Emmett several times.

He shook his head again. 'No. I know his thoughts on revolution too. And I can't sit by him and listen to it.'

'Sean, you should know . . .'

'What?' He stared at her.

She bit her lip. 'Emmett and I . . . we've been seeing a lot of each other . . .'

He nodded slowly. 'He's a good man. You could do a lot worse.'

'Do I have your approval then? Of my relationship with Emmett? That matters to me.'

'You do.' He squeezed her hand and she smiled at him, her wonderful, big-hearted but broken brother.

'And of the plans for a Rising?' she whispered.

He shrugged. 'I don't believe it'll happen in any meaningful way. Not until the war in Europe is over and the politicians in London can go back to discussing a way forward for Ireland. All this talk of revolution and Irish independence that Emmett writes about in his cryptic letters – it'll all come to nothing. It's all posturing. You should understand that.'

'Maybe you're right. Eat your sandwich, dear brother.' He wasn't right, but she couldn't tell him any more than she already had. He'd see for himself, when the Rising began, if he was still in Dublin then. But from what he'd said, he was likely to be somewhere out in the countryside by then, making sure he was far away from any authorities who might arrest him and send him back to his regiment. A thought occurred to her. He was dressed in his soldier's uniform. 'You'll need some different clothes.'

He looked down at himself, as though he'd forgotten he was in uniform. When he lifted his head again, he looked defeated, as though for all his conviction that he would not go back, this first small hurdle had defeated him.

'Sean, it's easily solved. Go and see Emmett. He'll sort you out with clothes, money, anything you need to get away. You know he will. I can tell him not to talk about the Cause to you.'

'Yes. I can't see another solution. Where will he be, now?'

She thought quickly. She could not take Sean to Surrey House, not today. Who knew who might be there! Connolly would not take kindly to her turning up with a British soldier. 'I'll send him to you. I know where to find him. You stay here, promise me?'

He nodded, then folded his arms across the table and rested his head on them. 'God I'm so tired, Grá. So very, very tired of it all.'

She watched him for a moment, then stroked his hair and kissed his forehead. 'I'll order you more tea, and Emmett will be here as soon as possible. I-I don't know when I'll see you again.'

He pulled a hand out from under his head and squeezed hers. 'Soon, I hope.'

'Yes. Until we meet again, my dearest brother.' She ordered another pot of tea for him, paid the bill, and hurried out of the café. As the door closed behind her, she glanced back to see him still sitting there with his head resting on his arms, his eyes closed. Her poor brother. What he must have seen and done over there in the trenches did not bear thinking about. It shouldn't be so, but it was. The Rising was the only hope of ending all that for Irishmen at least. It had to work.

Seeing Sean like that, knowing it was fighting for Britain that had broken him, only strengthened her resolve still further to do whatever she could so that men like Sean could come home and fight no more.

Back at Surrey House, Gráinne found Emmett presiding over an impromptu meeting in the dining room of various more junior members of the militant organisations. Connolly was there, doling out jobs and roles to everyone. Gráinne motioned to Emmett from the doorway and he made his excuses and left the meeting.

'It's all happening here! I can't believe what's going on, and that I've been a part of it! How's Sean?'

'He's all right . . . Come into the kitchen, Emmett. I need to ask you another favour.'

He frowned and followed her. She quickly explained about Sean's predicament. 'He needs a set of civilian clothes if he's to have any chance. And money. I gave him what I had on me, which wasn't much. I have more upstairs – let me fetch it. Will you go and see him? Lend him clothes and give him my money?'

He pulled her into a hug. 'Of course I will. I'd do it for him, even if I wasn't with you. I'll go now. He's at the Liffey Café, you say?'

'Yes. I told him to stay there until you arrive. He looked shattered. Let me get that money.' She ran upstairs and brought down her little pot of savings to give to Emmett.

'I'll add the same myself,' Emmett said, and she was filled with a rush of love towards him. 'I'll be away, so. I'll see you again tomorrow I expect.'

'What about your work?'

'Ah, one of the solicitors where I work is in the Volunteers. The office is closed this week, and for as long as is necessary. We're putting country first.'

She nodded, and kissed him goodbye. 'Stay safe, Emmett.'

'You too.' What would the next few days bring, she wondered. Easter Sunday was just three days away.

Chapter 15 – March 1998

Nicky wasn't sure whether she had consciously decided not to visit Seb at the sit-in the following morning. Somehow, she managed to miss her alarm going off, and by the time she woke up she needed to rush to get to a tutorial. There was just no time to get to the union bar first. If he was expecting her to bring him something for breakfast then too bad. She'd taken him enough food yesterday. It was his own fault if he hadn't made that last.

It was Wednesday and that was always a busy day for Nicky, with back-to-back tutorials and lectures. There was a talk at lunchtime that she'd diarised – not part of her course but, nevertheless, it was a subject she was interested in and she'd wanted to attend. She just had time to call Seb to let him know she'd be there at six o'clock, and she'd bring him something to eat then.

He sounded weary and resigned on the phone. 'Yeah, babe, see you then. If we're still in here.'

'You'll still be there, surely?'

He sighed. 'Only three of us left here now. Not sure how much longer this will go on. Anyway, if I'm not here, call me, yeah?'

'Will do. See you later. Looking forward to having you all to myself again, Seb.'

'Yeah, whatever.'

Nicky hung up feeling flat. She didn't care if the protest was winding-up – actually from her point of view, it'd be better if it did end today. She'd get Seb back, she wouldn't need to keep supporting him, and if she was honest, she didn't care for their cause. Why shouldn't people be able to choose to go to a smoke-free bar? Imagine going out for an evening, and being able to wear the same clothes the next day without them stinking of smoke? And for the asthmatic girl whose health kicked this whole thing off, surely she had rights too? Smokers could still go to the union bar, and simply go outside if they wanted a cigarette. How much was that really imposing on their rights? There were other bars they could choose to go to. It was all a balancing act. Nicky wished she could put all this to Seb and have a proper discussion about it. It wasn't that she wasn't brave enough to try – the problem was she couldn't really be bothered with it. He'd just bleat about his rights as a smoker, and would refuse to see any other viewpoint. He was, she realised, a little self-centred. Rather like a toddler who only cared about things affecting himself.

And yet, he'd taken part in bigger, more worthwhile protests. The road-building ones – the protesters had been trying to protect ancient woodland. They'd made the point that more roads are bad for the environment. Investment should be in public transport instead – better for the planet, better for everyone. Now that, she agreed with.

Nicky sat through the lunchtime talk with only half her mind listening to the speaker. The rest of her mind was beginning to question what she'd seen in Seb, besides his undoubtedly good looks. But she couldn't abandon him now, with the protest still limping on. He needed her. He'd done good things in the past. Perhaps this was just a blip. He deserved another chance. After all, she'd only known him a few weeks. She'd been with Conor for three years. It took a while to really get to know someone.

She spent a few hours in the library that afternoon, pushing ahead with her project. She read up on the Cumann na mBan and Constance Markiewicz. And she read some descriptions of what had happened during that fateful Easter week in 1916. Only a week – not even a full week – and yet the shockwaves of what the rebels achieved had reverberated across Ireland and Britain, and even America, for several years. It was those events that led, three years later, to the Irish War of Independence, the subsequent partitioning of Ireland, the Irish Civil War then decades of IRA activity. The peace process now, she read, since the shaky ceasefire that had begun last August, was currently at its most promising since 1921. Fingers crossed, she thought. Lasting peace in Northern Ireland would be almost a resolution, the end of the story of the 1916 rebellion. Well, not absolutely the end while Ireland remained partitioned, but a major step along the way. And she had a feeling Supergran would love to be around to see it happen.

By the time she'd finished working, been to her last lecture of the day and walked over to the union bar, she was tired but buzzing with excitement about her project again. It was progressing well and she couldn't wait to go back to visit Supergran and hear the rest of her story.

At the bar, the doors were wide open. The sit-in had obviously ended. Various university admin staff were inside, taking notes of damage and counting empty beer bottles. Some police officers were there too, taking statements from staff.

Seb, along with the three other protesters who'd stayed till the end, was sitting on a bench outside looking dejected.

There was a police constable standing nearby. Had they been arrested? Nicky walked over to be within calling distance.

'Seb? What's the news?'

He shrugged. 'All over, as you can see.'

'What's going to happen?'

'Dunno. We got to go to the police station and give statements. Don't think we can be charged with anything. We did no damage.'

'Just the drink,' said the guy sitting next to him.

'We can pay for that,' Seb snapped. Nicky suspected he'd get his parents to pay for it. He'd said something about that earlier. So much for the great freedom fighter, if he needed mummy and daddy to bail him out. She bit her tongue. Now was not the time for that discussion.

'You'll be glad to get a shower,' Nicky said. Despite her efforts fetching him clean clothes from his flat, he was still wearing the same shirt and jeans he'd been wearing at the start. 'And some decent food.'

'Think that'll all have to wait until after I've made my statement,' Seb said.

Just then a police officer approached and ushered Seb and his friends into a couple of police cars. Nicky took a step back – she didn't want to be mistaken for one of the protesters. Her part had been very minor. The officer only glanced at her and said nothing.

'Come and see me, later. Tomorrow,' she called to Seb as he got into the police car. He didn't respond, so she wasn't sure if he'd heard her or not.

And then, there was the slow walk back to her room, accompanied only by her whirling thoughts. How sure was she of Seb? Not very, was the unwelcome answer, but she'd promised herself she'd give him another chance. It was still early days for their relationship, and it had been an odd time, during the sit-in.

Back at her student flat, she checked the post. There was a letter there from Conor. It was the first he'd sent since she dumped him. She felt a flutter of nerves as she opened it. A million possibilities of what it might contain rushed through her mind. Did he miss her? Would he plead with her to take him back?

It turned out to be simply news. He'd applied for, and been accepted on, a Voluntary Service Overseas placement. During the long summer break, he'd be travelling to Uganda, helping roll out portable ultrasound equipment to medical centres. He was excited at the prospect, happy at the thought that he'd be doing something tangible, some real good that would make people's lives better in the long term. Nicky smiled as she read it. She could just imagine him doing this work. Good for him. Other than that, the letter contained just news about his course, some gossip about mutual friends, and wishes that she was well and happy and still enjoying her course. *As I'll be away most of the summer there won't be much chance to catch up with you in person,* the letter went on. *But if you're around in the last week of June we could meet then, for a drink and catch-up, if you like? No worries if you don't want to or if you're staying in Brighton for the summer break.*

She did want to see him then, she realised. It was still months away, plenty of time for him to get over losing her, and plenty of time for her to get her life in order. It'd be good to catch up. He was still a friend, wasn't he? Someone she cared about and wanted to stay in touch with, no matter what. She decided to wait a week or two, and write back to him. She could tell him about her 1916 Rising project – she knew he'd be interested in that. Unlike Seb.

Nicky remembered how, at the start of the Upper Sixth, she and Conor had spent hours discussing which universities to apply to and which courses they wanted to do. Conor had known for a long time that he wanted to study medicine, which, of course, limited his choice of university. Nicky took longer deciding what to study – she was definitely more interested in the arts rather than the sciences – but eventually her history teacher talked her into applying to study modern history.

One day she and Conor had been drinking milkshakes made with Maltesers that were Nicky's current favourite snack at a local café.

'So will we try to find a decent university that offers both medicine and modern history?' she'd asked.

'If such a thing exists.' Conor had looked doubtful.

'We should try.'

'Or else apply to unis that are easy travelling distance apart? We'd be able to hook up at weekends, at either uni. And we could make sure we go home to our parents at the same time so we can also see each other then.' He'd looked at her carefully as he spoke. 'We've a strong relationship, Nicky. We'll survive being apart . . . if we want it to last.'

'I know we will,' she'd said. 'And, of course, I want it to last! Don't you?'

'You know I do. But I also know people change when they leave home. And if that happens, and either of us wants to call it a day, well then, I think, we'd just have to accept it. Don't worry! I have absolutely zero intention of that happening. I just want you to know that if you find yourself feeling that you want . . . I don't know . . . a break or something, then you should just tell me, and I'll be cool with it.' He'd given her a twisted little smile. 'Heartbroken, of course, but cool with it.'

He'd been as good as his word, hadn't he? Nicky thought now. Cool with her wanting to break things off. But was he also heartbroken? She hated to think so. She hated what she'd done to him, hated herself for doing it.

She'd had good reasons to do it, she reminded herself. And he'd said if ever she felt that way, she should just tell him. She'd done what he'd said, and now . . . now she needed to live with that decision and make the best of it. Make the best of her life. In some ways, she owed it to Conor to do that.

The following day, Nicky had no lectures or seminars in the morning. She decided to work in her room for the morning. As well as her main project on rebellion, she had a couple of other essays to write, which were due within a week or so.

She was partway through writing one of them when there was a tap at her door. 'Nick? You there, babe?'

'Come on in,' she called, and a moment later Seb was flopped across her bed, his forearm across his eyes. She moved across the room to sit beside him, her hand in his. He'd showered and was wearing clean clothes, she was pleased to see. 'You all right?'

'No. Been kicked out of university. Just come from seeing the vice-chancellor. Bastard says I have to go. He refused to accept we were only standing up for our rights.'

'Was it the damage in the bar?'

'Yeah, that and the beer we drank, and the fact the bar lost revenue while we were there. Something about can't allow this sort of thing, got to make an example. Fucking bastard.'

'Shit.' Nicky had not expected he'd be thrown out. That seemed harsh. Students had a long history of rebellion, of organising protests and sit-ins and marches. Her own mother had condescendingly said it was 'all part of the student experience'. Surely all that was necessary was for him and the others to pay for any damage done?

'Yeah, I know, babe. But. My course sucked, anyway. I don't care.'

'What will you do?'

'Gonna stay here in Brighton. Get a job, I suppose. I'll still be able to see you, don't fret, babe.' He squeezed her hand, then pulled her down to him to kiss. As his hands snaked their way around her waist, under her T-shirt, Nicky tried to get herself in the mood for sex. But all she could think of was the state he'd been in at the end of the sit-in – unwashed, wearing four-day-old clothes even though she'd brought him clean ones, relying on her to bring him food. And smoking. All that endless smoking and coughing. Even now, he stank of it, he tasted of it, and suddenly she felt a revulsion towards the habit.

She pulled away from him, sitting up on the bed again. 'What's wrong, babe?'

'Not in the mood, sorry. I was deep into writing an essay when you came here. The impact of post-war austerity is not the best way to turn me on, I guess.'

'Hmph.' He spun round and sat on the edge of the bed, head in hands. 'Your bloody coursework. You still doing that Dublin nonsense? All that history – it's all looking backwards, ain't it? Whereas we should be looking forwards. Making the future a better place, not peering at the past.'

'"Those who fail to learn from history are condemned to repeat it,"' she quoted. 'It's by studying history that we're most likely to get the future right. I think it's important.'

'Bollocks to that. Well, I'm glad I'm off my course. University's a waste of time anyway. I'll have a job in a week, I'll have money coming in and I'll only have to work a few hours a day. You'll see.'

'Hope you get one.'

'Yeah, I will. And there'll be another protest. I won't be rolling over and accepting what the authorities tell me, that's for sure. I'll still be an activist.' He grinned at her. 'I'll have more time without having to do this studying shit.'

'Maybe not if you get a job.'

He shrugged. 'I was able before, when I helped out Swampy and his crowd at the Newbury bypass.'

'How many days did you live at the protest site then?' Nicky couldn't help herself. She had to know how big a part he'd played in that.

'Well, you know. I was back and forth.'

'How many nights?' She smiled as she asked, softening her questioning.

'Well, not nights as such. It was more like . . . the part you played these last few days. Took them food and stuff.'

'You bought them food?'

'Raided Mum's freezer. She'd always complained it was stuffed too full.' He laughed. 'I was helping her out by making space in it, and supplying the protesters at the same time.'

'So you didn't actually stay overnight? You just took them food your parents had paid for?'

'Yeah, babe, something like that. What does it matter, anyway? Ancient history. Like I said, we should look forwards to the next thing, not backwards.' He got to his feet. 'You've got my number. Call me, yeah? When you're in a better mood.'

With that he left. Nicky breathed a sigh of relief. Maybe he was right, and she was simply in a bad mood right now. Things would be better between them the next time she saw him, if she was less distracted by her studies, and if she didn't question him too closely about his activism.

Or maybe she needed to call it a day.

The one thing she was sure of, was that now was not the time to make a decision. Right now, she had an essay to write, and that needed to take priority. There was only another week and a bit of term and then she'd be off to Dublin again. Before then she needed to clear the decks of all her other work, so she could concentrate on the rebellion project.

And maybe she ought to call her parents. She hadn't spoken to Mum since before her trip to Dublin.

Chapter 16 – 21–23 April 1916

Gráinne went to the Countess's Henry Street flat on the morning of Good Friday. She had a pile of mail to take and several hand-delivered messages. And she wanted to find out if there were any further developments. People were constantly calling at Surrey House wanting to know. The policeman standing opposite must have a full notebook of names by now, she thought.

She managed to meet briefly with Emmett along the way, and he reported that he'd given Sean clothes and money, and had allowed him into his own lodgings to change. 'I need to dispose of his soldier's uniform, but that will have to wait,' Emmett said.

'And where has Sean gone?'

Emmett shrugged. 'Out of Dublin I expect, but he did not say where. He said to thank you for everything and to wish you well. After the war – both the wars – he'll come to find you.'

'Does he know much about the Rising?'

'I hinted there was something definitely about to happen and, therefore, it'd be safer for him out of the city. I said no more than that. You said he did not want to be lectured about Irish independence, so I did not do that.'

'Thank you. I said as much to him too. So he has an idea about it. Here is the Countess's flat. I will see you tomorrow, I hope.' She kissed him and then went up the stairs to the flat's entrance, where she knocked on the door.

The Countess let her in, and Gráinne was not at all surprised to see both James Connolly and Pádraig Pearse there, having an urgent conversation in the sitting room.

'Madame, I brought you these letters and messages,' Gráinne said, handing them over. 'There are people calling at all hours, wanting to know if there are any updates. Is there anything new I should tell them?'

'Not at present, Gráinne. But . . .' the Countess glanced at the men in the sitting room with a worried expression. 'But stay here a little while. They're talking . . . there's been something happening. Tell you what – make us some tea, would you? Let's be civilised about this, as we would have been in Surrey House. Maybe they'll have sorted things out by the time you bring it in.' She smiled at Gráinne and pointed the way to the flat's small kitchen.

Gráinne did as she'd been asked, rummaging in unfamiliar cupboards to find what she needed, and managed to put together a tray to take through. The three in the sitting room were looking thoughtful but satisfied, as though something had been resolved.

'The Rising is still on – that is the message to give anyone you trust who asks,' Connolly told Gráinne. 'We had a slight hiccup. Eóin MacNeill heard of it and was none too happy he'd been left out of the planning. He sent out a countermanding order to his Volunteers, calling it off.'

'Thankfully, I was able to talk him round,' Pearse added. 'But only by telling him about the arms shipment that's due in today. With those arms we'll have enough weaponry. He saw sense, and rescinded his countermanding order.'

'We've only told you this in case there are rumours that it's been called off,' the Countess said. 'Don't mention any of it unless you need to, to reassure anyone who's not sure whether we're going ahead.'

'Of course, Madame. And, Mr Connolly, Mr Pearse – you can absolutely rely on me.'

'I know. Well, you had better get back to Surrey House and man the fort there. If all has gone according to plan, those arms and explosives from Germany should be on their way across the country by now. We'll have time to distribute them among the units before Sunday.' Pearse nodded, dismissing her.

'Call here again tomorrow morning, in case there's more news,' the Countess instructed. 'It's safer to pass these messages on in person rather than put them in writing, at this stage.'

'Yes, Madame.' Gráinne left them to their discussions, and went back to Surrey House thinking on all that she'd heard.

The next day, Saturday, did indeed bring more news. Gráinne had gone to Henry Street with Emmett, although he waited outside while she went in to see the Countess. This time the Countess was alone and in an agitated state. 'Ah Gráinne. I waited to see you, to pass this on. We've had terrible news. The *Aud* – that's the boat that was bringing the arms shipment – was intercepted by the British navy.'

'What? But the guns—'

'Are all lost,' the Countess finished for her. She gazed at Gráinne sadly. 'The captain scuttled the ship rather than allow the British to take them. We needed those weapons. Without them we have only those we brought in at Howth two years ago. It was a good haul but there are not nearly as many as we need.'

'So does that mean . . .?' Gráinne couldn't bring herself to say it. Was the Rising to be called off, at this late stage? Just a day away?

But the Countess was shaking her head. 'No. James was here earlier and he says we are to go ahead. He says in one way this could work in our favour – the authorities may have heard a Rising is planned, and they'll assume we will call it off without those weapons. But we still have plenty of guns. And plenty of men, which is important. It's all still on. However, we don't need the men mobilised to distribute the weapons now, of course. It's a setback, that's all. Now then, I have to go to Liberty Hall. Can you be here tomorrow early, please? I want you by my side on the big day.' She smiled at Gráinne. 'Be here by seven o'clock, dressed for war.'

Gráinne was shaking as she left the flat and went to meet up again with Emmett. Dressed for war – how did one dress for war? The Countess had put together a uniform for herself, but most of the Cumann na mBan women had not. Some wore breeches under their skirts so they could hoist up their skirts to run, or even take them off. That seemed like a good idea. She wondered if Emmett might have any that fitted. She'd ask him . . . but there was the bigger news, of the loss of arms. She knew she should probably not talk about that, but she had to know what he felt, whether he thought it would ruin their chances.

'We've lost the guns. The arms shipment that was due to land yesterday has been lost. The ship was intercepted. The Countess says Connolly wants the Rising to go ahead regardless. I don't know what this means. Will we still have a chance?'

Emmett stopped walking and turned to face her. He gazed at her for a moment then wrapped his arms around her. 'Oh Gráinne, I don't think we ever really had a chance. Not to actually overturn the British government here. But we have to try. We have to take a stand, show them we mean business. This isn't the end, it's only the beginning. This Rising will fail, but we'll show what we can do.'

'It'll fail?' Gráinne gasped. She had not thought of it like this at all.

'Yes, I am sure it will. With or without those guns. But if we can take Dublin and hold it for a day or two, we'll have made our point. Striking a losing blow is better than striking no blow at all. And then the next time, the next time, we'll have more men, more guns and we'll rise up stronger and harder. And in the meantime, let's try to enjoy this last day together, for who knows when we'll next be able to enjoy these simple pleasures, walks together, quiet chats.'

She smiled at him and squeezed his hand. To live in the moment seemed like a good idea, in this last day of peace.

Gráinne barely slept that Saturday night. How could she sleep when there was to be a rebellion the next day? A rebellion that was destined to fail, according to Emmett. She spent the night tossing and turning, her mind playing over countless possible scenarios of what might happen in the days to come. Perhaps they'd all be arrested within hours. Perhaps there'd be gunfire. Perhaps they'd take the key buildings in the city that Connolly and Pearse had identified as targets, and would hole up for a few hours before having to surrender.

Her own primary role was to be a messenger running between the various targeted points in the city. She would travel by bicycle or on foot. She'd deliver commands, news, food and ammunition, as required. James Connolly had assured her and the other Cumann na mBan women in this role that they would be in no danger but would be performing an essential service in aid of the Rising. It would likely be a long and tiring day, and she would be doing it after a sleepless night. Not ideal. She wondered whether Emmett was able to sleep at all, or was he like her, lying wide awake in the early hours, staring at the ceiling and wondering what the day would bring? She had no idea when she would see him next.

She rose early, far earlier than she really needed to but what was the point lying awake in bed? There must be something useful she could do, at the Henry Street flat or at Liberty Hall itself. She dressed in the knee breeches she'd borrowed from Emmett and woollen stockings, and put a loose skirt over it. She'd sewn pockets into the inside of the skirt, to hide anything she might be asked to carry. A blouse and a light jacket on top completed the outfit. She looked like any other woman in Dublin going about her business. Her boots were low heeled and comfortable so that if she needed to run in them, she could. She forced herself to eat some breakfast even though her stomach was churning with nerves. Finally, it was time to make her way over to Henry Street. This early on an Easter Sunday morning no trams were running so she bicycled the route, arriving at Henry Street well before seven o'clock.

'Gráinne! Come in. We have time for a coffee, I think. A civilised way to start a rebellion.' The Countess, dressed in her Citizen Army uniform complete with munitions belt, went to the kitchen to make the coffee, while Gráinne paced nervously around the flat. A minute or two later, the letterbox was pushed open and a newspaper shoved through. 'Ah, the *Irish Independent*. What news will it be reporting tomorrow, eh?' the Countess said with a wink as she retrieved the paper and opened it.

'Oh my God. No!' the Countess gasped, and sat down hard, the half-made coffee in the kitchen forgotten.

'What is it, Madame?'

'There. Read that.' The Countess gestured to a notice prominently positioned in the paper. Gráinne read it quickly, her mouth dropping open with shock. *Owing to the very critical position, all orders given to Irish Volunteers for tomorrow,*

Easter Sunday, are hereby rescinded and no parades, marches or other movement of Irish Volunteers will take place. Eóin MacNeill, Chief of Staff, Irish Volunteers.

'That bastard! I thought Pearse had talked him round. He must have heard of the loss of the arms shipment. Damn it!' The Countess was pacing up and down, flapping her arms about.

'Madame, hundreds or thousands of the Volunteers will see this,' Gráinne said. It was one of the most popular papers in the country, and the Sunday edition especially was widely read. 'What can we do?'

'Well, we need to get straight over to Liberty Hall, first. So much for our little interlude drinking coffee. Come on. James will be needing us.'

'He'll call it off, won't he?' This on-off rebellion! The uncertainty was the worst of it, Gráinne thought.

'I don't know,' the Countess said, as she tugged open the front door. Gráinne quickly ran back to the kitchen to turn off the stove where the coffee pot was bubbling away, and followed her out. They half walked, half ran to Liberty Hall, where Gráinne was pleased to see many men already assembling. Either they'd not seen the notice in the paper or they had simply ignored it.

Inside Liberty Hall all was chaos. James Connolly was pacing up and down, cursing. He'd obviously seen the paper. The Countess ran to him. 'You've seen it? What will we do?'

'I don't know, I don't know! He's undermined us completely.'

'We've some men turning up – see out there?' The Countess gestured towards the congregating men out front, some of whom were looking confused, presumably wondering whether they should just go home or not.

'But we won't get the numbers. We'll be in our hundreds, not thousands. If all the Volunteers in the Dublin area turned up, we'd take the city. But we won't have them all. And who knows what the situation will be elsewhere in the country!' Connolly let out a roar, like that of a trapped animal.

Gráinne watched, wide-eyed. He wasn't the only one beside himself with anger. Several of the rebellion's leaders, including Pádraig Pearse were already there. One man was thumping the wall in frustration. 'James, we need a plan,' the Countess urged. 'We need to tell the men something. Are they to fight today or not? Are they to fight at all?'

Connolly turned to her, his eyes blazing. 'If we don't fight, we can only pray for an earthquake to come and swallow us and our shame. We have to fight.'

'Very well. So the question is, when? We can get messages out to the men in Dublin, if we're to delay it.'

Connolly nodded, calmer now, and strode across the room to Pádraig Pearse and the other company commanders. They discussed the situation quickly, urgently, and then there were nods from all of them. 'We fight. But we delay by a day, and fight with whoever turns up tomorrow. Muster here at midday. Send messengers out with the new instructions. And get the printing press up and running, to print off the Proclamation of Independence!'

The Countess began organising messengers as ordered. Gráinne went outside among the gathered men and told them group by group of the change of plan. Their demeanour was one of disappointment that they would not fire their guns that day. 'Tomorrow, midday, here,' she urged them, and they nodded their understanding and agreement as they dispersed to spread the word.

The morning passed by in a blur of activity interspersed by periods where everyone seemed dejected by the delay. Emmett came to Liberty Hall in the middle of the day. 'I thought I'd find you here. I heard the news. Couldn't believe it when I saw the notice in the paper. Just one day's delay.'

'Oh Emmett, it seemed like it was to be over before it'd even begun!' She wanted nothing more than to sink into his arms and feel his lips upon hers, but not here. Not in the middle of Liberty Hall.

'We'll be all right, the new orders will reach most of the men. You'll see. Have faith and be strong.'

'Gráinne, go down to the basement and see if they've printed off the Proclamation yet,' the Countess said. 'If they have, bring me up a copy. I want to check it over. Tomorrow we'll be pasting it up on walls and lampposts across the city.'

Gráinne went down to the room where the printing press was housed, and found that the printers had begun work on it. Copy after copy of the Proclamation was coming off the press. 'I need to take a copy for the Countess Markiewicz to check,' she said, and one of the men handed her a copy. 'There's a good clear one. Some are a little smudged but that one's good.'

As she took it upstairs, she read it herself, although she was pretty well aware of what was in it. Hadn't the precise wording been thrashed out at numerous meetings at Surrey House? It was the Countess and some of the senior Cumann na mBan women who'd insisted that it refer to Irishmen and Irishwomen throughout. 'It can't state that the Irish Republic guarantees equal rights and equal opportunities to all its citizens, but only refer to Irish men and not women,' the Countess had pointed out to Connolly, and he'd amended the wording accordingly.

Gráinne passed the printed sheet, the ink still wet, to the Countess. She scanned it, looking pleased. 'Come on. Outside. I'm going to read it out.'

'But we haven't . . . taken the city!' Gráinne was astounded. How could you declare the start of a new government when you hadn't yet seized control?'

'I know. This is a practice run. Let's see how well it sounds when it's read aloud.' The Countess marched out of the building and stood on the top step at the front.

'*The Provisional Government of the Irish Republic to the people of Ireland,*' she began, her voice loud and confident. She'd acted in many plays performed at the Abbey Theatre, Gráinne knew, and had made quite a name for herself as an actress in years gone by. '*Irishmen and Irishwomen: In the name of God and of the dead generations from which she receives her old tradition of nationhood, Ireland, through us, summons her children to her flag and strikes for her freedom.*'

A number of Irish Volunteers were still milling about, and a tentative cheer went up at these words. The Countess grinned at them and continued. '*Having organised and trained her manhood through her secret revolutionary organisation, the Irish Republican Brotherhood, and through her open military organisations, the Irish Volunteers and the Irish Citizen Army, having patiently perfected her discipline, having resolutely waited for the right moment to reveal itself, she now seizes that moment, and supported by her exiled children in America and by gallant armies in Europe but relying first on her own strength, she strikes in full confidence of victory.*'

Full confidence. Gráinne mulled over the words. Maybe there'd have been more confidence if the gun shipment had arrived, and without the disruptive actions of Eóin MacNeill. But what was done, was done. She remembered Emmett's words from the day before: it was better to strike a losing blow than no blow at all. And what proud Irishman or woman could fail to be moved by the stirring words of the proclamation?

The Countess was still reading – asserting Ireland's right to her freedom, the rights of the people of Ireland to ownership of Ireland and control of its destiny. The guarantee of religious and civil liberties to every Irishman and

Irishwoman. The resolve of the Irish Republic to pursue the happiness and prosperity of the whole nation, cherishing all the children of the nation equally.

Yes, Gráinne thought. That was all they wanted – the right to live as Irish Catholics in their own land. That was what the centuries under British rule had taken from them.

The final paragraph called upon God to protect and bless the Irish Republic, and asked that its children be ready to sacrifice themselves for the common good.

Those few Volunteers and Cumann na mBan members who'd listened gave a small round of applause as the Countess finished. She gave a small bow. It was almost as though she was back on stage at the Abbey Theatre, Gráinne thought. The rehearsal had gone well. The next time that proclamation was read aloud in public, the revolution would have begun.

Chapter 17 – March 1998

Nicky called her mum the next morning. She was giving herself a few days off from Seb, to see how she felt about him. But she couldn't put off telling Mum she wouldn't be home for the Easter weekend. It was not far off now.

Her father answered. 'Hello, pet. I'll put your mum on.'

Nicky rolled her eyes. It was the same thing Dad always said if he happened to answer when she called. She got on well with him – better than she did with Mum – but he had never liked talking on the phone.

A moment later she heard her mum's voice. 'Nicola! You've decided to phone us at last. I don't mind telling you, I've been worried, not hearing from you for so long. But your dad kept saying that no news was good news and if anything terrible had happened we'd have heard. So you've him to thank that I didn't get in the car and drive over to check on you.'

'Good old Dad,' Nicky said. She couldn't help but grin. There was a smile behind Mum's words. She could hear it. Mum wasn't really too annoyed.

'So, you went to Dublin and saw Gráinne last weekend? How was that?'

'Yeah, great. Got lots of info for my project. Supergran is fabulous. She remembers everything and is happy to talk – well for an hour or two at a time. Then she gets tired, and your aunt Eileen tells me to leave her alone. Your cousin Jimmy was great too – took me out in his car a couple of times.'

'Glad to hear they've all helped. They're a good crowd, my family. Well, you can tell me all about it when you come home for the Easter weekend.'

'Ah yeah, about that. Actually, I'm thinking of going back to Dublin. Didn't have time to get all the story from Supergran as she gets tired quickly. She said I could go back again, and Easter's a good time.'

'Oh, Nicola! We were so hoping to spend time with you. I'd booked a nice restaurant for the three of us for lunch on Easter Sunday. I thought you said you'd come home for the weekend even though I knew you couldn't come for the whole break?'

'But this is for my project. The one you suggested I do, Mum. So really, you've only yourself to blame.' Nicky rolled her eyes. Seriously, her mother couldn't have it both ways.

Mum sighed. 'Yes, I suppose so. I'm just so disappointed. Your dad will be too. Well, how about you come for the May bank holiday instead, to make it up to us?'

Nicky made a non-committal grunt at this.

'Well,' Mum continued, 'once again please give my love to your Supergran and good luck with the project. Let me know when you have flights booked. I'll help you a little with the cost again. We spoil you, you know. I suppose it's because you're an only child. Perhaps I'm partly to blame.'

'Blame for what?'

'Oh, nothing. Anyway, I hope the trip to Dublin goes well and you get everything you need for your essay.'

'Cheers, thanks, Mum.' She wasn't so bad, Nicky supposed. She was helpful, when she wanted to be. And she hadn't made *too* much of a fuss about Nicky missing Easter at home. Not nearly as much as Nicky had been expecting.

Nicky made a visit to the travel agent's again later that day, when she had some spare time in the afternoon. She booked her flights, then once more called her great-grandmother and then her mother from the station to tell them the dates and times. Supergran was delighted it was all booked, and promised to pass the news on to Jimmy so he could collect her from the airport.

When she'd finished making her phone calls, Nicky still had time to spare. Perhaps she should go and see Seb again. He'd likely be at his flat – now that he'd been thrown out of the university. She debated calling him, but his flat wasn't far from the station. It'd be just as easy to go straight there. If he was out, then she could leave a note.

She was lucky; he was there. He smiled to see her, a smile that lit up his whole face and seemed to bathe her in its power, and she was reminded again why she'd fallen for him and why she was giving him a second chance. 'Hey. Just thought I'd drop by and see how things are going for you.'

'Good to see you, babe,' he said, pulling her close for a kiss. She was pleased to find he didn't taste so strongly of cigarettes.

'What have you been up to these last couple of days?' she asked, as he led the way to the kitchen and began rummaging around for food and drink to offer her.

'Oh, you know. This and that. Beer?' He opened a can and passed it to her without waiting for an answer.

'Oh, well . . . yes, all right. Thanks.' She accepted it and took a sip. It was warm – it had not been in the fridge. 'Are you looking for a job yet?'

'Job? Ah, no. Not yet. There are other things I want to do first. More activism, you know? If I'm working, I can't do it, can I? I've got enough money for now. Parents have paid the rent this month and they'll keep paying it till the end of the academic year.'

'Do they know? That you've been chucked out?'

He looked sheepish for a moment then smiled. 'Nah. Haven't told them yet. I'll wait till I've got something else lined up. Soften the blow, like.'

Nicky wasn't sure she liked the idea of him pretending to them he was still a student. It seemed dishonest, especially if they were financing him. But it was his call and nothing to do with her. 'So anyway, what other things are you going to do?'

'Another protest. There's one on Saturday. Going to be big. There's a developer wants to build houses on green-belt land. Protected woodland, it is. We're going to march through the streets and stop them. There'll be thousands. Want to join us?'

'Tomorrow?'

'Yeah, afternoon. You're not off to Dublin again yet?'

'Not quite yet . . .'

He grinned. 'That's sorted, then. Be here by eleven and we'll set off then. I'll get some placards made up. It'll be fun. We'll end up with a party on the beach, I reckon. Do some good, then have a piss-up under the stars. A perfect day, eh, babe?'

Nicky smiled back happily. This was more like it. This was the kind of protest she could get on board with. Environmental protection, marching through the streets with placards, stopping a greedy developer who was only trying to line his own pockets.

They went into Seb's bedroom, to drink their beers. There was a letter lying opened on the bedside table. Nicky glanced at it without meaning to. It had the university's crest at the top. Seb saw her looking at it and handed it to her. 'Have a read of that. Bloody vice-chancellor.'

'What is it?' She scanned the letter quickly. It seemed as though the university was charging Seb for all the beers and all the damage during the sit-in, as he'd been the ringleader. The letter was signed by the vice-chancellor, and named an eye-watering amount that Seb was liable for. If he did not pay up within a month there would be criminal charges. 'Oh. That's a lot.'

'More than I can wrangle out of my parents. They'd have coughed up a couple hundred, no problem, but not that amount.'

'Will the other protesters pay some?'

'No. They say not, and the VC says it's down to me. Bastard.'

The second page of the letter was an itemised bill for the damage. Some furniture had been broken, carpet tiles needed replacing, and apparently someone had tried to force open the bar's till. 'Doesn't seem right that you should pay it all,' Nicky said. She hoped he wouldn't ask her for any money. She really didn't want to be put in the position of having to say no.

Seb shrugged. 'No. And I ain't gonna pay it. I'll go to the papers, tell them how a valid protest gets treated by that crappy uni. They're victimising me. But they'll be sorry. Especially that bastard.' He stabbed a finger at the VC's signature at the bottom of the letter.

Nicky was torn – although a part of her thought it was certainly unfair that Seb had been singled out and charged with all the damage, a larger part thought that he'd brought it on himself. The protest had been a bit pointless, if she was honest, and he'd allowed it to get out of hand. If he'd insisted the protesters had stuck to his original rules of no damage and no theft, there would have been no charges and maybe he wouldn't even have been thrown out of university.

'Anyway. Let's not think about it now, eh, babe? Come here.' Seb smiled at her and patted the bed on which he was sitting. 'Been ages since you and I got close. Fancy a bit?'

She'd promised herself she'd give him another chance, Nicky told herself as she crossed the room to sit beside him, and began kissing him. Today could be the start of a reset of their relationship, in her mind at least.

On Saturday, Nicky turned up at Seb's flat as they'd arranged, ready to pick up placards and join the march. Seb had used a pizza box to make a couple of placards. One read, '*Save Our Woodland*' and the other, '*Stop Illegal Developement*'. Nicky refrained from pointing out the spelling mistake. Dull slogans but they said it all, and she happily picked up the woodland one. This was what it was all about!

'What time does the march begin?' she asked.

'Midday. A few speeches first I expect, then we'll set off. You've done this sort of thing before? You must have!'

She grinned. 'No, it's my first time.'

'Bloody hell. You're what, twenty and only now going on a protest march? You've led a sheltered life. Good job you met me! I've been on loads. Best ones end with a *paarrrty*! Whoop whoop!' He punched the air.

Nicky laughed, then checked the clock on his kitchen wall. 'We'd best get going.'

'Yeah. Come on then, protest virgin!' They left the flat and walked through the streets to the starting point, on the seafront. Nicky was pleased to see handfuls of other people making their way there too, also armed with signs. Some were chanting slogans. When they reached the rallying point, she estimated there were several hundred protesters. It was a sunny but windy day, and the mood was upbeat. There were some police around, ready to stop traffic as the march set off, but they looked friendly and almost happy to be there. *This* was what she wanted to be a part of!

'If we get separated,' Seb said as the march set off along Marine Parade in the direction of the pier, 'meet up back at my flat this evening, yeah? You can stay the night.'

'All right. Here we go!' Nicky held her placard aloft and began joining in with the chants. 'Save Our Woodland! Save Our Woodland!'

Seb gave her what appeared to be an indulgent grin, but he joined in the chanting. Together, with the several hundred others, they made their way slowly along the road, with the police stopping traffic from side roads as they passed. Several drivers tooted their horns in support. The crowd was made up of young and old, men and women, families and teenagers. A real cross-section of society, all united in one aim to save a piece of woodland from money-grabbing developers. A worthwhile cause.

As she marched, Nicky thought back to a freezing cold day over a year ago, when she and Conor had sat huddled together on a park bench, sipping coffee in takeaway cups. Across the park, there had been a small demonstration going on – she could no longer recall what it was about. Approximately fifty people had gathered, a few held placards aloft, and some had children in tow. A man with a loud speaker was urging them to never give in, to hold on to what was theirs, whatever it was.

'Look at them,' Nicky had said. 'They've come out on a cold day, with their kids and homemade banners. Must feel good to believe in something strongly like that.'

Conor looked at her. 'You'd do it, I reckon, if it was something you cared about.'

'Like what? I don't really know what I care that strongly about, that I'd give up a Saturday afternoon on a day like this.' Nicky thought for a moment. 'I kind of wish there *was* something I care about that much. It'd give meaning to my life. I like the idea of peaceful protest, the solidarity and camaraderie with other protesters. Don't you?'

Conor smiled. 'Well, yes, but does it work? Or is it better to do something practical?'

'What do you mean?'

'Write to your MP, donate to a relevant charity. Better still, work for a charity that aims to right whatever wrongs you are protesting about.' He gazed across the park at the little demonstration. 'I have nothing against peaceful protests like that, but sometimes I think there are better ways of channelling energy to make the world a better place. Been thinking about this a lot, lately. After I've got my degree in medicine and qualified as a doctor, I'm thinking I'd like to work overseas, maybe in a war zone. For a charity like Médecins Sans Frontières.'

'Who are they?'

'Doctors Without Borders. They're an international charity providing medical and humanitarian help in conflict zones. I like the idea of working for them for a few years. I'd be doing some real good in the world, using my skills to help people who need it most.'

Nicky gazed at him in awe. He really meant it. He was so clear about his life, about what he believed in and how he could help the world. If only she was the same. But she was not good at the sciences, so medicine was not an option for her to study. She wanted, in a vague, undefined kind of way, to change the world. She just didn't know how to go about it or where to start.

She looked back over at the protesters. There were fewer of them now – those with small children were beginning to pack up and go home. Were they changing the world, even just a little? If their protest was listened to and taken note of by those in power, would that make it worthwhile? The average person could do so little in practical terms, but they could start small and escalate. Letters to MPs or to national newspapers, protests, marches, rebellions.

'It's great that you'll be able to do something real. But that's so many years away. And it won't be you changing the world – you'll just be repairing the damage done by others who are changing things, whether or not for the best. Don't you sometimes think you'd like to do something *now* to get your voice heard?'

'Get my voice heard about what?'

She shrugged, feeling a little exasperated with him. 'I don't know. Something, *anything*. We're young, we're supposed to be rebellious. We're supposed to kick against the status quo, to stir things up and work for change. I know I want to. What about you?'

'Hmm. Well, when I feel strongly about an issue, I'll do something about it. Something practical, that'll make a real difference. Not just standing in a park with a slogan on a piece of cardboard. Not just rebelling for the sake of it. Has to mean something.'

She'd turned away from him then, cross with him. She wanted to make her mark too, and protest marches were about as much as she'd be able to manage. Yet here was Conor being so dismissive of them. It was all right for him with his plans to study medicine and then work in conflict zones. But what about ordinary people like her?

Now, as she marched through Brighton on this fine spring day, with like-minded souls and Seb at her side, she felt fulfilled, as though she could taste revolution in the air. She'd been right to drop Conor and free herself up for experiences like this. Supergran had marched and fought for what she believed in, alongside the man she loved. And now Nicky was doing the same, albeit on a smaller, less dangerous scale.

Chapter 18 – Easter Monday 1916

Gráinne had expected that she would endure another restless night, but she had been so exhausted from lack of sleep on Saturday night that she fell into a deep sleep and did not awaken until the dawn chorus roused her. Her stomach gave a lurch when she remembered the events of the previous day, and she rose from her bed immediately. There was lots to be done, if she were to be ready to muster at Liberty Hall at noon as ordered. She said a quick prayer that word had reached all the Volunteers and other groups, and that there would be a good turnout for this momentous day. After the *will they, won't they?* of the last couple of days, she prayed also that there would be no more delays or miscommunication.

She dressed quickly and ate as much breakfast as she could manage, ensuring that all others who'd spent the night at Surrey House (several Volunteers who lived out of town had slept on the floors) had plenty to eat too. The day was bright and warm, with not a cloud in the sky. 'Nice weather for a revolution,' one man said to her with a grin, as she gathered up dirty plates and cups.

Nice weather indeed. And, yet, still the washing-up needed to be done before she could go to help liberate her country.

She left the house tidy and clean, wondering when she might come back to it, and made her way to Liberty Hall. It was a national holiday, so all shops and businesses were closed and people were out strolling, making the most of the unseasonably good weather. As Gráinne approached Liberty Hall, she could see that the message had thankfully reached many men, for there were hundreds there, milling about, wearing their uniforms, carrying weapons. Members of the public who passed gave them scarcely a glance – everyone was very used to seeing men drilling outside Liberty Hall. But this time there were more than usual, far more, and they'd been renamed. 'You are the Army of the Irish Republic,' Connolly proudly told them, as he organised them into companies that would each march to a different, strategic part of the city.

Gráinne was assigned to Connolly's company, to march initially to the General Post Office on Sackville Street. This was to become the temporary headquarters of the new Irish Republic. She was pleased to see Emmett was assigned to this company too. Although she'd be coming and going, working as a messenger between the various locations, she was glad she knew where he was to be based, and would be able to check on him now and again as things progressed. Her stomach flipped over as she imagined herself coming back from a mission and searching out Emmett, who'd be holed up with a rifle somewhere.

The atmosphere, as noon approached and more and more Volunteers gathered, was tense but optimistic. Men laughed and joked, boasting of how many British soldiers they expected to shoot at, telling each other how they'd remember this day for all time and what a story they'd have to tell their children and grandchildren! But Connolly, Pádraig Pearse and other leaders were more subdued. Gráinne heard Connolly say quietly to Pearse that they were going out to be slaughtered. Did he mean all the men, or just those few who were signatories to the Proclamation? There was no time to find out, for church clocks nearby were striking noon and it was time to begin. Connolly and Pearse were at the head of the march with Joseph Plunkett alongside them.

'Oh, Grace, what must you be feeling now?' Gráinne whispered. The day that ought to have marked the start of their honeymoon was instead the start of a rebellion. With Sean coming back and the confusion of the last few days, she realised she hadn't seen her friend for a while.

Along with a number of other Cumann na mBan women, Gráinne followed the men marching towards the GPO. She estimated there were about two hundred of them. Some were dragging handcarts loaded with weapons. It looked, on the whole, like a repeat of the St Patrick's Day march. That is, until they reached the GPO. At that point Connolly halted the company, then ordered them to turn to their left and charge the building. Gráinne and the other women hung back, out of the way, waiting until it was safe for them to approach.

The building was taken quickly and without incident. From Gráinne's viewpoint, across the street, it seemed the most difficult part was persuading bewildered staff and customers to leave. She watched as Pádraig Pearse, flanked by Connolly, came out and stood on the steps, holding aloft the Proclamation which he read out in a strong, clear voice. A handful of people, mostly post office customers who'd been evicted, stood to listen. They looked bemused by it all, Gráinne thought, as though they didn't understand what was happening. But then, why would they understand, at this early stage?

After Pearse had finished reading the Proclamation, Connolly turned to him and shook his hand. 'Thanks be to God, Pearse, that we lived to see this day.' Pearse nodded, and the two men went back inside the GPO.

On the roof, Gráinne could see the Union Flags being lowered, and two others hoisted in their place. One was the tricolour: green for the Gaelic tradition, orange for the Unionist tradition, and white for peace between them. The other flag, she was delighted to see, was the emerald green bedspread she had helped the Countess turn into a flag. Its gold-painted lettering could clearly be seen as the wind lifted its corners.

It was done. The rebellion had begun, and the birth of the Irish Republic had been announced. Pearse and Connolly attached the Proclamation to the foot of Nelson's Column, where a man approached, spoke to Pearse and then peered at the notice. He shrugged and moved away.

It was safe to approach the GPO, so Gráinne and the other women did so. There were a couple of nurses including Elizabeth O'Farrell, and some other messengers. Inside, the men including Emmett had begun barricading the windows, stacking heavy ledgers they'd found in offices on the windowsills to protect against bullets or blasts. Connolly was standing in the marble-clad main hall, directing proceedings. He beckoned Gráinne to him.

'All right, so your first assignment. The Countess has led a company to St Stephen's Green. I want you to go there and report that we have successfully taken the GPO and declared the Republic. This is now the seat of government for Ireland, and Pearse is our first President of the Republic. Find out how things progress there. Then report back here. If Sackville Street ever becomes unsafe, we will keep clear a side entrance on Henry Street. This will be your responsibility for as long as this lasts – running messages between these two locations. I shall send other messengers to the remaining rebel positions.'

'Yes, sir.' Gráinne fought against the impulse to curtsy and wondered whether she should instead salute. In the end she settled for a businesslike nod, and hurried off on her mission. She was pleased with what she'd been assigned – she'd keep abreast of developments and would also be able to keep check on Emmett and the Countess, the two people in this rebellion that she cared the most about. Emmett was still working on blocking the windows, and gave her a cheerful grin and a wave as she hurried past, towards the Henry Street exit.

There was a bicycle left in the entrance to the Countess's Henry Street flat, and she retrieved that, as planned, to set off on her journey. As she cycled, she kept an eye out for movements of British troops or police, so she could report back. Already it seemed that word of the revolution had spread, and people were hurrying through the streets. A group of men were engaged in smashing the windows of a gents' outfitters shop on Sackville Street and grabbing whatever merchandise they could. Just hours into the rebellion and looting had already started! It was not what she'd hoped to see, but nobody could blame them for wanting to get whatever they could out of the situation.

At St Stephen's Green, the park looked very different to the many previous occasions she'd strolled there or sat in the sunshine with Emmett. The rebels had quickly taken control of the square, and were digging trenches. 'Inspired by our lads over in France,' one Volunteer told her, as she looked around for the Countess.

'Have you seen Countess Markiewicz?' she asked him.

'Out in a motorcar, with Dr Lynn. Gathering up medical supplies. The doctor's going to set up a field hospital here in case of any injuries,' the Volunteer told her. 'Though it's all peaceful enough now. We had a bit of a job altogether persuading people to leave the park and go home.'

Gráinne nodded and carried on through the park. It was a shame the rose-beds had to be dug up for the trenches, she thought, but the rebels had certainly worked hard so far. She scanned the tall buildings that surrounded the park, and a sense of foreboding struck her. If the British army took control of any of those, gunmen on the roof or at the upper windows would surely be able to fire down into the green, picking off rebels one by one, even if they took shelter in the trenches? But, surely, better military minds than hers had thought this through.

Over to one side of the Green some trestle tables had been set up, and some Cumann na mBan women were there, making sandwiches and handing them out to volunteers with a smile. Almost as though it was a garden party, rather than a revolution, Gráinne thought, but, nevertheless, she took the opportunity to eat a couple. Who knew when or where she'd have the chance to eat next? She spotted Margaret Skinnider and ran over to her to pass on the messages, and as she was speaking to her a motorcar pulled up outside one of the park's entrances. The Countess came through a gate.

'We need to barricade the road up there. Get anything you can lay your hands on, men. We need to seal off the surrounding streets. This little oasis is ours, now!'

A cheer went up, and men ran off to do as she'd asked.

'Gráinne! I am glad to find you!' The Countess walked briskly over to her, looking excited and elated. 'It is going well, I think. I have been to City Hall, and the Jacob's factory and we have taken both. A constable was shot at the entrance to Dublin Castle; he is the first casualty perhaps. God rest his soul. Our boys have pulled back a little to City Hall rather than attempt to take the castle itself. You may report that back to Connolly and Pearse. I don't know if this was the right thing to . . .'

'Countess? We need you, and Miss Skinnider, to stay here as snipers. We can't spare you for liaison purposes.'

A gruff man in the Irish Citizen Army uniform had marched over to them. It was Michael Mallin, who was commanding the forces at St Stephen's Green alongside the Countess. Gráinne recognised him from meetings at Liberty Hall. 'Miss MacDowd?' he said to her, and she nodded. 'Report back to Connolly that all is well here, we've met no resistance as yet—'

He broke off as gunshots were heard, and Gráinne instinctively threw herself to the ground. The women who'd been serving sandwiches looked around in confusion before a Volunteer ran over to them and pulled them down under their trestle table. The Countess had already drawn her gun, and was firing in the direction the shots had come from.

'MacDowd, report back to Connolly that we are skirmishing but all is well,' Mallin continued. 'We are well established here. Once the trenches are complete, we will take one of the buildings to consolidate our position.' He motioned towards the Royal College of Surgeons on the west side of the Green.

'Yes, sir,' Gráinne said. She got to her feet and ran back to where she'd left her bicycle. The shots had unnerved her. It was all so very real now. But she had a mission to complete.

Gráinne cycled as quickly as she could, heading back over the Liffey and up towards the GPO. Sackville Street appeared very changed from how she'd left it. There'd clearly been some sort of attack by cavalry, and a dead horse was lying in the middle of the road. On it sat two women in their shawls, drinking some sort of liquor straight from the bottle and laughing at the situation. Looting had begun. Gráinne saw shop windows – including those of her former employer Clerys department store – that had been smashed and everything within reach grabbed. Everywhere, local Dublin women could be seen wearing silk scarves and flamboyant hats, with rings on every finger and lingerie streaming out of the pockets of looted fur coats. Children ran past her, carrying anything from toys to bottles of whiskey to whole legs of ham. On street corners, men had already set up stalls trying to sell gold watches for just a shilling a piece, the money being of more use to them than the watch.

It had been only a few hours, but clearly law and order in the city had broken down. 'We'll have to get that horse moved,' she muttered to herself, 'before it starts to smell in this heat.' The sun had shone all day and now, late afternoon, it was hot as summer.

Inside the GPO, she quickly found Connolly and passed on news of all she'd seen and heard. He listened intently and praised her. 'You've done well. Now take a rest, get yourself something to eat and drink. We're here for the duration, you understand, though I've had some fellas tell me they need to get home because they have to work tomorrow! I told them, there's no work tomorrow save for liberating the country, and sure isn't that work enough for them?' He shook his head. 'I don't think some of them understand what we're doing, even now.'

There was a fire in his eye that frightened Gráinne a little, even though she knew the man well. He would not give this up, he would never surrender. He'd rather die. She gave an involuntary shudder and went off in search of food and water. And in search of Emmett, whom she badly wanted to see.

He was upstairs, at a window that had been fortified with the ledgers, and bearing a rifle. There was a small gap through which he could see and shoot at any soldiers that came up Sackville Street. It might have been him, she realised, who'd fired the shot that killed the horse.

'Emmett!' She kept her distance from the window, in case there were snipers stationed across the street who might fire. Only then did she realise that she could have been in danger, cycling back up Sackville Street as she had done.

'Gráinne!' Emmett laid down his weapon and took her in his arms. 'You're back, you're safe. But you mustn't come up Sackville Street again. Look – there was a cavalry charge up the street. We fired on them and they retreated. What on earth did they think they were doing?'

'I don't know. It's mad out there, all right.' She told him of the trenches in St Stephen's Green, and of the Countess firing shots at what was probably a sniper, up on a roof overlooking the Green. 'They're not in a good place. It's not for me to say, but I think they've made a mistake.'

He nodded. 'You're right. Buildings are easier to defend than open spaces surrounded by buildings. Let's hope they stay safe. Have you heard much from elsewhere?'

'A policeman was killed at Dublin Castle. They're saying he was the first casualty. Pray God he's the last as well.'

Emmett sighed. 'He won't be the last, Gráinne. You must understand that. There will be more, and some on our side too. It's inevitable. We've started this thing, and we must see it through. I fear today was the easy part.' He stepped forward and took her in his arms. 'Let's make the most of this moment of peace. The days ahead will not be easy.'

She nestled against him for a moment and then lifted her face to his, and they kissed. 'Where will we sleep tonight?' she asked, when they parted. It was beginning to darken outside.

'Here. The basement is safest. Some of us will be on watch all night, of course. Get what rest you can.'

Chapter 19 – March 1998

The march was a long one, looping around Brighton. They made slow progress as there were so many people, and they frequently needed to wait while the police stopped traffic and cleared roads for the next section. Nicky found it tiring walking so slowly, and her voice soon became hoarse from chanting.

'I'm going to get us some bottles of water and something to eat,' Seb said in the mid-afternoon. He passed his placard to Nicky, and nodded at a nearby row of shops.

'Shall I come with you?' she asked, but he shook his head.

'Nah, you go on. You won't move far, and I'll find you again soon.' He kissed her quickly and ducked through the crowds. Nicky wasn't tall, and she lost sight of him almost immediately. She walked slowly, letting people pass her. He'd only be a minute or two, and he'd spot her by her placard, which she held high above her head.

But she was pushed along by the masses, and time passed with no sight of him. The march moved further along the road and round a corner, and still he did not appear. Half an hour passed, then an hour. The march began gradually to break up, as those with children peeled away, followed by older protesters. And then as they approached the starting and ending point, Nicky realised there were only fewer than a hundred left but still no sign of Seb. He'd said to meet at his flat if they got separated, so that was where she should go. She was hungry, so she bought herself a sandwich and a can of Coke along the way. So much for Seb buying her something! Maybe he was at his flat now, waiting for her, with a pizza to heat up in the oven and a six-pack of beers to drink. They could have a pleasant evening together talking about the march and how well it had gone.

But he wasn't there. His flatmates Ryan and Artie were in the kitchen making a vegetarian curry that made Nicky's mouth water. 'Not seen him since early morning,' Ryan answered, in response to her question. 'Wasn't he going on that march?'

'Yes, with me, but we got separated,' she said, and the two others just shrugged, not interested. She knew Seb didn't get on with them very well, so she decided not to ask them anything more. She took her sandwich and drink to his room. Perhaps there would be a note there. She imagined him coming back there looking for her, and leaving her a note when he failed to find her.

But, of course, there was no note. She ate her sandwich quickly. She should have phoned him, she realised. He'd have his mobile with him, and she could easily have used a call box. 'Stupid woman,' she told herself, as she left the flat again. At least now she'd eaten and drunk something she felt better. It was getting late, darkness was falling.

There was a pay phone in a pub on the corner of the road, and Nicky went inside to use that. Seb's phone rang and rang, and eventually she was connected. 'Hey this is Seb. Can't or won't – ha ha! – talk to you right now, so leave a message, yeah?'

'Hey Seb, it's me, Nicky. Where are you? I'm going to wait for you at your flat. Hope everything's OK?' She hung up, and cursed herself for asking was everything OK. He'd laugh at her for that. Of course there'd be nothing wrong – why would there be? He must have spent longer finding food than he'd expected, and the march had moved on, and then perhaps he spent a while trying to rejoin it. Perhaps, even now, he was with the stragglers. The die-hards would be drinking by now, having a bit of a party, probably on the beach as he'd anticipated. Seb would be with them, wondering where she was.

She decided to go to the beach and check that out. Perhaps he'd forgotten their arrangement to meet back at the flat. She'd find him by the pier with a can of beer in his hand, laughing at jokes around a campfire. Yes, that would be it. He'd put an arm round her and laugh that she'd missed him, because he'd rejoined the march at the tail end of it. It'd all be a big misunderstanding. And his phone? Out of charge, of course, as he'd been out all day and hadn't remembered to charge it last night.

Nicky headed down to the seafront and stood on the prom, looking left and right. There'd be a large group, a fire, some music . . . but she could see nothing. She walked to where the march had started and ended. Surely there'd be a few still around, with placards. She could ask . . . though what exactly she would ask she didn't know. *Have you seen my boyfriend, a good-looking chap in a leather jacket, who was with the march this afternoon? No, he wouldn't be holding a placard as he gave it to me . . .*

There was no sign of any protesters at the start point. But away from the sea, up a narrow side street, there was a commotion. Noise, shouting, chanting – that was them. The remains of the march were up there. She headed up the street but after a short way she was stopped by police – half a dozen of them in fluorescent yellow jackets stood in a line across the road. 'Not this way, miss. Road's blocked,' the nearest told her.

'I'm looking for my boyfriend,' she explained. 'He was with the march earlier.'

'If he's still with it, he's in trouble,' the policeman said. 'I'd keep away if I were you.'

'I need to find him . . .' She sounded pathetic, even to herself, but the policeman shook his head.

'Can't let you pass, miss. Go home. I'm sure you'll catch up with him soon.'

She had no option but to comply. Was it worth looping around to the next street? Or would police be there too? It certainly sounded as though there was trouble ahead. Sounds of smashing glass and angry voices reached her. Had the last protesters become violent? Was this always the way protests ended – starting peacefully with good intentions and then descending into riots? Was it that handful of troublemakers Seb had pointed out? Surely he wouldn't be with them.

She decided to go back to his flat. If he was there, then all was well. If he wasn't, she'd leave a note and then go to her own accommodation.

At the flat, Ryan and Artie had the TV on in the sitting room. The local evening news was on, reporting on today's protest.

'Several arrests were made as protesters turned violent after the main march ended,' the reporter announced, to a backdrop of a police cordon across a road, and a burning car. 'A police spokesperson said that the earlier march had been peaceful but a handful of troublemakers had apparently infiltrated it and deliberately tried to start a riot.'

'There's always some idiots that fuck it all up,' Artie said, and Ryan agreed. 'Reckon it was our Seb?' They laughed aloud.

'Seb wouldn't have done that,' Nicky said. It was her duty to defend him, wasn't it?

'You sure about that? Look at the mess he made up at the union bar,' Ryan replied. 'He'd love to be arrested. It'd add to his street cred, wouldn't it? Ha ha. I bet he was right in the middle of that riot.'

'Hmm. Well, I'm going to leave him a note and go home. Tell him I was here looking for him, when he comes back, will you?'

'Sure, whatever.' Ryan waved a hand dismissively.

Nicky wrote a note and put it on Seb's bed, then left the flat and made her way home. She'd just missed a train and at that time of the evening there was a long wait until the next one. She tried calling Seb's number again but once more there was no answer. Could he really have been arrested? She hoped not. She hoped he was not in any more trouble. But for now, she had no way of knowing what was going on.

For all of Sunday Nicky worried herself sick about Seb. She tried calling several times but only reached his voicemail. She called at his flat again in the morning, to be met by shrugs from Ryan and Artie. 'Didn't come back all night. Like I said, bet he was arrested,' Ryan said.

She told herself that he'd call on her when he could, and meanwhile, all she could do was keep trying to phone him. Sooner or later, he'd be released and would charge his phone.

It wasn't until lunchtime on Monday that Nicky was able to get through to Seb on the phone. 'What happened? I lost you . . . I was worried . . .' She bit off the words, scared to come across as too needy.

Seb sounded tired when he replied. 'Got arrested. Spent the night in a police cell. Phone was out of charge, which I didn't realise until today.'

'I guessed your phone was out of charge. Arrested! What for? I came looking for you late in the evening, but the police wouldn't let me near. There was a car on fire and lots of shouting . . .'

'Huh? No, that was nothing to do with me. I wasn't arrested because of the protest.'

'What, then?' But at that moment the pips went, and Nicky realised she had no more ten pence pieces and no credit on her phone card. She hung up, frustrated, and even more worried than before. Seb had sounded scared as well as tired. Was he being charged with something?

She needed more coins so she could call him again. She went to one of the campus coffee bars and bought a can of Coke, paying with a five-pound note to get some change. And then she ran back to a pay phone.

When Seb answered this time, it was clear there was someone else with him. She could hear a woman's voice in the background. She sounded upset. There was a man's voice too. 'Seb? I had to get more change. Are you all right?'

'Yeah, Nicky. I'm fine. Tired.'

'Who's there with you?'

'Parents.'

'Oh! You said it wasn't the protest . . .'

'No. Look, I can't talk now. I'll come and see you . . . in a few days, when this is sorted.'

'It'll be more than a few days, my lad,' the woman's voice said, sounding as though she was suppressing anger. His mother, Nicky supposed.

'Sebastian, whoever it is that keeps calling you, tell them to stop. Or turn your damned phone off.' This was Seb's father.

'Got to go,' Seb said, and hung up.

Great. Nicky was left none the wiser as to what had happened. But it was obviously serious, if both his parents were there, on a work day.

202

For now, there was nothing she could do, other than do some studying in the library and prepare for her next trip to Ireland, which was only a few days away. The university Easter break had begun so there were no lectures or tutorials to attend.

Nicky left it until the evening of the next day before trying to contact Seb again. But once more his phone went straight to voicemail. She decided to go into Brighton and call on him at his flat. Surely his parents wouldn't still be there? It was raining, but no matter. She had to see him and find out what was going on, discover the truth about what had happened after the march on Saturday.

When she rang the doorbell at Seb's flat, Artie answered and looked surprised to see her.

'Is Seb in?' she asked. 'I haven't seen him since Saturday, though I spoke to him the other day.'

'He's not here, no. Um, you'd better come in for a minute.' He showed her through to the sitting room where the TV was on, showing an episode of *The Bill*.

'You back again?' Ryan said, with a frown.

'She's still looking for Seb.'

'Hasn't he told her?'

'Told me what?' Now Nicky was definitely worried.

Artie sighed. 'He's not living here anymore. He moved out on Monday. His parents were here, furious with him. He got arrested and they had to bail him out. He's been dragged back to Hertfordshire – seems he hadn't even told them he'd been kicked out of university.'

'He's a pillock,' Ryan said, with a sad smile at Nicky.

She was shocked to hear it. Why hadn't he told her? If only she had a mobile phone and he could have called her. He could have sent a letter . . . maybe he had, and it just hadn't reached her yet. 'Do you know why he was arrested?'

Ryan nodded. 'During the march, the dickhead spotted the vice-chancellor getting out of his car in the town centre. He smashed the car window and pissed into it. That's what he was arrested for – criminal damage. He's been charged, he pleaded guilty, and is just awaiting sentencing. He might get off with some community service and a fine but he's likely to have to do time.'

Nicky sat down heavily into an armchair. She shook her head. 'What an idiot. I thought he had got caught up in the violence at the end of the protest.' It must have happened shortly after he left her, she thought. So . . . in broad daylight. Somehow that made it worse.

Ryan laughed wryly. 'Definitely an idiot. Fucked up his future, hasn't he? Listen, it's not my place to say, but you're better off without him.'

She nodded slowly. He was almost certainly right. 'Well, thanks for telling me. I can't get through to him on the phone.'

Artie got up and went into a bedroom, then returned with a piece of paper. 'Here. His parents' address and phone number. You can contact him there, if you really want to.'

'Ah, cheers. Thank you.'

She left the flat, feeling shocked at what she'd heard. She would write, she decided, and give him a chance to reply, to tell her himself what had happened. But as far as she was concerned, this was definitely the end of the relationship. However aggrieved he'd felt at his treatment by the university, causing criminal damage to the vice-chancellor's car was not justified, and not something she could defend or accept.

Conor would never have done such a thing, she thought. He wouldn't have staged the sit-in either. He'd have gone on the protest march, chanting slogans and trying peacefully to save the woodland, but he would have stayed well away from any trouble. And he definitely wouldn't have smashed a car window and then peed into it.

Chapter 20 – 25–26 April 1916

Gráinne spent the night of Easter Monday curled in a blanket, with several other women, in a room in the basement of the GPO. Unsurprisingly, she barely managed any sleep, as rebels were in and out all night, and there were frequent bursts of gunfire. Still, she tried to do as Emmett had said and rest as much as possible, wondering whether he was able to get any rest himself.

It was still early when she rose. It was a grey morning with rain falling, unlike the previous day's blue sky and sunshine. There was a supply of bread and butter for breakfast, and one of the other Cumann na mBan women had set up an urn to make tea. Gráinne gratefully drank a cup, then reported for duty to James Connolly.

'Gráinne, I need you to take that bicycle again and see how things fare over at St Stephen's Green. Beware it may not be as straightforward as yesterday. Take the back streets, and if you're stopped by the authorities, feign ignorance of the whole thing. Smile your pretty smile and pray to God that they let you get on your way or, at worst, make you turn back.'

'I'll be careful,' she said. 'Sir, if you see Emmett O'Sheridan this morning, tell him where I've gone, please?'

He smiled indulgently at her and nodded. 'I will. He's a good man, your Emmett.'

'Sir, yes he is that.'

She was about to go, when a tall young lad who couldn't have been more than about sixteen came rushing in. 'Mr Connolly, sir, I'm sorry I'm late. Me mam is after taking the valves out of me bike tyres, so she is, to try to stop me joining the Rising, so I had to run here. Couldn't come yesterday because me dad had taken us all out to the seaside.'

'And who are you?'

'Martin Walton, sir. I joined the Volunteers three weeks ago, so I did.'

'Well, Martin, we can put you to good use. Report to Jacob's Biscuit Factory. We took it yesterday, but they need more men there. Do you know where it is?'

The boy looked confused. 'Not too sure, sir.'

'South of the river. Go along Dame Street, past the castle, then head south. You can't miss it.'

'South of the river? Sure I've never been south of the river in me life!'

Connolly turned away, looking a little irritated, Gráinne thought. She took the boy's arm and led him away, giving him some better directions. 'And be careful. Stay out of sight of any police or soldiers.' His expression turned from one of excitement to fear, and she took pity on him. 'Perhaps you should have stayed home with your mam.'

'Ah no, miss, my place is here, fighting for our freedom.' He pulled his shoulders back, and before she could say anything more to him, he was off, his long legs carrying him quickly out of the building on the Henry Street side. She wondered if she'd ever see him again, and offered up a silent prayer that he'd stay safe and eventually return home to his mam.

* * *

Gráinne had left her bicycle inside the GPO so she retrieved it and set off. She took a long and convoluted route through the city to St Stephen's Green. It was obvious there were far more soldiers in the city today. Once, as she turned into a street, she saw columns of them, marching four abreast, in the direction of the castle. She'd had to duck back the way she'd come and find another way around them. That was one thing to report back to Mr Connolly. Clearly, troops had been arriving all night, by train. If the Volunteers had had the advantage of numbers yesterday, they certainly didn't today.

As she cycled along Grafton Street approaching St Stephen's Green, she could hear gunfire. It was almost continuous, and she realised there must be a machine gun somewhere. That must belong to the British military – the Volunteers possessed no such weapons. She stopped and ducked into a shop doorway, trying to work out where the firing was coming from. She could just see the Green, and as far as she could tell, it was deserted, though the thick bushes could have been hiding rebels.

The gunfire was coming from the Shelbourne Hotel, which appeared to be occupied by troops. What of the Countess and Margaret Skinnider, and the others? She scanned around and realised there was someone on the roof of another building, on the western side of the Green. Someone in the dark green of the Irish Citizen Army, and above that person flew a tricolour. Now she knew where they were. She left her bicycle in the shop doorway, and made a run for a side entrance to that building – the Royal College of Surgeons. As she approached, a door opened and she was pulled inside.

'We saw you approaching. It's not safe out there in the street altogether,' a Volunteer she'd seen the day before told her. 'The Countess is on the roof. I'll ask her and Commander Mallin to come to you and hear your news. Follow me.'

She followed him to a room deep inside the building where she was asked to wait. A few minutes later, Mallin and the Countess both arrived, looking tired and dishevelled. She told them news from the GPO and of the columns of troops she'd seen marching through the city.

'We knew more would come,' the Countess said. 'I was hoping for another day . . . but we'll see. Tell Connolly we have a good position here. It seems the military occupied the Shelbourne overnight. As soon as it got light, they began firing on us in the Green, so we had to retreat to here. But this is good – we have snipers on the roof and we're picking off their machine gunners one by one. For every hundred bullets they fire, we fire one, but ours hits its target.'

'And have we lost any of our men?' Gráinne hardly dared to ask but Connolly would want to know.

The Countess rubbed the bridge of her nose. 'Yes. There are four Volunteers lying dead in the Green. We cannot retrieve their bodies yet. There is too much gunfire. Bless them, they gave their lives for Ireland.'

They were the first Volunteer casualties Gráinne had heard about and the news saddened her immensely. She thought of that boy, Martin Walton, whose mother had tried to stop him joining the Rising. The men lying dead in the Green might be simply boys like him, caught up in a conflict too big for them. And was it too big for *her*, now? She wasn't much older than that boy. She'd believed so fervently in the Cause; she still did; but this – the violence and bloodshed? She wasn't sure she was made of stern enough stuff to cope with it. Yet here she was, in the middle of it as she'd wanted to be, and she had her duties to carry out. There was nothing else to do other than stiffen her spine and get on with it.

She stayed at the Royal College of Surgeons for a while. There were a few injured Volunteers lying on makeshift beds in a room at the back, so she helped nurse them, cleaning and bandaging wounds. When there was nothing more she could do, the Countess told her to continue on her way as instructed by Connolly. She caught hold of Gráinne's hands. 'And for God's sake be careful. It's becoming dangerous out there.'

'I will, I promise.' Gráinne followed the Countess to a back door that led out of the college on the opposite side to St Stephen's Green, well out of reach of gunshot from the Shelbourne.

'If you come again, come to this door. We will be watching and will open it for you. Good luck.'

Gráinne took a deep breath and left the building, then realised she could not retrieve her bicycle without being in danger of being fired upon. 'On foot it is, then,' she told herself, as she set off back to the GPO.

En route, she realised the gunfire she could hear now was heavier; not machine guns or rifle fire but heavy artillery. From a street corner, she could see troops storming City Hall, and as she watched, keeping herself as hidden as possible, she saw women being led out of the hall and up towards the castle. They were Cumann na mBan women, and she recognised a few of them. They were under arrest. City Hall was apparently lost.

She left the area, running as fast as she could, and made her way back towards the river. In a back street she heard her name called from an upstairs window.

'Gráinne! Up here!' It was Grace. 'I'll run down and open the door to you.'

A moment later, a door opened and Grace's face appeared. 'Come in, do. Tell me the news. I've not left this house for days.'

'Do you have food?' Gráinne asked, as she followed Grace

into the front room of a small house. Someone had put boards across the downstairs windows so it was dark and gloomy inside. She knew some people barricaded in their own homes were already beginning to go hungry. Shops in the city centre were closed and many had been looted.

'I have enough. Gráinne, what news? Have you seen Joseph?' Grace's eyes were wide with worry.

'Yes. He's at the GPO, the headquarters. It's all right, Grace. He's safe there. He, Pearse and Connolly have set up an office in the basement where they are away from any gunfire, and they are leading the Rising from there.'

'He's not being shot at?'

'No, not down there. He doesn't venture out into the street.' At least, Gráinne thought, not as far as she knew.

'And is he well?'

'He's well. Uninjured, thank the Lord.' Gráinne took the other woman's hands and squeezed them.

Grace seemed reassured by this answer, and nodded slowly. 'I'll make you some tea.'

'No, I have to get back. I have news and messages for Connolly.'

'Then take another message for me, please? For Joseph. Tell him I love him so much. I pray for him every hour, and I am waiting for him. When all this is over, we will keep our promises to each other. Ireland has him now, but I shall have him after.' She smiled a tight, sad smile, and Gráinne embraced her, squeezing her tightly. She had her own lover, Emmett, to worry about but at least she was able to see him daily and she was aware of all that was happening. She couldn't imagine how much worse it must be for Grace, not knowing how the rebels were faring, not being able to see her fiancé and having had to postpone her own wedding.

'I'll tell him. Your words will lend him strength and courage,' Gráinne said.

'We should have been married by now. I should be Mrs Plunkett. I should be with him, looking after him, loving him.' Grace whispered these words, her eyes glistening with tears. Gráinne hugged her one last time. She should go, she knew, before the other woman broke down entirely. For it would be far more difficult to leave her then.

'I'll return again, Grace, if I am able to. Keep safe.'

As she left the house, she heard gunfire in a neighbouring street. She ran quickly along the road, praying that no sniper had taken up a position in this street, imagining at any moment the sting of a bullet in her back.

She crossed the Liffey by the Ha'penny Bridge which seemed the safest route back to the GPO. If she was stopped by the military, it would no longer be possible to feign ignorance of the Rising. Not with the constant sound of artillery, and the numerous fires that she could see burning in different parts of the city. Anyone truly innocent of any part in this would be hunkered down at home, waiting it out, not running around the streets. She concocted a story in her mind, of an invalid elderly aunt who needed nursing care, as the reason she was out and about. It might work, at a pinch.

Halfway back to the GPO, she was stopped by a man in civilian clothing. 'Get yourself inside, girl,' he said. 'Haven't you heard what's happening? The Sinn Féiners have taken the city, and they say the Germans are landing! Over in England, the Zeppelins are dropping bombs and Germans are coming to invade. We're finished! Get inside, take cover, is my advice!'

'Thank you, sir, I will. I just need to . . .' But he had gone, hurrying along the street, keeping to the sides, with his jacket pulled up over his head as though that would protect him.

Germans landing? What was he talking about? Surely it was just a crazy rumour?

And then, down a side street, she noticed a group of armed rebels making a run for it, repositioning themselves. For a moment, she thought she saw Sean. But it couldn't be him. Emmett had said Sean would be out of Dublin by now. Long gone. She'd only had a glimpse of the back of a man with similar build and hair to Sean. That was all. She whispered a quick prayer that wherever her brother was, let him be safe and well.

She was nearing the GPO now. The side door she'd been told to use was closed – she had to rap on it to gain attention. 'Who's there?' came the call. She was irritated that no one was watching out for her. Everyone inside knew her.

'Jesus, Mary and Joseph, it's me, Gráinne MacDowd. Open up!'

The door opened, and a sheepish-looking young Volunteer let her in. He grinned. 'Just you? Jesus, Mary and Joseph not with you, then?'

She couldn't help but smile at his joke, now that she was inside, safe from the gunfire. Or was she safe? As she moved into the building, it was rocked by a blast, and plasterwork from the ceiling fell down on them.

'Been happening all day,' the lad told her. 'They know this is our headquarters.'

'Probably because we raised a flag above it, to give them something to aim at,' she said, wryly. She'd been proud of the flags but were they really sensible? Didn't they proclaim to the troops: *Look, here we are, aim at this flag and you'll hit us?* She brushed plaster dust off her clothes and hair. 'Do you know where Mr Connolly is? And Mr Plunkett?'

'Basement, I last saw them.'

'Thank you.' She hurried off to report on what she'd seen and heard, and pass on Grace's message to her fiancé. And she'd feel safer in the basement.

213

As she made her way to the stairs that led to the basement, she heard a series of small explosions coming from Sackville Street. She spotted Emmett, still in position at one of the windows. 'What's happening? Is it safe to be by the window?'

'Gráinne! I'm glad you're back. It's safe enough. Some fools are after looting a fireworks shop. They've piled the fireworks up in the street and set fire to them. There're rockets firing in all directions.'

'Fireworks! Well at least those can't harm the building.'

'Hmm, not unless one hits the explosives we've got stored here,' Emmett said. 'There're men moving them away from this side of the building, just in case a stray firework comes inside. Look, there's a Catherine Wheel going off, rolling up the street!'

She glanced out and saw what he meant. It was mayhem out there, with spurts of colour flashing and banging, rockets shooting sideways and hitting buildings and a huge fire taking hold in the middle of the street. The dead horse still lay where it had fallen, though nobody was picnicking on top of it today. Gangs of boys were laughing and pointing as the fireworks went off.

'Why don't they realise we are doing this for them? It's awful that they looted shops at the first chance they got. Makes me sick to my stomach, so it does.' Gráinne spat the words out. She'd been scared by all she'd seen and heard.

'Oh, love.' Emmett took her in his arms. 'I know. But we're doing what is necessary, for the greater good, for the long run. Don't lose sight of that.'

'I'm trying not to. But it's so very hard. Emmett, I met a man outside who said there were Germans landing. Is there any truth in that?'

He laughed. 'Not that I know of. Just a rumour. The people are scared and making up stories to tell each other.'

'I thought so. I need to report to Mr Connolly now. I'll find you again soon.'

'All right, so. There's some food downstairs. A couple of the women went out and raided a bakery and a delicatessen.'

'Thank you.' She realised then that she was hungry. She'd eaten nothing since breakfast and that was a long time ago. She headed off to the basement.

Connolly was there, sitting with Pearse and poring over a map of the city and some other papers. He looked up as she approached and she quickly reported on what she'd seen and heard. Some of it she suspected they already knew – such as the loss of City Hall – but they listened carefully to everything she said. She mentioned also the man who'd told her the Germans were landing, and they laughed and as Emmett had said, confirmed no such thing was happening.

'Thank you, Gráinne, for your work today. Once more you have done well. Pearse, what of this will you put in your news-sheet?'

Pearse rubbed his chin. 'We shall say that the Republican forces everywhere are fighting bravely.'

'With splendid gallantry,' Gráinne added, and immediately blushed. Who was she to tell the great man what to write?

But he nodded. 'A good phrase. I shall use it. We will print the news-sheet at Liberty Hall today, along with the manifesto to the people of Dublin. I want to encourage more people to rise and fight, and I shall stress that the freedom of Ireland is only days away. The Irish regiments have refused to fight against their fellow countrymen.'

Gráinne left the two men discussing their manifesto. Pearse's comment had made her think of Sean once more. Had he managed to get out of Dublin, and find somewhere safe to stay? Would he have heard about events in Dublin, and was he thinking of her and Emmett, hoping they were safe too?

Remembering Grace, she went in search of Joseph Plunkett. She found him counting out rounds of ammunition into boxes. 'Mr Plunkett, I ran into Grace while I was out.'

He looked up at her with concern. 'Is she well? Is she safe?'

'She is both. She is hiding in a small house south of the river, and she has food. She asked me to tell you she loves you and she's waiting until this is all over and you can . . .' Gráinne broke off, at the look of agony in Plunkett's eyes.

'I made her a promise. A solemn one. Somehow, I have to keep it,' he said, his voice barely more than a whisper. 'I signed the Proclamation. I fear that in doing that I have signed my own death warrant, and Grace . . . poor Grace . . .' He stared down at the ground for a moment and then seemed to rally himself. 'Well, thank you, Gráinne. Please, go and rest, find something to eat.' He gave a short nod and she was dismissed.

His own death warrant? What did he mean? Surely he had as good a chance as any man to stay safe and survive the rebellion? And after, when it was all over, there would be a chance for him to marry Grace as he'd promised. Unless, as a leader of the rebellion he'd be imprisoned? Or worse?

And what of Emmett?

Chapter 21 – April 1998

That week, the week after the protest march, was the first week of the Easter break. After Seb was dragged back to his parental home, Nicky spent more time with her other friends. She had to apologise for the way she'd more or less ignored them in recent weeks. 'The project, the trip to Dublin – it's all kind of taken up my time,' she said to Sabina one afternoon, as they walked across the campus.

'Rubbish. It's that new boyfriend of yours that's been the problem,' Sabina replied, and there was a seriousness to her tone. 'How's that going, anyway?'

Nicky shrugged, and was quiet for a moment, deciding how much to confide in her friend. Sabina said nothing, but gave Nicky a questioning glance and then steered her towards a bench. 'Sit down, mate. You look like you need to talk.'

'I-I suppose I do. I think it's all over with Seb. We haven't talked about it, but . . .' She took a deep breath. 'He's been kicked out of university, arrested and charged with criminal damage, and his parents have taken him home in disgrace.'

Sabina gasped. 'Oh my God, mate. Was this because of the sit-in? I did think that was a bit stupid, if I'm honest.'

'Not just that,' Nicky said, and then she told the full story.

Sabina listened quietly and when Nicky had finished, she put a comforting hand on her shoulder. 'You are far better off without that loser. You know that, don't you? After Conor – I mean that Seb just doesn't measure up at all. Nice-looking but that's all he has going for him, in my opinion. Listen, whatever happens, don't forget I'm here for you. So's Jez, I know I can speak for him too.'

Nicky blinked back tears, grateful for the support. 'Thank you. I guess I'm learning who my true friends are. I've been a bit stupid, I suppose.'

'Hey, we all make mistakes,' Sabina said, giving her a hug. 'Anyway, welcome back.'

On Saturday that week, Nicky was making her way through campus to the library, when she spotted a familiar figure walking up towards her student flat. He hadn't seen her yet, and she was tempted to duck behind a tree and hide, but stopped herself. He looked up and waved, then walked over to where she stood waiting.

'Hey stranger. Thought you were going to Dublin again?' Seb said, a slight frown between his eyes as though he wasn't sure of the reception he'd get from Nicky.

'I am, on Wednesday. And you've been with your parents?' She was trying to read him. Did he think their relationship still had a chance?

'Er, yeah. They're not paying my rent anymore, and I had no real choice.'

'What happened about your arrest?'

He shrugged. 'Oh, that. Waiting for it to come up in court. I'll plead guilty, look contrite, and my lawyer says I'll get community service. No biggie.'

'Not good though . . .'

'Better than three months in prison which is the other possibility. Parents would be furious if that happened.

The shame, their little boy in jail.' He laughed. 'Would almost be worth doing, just to bring them down a bit.'

'Seb, they're doing all they can for you. Who's paying for your lawyer, for a start?'

'Well, yeah, they are . . .'

'And they paid your bail, and they were paying your rent, and you said they'd pay for the damages caused to the union bar.'

He simply shrugged at this, as though it was his due, as though he just accepted it all as his right. 'They're my parents, yeah? They care about me, they support me.'

'You're an *adult*, Seb. Not a five-year-old. Don't you think you should ease off a bit, expect less from them? Isn't it time to stand on your own two feet and pay your own way?'

'I'm a student! I don't earn anything! How am I supposed to do that?'

'You're not a student any longer,' she reminded him. 'You could get a job.'

'While I'm awaiting the court case? Who's going to employ me?'

Now it was Nicky's turn to shrug. 'I don't know. Maybe you should have thought about that before trashing the vice-chancellor's car, Seb? Whatever possessed you to do that?'

'Dunno. Saw him getting out of the car and found myself in a red rage. He threw me out – he didn't have to do that, but he's fucked up my life. I thought he deserved it.' Seb ran a hand through his hair. 'Anyway, babe, why are you having such a go at me? I don't need it! Had my mum on at me the whole week. I came here today to find you, hoping to find someone a bit more sympathetic.' He tilted his head on one side and smiled at her. 'Listen, shall we go to your room? Have a bit of a lie-down? You've no lectures or anything, have you, so we could . . . take our time. Fancy that, babe?' He reached for her and ran a finger down her cheek.

She stepped away and stared at him. He was a spoiled brat, she realised. Someone who took advantage of those who loved him, but only cared about himself. All that talk of activism, of standing up for his rights – it was all just attention-seeking. He was trying to look big and tough but, in reality, he was just a little boy who went crying to mummy and daddy when things went wrong. His big protest in university had been pointless and damaging. He'd only half-heartedly joined in with the environmental march, and had left it – left her! – at the first opportunity. Then he'd done something so stupid she couldn't believe it, even now, and yet he was showing no remorse. Not a shred of it. And he'd come here today to see her, not to explain or apologise or find out how she was. No, he'd come here in the hope of getting laid. Well, not with her, he wasn't.

'No, Seb. No, I don't fancy it. It's over between us, you get that, right? I can't carry on seeing you, after all that's happened. I just can't.'

'What, just because I don't live nearby? It's only an hour's travel, babe. Look, I left this morning at nine and here I am. Next time you can come to me. When my parents are out.'

'Seb, it's nothing to do with where you live. It's—'

'Because I'm not a student?'

'No, it's because—'

'Ah-ha.' He nodded his head smugly. 'I get it. You're ashamed too. You're as bad as they are. You say you support me, you say you're a freedom fighter too, but when it comes down to it, when it all gets *serious*,' he stabbed a finger at her chest as he spoke, 'you run a mile. Well to hell with you, little miss history student. You get back to fretting about the past while I deal with the future. You go and find yourself a spotty nerdy history geek, and get out of my life, hey? I've come all this way to see you and you're just brushing me off. With not a word of explanation.'

Nicky blinked. She'd been trying to explain but he'd kept interrupting her. She realised then she didn't care what he thought, he didn't deserve an explanation. It would make no difference. 'Well, Seb, it was fun while it lasted. Bye, then.' She purposely made her voice sound nonchalant, as though she didn't care. And she didn't. Not about him, anyway.

He looked shocked, as though he hadn't believed it really was the end, as though he'd expected her to plead with him to stay with her. 'Fuck's sake. *No one* dumps me. You don't know what you're doing. You'll be sorry, and you'll come begging me to take you back and you know what, little miss playing-at-being-a-rebel, you know what? I won't take you back. You hear? This is it, babe. The end. We're done.' He turned on his heel and walked off, still muttering, in the direction of the station.

Playing at being a rebel? He'd just described himself. It was clear to her now – Seb liked the idea of being a rebel for its own sake. Not because he was trying to make the world a better place. It was all about him, no one else.

Nicky rummaged in her bag and found the piece of paper with his parents' address on it. She tore it in half, screwed the pieces together, and dropped them in the nearest bin. Then she opened her student diary, turned to the page where she'd written Seb's phone number, and crossed it out, thoroughly, ensuring it was no longer readable at all.

And then she took a deep breath, made a resolution that she'd never again allow someone to call her 'babe', and continued on her way to the library. She had work to do.

Chapter 22 – 27–28 April 1916

After a second night in the GPO basement, Wednesday dawned bright and sunny once more. But as the morning wore on, a bombardment of artillery fire started up. A scout reported that a gunboat had come up the Liffey and was firing on Liberty Hall and up Sackville Street to the GPO itself.

'Good job we evacuated Liberty Hall after printing those documents yesterday,' Connolly said, as the scout reported that Liberty Hall was in ruins. 'They knew that had been our headquarters before this week so it was always likely to be a target.'

Food was becoming scarce at the GPO, and some of the Cumann na mBan women were asked to go out and find what they could. There were still well over a hundred Volunteers based there. At the back of the building, a make-shift hospital for the wounded rebels had been set up and Gráinne spent part of her time nursing there. Every time a man was brought in on a stretcher her heart lurched and she prayed it would not be Emmett. So far, thank God, he had escaped injury.

The building seemed to rock on its foundations every time an artillery shell landed nearby. Everyone was covered in plaster dust and in some areas, rooms were unusable after direct hits. It was a shame, Gráinne thought. The GPO had been rebuilt only the previous year. It was a fine-looking building, but how much of it would be left when this was over? She risked a glance through windows at the front and gasped to see the state of Sackville Street. Further down the street a barricade was burning, and the fire was spreading into nearby buildings.

Connolly came to check on the wounded. 'Martial law's been declared in the city,' he told them. 'No one's to be out between seven o'clock in the evening and five in the morning. The authorities are worried. We're making progress.' He spotted Gráinne, who was leaning over a man who'd caught some shrapnel in his upper arm. The nurse Elizabeth O'Farrell had picked out the pieces and Gráinne's job was to clean and bandage the wound. She'd taken several first-aid courses with the Cumann na mBan and was using everything she'd learned. 'Gráinne, when you have finished here, can I ask you to go out again on your rounds? I've messages for the Countess. And we need to know what's going on, what's the mood like among the people.'

'Yes, sir, I'll go as soon as I've seen to this fellow,' she replied, although her heart gave a flutter at the idea of going out there again, with the bombardment still going on. But there were Volunteers coming and going all the time. They weren't frightened, or if they were, they didn't show it. So why should she?

She headed out in a different direction. No need to go anywhere near City Hall now, as they knew that position had been lost. She headed straight to the Liffey and then turned eastwards along its banks. There was the gunship Connolly had heard about, its guns trained on Liberty Hall which was now nothing more than a mound of rubble. She could see troops going through the gatehouse of Trinity College. It had been requisitioned as a temporary barracks by British troops, she knew, so she kept away from there. A little further on she saw lines of troops – hundreds of them! – marching in from the direction of the docks. The British must have sent half their army over. Was there anyone left fighting the Germans? She watched from a side street as the soldiers passed. Local women opened their doors and handed out mugs of tea and packets of sandwiches to them. Some were pointing up the road, as though telling the troops where the rebel strongholds were.

Well, that's a good indication of the mood of the people, she thought wryly. They don't like us or what we're doing. One woman called out to the soldiers, 'Shoot the whole lot of them. I hope every last man of them is killed.' A man, presumably her husband, shushed her. It was the women who seemed most hostile to the Rising. Women were generally hostile to all fighting. If she hadn't believed so strongly in the Cause she might be like that herself.

Gráinne made her way via back streets to St Stephen's Green, to deliver the messages to the Countess. There, a battle was going on from the rooftops, with snipers on top of the Royal College of Surgeons firing upon the Shelbourne Hotel, just as they had been the day before. Boys were lurking at the corners, daring each other to run into the Green itself, dodging the bullets.

'Don't, lads,' she told them. 'Go home. This is too dangerous.'

'Ah, sure they won't shoot at us, we're just kids,' one boy said.

Gráinne grabbed at his arm. 'They won't look to see the size of you. They'll shoot first and look later. Now go home, if you know what's good for you.'

'She's right, so she is. We should go,' said another boy, and reluctantly they turned away.

Gráinne made her way to the back of the Royal College of Surgeons, the door she'd used the previous day. She was admitted on giving the password the Countess had told her.

'The Countess?' she asked the man who let her in.

'On the roof.' The man pointed helpfully at the ceiling.

Gráinne went up the nearest stairs to the top floor. A door stood open, leading onto the roof. The Countess and Margaret Skinnider along with another two rebels had taken up positions crouched behind a balustrade, their rifles pointing towards the Shelbourne Hotel. Gráinne could just see figures moving about on the roof of that building. The Countess and Miss Skinnider took shots whenever they had a clear line of sight.

'Countess?' Gráinne called from the doorway.

'Gráinne? For God's sake, get down! If you can see them, they can see you.' The Countess flapped her hand and Gráinne dropped to her hands and knees, and crawled over.

'I have messages for you from Mr Connolly. He says to—' She broke off amid a volley of shots and then a scream. Looking round, she saw Margaret Skinnider had been knocked backwards, and was lying on the roof clutching at her side.

'Margaret!' The Countess crawled over to her friend. 'Oh God, she's been hit! We have to get her below.'

'It's not bad—' Miss Skinnider began saying but then she screamed again as the Countess tried to move her.

'Cover us!' The Countess shouted at the two Volunteers who were on the roof with them, and they immediately began firing towards the Shelbourne. 'Help me, Gráinne. We have to drag her towards the door, but stay as low as possible.'

It was with enormous difficulty that the two of them managed to manoeuvre their comrade nearer the door. Using a mix of crawling and walking in a deep crouch they'd half dragged, half carried her across the roof. At the door, the Countess shouted down for help. They pulled Margaret inside and closed the door.

Gráinne stood up, grateful to be able to stretch her legs, while Margaret lay at the top of the stairs groaning and clutching her wound. A Volunteer ran up the stairs with some dressings and bandages, and Gráinne put to use the first-aid training she'd learned at Cumann na mBan meetings.

With the bleeding staunched, two Volunteers were able to carry Margaret downstairs to a room they'd turned into a field hospital. A Cumann na mBan nurse took over her care. The Countess stroked her friend's forehead. 'There are those who say we women shouldn't be involved in the shooting, Margaret. But you were never going to listen to them, were you? Now, rest.'

'It's not so bad,' the injured woman said, but her voice was weak and she looked to be in shock.

'Madame, is there anything more I can do for her?' Gráinne asked. She felt oddly shaky, and all she really wanted to do was lie down somewhere safe and drink sweet tea. But now was not the time.

'No, Gráinne, you did well. Poor Margaret. But she is a firm believer that women have the same right to risk their lives as men, under the new Irish constitution.'

'Madame, I will pray for her recovery.'

'Thank you. It is all we can do.' The Countess leaned for a moment against the wall. She looked ten years older than at the start of the week.

Gráinne quickly passed on the messages she had for the Countess, who listened carefully and nodded. 'Thank you. You can tell Connolly we are holding out well here but we are taking casualties and I don't know how much longer we can last. Our spirit is still strong, but our numbers and position are weak. It's only a matter of time.' She leaned closer to Gráinne. 'But if we can make it to the end of the week, if we can hold Ireland free for a week – what an achievement that will be! Surpassing all rebellions in the last century and even the 1798 United Irishmen uprising!'

An achievement, yes, Gráinne thought, but a far cry from a sustained, peaceful independence for her country.

As she headed back to the GPO later that day, it felt as though, slowly but surely, the revolution was slipping out of their grasp. As the Countess had said, it was only a matter of time before they'd have to give in and surrender. For all Connolly's and Pearse's talk of there being no question of surrender, it would surely happen in the end. But how many lives would be lost, on both sides, before then? She found herself wondering if it would have been better for it all never to have started. Instead of rising up they might have waited for the political solution as Sean had wanted. Then these lives would never have been lost and Miss Skinnider would not be lying in a pool of her own blood.

Gráinne spent an uncomfortable third night in the basement of the GPO. The bombardment of artillery was relentless but, somehow, she managed to get a few hours' sleep, from sheer exhaustion. She was hungry too; there'd been very little food to go around. All the nearby shops had been emptied by looters. The sky glowed red from the many fires across the city and still the rattle of machine guns and the booming of larger artillery was never-ending.

On Thursday, the fires in Sackville Street worsened. The whole of the east side of the street was on fire, including Clerys department store. The huge plate-glass windows in its frontage had shattered and melted in the flames. It was impossible now to go out into Sackville Street.

Halfway through the day, Gráinne was sent to the upper floors of the GPO, taking bottles of water to the Volunteers stationed up there with rifles, whose number included Emmett. It would be a chance to see how he was.

She was partway up the last flight of stairs when she realised something was wrong. There was shouting coming from above, and the sound of feet clattering down the stairs. A half-dozen Volunteers ran past her. Emmett was among them. 'Gráinne! It's not safe. The whole of the roof is on fire, and it's spreading down. We need water, and fast!'

She gasped. 'I have these.' She held up the bottles she'd been bringing up.

'No, keep the drinking water. We need buckets, and a chain of men. Go down, pass the message on, and keep away. It's too dangerous.'

She turned around and ran back down, doing as he'd asked. For the rest of the day Volunteers ran up and down stairs with buckets of water trying to control the flames, but it seemed that all they could do was slow the spread, not quench the fire.

Gráinne did not go out at all that day. Indeed, she was wondering how any of them were going to get out alive. All she could do was focus on the tasks at hand – seeing to the wounded, doing her best to make them comfortable. Thankfully, Emmett was still safe, though his face looked haggard and whenever she caught his eye, he just shook his head sadly. It would only be a matter of time before it was all over, and Gráinne could only hope that some of them at least, please God including Emmett, would be saved.

She was dressing a Volunteer's wounded leg when James Connolly was brought in on a stretcher. He had been out into one of the side streets and a ricocheting bullet had hit him on the ankle, shattering the bone. He was clearly in immense pain but seemed determined not to show it.

As Elizabeth O'Farrell rallied first aiders around him to do what they could, he announced that he could still lead the rebellion from his sickbed, and lead it he would, until the last moments.

Gráinne brought him a cup of water, which he took gratefully. 'You'll be all right, Gráinne. We have a way out, and soon I will start to send people to safety.'

'Sir, what is the way out of here?' With the fire burning above them, the snipers and the continuing shelling, it had felt to Gráinne that they were trapped.

'I've had men digging tunnels from here into neighbouring buildings, through their basements. That's our escape route, if, or when, the fire here takes hold any lower down the building. Arrggh, my damned leg!'

'Can I do anything?'

'No, I just have to bear it. The good Lord knows other men have suffered worse. How many times have you women been up and down that laneway and nothing ever happened to ye. I do it once, and look at the result.'

Connolly's injury sent the mood of the Volunteers spiralling downwards, if that was possible. Pearse tried to rally them by telling them police had been captured in the north side of the county, and that many more rebels were even now marching to join them in the city. Cheers went up at this, but privately Gráinne wondered if he was simply making it up.

Certainly, Joseph Plunkett seemed to think so, for he gave Gráinne a wry smile and small shake of the head as he heard Pearse speak.

Later, who knew whether it was day or night down there in that gloomy basement, Connolly gave the order that all Cumann na mBan women who weren't trained in first aid should evacuate the building, via the tunnels. Gráinne half

229

wished she could go with them, but she was still able to be of use tending to the wounded. Besides, she wanted to stay where Emmett was, for as long as possible.

The atmosphere now was one of grim determination. They were hanging on for as long as possible. With the other women – messengers and those who'd been in charge of food and supplies – gone, there were only a handful of nurses and first aiders left. Elizabeth O'Farrell was doing her best to keep everyone employed. 'Stay busy,' she said to Gráinne. 'It stops you thinking of what might happen next.'

The fires in the upper floors of the building were now out of hand, and the men had stopped trying to dampen them down, instead retreating down to lower levels.

Connolly gave the order to evacuate as many of the wounded as possible, via the tunnels into neighbouring buildings. Stretcher after stretcher was carried out, with some of the first aiders going too. Gráinne had been asked by Elizabeth O'Farrell to stay until the end, to help nurse Connolly.

But the fire was too intense, and the moment came for Connolly and Pearse to evacuate too. Connolly by stretcher, via the tunnels, but Pearse, Plunkett and others were to go at street level, with orders to reconvene at a house on Moore Street.

Gráinne went with Connolly. The tunnels were roughly dug: bricks in the basement wall had been pulled away to make an opening through to the next building's basement. Emmett and a tall handsome man named Michael Collins carried Connolly, while Elizabeth O'Farrell and Gráinne hurried along behind, carrying the last of the first-aid equipment and a small amount of food. It was a difficult journey but at last they emerged into the basement of a fishmonger's shop in which a couple of other Volunteers were waiting. 'Upstairs, sir,' one said to Connolly. 'There's a safe room for you there.'

They carried Connolly upstairs and laid the stretcher in the middle of the room.

'How are you feeling?' Gráinne asked him.

'Bad,' came the reply. 'The soldier who wounded me did a good day's work for the British government.'

She made him as comfortable as possible, then looked around the room at the last few of them, from the two hundred or so who'd originally marched to the GPO back on Easter Monday. How long ago that seemed! And now here, this small room behind a fishmonger's shop, was the last headquarters of the Irish Republic.

Soon after, Pearse came in looking grim. He crouched down beside Connolly. 'As we crossed the street I saw a civilian family, the man waving a white cloth, trying to make their escape. God rest their souls; they were shot at. They fell. Man, woman and child. There are innocents being killed now, James, and I don't think it's fair for us to carry on.'

He'd spoken quietly but not so quiet that Gráinne couldn't hear. She turned her face away. Innocent civilians, and a child! Mowed down as a result of this rebellion. It wasn't her side that had shot them, but it was her side that had started the conflict, and so, in a way, it was their fault. And she was a part of it. A part of a rebellion in which children were killed for being in the wrong place at the wrong time.

'It is time?' Connolly asked.

'It is time.' Pearse nodded.

And Gráinne quietly heaved a sigh of relief.

Connolly called for paper and pen, which Gráinne fetched for him from another room in the house. They helped him into a chair with a small table at the side, so that he could write. Gráinne sat by while he wrote a series of notes. He handed them out to the few Volunteers still with them,

231

with orders for each to go to a different rebel outpost, taking the notes which were the last orders he would give as commander of the Army of the Irish Republic. The final note he gave to Elizabeth O'Farrell.

'This is our surrender notice. Take it to whoever is in charge out there, on the British side. They won't shoot at you, being a woman. Hand it over. We will accept . . . any terms. It's unconditional.'

And with that he sighed heavily and hung his head, forearms resting across his knees. The exhaustion, the stress, the pain of his injuries – it was as though all of it hit him at once at that moment.

Gráinne's heart bled for him but there was nothing she could do or say that would make even the slightest difference. It was over. They had risen, and they had been brought down.

As Elizabeth got ready to leave the shop, Gráinne put a hand on her arm. 'Take care. Wave your white flag.' Connolly had said they wouldn't shoot a woman, but they had, hadn't they? And a child. She prayed silently that Elizabeth would be safe.

Chapter 23 – April 1998

It was a relief to simply concentrate on her university work, especially her rebellion project, for the next few days. Nicky felt oddly free now that the relationship with Seb was over. It had only lasted four weeks, she realised. A mere drop in the ocean of her life, unlike her relationship with Conor.

At last, the day arrived when she was due to go back to Dublin – on the Wednesday before the Easter weekend. She was surprised at how much she was looking forward to it – seeing Gráinne again, also seeing Jimmy, Eileen and any other relatives. She'd hear the rest of Supergran's story. And she'd made a list of places in Dublin that had played a significant part in the uprising. Her plan was to take at least one trip into the city, to tour around and see them at first hand. The GPO, which she knew had been the headquarters of the rebellion, was, of course, right at the top of her list.

The journey was easier this time, now that she knew what she was doing and where she was going. When she went to a cashpoint a day or so before, to get some money she could change for Irish punts in Dublin, she was pleased to see her bank balance had gone up. Mum must have transferred some money to cover the cost of the flights, again. That was kind of her, and would save Supergran from having to pay.

She emerged into the Dublin airport arrivals hall and looked around for Jimmy who was supposed to be meeting her. She spotted him, standing with a huge grin on his face. He gave her a brief hug and kiss when they met, as though they were old friends. 'Good to see you again, Nicky! I've something to show ye. Come on, follow me.' He took her bag from her and led the way out of the airport and into the short stay car park. There was his car, the familiar Ford Galaxy, and he stood in front of it. 'Ta-da!'

She grinned, but couldn't understand what he was showing her. It was the same car. Cleaner, perhaps. Tidy inside. 'You've cleaned it?' she said.

'Yes, and . . .' Jimmy pointed to the back of the car, beside the numberplate.

'Oh wow! You've registered as a minicab driver!'

'Yes! I was after thinking about what you said, about people wanting the bigger cars for airport runs and me living so close and all, and decided to go for it. And it's working! I've done a half-dozen trips this week already, made myself a few quid, and kept myself off the streets, as my auld mammy would say. It was all your idea, cousin Nicky, so I must thank you for it.'

'I'm so glad it's working out.' He was such a genuinely nice man, he deserved some good luck.

'Well, in you get, so. I've a booking in an hour, so I need to get you to Gráinne's now.'

He was his usual cheerful self, but Nicky thought he stood a little taller and seemed a touch more confident than he had on her last visit. A steady income would be helping with his self-esteem, perhaps. She felt proud to have played a small part in that.

* * *

234

Her great-grandmother was delighted to see her again, and there was a homemade vegetarian pizza waiting to be heated up, and a bowl of salad. 'Eileen was round earlier with these,' Supergran said. 'I wasn't altogether sure about the pizza, but she said it's what you young people eat, so who am I to argue?'

'I love pizza,' Nicky said. 'I'll thank Eileen for it when I see her.'

'And I've been busy,' Supergran said, 'writing down places you should visit, with a few notes on what happened in each one. Not much, mind, I'm not a one for writing. Not with these hands.' She held up her misshapen, arthritic hands. 'Anyway, here it is, and I hope you can read it.'

Nicky took a sheaf of papers from the old lady, and glanced through them. Gráinne's handwriting was spidery and wobbly, but easy enough to make out. She'd listed plenty of sites in Dublin, many that Nicky knew of from her own research and that she'd already earmarked to visit, but also others that were unfamiliar. 'This is marvellous, thank you Supergran!'

'You said you'd want to go into the city, and now that Jimmy's busy as a taxi driver he can't spare the time to take you. But he did get this for you, and I've marked the spots on it.' Supergran handed Nicky a map of Dublin, and there were red pen rings around a few locations.

'That's me sorted for tomorrow then. Thank you so much!'

'Ah yes, and Jimmy's going to call at nine o'clock to give you a lift to Malahide station. He says he can't do any later as he has bookings.'

'Nine o'clock's perfect.' Well, it was a bit early for Nicky's liking but she'd manage. She was touched by the efforts everyone had gone to, to help her with this project. She owed them a lot.

* * *

Nicky caught a train the following morning as planned, with Jimmy dropping her off at the station. He promised to pick her up as well if he was free, if she called to tell him what time she'd be getting back. 'I have one of these mobile phone yokes now,' he said, waving it at her. 'So I'll give you the number and you can call and let me know. As long as it's before six o'clock. I've tickets to the rugby this evening. No doubt Leinster will be given a hammering by Munster, but even so, I need to be there to cheer on the boys in blue.'

She smiled. 'Enjoy the match. I can walk back. It's not so far.'

'Ha. You'll be tired, so you will, after a day stomping around the city. Well, I'm here if you need me, if it's not too late.'

The journey into Dublin's Connolly station took around half an hour, with the train passing through industrial and residential areas of north Dublin. Connolly station was named after one of the leaders of the 1916 rising, Nicky realised, along with Pearse and Heuston, the other principal railway stations in the city.

From there she walked the short distance to O'Connell Street, the main shopping area of Dublin. This had been called Sackville Street back in 1916. Supergran's map had the GPO prominently marked, about halfway along. It had been the headquarters of the Rising, the place from where Connolly and Pearse had established the first government of the Irish Republic. It had only lasted a few days, until the Rising was quashed, but still, this was where it had been based.

When she reached the GPO she stood outside for a moment, gazing up at its neo-classical facade. It was an imposing building, with a huge portico in front, supported by Ionic columns. There was a plaque on the wall commemorating the Rising, which she read, and then she headed inside, not at all sure what she expected to see. Some sort of museum, perhaps? Display boards, reconstructions? But no – it was a working post office, with a row of counters behind glass, and a queue snaking back and forth in front. There were a number of leaflet stands holding forms for passport applications, motor tax payments and the like, and a photo booth near one entrance.

Nicky gazed around, taking in the marble floor and the high windows, but really there was little there to help her imagine what it would have been like in 1916. She knew from her research that heavy ledgers had been piled against the windows as protection, and that by the end of the week the building had been on fire and the remaining rebels had had to evacuate. There were a few old photos in the foyer, showing the building in near ruins. She studied these carefully.

From the GPO she headed down O'Connell Street, past the department store Clerys where Supergran had worked before getting involved with Constance Markiewicz and the Cumann na mBan. It was a grand-looking building, with an array of fashions and household goods in the windows. If Mum was here, Nicky thought with a smile, she'd want to go inside and browse for hours. But she wasn't here to shop. She was here to research. She headed on down the street, past the Anna Livia statue and fountain, that Jimmy had told her was nicknamed the Floozy in the Jacuzzi. She laughed, liking that name. Anna Livia, an information plaque read, is a character from James Joyce's *Finnegans Wake*, supposed to represent the spirit of the river Liffey.

A few minutes later, she reached the banks of the Liffey. Referring to Supergran's map, instead of crossing it she turned left along the northern bank and walked a short way. Here was a tall building that stood on the site of the old Liberty Hall. James Connolly had used Liberty Hall as the headquarters of his Irish Citizen Army in the run-up to the Easter Rising, Nicky knew. She'd seen a photo of it with a banner across the entrance, reading *We serve neither King nor Kaiser but Ireland.* Stirring words for the middle of the Great War, designed to boost Irish nationalism.

The building had been flattened during the Easter Rising, as British troops had assumed it was the headquarters of the rebels. It had been rebuilt, but later demolished and the current sixteen-floor tower built in its place.

Once more, not much to see or imagine from the Rising, but it was good to get a feel for distances between the various locations. Nicky checked her map, crossed the river and walked along Grafton Street. Here there were more shops, and on impulse, she nipped into Bewleys and bought a couple of boxes of chocolates. One for Supergran, and the other to take home and give to her mother. She'd paid for two lots of flights, and given her the idea for the project. She might be an annoying, controlling, overly fussy mother, but, Nicky was gradually beginning to realise, she really did have Nicky's best interests at heart. She wasn't all bad, not by a long way.

Nicky smiled to herself. Was this a sign, could it be that she was ready for a new, better relationship with her mother? Those weeks with Seb had changed her. And the work on the rebellion project was changing her too. You fought for what you believed in, but some things were worth fighting for more. Hadn't Mum said something similar, on her last visit to Brighton? And change – even when imposed from outside, even if not everyone agreed with it – was sometimes for the better. Like banning smoking in one campus bar.

At the end of Grafton Street, she reached St Stephen's Green, and walked through a gate in the iron railings to reach the park. Ah, this was better. This square hadn't changed much since 1916. It was flanked by Georgian and Victorian buildings, with a more modern shopping centre on one corner. There was a lake, rose beds, a fountain and several paths criss-crossing the area. Here was where Constance Markiewicz and her company had dug trenches, thinking that was the best way to hold this area. Nicky glanced up at the Shelbourne Hotel on the northeastern corner.

'Oh Constance, was it not obvious that you were sitting ducks down here, with the British army shooting from that hotel's windows?' Nicky muttered. Elsewhere in the city, the rebels had set up their strongholds in buildings, but here, for unknown reasons, they'd chosen open land and been unable to defend it. They'd had to retreat, in the end, to the Royal College of Surgeons on the west side of the Green. Nicky looked around and noted that building – she'd walk past it later, when she'd been round the park itself.

There was a plan of the park and its features, and Nicky wandered over to study it. It showed the location of a number of statues; one of which was a bust of Constance Markiewicz. Supergran hadn't mentioned that being here. Nicky found the bust, and stared up at the bronze features of a woman who'd believed so strongly in her cause she'd taken up arms along with the men and been imprisoned for it. All of this back in 1916 when women didn't yet even have the right to vote.

Nicky took a few photos of the Green, the bust, the buildings around it. She'd get the film developed back in Brighton, and the photos would help her picture the locations she was writing about.

She consulted her map. Where to go next? A bridge on Mount Street was ringed – she recalled the name as a place where a couple of Irish Volunteer gunmen had held out for a long time against repeated attacks by squadrons of British soldiers. They'd shot many – it was the worst loss of life of the conflict. Near there was the bakery where Éamon de Valera, who she recalled Jimmy had told her later became Ireland's Taoiseach and then President, had commanded a unit against the British. But in the other direction was Dublin Castle and City Hall. She decided to go that way – a castle sounded more interesting than an old bakery and a bridge over a canal. She headed back up Grafton Street, intending to turn left along Dame Street when she reached Trinity College.

Her stomach rumbled and she realised it was mid-afternoon. Time to get some lunch in a pub, perhaps? Down a side street off Grafton Street, she spotted an inviting-looking little pub – McDaid's. Its small frontage was painted in dark colours surrounding arched windows. Inside there were a series of snugs and dark wood panelling. It was the kind of place that probably hadn't changed at all since 1916. Nicky ordered a veggie burger and chips and a glass of lager, and sat at a table near the window. She could imagine the 1916 rebels meeting in a place like this, poring over maps and discussing tactics. She pulled out a notebook and jotted down a few points.

A middle-aged woman, who'd been sitting on a stool at the bar, picked up her pint of Guinness and moved over to Nicky's table. 'Hello there, would you mind if I sit with you? You look to be on your own, and so am I, and I'm after fearing we'll pick up all the local nutters if we don't join forces. I'm Céline.' She gave a friendly smile.

Nicky laughed. 'Sure, sit down, please. I'm Nicky.' She gestured to a spare chair at her table.

'You're working, I won't disturb you, sure I won't.'

'It's all right. Just jotting down a few thoughts before they disappear.'

'Writing a novel?' Céline asked.

'No. University project on rebellion, for my history degree.'

'The 1916?'

Nicky nodded. 'Great guess!'

'Ah so, you're English, you're here in Dublin, what else would it be? So you're checking out the locations? What a great idea.'

'Yes. And I'm hoping to write about the part women played in the rising.'

'Countess Markiewicz, Elizabeth O'Farrell who handed over the surrender note, Margaret Skinnider the only woman to be injured?'

Nicky smiled. 'Yes, all those.' Supergran had mentioned those names. 'You know a lot about it all?'

Céline laughed. 'Sure aren't I a history teacher, teaching at Leaving Cert level. Delighted to meet a fellow history lover!'

Nicky grinned. She couldn't believe her luck. She opened her notebook to a fresh page, picked up her pen and looked expectantly at Céline. 'Right then . . . shoot!'

The next hour passed quickly, with Céline telling Nicky lots of details about the Easter Rising that she hadn't previously heard. Céline was delighted to hear that Nicky's great-grandmother had played an active part, and offered to read and comment on Nicky's essay when she'd written it. Nicky wrote down her email address and thanked her.

As Céline was leaving, she stopped and turned back to Nicky. 'Don't forget the ducks in St Stephen's Green.'

'What about them?'

'During the Rising, there were occasional ceasefires in the Green to allow the park-keeper access to feed the ducks. Rebellion or no rebellion, someone had to think of the animals.' Céline grinned and gave Nicky a wave as she left the pub.

Nicky wrote that last little snippet down. It would all help to add colour.

* * *

That evening, Nicky watched the news on TV with Supergran. The British Prime Minister, Tony Blair, was in Belfast, attending talks at Stormont in Northern Ireland. The newspapers were reporting that there might be a breakthrough in the peace talks, and an agreement could soon be reached.

'Do you think it'll happen?' Nicky asked Supergran.

'I hope so, my dear, I really do. A lasting peace in the north is my greatest wish for this country.'

As they watched, Blair emerged from talks and stood at a podium to say a few words to the reporters gathered there. He was surrounded by reporters and photographers, and dozens of flashes went off as he began to speak.

'Now is not the time for soundbites,' he said, 'but I feel the hand of history upon our shoulder.'

Nicky snorted with laughter. 'Listen to him! "Not the time for soundbites" and then he comes up with a really cringeworthy one. "The hand of history upon our shoulder." I'll tell you what, if this set of talks comes to anything, he'll be remembered for saying that.'

'He'll be remembered for achieving peace in Northern Ireland,' Gráinne said. Her tone was wistful. This really meant a lot to her, Nicky realised. Her fight for Irish independence as a young woman had ended with a divided country and conflict on and off over the decades. Now it looked as though there was a major step towards lasting peace at long last.

Chapter 24 – 29 April 1916

They held their breath, all of them, as Elizabeth O'Farrell, holding Connolly's surrender notice and a piece of white cloth to serve as a flag, cautiously opened the door of the shop on Moore Street. Immediately there was a volley of gunfire, but she stuck out an arm and waved the white flag, and the gunfire ceased amid shouts from the British military.

Gráinne stood beside Emmett and watched as Elizabeth took a deep breath, crossed herself, and walked out into the street, waving the flag in front of her. A brave woman. Would Gráinne have dared be the one to go out there? She wasn't sure. She was too young. This was a job for a more mature woman whom the British army general would take seriously. She was just thankful Connolly hadn't asked her to do it.

The wait, while Elizabeth was away from the building, was interminable. The seconds ticked by so slowly that Gráinne, glancing frequently at a clock on the wall, was convinced it had stopped. But, at last, she returned, tapping on the door and giving the agreed password.

'The first fellow I spoke to told me to come back and fetch the women. But then he realised he needed to report back, and took me to General Lowe. There is a motorcar outside that brought me back here, and Commandant Pearse is to go in it to surrender to the General.' At that, Elizabeth sat down heavily. She looked, Gráinne thought, completely defeated.

Pearse nodded. 'I shall go.' He turned to those assembled, the last rebels. 'Gentlemen, ladies, it has been my pleasure fighting alongside you. This is the first step towards Irish independence, and we shall be remembered for it.' With that he put on his hat, took the white flag from Elizabeth, and exited the house.

There was silence in the room as they all contemplated what would happen next. Gráinne caught a glimpse through the window of Pearse getting into the motorcar at gunpoint, and being driven away, God only knew where to.

'What do we do now?' she asked.

'We put down our guns. We go out into the street with our hands held aloft,' Connolly said. 'Tell the first officer you see that I am in here, unarmed, and in need of medical assistance.' His tone was grave, but somehow reassuring. He was accepting defeat, accepting his fate with a dignified grace, despite his injuries and despite his losses.

Emmett took hold of Gráinne's hand and squeezed it. There was no need for any words.

The group were silent as they did what Connolly had ordered. Weapons were placed in an attic, away from Connolly. Joseph Plunkett opened the door and stepped out, arms held high, waving a white flag. Behind him, all those who could walk, followed. One or two had their heads down, as though shamed, but Gráinne held hers up with pride.

Outside there were a dozen soldiers, who herded them along the street and into Sackville Street. Gráinne gasped to see the state of it: the whole of the east side was reduced to smouldering rubble, and the west side was still burning.

They had to move to the centre of the street to avoid the debris that fell from the ruined buildings.

All around, troops were going from building to building, calling for rebels to surrender. The few who were in other houses in the area came out, looking scared and worried, and joined Gráinne's group in the centre of the street. Gráinne and Emmett found a patch of tarmac, clear of rubble, and sat down, back to back, using each other as support.

'How long will they keep us here?' Gráinne asked.

'I don't know. Until they're sure they've cleared the area. And then who knows where we'll be taken. I suppose we might be separated. They'll keep the women separate from the men, and I hope they'll let the women go.'

'We're as much a part of it as the men,' Gráinne said. She was proud of the part her sex had played in it all. They'd proved their worth, she thought.

'You are, I know, but they don't know that. And if there's a chance for you to be set free, take it, without any argument. Promise me that.'

She could not see his face as he said those words, but she could imagine the look of love and fear for her in his eyes. She nodded, and reached behind her to find his hand. 'I promise. And you, promise me the same.'

'I do.'

From where she was sitting, she could see down the side street where two soldiers were carrying out the stretcher that held James Connolly. They loaded him into the back of a vehicle and drove away. To a hospital, she hoped. Somewhere his shattered ankle could be properly treated.

'At least the flag's still flying,' a voice said, and Gráinne turned to see Michael Collins who was sitting alongside Joseph Plunkett. He smiled at her and pointed up at the roof of the GPO where the Countess's burnt and tattered emerald flag somehow still fluttered in the wind.

It had been shortly after midday when Elizabeth O'Farrell had left the house with the order to surrender. Now, Gráinne thought, it must be late afternoon. She was hungry and thirsty, but there was nothing on offer so no point complaining about it. Armed soldiers stood in a ring around the rebels, who like her and Emmett, were sitting on the ground, trying to make themselves comfortable. A few were lying down. Some were injured, but the most seriously hurt were being taken away to hospitals.

Later, an army officer called out a list of names. They were the signatories of the Proclamation of the Republic. Joseph Plunkett's name was among those called out. Gráinne watched as he stood slowly, and raised a hand. He was led away into an army vehicle. She caught Emmett's eye, and he shook his head sadly.

Gráinne wondered where Grace was now. Was she still hiding in that little house? Did she know of the surrender, the failure of the Rising? And the Countess, what of her? She prayed her friends were safe, wherever they were.

As afternoon wore on into evening, canteens of water were passed around by their guards. Gráinne drank gratefully and tried to ignore the pangs of hunger and the numbness of her bottom from sitting on the hard ground. There were a hundred or more rebels there now, in Sackville Street, guarded by around fifty soldiers. When would they be taken elsewhere? She supposed they would all have to be formally arrested and questioned and imprisoned. And what then? She could not imagine how the military would deal with them all.

As evening fell, at her side Emmett began to sing, quietly, so that only she could hear. He sang rebel songs and folk ballads, songs of love and longing and loss. Listening to his voice soothed her and for those moments she was able to forget where she was and why they were there.

Once the sun had sunk below the horizon it became cold, and Emmett took off his jacket to wrap around her shoulders. She tried to say no, he needed it more than her, but he insisted. He shifted so that she could curl up against him, her head in his lap, and she closed her eyes.

But there was no chance of sleep. Apart from the discomfort there was a constant murmuring from the rebels as they discussed what might happen to them, and the occasional shout from a soldier telling them to keep quiet.

'They are worried we are plotting something,' Emmett whispered to her. 'But, of course, no one is thinking that. There is nothing we can do. If anyone made a move they'd be shot immediately.'

She did not want to imagine that scenario. 'Sing to me again,' she said, and he did, his voice sweet, soft and low. 'I wonder if they'll write songs about us,' she said, when he had finished.

'They will, to be sure.' His voice cracked as he spoke, with exhaustion and pent-up emotion.

And all through that long, terrifying and uncomfortable night, he held her and sang to her and she knew that she would not have got through the night without him. She knew too that she loved him and she wanted them to spend the rest of their lives together. She made herself a resolution, that when it became possible, when this was over and they were free again – if that day ever came – she would ask him to marry her. It did not always have to be the man who asked, did it? The idea, the plan, made their suffering more bearable. She spent the night dreaming of possible futures, in which they married in a city church on a summer's day, or a country church in the autumn; they lived in a Dublin flat, or an isolated cottage with a view of the sea . . . it didn't matter what or how or when, as long as they were together.

Chapter 25 – April 1998

Before this project, the last time Nicky had been in Ireland was the previous summer. Mum had invited Conor on holiday with them. They'd booked a holiday cottage somewhere on the Ring of Kerry, but before that, they were visiting Irish relatives based in the Dublin area. They couldn't all stay with one relative so Mum and Dad had opted to stay with Eileen, while Nicky and Conor stayed for two nights with Supergran.

Conor had been nervous about meeting Gráinne. 'I just can't imagine how I'll get on with someone in their late nineties,' he'd said, but Nicky had dismissed his worries.

'Honestly, she's lovely. And you're lovely too. You'll get on like a house on fire.'

And she'd been right. Conor had quickly relaxed in Supergran's company. As she washed-up on the second day, she looked over to where her boyfriend and great-grandmother were sitting with their heads together, puzzling over a crossword in the local newspaper and giggling over a rude word that seemed to fit the clue. Later, Supergran had taken Nicky to one side and told her, 'This one's a keeper, as I believe you young ones say. Don't let him go.'

'I won't.' Nicky had smiled, and at the time believed it to be true. Why would she ever want anyone else in her life other than Conor?

That had been a good holiday. Unusually for Ireland, the sun had shone most days. They'd swum in the sea, played on the beach as if they were children again, explored caves and clifftops and villages with winding streets and brightly painted front doors. Looking back, Nicky considered it the height of her relationship with Conor. The best time. The time when she felt completely at ease with him, she loved him so much, she knew nothing would ever part them.

It was the summer before they went to university. The summer before they went their separate ways.

'I think it's a shame,' Supergran told her after breakfast on Good Friday, the day after Nicky's tour of Dublin, 'that you and that lovely young fella Conor split up.' She waved a hand vaguely in front of her. 'Oh, you'll say it's none of my business and sure it's not, but he was a nice young man and I liked him that time you brought him here. I hope he's all right and you've not upset him too much. There. I just wanted to say that.' She turned a bright smile on Nicky, who felt a little taken aback.

'He is nice, you're right. I just wasn't sure . . . I mean, we're still so young . . .'

'As was I when I got together with my Emmett.' Gráinne looked wistful for a moment. 'Anyway. We've a story to tell, haven't we? Make some tea, fetch the biscuits and your notepad, and we'll get to it, so.'

Nicky went to do as she'd been asked, her mind running over what her great-grandmother had said about Conor.

'Where did we get up to the last time?' Supergran asked when Nicky returned with a tray of tea and biscuits and they'd settled down on the sofa to talk.

Nicky checked her notes. 'We'd talked about you working with the Countess Markiewicz, and the rebellion being planned in her house.'

'Ah yes. Sure and now I need to tell you all about the Rising itself, don't I? See, I call it a Rising, some call it a rebellion, and there were some British newspapers that just called it a riot. How much you can tell about a speaker by one word!' She chuckled. 'Now, let me tell you it from the start, from the muddle over whether it was on or off, that caused us all so much worry. And the start of it when didn't we all march through the streets with our weapons and uniforms and the people thought it was just practice, and we went to the GPO itself and ordered everyone out. And the proclamation was read on the steps of the GPO by Pearse, but it wasn't the first time it was read in public, for hadn't the Countess already read it out the day before, when it was hot off the press?'

Supergran smiled. 'Sure, there were some fine moments at the start of the week, Nicola. Moments when it was all going well, and we were proud to be a part of it. The weather stayed fine for the whole week. You know, for many years whenever we had a spell of sunshine in spring people would call it "rebellion weather". We were lucky with it, and I was thankful it wasn't raining when I was back and forth on my bicycle, then on foot delivering messages and finding out how things were going. St Stephen's Green, where you went yesterday, now wasn't that the frightening place to go? What with those British soldiers holed up in the Shelbourne Hotel and shooting down on everyone.'

'I met a woman in a pub when I was eating my lunch – a history teacher. She said there were ceasefires at St Stephen's Green so that the park-keeper could go and feed the ducks.'

'Were there?' Gráinne smiled. 'Well, not any time that I was in the area, that's for sure. I was glad when they pulled out of the Green and into the Royal College of Surgeons. I could get in and out the back way there, and it felt a bit safer all round.'

'It's hard to imagine what it must have been like. You were only about the age I am now. I couldn't have done what you did that week.' Nicky reached across the table and squeezed her great-grandmother's hand. It was too easy to see someone like her only as she was now – old and frail, easily tired, sometimes confused – and forget that once she was young and full of fire.

'Ah, you would, Nicola, if you were put to the test. I think we all have more in us than we realise. Some of us are never tested, that's all. But don't be wishing for such a thing to happen in your life. It's much easier to have a quiet life with no drama!' Supergran chuckled again, then looked sad and thoughtful. 'Especially when I think on all those who were lost that week. Those killed in the fighting on both sides, and those executed afterwards. And others, who went missing. My brother, Sean.'

'What happened to Sean, Supergran?' Nicky asked gently.

'I don't know. I saw him a few days before the Rising.' The old lady sighed. 'He was home on leave from the trenches, and he said he couldn't go back. He was going to desert. He was so shaken up by what he'd seen and done, and he said he couldn't take any more. Emmett helped him. Gave him some civilian clothes and money, so he could go away somewhere, lie low and try to make a new start.'

'And did he?'

'Ah, that I don't know.' Gráinne shook her head sadly. 'I never saw him again, nor heard of him. I tried to find him, I did all that I could after the Great War was over and there was no danger of him being court-martialled, but there was no trace of him. My father tried too, so did Emmett, but there was simply no sign of him. He didn't return to the army, we know that. He was listed as a deserter. That was something many families were ashamed of, but we weren't, my father and I. We knew he'd suffered out there, fighting for a country that wasn't even his own. We didn't blame him for not wanting to go back. But I do wish I'd found him, or found out what happened to him. All these years, not knowing.' She gazed at Nicky with watery eyes. 'It's hard, even after so long, the not knowing. He'd be long gone now I expect, whatever happened to him. He was older than me, and sure aren't I old enough now. But I do wish I knew. He just disappeared, so he did.'

'That's so sad.' Nicky squeezed the old lady's hand. If only there was some way she could find out what became of Sean . . . but after all these years it'd surely be impossible.

Gráinne sniffed, then smiled at Nicky. 'It is, but I'm resigned to never knowing. Anyway, we should get on with the story. What happened to Sean is nothing to do with the Rising, after all. It's just that he went missing at the same time.'

She began to recount day by day, as far as she could recall, the events of Easter week. As she reached the end of the story, the final hours of the rebellion, the imprisonment and then executions of its leaders, her voice fell solemn and quiet, and Nicky had to strain to catch everything. But she didn't dare interrupt or ask Supergran to repeat anything. It was clearly a strain for the old lady to talk for so long, to remember so many upsetting events, so once was enough. Nicky scribbled down everything she heard, as fast as she could. She'd considered using a tape recorder but had thought it might inhibit Supergran's flow. Pen and paper worked better.

The old lady had a nap in the afternoon that day, but woke in time for the evening meal, which Nicky had prepared. Now that she knew where everything was in the kitchen, she was happy to prepare meals and save Eileen and the others from having to come every day. Tonight, they were having a cheese and leek quiche with some new potatoes and broccoli. Nicky found she quite enjoyed preparing food for Supergran, who always seemed most appreciative.

'What have we got today?' Supergran asked as she came to the table. 'Mmm, it looks good, so it does. Thank you.'

They watched the evening news while they ate. The lead report was about the signing of the Belfast Agreement. Tony Blair was once more on the TV, looking pleased with himself as he stood beside the Irish Taoiseach, Bertie Ahern. 'The burden of history at long last is lifted from our shoulders,' he said.

Nicky was about to comment on his use of yet another cheesy sound-bite when she remembered how important it all was to Supergran. She looked over at the old lady, who was fumbling in her sleeve for a tissue. Nicky got up and pulled one from a box on a side table and handed it to her.

Gráinne took it with a weak smile, and dabbed at her eyes. 'I can't believe it. They're after signing an agreement, after all these years. After all these long years.'

They listened to the news report. The British and Irish governments, and most of the political parties of Northern Ireland, had at last come to an agreement regarding how Northern Ireland should be governed and what the relationship between Britain, Ireland and Northern Ireland would look like in the future. With both the UK and Ireland being part of the European Union, in the same customs union and single market, it meant removing the physical border between Northern Ireland and the Republic of Ireland was simple, if both sides agreed to it. Without any border infrastructure, it was almost as though the two areas were one single country – as the Republicans wanted – and yet Northern Ireland still remained part of the UK – as the Unionists wanted.

'Oh, that's clever,' Nicky said, as the contents of the treaty were explained and their implications sank in. 'Both sides get what they want, and we all get peace.'

'As long as it sticks,' Supergran whispered.

'I think . . . I hope it will.'

It had to be ratified by referendums – both Northern Ireland and the Republic of Ireland would hold one, to be sure the people of both regions were happy with it. But it sounded as though the architects of the treaty were confident this would happen. The agreement stated that a devolved government would be set up for Northern Ireland, and that the IRA would begin the process of decommissioning their weapons. This had always been a sticking point in the past. Nicky grabbed her notebook and scribbled down some notes. She'd go out and buy a stack of newspapers tomorrow.

'This all ties in with your project, doesn't it?' Supergran said. 'The Easter Rising of 1916 began it all, and the Good Friday Agreement of 1998 is another big step in Ireland's history. One that we'll never forget, as we've never forgotten 1916.'

Nicky nodded. The hand of history, indeed. Nicky was not a religious woman, but she found herself praying silently to any gods who might be listening, that this agreement signed on Good Friday might lead to lasting peace in Ireland.

Chapter 26 – 30 April–3 May 1916

In the morning, water was handed round to the rebels, but once again there was no food. And then they were ordered to stand, to line up three by three and march. Gráinne's whole body was stiff and sore from the night spent on hard tarmac, and she groaned as she forced herself to her feet. She staggered a little, and Emmett caught her, steadying her. 'Easy, now. Straighten up slowly. Try to stretch a little.' She did, and it helped.

Everyone was the same – there were groans aplenty as they formed into lines. They were ordered to walk south-ward along the devastation of Sackville Street, towards the river. It had only been a few days since she'd marched with the Volunteers in the opposite direction, at the start of the rebellion. Then, they'd marched smartly and proudly. Now, they were a ragged bunch, dirty, injured, and more tired than she had ever thought possible. Defeated.

They crossed the river and walked along streets Gráinne had used so many times running messages. As they passed through residential areas, people turned out of their houses to watch. Some were downcast, caps in hand, nodding with respect at the rebels. But others – and she had to admit it was the majority – openly jeered and mocked them.

'There they go, the eejits,' one woman said. 'I hope they shoot every last one of youse.' She said it with such venom it made Gráinne gasp and clutch at Emmett's hand. He was looking straight ahead, his head high and his jaw set firm.

'Take no notice. No notice at all,' he muttered to her.

But the woman's words and hatred had scared Gráinne. What if it was indeed the firing squad that awaited them all at the end of this march? They were approaching Dublin Castle, its guard at the gates trebled since before the Rising. Were they to be taken into its courtyard and simply shot? Gráinne felt her knees go weak. But they were marched straight past, heading west.

'Kilmainham, I'm guessing,' Emmett said.

The jail had a reputation for appalling conditions. If that was where they were being taken . . . well, there was nothing they could do about it. Gráinne steeled herself. It could not be worse than spending another night in the open in Sackville Street. And, surely, they'd be given something to eat, eventually, if they weren't to be immediately shot.

It was a long and weary march to the jail, and the taunts from crowds continued. Some people threw things at them – stones, pails of water – but this stopped when the soldiers guarding them threatened to arrest anyone throwing anything. They were only hit by insults after that, and the occasional gobbet of spit.

At last, they reached the jail, and were herded into its court-yard. They weren't the only revolutionaries there – rebels from other parts of the city had been rounded up and brought there too. Gráinne spotted the Countess Markiewicz across the yard, and managed to work her way over to her.

'I am glad you are safe, Gráinne,' the Countess said, giving her hand a squeeze. 'I could not believe it when we received Connolly's orders to surrender. There were some with me who wanted to fight on, but I told them we have to trust James and obey his orders. And here we are.' She looked around the bleak walls of the courtyard. 'And here I suspect some of us may end our days.' She shook herself and gave Gráinne a forced smile. 'Ah, don't mind me, being so downbeat. Tell me, how is James? I hear he was wounded?'

'He was – a bullet ricocheted into his ankle, Madame. But it is not a life-threatening injury and I think he and some others were taken to hospital.

The Countess nodded. 'Well, that is good. Margaret too was taken to hospital.' She looked tired and defeated, and seemed to have run out of words so Gráinne returned to Emmett's side. Across the yard, soldiers were beginning to organise the prisoners into groups and leading some away. It would not be long, she knew, before she was separated from Emmett.

And, indeed, before long a soldier approached them. Emmett touched her face. 'Stay strong, my love. I'll see you on the other side.'

Other side of what? she wanted to ask, but there was no time. 'All women, follow me,' the soldier said, and led her, along with the other Cumann na mBan prisoners, into the main hall of the jail. She glanced back once more at Emmett, who stood resolute, awaiting his fate.

Inside, she glanced up at the high ceiling with its glass roof and steel beams, which reminded her of a railway station. There were suspended walkways off which the cells were accessed, and steel staircases at each end connected all levels. In the middle was a table at which a sergeant sat in front of a ledger. The women were instructed to line up and give their names and statements to him.

Gráinne had hoped they'd be given something to eat first, but it was not to be. One by one they approached the desk and gave the details.

'Gráinne MacDowd. Messenger and nurse,' she said, when it was her turn.

'Based where?'

'The GPO.' She would answer the questions honestly, she'd decided, but she would not give any more details than she had to, and she would say nothing that would incriminate anyone else.

'Who was in charge?'

She gave a little shrug, as if to say she didn't know any names. But the sergeant put down his pen and glared at her. 'We know already who was in charge at each rebel stronghold. We have arrested all of them. I suggest you answer me fully and honestly. It will go better for you if you do.'

She took a deep breath. She had no choice, and if they already knew, there was no point keeping quiet. 'Our commandant was James Connolly, and Pádraig Pearse, the President of the Republic, was there too.'

'President of the Republic. Huh.' The sergeant scoffed, and made a note. 'And who else did you see there? Who did you see with guns, shooting, perhaps?'

'Sir, I was mostly out in the streets delivering messages, or in the basement nursing the wounded. I did not see anyone shooting.' It was more or less true, and the sergeant seemed to accept it.

'And to where were you delivering these messages?'

'To St Stephen's Green on the first day, and later the Royal College of Surgeons.'

'To whom did you pass on the messages?'

'To the commandants,' she replied.

'Names?'

They knew anyway, she told herself. 'Commandant Michael Mallin and Countess Markiewicz.'

'A bloody woman.' The sergeant made another note, handed her a sheet of paper and a pencil and told her she could write one letter to family or friends, and then she was dismissed. She was taken to a large cell in which there were a dozen or so women, sitting on benches that lined the walls, some of them already taking the chance to write their letters.

She sat down, and nodded at those she recognised. It was good to see Elizabeth O'Farrell was there. They sat in silence, each lost in their own thoughts. Twice the door opened to admit more prisoners.

Gráinne used her sheet of paper to write a letter to her father, telling him a shortened version of what had happened. The letters would no doubt be censored but at least he'd know she was alive and where she was being held. She'd barely finished writing when a warden came round to collect the pencils and letters.

At last, at long last, food was brought in to them. They were each given a bowl of stew and a hunk of bread, with weak tea to drink. The meat was sparse and stringy but the stew was edible enough.

'At least they're feeding us,' Elizabeth O'Farrell said. 'Eat every scrap, girls. We need to keep our strength up.'

Gráinne did not need telling twice. She realised it was the largest meal she'd eaten since the Rising began.

They were issued with rough bedding: a thin rolled-up mattress and a blanket. The room they were in was barely big enough for the eight women it held, but Gráinne managed to get a spot beside a wall and away from the door. It didn't matter – she was so exhausted she knew she would sleep, no matter what. They were given a fifteen-minute warning before lights out, and each of them used the lidded bucket that served as a toilet, then laid out their bedding. Gráinne's eyes closed almost as soon as she put her head down, and she was only dimly aware of the lights going out.

* * *

259

She woke at first light, and lay on her back listening to the other women breathing and shuffling around. She wondered in which part of the prison Emmett was, or whether he'd been taken anywhere else. Had he slept? Had he eaten? And the Countess?

As everyone in her cell gradually woke up, they began to talk. Yesterday they'd all stayed silent, too tired, too traumatised to be able to put any thoughts into words. But today was different. It was as though each woman wanted and needed to talk about her experiences of the last week – get the words out there, share among the group, as though doing that made it real, made it worthwhile. The women listened carefully as each in turn recounted her part in the Rising. When they'd finished, Elizabeth O'Farrell, as the most senior Cumann na mBan member among them, addressed the group.

'There is not one action any among us could have taken, that could have changed events for the better for our cause. We go forward knowing we did all we could. And, girls, this will not be the end of Ireland's fight. Not even the end for our generation. We must and shall rise again.'

Gráinne gave a small smile. Right now, she could not think of the future of Ireland. She was too preoccupied with her own immediate future, and that of Emmett. And Sean. With a start, she realised she had not thought of him for a couple of days now. Not since that time she'd thought she'd glimpsed him. Was he safely out of Dublin, hiding somewhere where he could remain until the end of the war in Europe? Now that the Rising had failed, he would need to keep out of the way of the authorities for much longer. An independent Ireland could have protected him. An Ireland still under British rule would not. She offered up a short, silent prayer to keep him safe.

* * *

It was on the morning after her third night in prison that she and the other women were awoken early, at dawn, by the sound of gunfire. Her first thought was that, somehow, the Rising had restarted, and that any moment the door to their cell would burst open and Pearse or Plunkett or one of the others would shout to them to rouse themselves and come out once more to join the fight. But then she realised it had been a volley of shots, as though several guns had been fired at once. That could only mean one thing.

She scanned the faces of the other women. All were silent, shocked and sorrowful, heads bowed as they too realised what the sound had meant. It was a firing squad. Someone, one of their comrades, had just been executed. All of them crossed themselves and muttered prayers for whoever it was.

Minutes later, there was another volley of shots. Gráinne could not stop herself from flinching.

'Oh, Jesus, Mary and Joseph,' one of the women muttered. 'Who are they shooting?'

'The leaders, they'll be shooting the leaders,' Elizabeth said quietly.

And then there was a third volley.

Gráinne turned her face to the wall and wept quietly, allowing the tears to stream down her face. How long would this go on? How many would be executed? Among the leaders were people she'd come to think of as her friends. James Connolly. Joseph Plunkett. The Countess.

Chapter 27 – April 1998

Nicky spent the next two days with Supergran in Malahide, taking occasional short outings with Eileen and Jimmy, including an Easter Sunday lunch in a restaurant that overlooked the beach and Irish sea. Around these outings, there was time for Gráinne to complete the story of the Rising, while Nicky once more took copious notes.

This was the sad part of the story. The end of the Rising, the arrests, the imprisonments and executions. While Nicky had read about it in dry textbooks, it was completely different hearing it at first hand from someone who had actually been there, closely involved. Someone who had been arrested and put in jail along with so many others. Nicky listened intently as Gráinne told this part of the story. She hadn't known her great-grandmother had been imprisoned.

'Oh, those executions,' Gráinne said. 'Even now, all these long years later, I can still hear the shots in my head. As dawn broke, there came the shots and I'd know another brave soul, who wanted only independence for his country, had been killed.' She shook her head. 'Tragic, so it was, but it backfired in a way. They executed so many that it turned the tide of opinion against them. The ordinary people of Dublin got sick of hearing the dawn shootings too.' Supergran gave a little, wry laugh. 'Funny, they executed the leaders of the Rising in an attempt to deter others from future rebellions. To make an example of them. But it worked the other way – more joined the Cause after the executions than we'd ever had. Many more. It paved the way for the War of Independence.'

Gráinne fell silent for a moment. She was remembering those, Nicky guessed, who'd given their lives for the Cause. And then she looked up at Nicky. 'I was fearful they'd execute the Countess as well. She was my friend as well as my employer, and I didn't think I could bear it if they shot her too. She'd been one of the leaders, after all.'

'They didn't, though, did they?'

Gráinne shook her head and gave a small smile. 'No, and I suppose it was because she was a woman. How would it have looked to the rest of the world, if they'd executed women? The Countess said afterwards, that she'd been ready to die, ready to be shot at dawn like the others. Hadn't she wanted equal rights for women? She was prepared to accept equal responsibility and fate for what she'd done. Thankfully, the British authorities didn't see it like that.'

'What happened to her?'

'She was in jail for some time. When she was released in 1917, there were hordes of people who turned out in Dublin to welcome her home. Sure, wasn't it an astonishing sight to see how well she was loved? But she was imprisoned again in 1918. And then there was the general election of November 1918, the one where women had the right to vote for the first time, you know?'

Nicky nodded.

'Well, women could also stand for election then, for the first time. The Countess did so, as the Sinn Féin candidate for a Dublin constituency. And she won by a huge majority. She never took her seat in the House of Commons though, because, as you know, Sinn Féin politicians refuse to swear the oath of allegiance to the queen, or king as it was back then. Besides, she was in Holloway prison at the time so it would have been impossible anyway! She was a member of the Dáil – the Irish Parliament. And she was made Minister for Labour later on. She was the first elected woman politician in Britain and Ireland, the first female minister.' Supergran chuckled. 'Oh, there was nothing that woman couldn't do, if she set her mind to it.'

Nicky was scribbling all this down. With the focus on women in rebellion that she wanted to bring to her essay, this was perfect. It wasn't strictly about the Rising itself, but was a fabulous footnote to the story. 'Thanks, Supergran. I didn't know all that.'

'You'll need to look it up to get all the dates and everything right. Can't be relying on my old memory completely.' Gráinne patted Nicky's hand, and then turned serious again. 'And now I need to tell you the last part of my story. Pass me a tissue, would you? It's the part I find hardest to talk about – what happened in the jail on the night of the third of May. That's a date I never forget, even after so long.'

'If it upsets you, you don't need to tell me,' Nicky said. 'I have enough material already for my project.'

But Supergran was insistent. 'I need to tell it you. I need to tell it all – I think, in a way, it'll be good for me.'

And she continued talking about events that happened while she was in Kilmainham jail, events that she witnessed. Nicky made a few notes but mostly sat in silence, listening intently. She knew she'd never forget this part of the story. By the time Gráinne had finished speaking, both she and Nicky had tears streaming down their faces.

* * *

Nicky went back to England on Easter Monday. There were still two weeks of the university holiday left but she hadn't planned to go to her parents, preferring to stay on campus and get her project written up, now that she had completed the research. A few days working in the library would get it done, and then she'd be free for the rest of the Easter break.

Campus was quiet as there were no lectures or seminars on, and many students had gone home for the break. There were just a handful of students arriving each morning to use the library or the banks of computers. Some of the faculty coffee shops were closed outside of term time but the main ones were open and for this Nicky was grateful. It was good to sit and drink a coffee before going into the library. A chance to gather her thoughts for the day's work ahead. She was pleased with the way the project was turning out, and proud of what she'd accomplished so far. Now it was just a case of pulling the story out of her notes, focusing on the role of women during the Rising and writing about what that meant for future generations, and then if she could, tying it to the newly signed Good Friday Agreement. 'Just a case of doing all that,' she said to herself, rolling her eyes. The research – reading books and talking to Supergran and walking around Dublin – had been the easy part, the enjoyable part. Now the hard work began as she had to find the right words to tell the story, and put them in the right order.

But there was nothing to distract her – her coursemates were home with their parents, there were no lectures, no social events on, and only a couple of others in her flat. No Seb disrupting her life, thank goodness. Nothing to stop her getting on with the work.

Nothing, that is, other than the letter that arrived for her the day after she returned from Dublin. She collected it from the bank of pigeonholes in her student flat, and smiled.

That familiar handwriting was so good to see. She'd hoped he might write again. She'd thought about him a lot while she was in Dublin, and had found herself wanting to share her news with him. And here was a letter.

She saved opening it until she'd reached the library where, instead of going straight to a study desk, she went downstairs to the café and bought herself a cup of coffee. She settled herself at a corner table and only then opened the letter.

Hey Nicky, hope all is well with you. I got your letter, it was lovely to hear your news. Your project about the Dublin rising sounds fabulous. I can imagine you getting well stuck into that, especially as your great-grandmother played an active part in it all. I hope you're enjoying the research. Your mum said you'd been over to Dublin to research – that's amazing. Makes me kind of wish I was studying something that gave me an excuse to travel. You know how much I enjoy going to new places. But a medical degree doesn't really lend itself to that. At least I have the VSO work in Uganda to look forward to this summer. It's a huge project – I think they are taking on all sorts of people, not just trainee doctors. There's a girl from my university who studies English who's applied to go as well, her role would be to do some of the admin.

Anyway, I saw your mum just before Easter, and she said you were staying in Brighton to get your project written up. I had been hoping to catch up with you, but I guess that'll need to wait, unless by any chance you are coming home to celebrate your mum's 50th birthday next weekend? She didn't say you were and I dared not ask in case there's any kind of surprise planned.

I'm at my parents until the start of next term so if you wanted to ring me for a chat, you can. I'll understand if you prefer to keep your distance. Your mum said you were seeing someone new. I guess you didn't mention him in your letter because perhaps you weren't sure how I would take it, but I'm fine with it, honestly I am. We were so young when we got together. Maybe if we hadn't met each other until we were in our mid-twenties it might have lasted. Who knows.

So, I'd better go. Dad wants me to cut the lawn, and Mum wants me to paint the banisters. Got to do something to earn my keep here, haven't I? They do so much for me. Right, well, let me know when or if you're at your parents and if you'd like to meet up. No pressure, no worries if you'd rather not, but please do write to me now and again. We shared so much for so long – I do want to stay in touch with you.

Hope you're happy, enjoying life and having fun,
Conor

As with the previous letter from him, Nicky read it several times. This one seemed more heartfelt, more genuine than the previous one, which wasn't much more than a newsletter and which had seemed a little stilted, as though Conor wasn't sure she'd be happy to hear from him. Obviously, the fact she'd replied had given him confidence that she *did* want to hear from him and stay in touch.

And as she read the letter for the third time, she realised it was more than that. She wanted to see him again, she wanted to sit with him in a pub over a pint of bitter and properly catch up. She'd like to find out who this girl was that might be on the VSO placement with him – was she someone special? Someone he hoped might become someone special?

'Hang on a minute, Nicola Waters. Are you possibly a smidgen jealous of this unknown person?' she muttered, earning herself a snigger from some girls at a nearby table. She gave them a hard stare back, drained the last of her coffee, then gathered her things and left the café. She needed to examine her feelings about the possibility of Conor finding someone else. He was free to do so, of course he was, and hadn't she rather quickly found Seb and immediately jumped into bed with him? But Conor doing the same thing, Conor finding a like-minded person to do a VSO placement with . . . that was not something she'd considered. Before she wrote back, or phoned him, or saw him again, she needed to get her thoughts in order.

The last thing she wanted was for Conor to feel guilty or somehow constrained, not able to find a new girlfriend. All she wanted was for him to be happy, whatever that took. If this new girl made him happy, then she was fine with that, wasn't she?

Chapter 28 – 3–4 May

There were no further executions that morning. Just the three volleys of shots. 'Just' three? Gráinne chastised herself for downplaying it with that word. Three. Three of their brave leaders had been killed. She remembered how Plunkett had said he knew he'd signed his death warrant, by signing the Proclamation. She prayed to God it had not been him who'd been shot. What of Grace? How would she take it, losing her fiancé in such a brutal way? She shed silent tears for the loved ones of all those who'd been executed. And she prayed there would be no more.

The women were allowed out into the central hall of the prison later in the day, and given a mid-morning breakfast. Rumours abounded as to who had been shot. A prison guard, one who Gráinne thought had some sympathy with the rebels' cause, confirmed one of them had been Pádraig Pearse. Gráinne nodded. If anyone was going to be executed it was always likely to be Pearse, who'd been the overall leader of the Rising, the one who'd read out the Proclamation and had been nominated president of the short-lived Republic.

The mood was subdued that day. There was no more talk of having played their part. Only fear, a deep fear, that there would be more executions.

The women were not allowed out into the prison yard for exercise. 'It's where they shot the men,' Elizabeth O'Farrell said. 'They won't let us out to see the evidence.'

Just as well, Gráinne thought. She knew she would not have been able to bear seeing blood upon the ground, knowing whose it was.

The women were herded back into their cells without getting the chance to see anyone else. Gráinne's thoughts ran wild all day, wondering how Emmett was faring and whether the Countess might also be shot, for she too had been one of the leaders.

They had settled down to sleep, the lights were out, and Gráinne was once more curled on her thin mattress on the floor by the wall of the cell. She was not asleep – after that first night when she'd slept off the exhaustion of the week, she'd found it difficult to relax enough for sleep to take over. She heard the turning of a key in the lock and sat up, staring at the door.

A warder stood there, silhouetted by the light shining behind him. 'Any of you women know Grace Gifford?' he asked.

Gráinne glanced around at the other women. Was this some sort of trick? Surely Grace could not be in the prison. She'd had nothing to do with the Rising beyond being engaged to one of its leaders. Of the women in her cell, she was probably the one who knew Grace best. Tentatively she raised a hand. 'Yes, sir. I know Grace.'

He stared at her for a moment as if working out who she was, and then nodded. 'Right, come with me. Just you.'

She scrambled to her feet, straightened her clothes that she'd been sleeping in, slipped her feet into her boots and followed the warden out. He locked the door behind her. 'Sir, what is this about?' It was, she thought, quite late at night. Maybe midnight, or thereabouts.

He didn't answer, but led her through the prison to a wing she had not visited before. He opened a door and ushered her through. It was a chapel, and inside was a prison chaplain, another warden and Grace.

'Gráinne! I didn't know if you'd be in here. Are you all right?' Grace rushed towards her and embraced her.

'I am, I'm fine, but why are you here? Surely you were not arrested?'

'No, not at all. But look . . .' Grace pulled out a small box from her pocket, opened it, and showed Gráinne what was inside. It was a plain ring – a wedding ring. 'They have given permission for Joseph and I to marry, here, tonight.'

'Tonight!'

'Yes. It *must* be tonight.' There was an odd expression in her eyes, part excitement but also fear and a profound sadness. And all at once Gráinne understood the significance of what was happening.

'Oh, Grace,' she said, and hugged the other woman tightly. Grace was struggling to control her emotions. Her breaths were coming in short gasps and her body was tense as she fought against the tears that Gráinne knew must be so close to falling. Her own face was already damp.

'I wanted someone I knew to be a witness to our marriage. They agreed to ask among the women prisoners. I am glad it is you. You were with Joseph for much of the week. How was he, when you saw him last?'

'He was well, and uninjured, and proud of what he had done. So proud. You must cling on to that, Grace, whatever happens.'

'I know. I know. But . . .' The words did not need to be spoken.

A second woman was then brought in. It was Bridget Kelly, a member of the Cumann na mBan who Gráinne didn't know well. She was housed in a different cell to Gráinne.

Bridget stepped forward and hugged Grace. In her face Gráinne could see the anguish that must surely be written across her own features. 'Be strong, Grace,' Bridget whispered. 'Be strong for him.'

Grace nodded, and a moment later the chapel door reopened and Joseph Plunkett was led inside, his hands shackled together. As he saw Grace, he lifted his hands to the warden who'd escorted him, and the guard selected a key from the chain that hung from his pocket and unlocked his handcuffs.

Only then did he speak. 'Grace, my love!'

Grace stepped forward and embraced Joseph, holding on to him as though she was drowning and he was her rescuer. They stood like that in silence for a minute, while Gráinne and Bridget moved to one side, and then the chaplain gave a discreet cough.

'Ahem. We should begin. There is not much time, as I understand it.'

The bride and groom separated, but remained holding hands, as the chaplain spoke the familiar words of a marriage ceremony. Gráinne stood alongside Bridget, listening carefully, feeling honoured and humbled to be a witness at this extraordinary wedding. By rights, Grace should have been wearing a white dress with flowers in her hair, they should be marrying in a church, there should be scores of guests and it should be the most joyous occasion, the start of many years of happiness for them, together. Yet here they were at midnight in this dark, austere prison chapel that was lit only by candles as the gas supply had failed, with only herself, Bridget and a warden to witness the wedding. Even so, it was what they both wanted. Joseph was keeping his promise to Grace that he would marry her, and Grace would become Mrs Plunkett, even if it was only for a short period. No, Gráinne told herself, do not dwell on how long this union might last. Think only of this moment.

'Do you, Joseph Mary Plunkett, take Grace Gifford as your lawful wedded wife, to have and to hold, from this day forward, for better or for worse, in sickness and in health, until death do you part?' the chaplain was saying.

'I do,' Joseph said, and his voice was strong and firm, his eyes fixed on Grace as though he was trying to lend her strength by the force of his words.

'And do you, Grace Gifford, take Joseph Mary Plunkett as your lawful wedded husband, to have and to hold, from this day forward, for better or for worse, in sickness and in health, until death do you part?' Grace nodded and squeaked out a reply, then repeated it with a stronger voice. 'I do. Yes, I do.'

Those words – until death do you part – were spoken at every wedding but this time, death for one of them was but hours away. Gráinne stifled a sob and Bridget caught hold of her hand as Grace passed Joseph the ring, and he gently pushed it onto Grace's finger. The chaplain pronounced them man and wife, then stood back to give them a little space.

Grace's knees seemed to buckle, and Joseph had to catch her to stop her falling. There was a stool in the chapel, and the warden moved it closer to the couple.

'Sit down, Grace my darling,' Joseph said, and she did. He dropped to the floor on his knees, by her feet, and wrapped his arms around her waist. She placed her hands upon his head, stroking his hair.

'We've done it, we are married,' she whispered.

'Yes. I wish, I wish so much that we could linger in this moment for all time, my darling. I just want to hold you for ever.'

Gráinne glanced at the warden, wondering whether he would allow the couple a few moments alone, but he was making no sign of leaving the chapel. He too, she could see, was choked with emotion. Tears were streaming down Bridget's face as she held tight to Gráinne's hand. The chaplain too was dabbing at his eyes. Grace and Joseph were fully focused on each other. Gráinne realised it would make no difference to them whether they were alone in the chapel or not – for them the chapel, the prison, the events of the week had all melted away and there were only the two of them and their everlasting love in the whole universe.

She wished too that they could linger here in this moment, but it was not to be. After too short a time, minutes only, the warden looked at his watch and cleared his throat. 'Mr Plunkett, come with me. It is time to return to your cell.'

Joseph rose, and leaned over Grace for a last time, a last kiss, while the warden looked away. Grace had given in to her tears now, Gráinne saw, and Joseph reached into his pocket for a handkerchief. 'Dry your eyes, my love. I did what I did for Ireland. I go proudly to my death. Goodbye, my love.'

Grace's response was the quietest whisper, 'Goodbye. I will always love you.'

He turned and nodded to the warden, who fastened the handcuffs around his wrists and led him out of the chapel. Grace stayed on her stool, staring after him, twisting the ring around her finger, allowing her tears to fall freely now. The handkerchief Joseph had given her dropped unnoticed to the floor.

Two other wardens entered – the one who'd brought Gráinne and then Bridget to the chapel and another, presumably to escort Grace out. One beckoned to Bridget who kissed Grace's cheek before following the warden out. She was too choked by emotion to be able to say anything more.

Gráinne stepped forward, hoping that, somehow, she could offer some crumb of comfort, though what comfort could there possibly be for a woman who'd just married her love, and who knew he was to be shot in a matter of hours? What comfort could there ever be? Even so, she stood beside her friend and put a hand on her shoulder to show she was there.

'Thank you for being here,' Grace said, reaching up to take Gráinne's hand. 'I am glad we have done this, though I wish – of course I wish! – that things could have been different.' She took in a deep breath and stood, thanked the chaplain, and left the chapel.

Alone for a moment until the warden returned for her, Gráinne bent and picked up the handkerchief. Maybe there would be a chance to return it to Grace at some point. She tucked it into her pocket and waited for the warden to take her back to her cell.

There was no sleep for her that night, as the events of the evening played out in her mind, over and over, and her thoughts stayed with Grace. Gráinne held the handkerchief tightly. It had initials embroidered in a corner – JP and GG, intertwined. Grace must have embroidered it for Joseph and given it as a gift. When she got out of the prison, Gráinne promised herself she'd return it. It would mean something to Grace.

The women were woken at dawn, once more, by the sound of the firing squad. The volleys of shots rang out four times that morning. One volley was for Joseph Plunkett.

Chapter 29 – April 1998

It wasn't easy to get on with her project that day. Nicky had a lot to think about. The letter from Conor. Her feelings about him possibly finding someone new. His comment about her mother's 50th birthday – that had entirely slipped her mind. Of course, she ought to mark the occasion and do something more thoughtful than simply posting a card home.

In her project, she'd reached the part where she wanted to write about Joseph Plunkett's wedding to Grace Gifford, in Kilmainham jail. The event was, of course, only a footnote in the history of the Rising, but Nicky wanted to cover it. It helped illustrate the impact of the rebellion on women. Supergran had been there, and had witnessed it. And Grace had continued fighting for her country, during the War of Independence and the subsequent Civil War. Indeed, she'd been imprisoned for a while in Kilmainham, during the civil war in 1923. What must that have felt like, being incarcerated in the place where she'd been married and where her husband of only a few hours had been executed? It was an emotional piece to write, and Nicky found herself swallowing back tears as she covered the story.

They'd been childhood sweethearts, Joseph and Grace. As had she and Conor. She'd known Conor so long, as a childhood friend first and then they'd become closer in their mid-teens until eventually going on that fateful school trip. They'd been inseparable, and all their friends had assumed, as the years went by, that they'd be together for ever. Nicky had thought that too, until she'd gone to university and decided she was missing out on something by being tied to a boyfriend from home.

Even if that boyfriend was someone she'd loved. Someone she still loved, if she was honest with herself. But it was too late now. She dashed away a tear, and concentrated on writing the story of that night in Kilmainham jail.

Supergran had never told her how she got hold of that embroidered handkerchief, Nicky realised. She'd have to ask about it next time she saw her, though she had no idea when that might be. In the summer, perhaps.

The other thing playing on her mind, while she wrote, was the part of Conor's letter in which he'd written that he needed to do jobs for his parents to earn his keep. *They do so much for me*, he'd written. She thought about how Seb's parents had done a lot for him – financing him, bailing him out. Yet Seb took his parents for granted. Unlike Conor, who understood how much he owed them and did his best to pay them back, however he could.

What about her? Nicky put down her pen and stared across the bank of desks in the library. Was she like Conor, or more like Seb, taking advantage of her parents' generosity? She felt herself redden as she realised that, being honest, she was far nearer Seb's end of the spectrum. Her mother only wanted to see her once or twice each term, but Nicky had denied her that. Yet Mum had paid for her trips to Dublin, without hesitation. Dad too, although he stayed quietly in the background, supported her in everything she did. Mum might be more outspoken about her choices, and sometimes that might come across as nagging, but it all came from a place of love. Nicky realised that now.

She'd been selfish, this year at university. She'd tried to be the stereotypical rebellious student, and had pushed her parents away at the same time. But those visits to Supergran had proved that the older generations were good people, with a lot of life experience and a lot to teach her own generation. Seb was wrong in writing them off the way he did, especially as he then so quickly accepted their help and money whenever he ran into trouble.

Whereas Conor didn't take his parents for granted at all. He couldn't help financially, but he did jobs for them around the house, and prepared little surprises like that cake he'd made for his dad, the bunch of wild flowers picked for his mum on a walk, the house-cleaning he'd done while they were on holiday so they'd come back to a sparkling house. He was kind and thoughtful, and paid them back by being an excellent son.

Maybe her mother was right, Nicky thought. She had a whole load of growing up to do. Somehow, learning about her great-grandmother's actions all those years ago, when she was about the age Nicky was now, had made her realise how immature she still was. And then her experiences with Seb, and Conor's letter had also helped clarify things.

'Oh God. I've fucked everything up,' she muttered. The student at the next desk looked up and glared at her, but his expression softened when he saw her tears.

'Are you all right? Want to get a cup of tea and talk about it?' he asked quietly.

'No, it's all right. But thank you.' She gave him a weak smile, grateful for his offer of support. This was something she needed to work through by herself, not talk about with a stranger. She took a deep breath, dabbed at her eyes with a tissue, and forced her mind back onto her project. If she achieved nothing else, she needed to get that written up this week. Then perhaps she'd have time to go home for a short visit before the next term began.

Conor's letter was still playing on her mind. He wanted to catch up with her, he'd made that clear. More than once, he'd said perhaps they could meet up if she went back home, or she could phone him at his parents'. As she left the library to get herself something to eat, she had a sudden desire to talk to him. Steady, dependable Conor. And maybe she'd be able to find out more about this English student he seemed keen on . . .

She had a hurried lunch of pizza and chips from the student union bar, which had been cleaned, repaired and reopened. It felt strange going back in there after Seb's protest. But he was gone, his protest long over. She'd always liked that bar. And now that it was a smoke-free zone, it was even better.

With her late lunch eaten, she went to the nearest bank of pay phones. She dialled Conor's parents' number. She did not have to look it up – it was seared into her memory from all those teenage years of calling him almost every evening, even if she'd seen him during the day. It was only as the phone started ringing that she wondered what she'd say if his mum answered. What did Beatrice think of her, after she'd dumped her son for no good reason? She'd get a cold reception, of that she was certain.

She heaved a sigh of relief when the phone was picked up by Conor himself. 'Hey, Nicky! Good to hear from you. How are things? How's the new fella?' His words were upbeat, but Nicky knew him so well she could detect the faint hesitancy behind them, the uncertainty as to what their relationship now was.

'I'm fine, thanks. I got your letter. You said you wanted to catch up, and I was working in the library today and, well, I thought that I'd like to catch up too.' She allowed a wistful tone to creep into her voice as she spoke, surprising herself with how sad she felt that their relationship was over. Even though it had been her choice, and she'd thought through the reasons behind it carefully.

'Glad you've rung! So how was Dublin?'

'Great. Supergran knew so much. I wrote stacks of notes and am now trying to pull them all together. She asked after you, you know. She liked you, that time we went over and stayed with her.'

'Ah. I liked her too. Wonderful old girl. So, Nicky, your mum's birthday . . . were you planning on coming home for it? Only . . .'

'What?' He was going to ask if they could meet up, she thought. And she found herself liking the idea.

'Your mum thinks you won't come home, as you prefer to stay in Brighton. But your dad . . . well, I don't know if I'm supposed to say anything because they, well, they have a policy of leaving you to do your own thing . . . but he's planning a bit of a surprise party for your mum's 50th. Nothing huge, but we're invited – me and my parents – and some of your extended family, and your neighbours and some of your parents' friends. And I thought . . . you should know about it, and decide whether to come home for it or not. Your dad was going to talk to you about it next time you phoned home. It's supposed to be a surprise for your mum.'

'Oh! I haven't heard anything about it.' Nicky remembered guiltily that, actually, she hadn't called home for a couple of weeks. Not since before Dublin. So her father hadn't had a chance to tell her.

'I hope I haven't messed things up . . . Anyway, it's on Saturday. From 2 p.m. Are you going to come?'

'Um . . . I hadn't . . . Well . . . Yes. I'll be there.' She made a snap decision. She could catch a train in the morning and be there in time.

'Fantastic. I'll see you there th—.'

Nicky cursed as the pips went, cutting him off. She scrabbled in her pockets for more change but there was none. She needed to call her father and find out the details. What day was it? Thursday! So in fact, the party was the day after tomorrow. Maybe she could just turn up . . . and surprise her mum. She could apologise for being the kind of newly adult offspring who takes her parents for granted. Try to be a better daughter. Try to be a better person.

She could also catch up properly with Conor.

Nicky's decision to go home for her mum's birthday weekend meant she only had another day to finish her rebellion project. She did not want it hanging over her when she returned to Brighton. Depending on how things went at home, she thought she might stay there until the start of the new term a week later. Mum would like that.

It was surprising how much she was looking forward to it all. To spending a bit of time with both her parents. To seeing Conor. Her stomach gave a little flip at the thought of him, but she quashed the feeling quickly. He wasn't hers anymore, and that had been her choice, her action.

She went back to the library and worked hard for the rest of the day, and the following day too. She managed to find a 10p lurking in a drawer in her bedroom, and used it to call home at a time she knew her mother would be out. Dad answered.

'Dad? Listen, I spoke to Conor earlier and he said something about you having a little party for Mum?'

'Yes, pet. It's tomorrow. I was hoping you'd call so I could tell you . . . but we would both understand if you want to stay in Brighton. Especially after all your busy time with those trips to Dublin, and with that new boyfriend to see. Your card for Mum arrived and I've hidden it away till tomorrow. She'll be delighted you remembered.'

'Glad it got there. But . . . is it all right if I come home? For the party? I'm not sure if . . .'

'Oh love, it'd be marvellous if you can make it! If you're sure?'

Nicky had never felt more sure of anything. She grinned. 'Dad, I'd love to come. Two o'clock, right?'

'Yes. What time shall I pick you up from the station?'

'I'll make my own way. You'll be busy getting things ready for the party, won't you?'

'Yes, your mum will be out for a couple of hours from midday – I booked her a spa treatment – and I've to do it all then.'

'I'll get there just after midday, and help.'

She could hear the broad smile in her dad's voice. 'That would be marvellous. Thank you, love.'

'See you tomorrow.'

And then all she needed to do was get the last part of the project written up. There were a couple of facts she wanted to check. How many people had been killed, on both sides, in the conflict? Were any of them women? There were some books in the library that probably contained the answers; as during her reading on the subject, she hadn't noted down the exact numbers. She slung her bag over her shoulder and headed off to the library, to her favourite spot there: a desk that overlooked the central light well and which was tucked away from the main thoroughfares. She'd got a lot of work done there over the week.

She fetched the books she wanted to refer to and piled them on the desk, then sat down to start working her way through, looking for the information she needed and the final facts to check. One of them looked promising for numbers of casualties – it had a section listing all casualties according to where in Dublin they were fighting, on either side. Nicky opened the book at that page and began jotting down the numbers. She found herself scanning through the names too. All those Irish Volunteers, willing to die for what they believed in. And the British soldiers, fighting because they'd been ordered to, when perhaps they felt the real enemy, the war they should be fighting, was the one still raging in Flanders.

Each casualty was listed along with his rank and age. They were so young, Nicky thought. Many were barely older than she was. She spotted no female names, however. Just a note at the bottom of a page that said that there were several civilian casualties too, caught up in crossfire or in the fires that ravaged Dublin towards the end of the week. There was no definitive list of these names.

But then, in a list of names of Volunteers killed at Boland's Bakery, Nicky spotted a name that leapt out at her. Sean MacDowd, Volunteer, aged 23, killed on the last day of the Rising.

Gráinne's brother, a Volunteer? Supergran had said he was in the army, fighting for Britain against the Germans. He'd disappeared after coming home on leave, telling his sister he couldn't go back and he was going to desert.

No wonder Gráinne had never been able to find Sean after the Rising. He'd been killed. And, somehow, she'd never had access to any lists of the dead Volunteers. Presumably she hadn't thought to check those anyway. She hadn't thought Sean would be fighting. She'd expected him to be lying low, or getting himself out of the city, into hiding somewhere else in the country. But it looked as though he'd joined the Cause.

And Gráinne had lived the rest of her long life not knowing what had happened to him. She'd believed he was a deserter, and never found out his fate. Nicky grabbed the book and took it to a photocopier. She made copies of the page with Sean's name on, and the preceding page for context. She'd write to her great-grandmother, she decided, and send her this page, explaining what it showed. She wasn't sure how it would be received – Supergran had said she longed to know what had become of her brother, but would she want to know this? That he'd died so soon after coming back to Ireland?

She folded the photocopied pages and tucked them into her bag. Gráinne deserved to know. Nicky would write to her as soon as she could, taking time to word the letter just right.

Chapter 30 – May 1916

Gráinne stopped counting the days after the wedding of Joseph and Grace. Some days began like the others – with the hideous sound of the firing squad and the almost unbearable knowledge that another of their number had been shot. The women, by unspoken agreement, would keep quiet at this time, squeezing each others' hands and silently mouthing prayers that helped no one but perhaps brought the women a crumb of comfort. For a couple of days there were no executions, and then a day came on which they counted another four volleys of shots. Later, they'd ask around and find out who had been executed.

She estimated she'd been in Kilmainham for about a fortnight when, finally, she and the other women in her group were called out and told they were free to leave. She emerged into a grey and damp Dublin day, blinking and confused, wondering what she should do and where she should go. Emmett was, as far as she knew, still incarcerated, though whether in Kilmainham or elsewhere she did not know. There had been rumours that some rebels had been taken elsewhere.

Walking out through the gates of the prison, she recalled the day they were marched inside amid the jeers of the crowd, and remembered some women who were calling for them all to be shot, every last one. Well, many of them had been. Were the people of Dublin happy now? She, and the others released with her, began to walk, slowly, away from the jail, all of them working out where to go, what to do. A small crowd gathered as they left, and Gráinne steeled herself for jeers and taunts. But to her surprise they applauded the women. One man stepped forward and patted her shoulder. 'Well done, all of you. You've done Ireland proud.'

The change of mood of the Dublin people was astonishing. Gráinne couldn't quite process it, and the others with her simply shrugged and went on their way.

Dad. She needed to get to her father. He'd know what was going on. And maybe he'd have news of Sean and Emmett. She made her way into the city and then turned southward. With no money for trams or buses she had no choice but to walk. She passed by some areas that had been rebel strongholds. The devastation in the city was immense – whole blocks of buildings had been reduced to rubble or blackened and gutted by fire. Still people were going about their daily business – working, shopping, patching up shop windows and reopening businesses. It was almost as though the Rising had never happened, and yet there was a shift in the mood of the city that she couldn't quite put her finger on. It was as though the Rising, or the aftermath of it, had turned the tide of opinion and now, only now! the Republicans had the support of the people. Why this had happened she didn't understand. But it was a good sign, for any future fight.

Slowly, surely, and with the help of a lift from a tradesman in his cart, she made her way to St Enda's school. With Pearse executed, would it even be open? Who would be running it? Would her father be there?

She approached the grand building with some trepidation, but was pleased to see its doors were open and there were boys milling about. So it was open, and functioning, and surely her father would be there. She went up to his rooms and tapped on the door. It opened almost immediately.

'Gráinne! Oh, my darling girl! I saw you walk up the drive and I was coming down to meet you.' He wrapped her in his arms and for a brief moment all her cares melted away, she was a child again and her father could make everything all right.

Except she wasn't, she was a grown woman, and her cares and problems were bigger than anything one man could fix. She found herself sobbing, the trials and intense experiences of the last few weeks overwhelming her. He led her into his rooms and bade her sit on a sofa, while he made tea – the Irish cup of tea that could make anything better, even if only by a little.

As he put the cup beside her and sat opposite, his eyes were kind and concerned. 'I received your letter from Kilmainham but was not allowed to see you or send a reply. Thank the good Lord you are now out. When I heard about the executions, Pearse, and MacDonagh! Both were friends of mine. Both gone. A terrible thing.' He shook his head sadly. 'So tell me, Gráinne, all that has happened, all that you have done.'

She told him, in stuttering sentences, of her part in the Rising, of the surrender, the night in the open, the march to the prison and the agony of hearing the firing squads each morning. As she got to that part, he came to sit beside her, holding her tightly as she sobbed into a handkerchief. She told him too of Grace and Joseph Plunkett's wedding. Partway through telling him that, she realised the handkerchief she had pulled from her pocket was the embroidered one with their initials entwined. The one she ought to give back.

'Have you heard, Dad, anything from Sean? Or Emmett? Or any other news?'

He nodded. 'I have plenty to pass on to you. Emmett was kept at Kilmainham for a few days but I understand he has been moved to an internment camp in Wales. I have an address, and you will be able to write to him.' She gasped, but he patted her hand to reassure her. 'He will not be executed, you can be certain of that. I expect he will be released after a little while.'

'And Sean?'

'He has been classified as a deserter. He will face a court-martial if he is found by the British army, but frankly, I think they have more pressing problems here in Ireland than searching for him.' Dad shook his head sadly. 'It is not a label I would have wanted for him, though I understand why he could not return to the Front. I do not know where he is or how he is, I only hope he is safe and in time he can return to us.'

She nodded, it was how she felt too. 'I'll look for him, when I am recovered.'

'No, love, don't. If you go enquiring after him and you find him, you will put him in danger of being found by the authorities. It's better just to leave him be until the war in Europe is over. He will contact us then. He knows where to find me.'

She'd do it discreetly, Gráinne thought. She'd go to places he knew and look for him in person. She had to at least try. 'What news of the Rising, and its aftermath?' Gráinne asked next. It was still puzzling her how the rebels had been jeered at when they were arrested but cheered when they were released.

'There is a feeling that the authorities are going too far with these executions. There are protests – people are saying enough is enough. But General Maxwell is in charge and it seems he has a bloodlust, and won't stop until all those who signed the Proclamation, and all those who were commandants are executed.'

Gráinne shivered. 'That would include the Countess.'

Dad shook his head. 'If he had a woman shot, the outcry would be immense. I don't think he will do it. I think she will be safe. Likewise, Éamon de Valera who was in charge at the Boland's Bakery outpost – because he was born in the United States, I think he too will be spared. His execution would simply bring Republicans even more support from our American friends. They will not dare to shoot him.'

'I hope you are right. They have shot enough.' Gráinne shuddered again, thinking of the horror of those mornings waking up to the sound of firing squads at dawn.

They sat in silence for a while, Gráinne sipping her tea and trying to picture how life might go on. As if reading her thoughts, Dad asked, gently: 'What will you do, now? And where will you live?'

Gráinne shrugged. She had no plans. In prison she had not been able to imagine her future; she could only live from day to day, minute to minute. The Countess was still in jail, and likely to be for some time. So she could not go back to Surrey House. Her old job at Clerys was not an option; the department store had been razed to the ground during the Rising. No doubt it would be rebuilt, but that would take time. Her father had only one room.

'You must stay here,' he said, when she did not answer. 'Take my room, and I will make up a bed on the sofa. Until something else comes up, I will look after you.'

She felt a rush of love for him. 'Thank you, Dad. Thank you so much.' It was what she needed now – simply to be looked after by someone, just for a while, until she could get back on her feet.

A few days later, the newspapers reported that another two rebels had been executed. One was James Connolly, who'd been carried out to the prison yard and placed on a chair to face the firing squad as his injured ankle meant he could not stand. Gráinne wept and said a prayer for him. 'He was a gentle, kind man,' she said to her father. 'I know he was at the forefront of it all, so he could not expect to escape, but even so.' He held her while she wept, and tried to comfort her.

Thankfully, those were the last executions. Her father had been right that they didn't dare execute the American-born de Valera or a woman. The main effect of the executions had been to rally the Irish people to the Republican cause. Gráinne discussed this with her father over many a pot of tea.

'We rose up and they condemned us, but if we did so now, they'd support us,' she concluded.

He nodded. 'Yes, you are right. It is only a matter of time, now. There will be more bloodshed but Ireland will be independent eventually.'

'Do you think now that it is the only way?'

He smiled sadly at her. 'I wish it weren't.'

Gráinne stayed with her father for two months, and then, in the summer, felt well enough to find lodgings in the city and a new job, working in a women's outfitters on Grafton Street. It was odd being back in the city centre, walking past City Hall and St Stephen's Green, and all those other places where the fighting had been intense. Liberty Hall had been flattened by the artillery bombardment, and Sackville Street, including the GPO itself, was still in ruins though there were plans to rebuild it and work had already started.

She came across Grace once, shopping in Grafton Street. The two women stood staring at each other, oblivious to other shoppers passing either side of them. Grace looked drawn and tired. Her usual sparkle was gone, at least for now. Gráinne struggled to find anything to say, and in the end, they simply embraced, sharing via their hug all that they wanted to say, all that there were no words for. Gráinne realised that to Grace she was a reminder of those dark days, a reminder of all Grace had lost. It was better, perhaps, if they did not continue their friendship. They parted, with a last squeeze of each other's hand, and a lingering glance that told of sorrow and understanding.

She wrote to Emmett twice a week at his internment camp in Wales, and received many letters in return. Some had been censored, but she was able to deduce that he and others held with him were already making plans for the next stage in Ireland's fight for independence. He mentioned the name of Michael Collins frequently. Gráinne remembered the tall handsome man who'd been Joseph Plunkett's aide-de-camp at the GPO. It seemed as though Collins was emerging as a possible future leader.

As the year wore on, and autumn and then winter came around, Gráinne settled into her new life. At last, in early December, a letter arrived for her that changed everything. It was from Emmett, and it confirmed that he was to be released. He was due to arrive in Dublin in just two days.

Gráinne arranged for time off from her work so that she could be at Dublin Port to meet him off the ferry. She washed her hair, put on her best clothes, and left on a cold but sunny morning in good time. Her stomach was churning with excitement and also nerves – how would things be between them, after all this time and after all they had been through? What if he no longer felt the same way about her? Would he be well, or would he need nursing back to health? He had given little indication in his letters of his physical wellbeing. The one thing she was sure of was that his Republican beliefs were as strong as ever, stronger even than they had been before the Rising, and that he was not about to give up the fight.

She stood at the docks, watching as the huge ferry made its approach and docked. She peered up at the railings – was he on deck, looking out for her? But she did not see him then. She remembered the last time she'd been here, to meet Sean, back in April. Just a few days before the Rising began. So much had happened since then! Sean had come home changed, damaged by the war and disillusioned by his part in it. And he had never gone back. What would Emmett's state of mind be?

At last, the gangplank was lowered and people began to stream off the ferry. She saw businessmen, plenty of soldiers home on leave, families with children and then – there he was! Almost last off, dressed in shabby clothing that didn't fit, his hair long and unkempt but his eyes were bright and shining, his mouth smiling, and his bearing upright and proud, unbeaten by his months of incarceration. He spotted her at almost the same moment she saw him, and he began to hurry down the gangplank as she ran across the tarmac towards him.

He dropped the small bundle he was carrying as they neared each other, and held out his arms to her. She allowed herself to fall into them, wrapping her arms around his back as he pulled her close and leaned over, resting his cheek on her head as she leaned against his chest. 'Oh, my Gráinne! I have dreamt of this moment. It is what kept me going. And now, here you are!'

'Emmett! Oh, Emmett!' All the words she'd thought she would say to him deserted her and all she could say was his name, over and over, as she relished the feel of his arms about her. He felt thinner than she remembered, yet beneath the clothes there was toned muscle. She pulled away a little to gaze at his face. He looked older, more lined, and there was a streak of grey hair above his ear; but he was still handsome, sparkling, and full of love for her. All her doubts about whether he would feel the same melted away. She knew, without him having to say it, that his love for her had grown rather than diminished over the months. As had hers for him.

As she gazed at him, he smiled at her. She pulled him close and, remembering the promise she'd made herself during that terrible night in Sackville Street, whispered in his ear. 'We'll never be parted again, Emmett. We'll marry, and we'll marry soon, my love.' He nodded and returned her smile.

Her eyes dropped to his lips and then he was kissing her and she was remembering the feel of him, the taste of him, the joy of him, and she knew that she was his for ever and that nothing else mattered. The years stretched ahead, years of love between the two of them, of renewed fights for Ireland and in the fullness of time, independence and peace.

Chapter 31 – April 1998

Nicky packed a bag with enough clothes for at least a week, but with no dirty washing. On her previous visits home, she'd taken a huge bag of dirty clothes, dumped them in the utility room and waited for Mum to wash, dry and fold them. That couldn't happen anymore. She'd realised, better late than never, that if she wanted to call herself a grown-up, she needed to start acting like one. She should think of others, look after herself, and not expect her parents to do everything for her. Give something back. In other words, be more 'Conor' and less 'Seb'.

She'd already posted a card for Mum's birthday, but had no gift for her other than the chocolates she'd bought in Dublin. At such short notice it was going to have to be whatever she could pick up at the railway station. She left early on Saturday morning, catching a train from Falmer and changing at Brighton. There was a flower boutique there, and she had a bit of time, so browsed the displays. They were all so expensive, and for something that didn't last! Eventually she chose a simple bunch of yellow roses, then headed out of the station to a nearby patisserie where she bought a chocolate cake, all prettily boxed up. Both gifts were a bit unimaginative and definitely overpriced, but she hoped Mum would appreciate them.

The train journey passed quickly and Nicky arrived home, walking the two miles from the train station, just after twelve. Her mum's car was gone from the driveway which meant she must be out at her spa treatment, as planned.

'Nicky, love. You're here!' Dad came out to greet her and enveloped her in a huge hug. 'I should warn you, she was muttering crossly about you not phoning her this morning. Of course, she doesn't know you're coming, and thinks you've just forgotten.'

'I'd have had to phone pretty early before I left, and that would have made her suspicious. Well, here I am. Ready to help with whatever you need. Can I put these roses in water?'

'Of course. They're very pretty. And then perhaps you could help me get the table ready. There's a delivery of party food expected in about half an hour.' He pulled a face. 'Bit lazy of me to order it all in, but it seemed the easiest thing to do. I'm no great shakes as a cook, as you know.'

'I think it was a wonderful idea.' Nicky followed him through to the dining room where he'd begun clearing off the plants and vases that normally adorned the table. Together they pushed it against one wall and arranged the chairs around the edges of the room.

'It'll work better as a buffet,' Dad said, and Nicky agreed.

The food delivery arrived soon after, and they were kept busy laying it all out on the table, along with napkins, bundles of cutlery and piles of plates. Dad had champagne cooling in the fridge and an array of alternative drinks on a kitchen work surface. Nicky put the vase of roses on the dining-room table on the side against the wall, and transferred the cake she'd bought to a pretty plate. There were golden balloons marked with the number fifty and a Happy Birthday banner that she tied above the front door.

'It all looks good,' Nicky said, and Dad nodded. 'Mind if I go and change now, before she gets home?'

'Of course, off you go. And thanks, love. I don't think I could have got this done on my own in the time.'

Nicky went to her old bedroom and changed into a floaty skirt she'd left in the wardrobe there (a birthday present from Mum) and a lacy top. There – she was wearing Mum's taste in clothes. That would send the right message. She looked at her footwear – her usual Dr. Martens were firmly on her feet, and decided to leave them on, liking the juxtaposition of feminine clothes with no-nonsense boots.

The doorbell rang. Was that Mum home? No, surely she'd just let herself in with her key. Nicky glanced in the mirror, smoothed down her hair, and went downstairs. Dad had answered the door, and it was Conor, holding a card and a bunch of flowers.

'Hi David. Hey, Nicky. Thought I'd come early and see if there's anything I can help with. Mum and Dad are coming a bit later.'

'Conor, good to see you,' Dad said. 'I think we have everything done. Nicky's been a great help.' He gave her an odd look, and went through to the kitchen leaving them alone in the hallway.

'I'll find a vase for those, or do you want to give them to Mum as they are?'

Conor was staring at her, and looking a little lost for words. 'Er, yeah. Whatever you think.' He swallowed. 'You look good, Nicky. Glad you were able to come back for this.'

'I'm glad you told me about it,' she replied, and held his gaze for a moment.

But only a moment, because there was a rattle at the door behind him, and then it opened and Mum came in. 'David, you've put up a banner! Oh! Conor! What are you . . . and Nicky!' She clapped a hand to her mouth.

'Happy birthday, Mum,' Nicky said, stepping forward to hug and kiss her.

'Happy birthday, Karen.' Conor held out the flowers which she took.

'Oh my goodness, what a surprise! Lovely flowers!'

Nicky grinned as Dad came forward to embrace his wife. 'There's more, love. I've invited a few people round. The food's all set out, and there's champagne chilling, but if you want a cup of tea first?'

'I most certainly do *not*! Get that bubbly open, David. I want to start the celebrations. Oh, those yellow roses are gorgeous!'

'They're from me,' Nicky said, and was rewarded with a look of surprise and pleasure from Mum. 'There's a posh cake in the fridge too. Sorry it's nothing more imaginative.'

'Flowers and cake. Perfect gifts, in my opinion. Something to be enjoyed that then doesn't clutter up the house for years to come.' Mum smiled. 'Thank you. Oh, I'd better go and change!' She was wearing yoga pants and a sweatshirt. 'Come with me, Nicky, and choose me an outfit. I like what you're wearing, by the way. Looks great with those boots.'

Nicky grinned. This was better. They weren't trying to score points over each other for once, but were each giving ground and noticing when the other had done so. It was a start, and perhaps something that they could build on. She followed her mum upstairs and into the bedroom.

'So how long ago was this planned?' Mum asked, as she opened a wardrobe door and began rummaging through.

'I don't know. I only heard about it two days ago.'

'Did you ring Dad then? I was in all day, never heard the phone.'

'Actually, I phoned Conor. He'd written to me, and I wanted to catch up with him, and he told me about it.

297

Then I called Dad yesterday.' Nicky took a deep breath. 'I'm sorry I haven't called you very often. I should have, after coming back from Dublin. I just got caught up in things.'

'It's all right. Your new boyfriend and everything . . .'

'I dumped him,' Nicky said quickly.

'Oh! That didn't last long.'

'No. I realised . . . well, I realised he wasn't quite what I thought he was. Mum, I've . . . I hope I've matured a bit, these last few weeks. I've been a bit self-centred, I suppose.'

'You've been a typical young woman, just coming out of her teens.' Mum said. 'You've been no worse than others I hear about from my friends. And maybe I've been a bit clingy, you being an only child and all.'

'Well, at least I could have called home more often.'

'Yes,' Mum sounded thoughtful. 'You could have. I think I might help you with that. If I buy you a mobile phone, on a pay-as-you-go contract, I'll be able to call you when I want to speak to you.'

'Would you do that? Buy the phone, I mean?'

Mum grinned. 'I think it might be the best answer all round. You'll have to pay for the top-ups though.'

'I will. Oh wow, thank you. And sorry . . . for my behaviour. For some reason I felt the need to be a bit of a rebel, you know? Maybe it was something I had to work through. Researching that project, talking to Supergran about a real rebellion, helped somehow.'

Mum smiled. 'I think we all have a bit of a rebellious streak in us, in this family.'

'Except you. You've always toed the line, haven't you?' Nicky couldn't imagine her mother getting caught up in any kind of protest.

'Oh, you'd be surprised,' Mum said, with a sideways glance at her. 'You were only tiny so you wouldn't remember, but I spent a few weeks at Greenham Common back in 1983.'

'You did *what*?' Nicky had read about the protests at Greenham Common, the women's 'peace camp' protesting against the decision to house nuclear missiles at the RAF base near Newbury. There'd been thousands of women involved at times, forming human chains around the base. Protests were ongoing all these years later, and there were still some women camped out there.

'I was part of the group that formed a chain from Greenham to Aldermaston. And I slept in a tent at the base for about three weeks. Your poor father had to look after you by himself, but he knew that I believed in what I was doing, and that I wanted – and needed – to do my bit. Perhaps I too needed to work through a rebellious phase in my life.' Mum laughed at Nicky's expression. 'There. That's shocked you, hasn't it? Didn't think your old mum had it in her?'

'Shocked, no. Surprised and . . . well, proud, I suppose. You're amazing.'

Mum looked pleased by the compliment. 'Ah, not amazing, love. Just doing what felt right. Exactly as you've been doing, I see that now. Come here.'

Nicky crossed the room and let herself be enfolded in her mother's arms; not as a child is held by a parent but as one woman is held by another who loves her. It felt good, secure, and loving. As though they were supporting each other and holding each other up. Just as it needed to be, as it should be, from now on. It would no longer be all one-way traffic, Nicky decided. It would be a long time, she hoped, before Mum and Dad needed practical help with day-to-day living from her, but in the meantime she could, and *would*, change her attitude. She'd be less of a teenager and more of an adult, taking on her share of the chores around the house and not simply expecting them to do everything for her. 'Sorry Mum. For being a rubbish daughter lately.'

'Ah, not so rubbish, really. Don't be hard on yourself. I think we've both rubbed each other up the wrong way at times.' Mum rubbed her nose and blinked. 'Anyway, the blue dress or the black silky trousers with that green top?'

Nicky understood her mother's need to change the topic before they both ended up with reddened eyes and tear-stained cheeks; not a good look for a party. 'Black and green. With a pair of heels.'

'Right then. I'll get dressed and then I'd better join the party. Who else is coming?'

'No idea, other than Conor's parents. And I think Granny and Grandad.'

'Great, will be nice to see Beatrice and Mark and my parents. You go down, I'll be there in a moment. You probably want to speak to Conor? Tell him . . .'

'Tell him what?' Was this the old, interfering Mum back again? Nicky hadn't decided when or how to tell Conor that it was all off with Seb.

'Oh, nothing. Ignore me. I mean, just catch up with him. It's nice that you two are remaining friends.'

Nicky smiled at the climbdown and went downstairs, just in time to hear a car pull up outside. She opened the front door and was amazed to see a familiar dark red Ford Galaxy with Irish numberplates parked in the driveway. Jimmy was helping Gráinne out of the passenger seat. Nicky ran outside to them.

'Supergran! Jimmy! Wow!'

'Ah Nicky, good to see you again, and so soon!' Supergran's eyes sparkled. 'Well, I was invited to your mum's party, but I wasn't prepared to fly, so Jimmy here said we'd take the ferry and drive. All a bit of a last-minute decision, like. I'm paying him, of course, now that it's his business. We spent a night at a lovely little hotel somewhere in Cheshire, and now here we are.'

'Come on in! I'm only just here myself.'

Mum was delighted and surprised to see her grand-mother, who quickly became the guest of honour. Soon, Conor's parents arrived, then Nicky's grandparents, and a host of other guests. The house filled up with chat and laughter, and every time Nicky caught her mother's eye, they both gave each other huge supportive happy smiles.

It was a fun party, and Nicky was kept busy chatting to people she hadn't seen for ages. In the past, she might have rolled her eyes at this kind of parental birthday party, but this time she found herself enjoying it. OK, it wasn't at all like raucous student parties that involved large quantities of drink, loud music, dancing, possibly some illegal substances and maybe a snog or two, but it was enjoyable in different ways. She sat with her grandparents for a while, catching them up on all that she'd done at university. She greeted several old friends of her parents who all wanted to know how she was getting on. Even Conor's parents were friendly towards her, and seemed not to be holding any kind of a grudge towards her for dumping their son.

In the late afternoon, Dad made a little speech thanking everyone for coming, and led the party singing Happy Birthday. Mum tried to make a speech, got tearful and ended up simply raising her glass and saying, 'Cheers, all! Sláinte! Hic!' which made everyone clap and laugh.

Later, as people began to leave, Nicky went around the house and collected empty glasses. It was not something she'd have even thought of doing on previous visits home. She took them to the kitchen and put them beside the sink. Conor came to join her. 'Shall I help you wash them?' he said.

She hadn't considered washing them up, but the idea of doing a small helpful job alongside Conor held an odd appeal. She smiled at him. 'Yes, why not?'

'I'll wash, you dry, then.' He pushed up his sleeves and began filling the sink with water, while Nicky found a clean tea towel in a drawer.

'Glad you came?' Conor asked, as they got to grips with the task.

'Yes. Thank you for telling me about it.'

'You've changed, a little. Must be the influence of your new man—'

'That's all over.' Nicky blushed as she interrupted him.

'Really? Oh, I thought . . .'

She shook her head. 'It was just a brief fling, really. He turned out not to be my type. Conor, I'm not sure what you think, but I only met Seb after you and I broke up. There was no overlap, at all.'

'I'd wondered. Sorry to hear it didn't work out.'

They worked in silence for a few minutes. Nicky had a question for him that she was dying to ask, but was struggling to work out how to phrase it. At last, she pulled herself together. This was Conor, whom she'd known all her life, whom she probably knew better than anyone. She should just *ask* it, straight out. 'So, who's the English student going on the VSO placement with you? How long's that been going on?'

'Sorry, what? Who?'

'You wrote in your letter, about a friend studying English who's applied to do VSO with you?'

'Oh, you mean Helen. She's applied, yes, but not sure she's going to the same place I am.'

'Ah, that's a shame for you both.'

'Shame? Why?'

'Aren't you . . .?'

He laughed. 'Ah, you thought we were together. Not at all. Helen's a good friend but I'm not her type. Not even the right gender.'

302

'Oh. I thought . . .'

'You read a lot into a throwaway comment in my letter.' His tone softened. 'Did it bother you? Thinking that perhaps I was seeing someone new?'

'No . . . not really . . . I mean, you had to get used to the idea I was seeing someone else, so I . . .' Where was this conversation going?

They fell silent again as Dad brought in a clutch of dirty glasses and put them beside the sink. 'Good job, kids, thank you,' he said, then seemed to realise he'd interrupted something, for he muttered something else and quickly left the room.

Conor waited until he'd gone. 'I was OK with you seeing someone else. It was what you wanted – a chance to live the student life to the full, and not feel constrained by anything. I got that.'

'You were really good about it. When I called it off, I mean.'

'I won't deny it felt shit, Nicky. I'd always thought . . . we'd last. Even though we'd talked about it and said that if either of us wanted to end things that was OK. It was a bolt from the blue when it happened, if I'm being honest. But I've thought about it a lot since, and you're right. We should – we must – make the most of our time at uni, and if that means seeing other people then that's what we should do.'

'Thanks for being good about it. I felt awful when I told you, but at the time it seemed right . . .'

'At the time? And now?' Conor took his hands out of the sink and turned to face her. 'Is it still the right thing for you now?'

'I-I don't know. It's only been a couple of months. I wanted time . . . and then the thing with Seb happened so quickly, and now . . .' She stopped talking, realising she was blushing and babbling and making no sense, and worse, her eyes were filling with tears.

303

Conor had almost finished washing the glasses. He dried his hands quickly on the tea towel she was holding, and then pulled her towards him in a hug. A friendly, supportive hug. 'Hey, it's all right. I don't know either what I want right now.' He squeezed her close and for a moment it felt as though she was back where she belonged.

But was she? They'd got together so young. And those reasons why she'd dumped him were still valid, mostly. She still wanted to feel unrestricted, able to do what she wanted and see who she wanted. She no longer dismissed Conor as boring and staid, though. He was anything but. She was sorry she'd ever thought that of him.

'Why don't we just let it ride for a bit?' he said. 'We've proved we can still be friends and can still see each other. Why don't we continue as we are next term. Then in the summer we could meet up, before I go away. Let's just take things as they come. Remain as we are, but stay in touch.' He gently pushed her away so she could look at him and see the love in his eyes.

She couldn't trust herself to speak. She simply nodded her agreement.

He smiled, and let her go. 'Good. I'm glad we had this talk. We'd better finish this washing-up now, eh?' He put his hand back into the soapy water and flicked a few bubbles over her.

'Oi! I'm all wet now!' she squealed, laughing. Conor had always been good at defusing intense situations. As they finished the washing-up, laughing and joking and with a fair amount of flicking of bubbles at each other, Nicky felt happier than she had done for a long time. She had worked out what was wrong with her life. She knew how to fix it, and had made a start by coming home for this party. There was the possibility of restarting her relationship with Conor, if, in time, they both decided it was what they wanted. But for now, she had the freedom she'd wanted, and so did he.

She'd miss him over the summer, when he was away doing his VSO placement.

As though he'd read her mind, he turned to her again. 'Nicky, if you've nothing planned for the summer, you might consider the VSO scheme too? Not necessarily the same one I'm doing, although they could make use of someone like you. It's just . . . you know . . . a way of doing some good in the world. We're so privileged, and it's a small way of balancing things out a bit.'

She smiled. 'I'll think about it.'

'I'll drop round the prospectus so you can take a proper look.' He seemed pleased she hadn't dismissed it. And actually, it wasn't a bad idea at all. Maybe voluntary work was a way of fighting injustice, of being an activist of sorts? Maybe it would help her fulfil that urge to do something meaningful?

Chapter 32 – April 1998

By eight o'clock the party was over, and most guests including Conor and his parents had left.

'To think our daughter is 50!' Nicky's grandmother exclaimed as she hugged Mum goodbye. 'Makes me feel so old. And our granddaughter almost 20! All grown up.'

'*Trying* to be a grown-up,' Nicky said, and Mum laughed and nudged her playfully.

At last, there were just Supergran and Jimmy left – they were staying the night. Gráinne would take the spare room, and Jimmy was to use the sofa bed in the sitting room.

Nicky was sitting with Gráinne on that sofa bed, while at the other end of the room, Mum and Jimmy were reminiscing over their childhoods when their families had often met up for holidays. Dad was with them, listening and laughing occasionally.

'So, are you after finishing your project now?' Gráinne asked Nicky. 'Is it all written up?'

'Yes, all done, though I need to type it up on a computer before I hand it in. When I've done that, I'll send you a copy.'

'That would be lovely. I'm so glad I was able to help.'

Now was the moment, Nicky thought. She reached out

and took her great-grandmother's hand, pulling it into her lap. 'I hope I can help you too, a little. In my research, I found out something about your brother.'

'About Sean? But how?' Gráinne frowned, but her eyes were bright and she sat up a little straighter, as though eager to hear whatever Nicky had to say.

'Let me just fetch something . . .' Nicky quickly went up to her bedroom and found the photocopied page in her bag. She came back down and resumed her place beside Supergran. 'Here it is. I photocopied this page from a book that included lists of Volunteer casualties during the Rising.'

Gráinne glanced at it but didn't take it. 'But Sean wasn't a Volunteer. I told you, he was in the British army, before he deserted.'

Nicky took her hand again. 'It looks like he must have decided to join the Volunteers. He got involved in the fighting at Boland's Bakery.'

'He was fighting? During the Rising?'

Nicky nodded. 'Yes. And I'm so sorry, Supergran. He's listed here as having been killed that week. Look.' She pointed at Sean's name on the photocopy.

'Sean MacDowd, aged 23, Irish Volunteer,' Gráinne read out, her voice barely a whisper.

Nicky became aware that across the room, her parents and Jimmy had fallen silent and were listening intently. 'That's him, isn't it? That's your brother?'

'Yes, that's him.' Supergran ran her gnarled fingers over the name, as though touching it brought him closer to her. 'So he joined the Cause after all. But he didn't tell us. We didn't know. Not I nor Emmett nor my father knew anything about what he was doing.' She gave a little gasp. 'Sure and this is why we couldn't find him, isn't it? We didn't for a moment think to check with the Volunteers. We were in prison after the Rising as I told you. By the time we were all out, the dead had been buried and the newspapers weren't talking about it anymore.'

'It would have been hard, back then, to get a definitive list of the casualties, even if you had thought of it,' Nicky said gently.

'We concentrated on looking outside the city, in all the places where Sean knew someone, where he might have gone to hide out. We looked everywhere, so we did. I wanted to put a notice in the paper, asking him to contact me, but Emmett said no, that Sean was a deserter and that's just the kind of thing the authorities would be looking for in order to find him again. They'd have court-martialled him if they found him. So I didn't. Not till after the Great War was over. But then we were into the War of Independence and then the Civil War right after, so it was years until there was true peace in Ireland.'

Tears were running down Supergran's face as she spoke. Without a word Nicky reached for a tissue from a box on a side table and handed it to her. Gráinne dabbed at her cheeks. 'But I never gave up, Nicky. Never. I kept looking, hoping, praying that one day he'd turn up, same old Sean with his twinkling eyes and cheery laugh. And all along, he was dead and buried.' She glanced up at Nicky with a sudden look of hope in her eyes. 'Do you know, or do you think it's possible . . . to find out where he was buried? If I could see his grave . . . it'd be like I was saying goodbye to him properly now, wouldn't it?'

Nicky squeezed her hand. 'In the book, it said that most of the leaders of the Rising, those who were executed, were buried in Arbour Hill Cemetery in Dublin. He might be there, or else in Glasnevin.'

'He had no mourners at his graveside,' Supergran said, in a whisper, and it was this that brought Mum and Jimmy rushing across the room to her side.

'Hush, Grandma,' Mum said. 'Don't upset yourself.'

'Oh, Karen, love. I'm not upset. I'm sad that my brother had no one there to mourn him. No one who loved him even knew that he was dead. But I'm happy that at last I know what happened to him. And if I can visit a grave, even an unmarked one, and know that it is his last resting place . . . well then, I shall be able to go to my own grave happy, so.'

'Don't talk like that, Gran,' Jimmy said. 'You're not about to go to your grave, sure you're not.'

Supergran smiled. 'I'm 100. I have no intention of leaving you all just yet, but I'm after supposing I can't have too many more years left in me. Nicky, I've enjoyed helping you with your project, so very much. Now, if you are planning to do another one, might I suggest something about the War of Independence? Emmett and I were active in that too, you know, and oh, the stories I could tell!' She sighed. 'But that's for another time. I'm tired now. Will someone help me to my bed?'

'Of course!' Mum and Jimmy spoke at once but it was Nicky who Supergran looked towards, and Nicky who was first to her feet to help the old lady up.

'I'll do it, Mum,' Nicky said. She registered the hastily disguised look of surprise on Mum's face, but she found herself looking forward to a few more moments alone with her great-grandmother.

Upstairs, as Nicky helped her get ready for bed, Gráinne turned to her and clutched her hand. 'I never told you about that handkerchief, did I? The one in my box of mementos.' She took a deep breath. 'It was Joseph Plunkett's, that Grace had given to him, but he gave it back to her to mop her tears at their wedding. She dropped it. I picked it up, and I should have returned it to her when I was released.' Gráinne shook her head sadly. 'But somehow I never did.'

309

'She's buried in Glasnevin Cemetery,' Nicky said. 'When we go looking for Sean, we could go to see her grave too, and you can apologise for keeping her handkerchief.'

'We? Does that mean you're coming back to see me again, even though your project's over?'

Nicky smiled. 'Too right I am. It'll have to wait till the end of the summer term, though. Early July?'

'Ah yes. I'm planning on being at home then, so I am. I'll keep the room free for you.' Gráinne smiled happily as Nicky pulled back the bed covers for her, and then tucked them gently around her.

'Good night, Supergran. Sleep tight.'

'I will, now I know Sean sleeps too.' And with that the old lady closed her eyes and was asleep in seconds. Nicky tiptoed out, turning out the light. She was lucky, she realised, being a part of this family. Supergran, her grandparents, her numerous aunts, uncles and cousins. And most of all, her parents – supportive, kind and loving. It had taken her a long time to understand how good they were to her, but now she knew, she was not going to forget it again.

You could be a rebel, as long as the changes you were fighting for were worthwhile. You could make mistakes, as long as you learned from them. And you could be independent, and yet still remain close to those you loved.

I hope you have to the Girl with the Emerald Flag and

Kathleen McGurl

A Letter from Kathleen McGurl

Thank you so much for choosing to read *The Girl with the Emerald Flag*. I hope you enjoyed it! If you did and would like to be the first to know about my new releases, sign up to my mailing list: http://signup.harpercollins.co.uk/join/6n7/signup-hq-kathleenmcgurl.

This book required a lot of research, and it was difficult to get the balance right in the historical strand between the real-life events and the emotional story arcs of the fictional characters. I'm married to an Irishman and we have dozens of books on Irish history, plus biographies of prominent Irish people, on our bookshelves. I spent a long time reading them all before embarking on this novel.

For the first time in my novels, the 'contemporary' strand isn't actually contemporary because I wanted my historical fiction character to still be alive. 1998, the year the Good Friday Agreement was signed, seemed the obvious date to use. I set this part of the book in Brighton and Sussex university, because that's where I was a student (in the 1980s) and I have happy memories of that time.

I wrote a lot of this novel while touring Spain in our motorhome, trying to channel the joys of Irish weather while sitting in the Spanish winter sun. An author needs a good imagination!

I hope you loved *The Girl with the Emerald Flag* and if you did, I would be so grateful if you would leave a review. I always love to hear what readers thought, and it helps new readers discover my books too.

Thanks,

Kathleen McGurl

https://kathleenmcgurl.com
https://twitter.com/KathMcGurl
https://www.facebook.com/KathleenMcGurl

The Girl from Bletchley Park

Will love lead her to a devastating choice?

1942. Three years into the war, Pam turns down her hard-won place at Oxford University to become a code-breaker at Bletchley Park. There, she meets two young men, both keen to impress her, and Pam finds herself falling hard for one of them. But as the country's future becomes more uncertain by the day, a tragic turn of events casts doubt on her choice – and Pam's loyalty is pushed to its limits . . .

Present day. Julia is struggling to juggle her career, two children and a husband increasingly jealous of her success. Her brother presents her with the perfect distraction: forgotten photos of their grandmother as a young woman at Bletchley Park. Why did her grandmother never speak of her time there? The search for answers leads Julia to an incredible tale of betrayal and bravery – one that inspires some huge decisions of her own . . .

Gripping historical fiction perfect for fans of *The Girl from Berlin*, *The Rose Code* and *When We Were Brave*.

The Forgotten Secret

Can she unlock the mysteries of the past?

A country at war

It's the summer of 1919 and Ellen O'Brien has her whole life ahead of her. Young, in love and leaving home for her first job, the future seems full of shining possibility. But war is brewing and before long, Ellen and everyone around her are swept up by it. As Ireland is torn apart by the turmoil, Ellen finds herself facing the ultimate test of love and loyalty.

A long-buried secret

A hundred years later and Clare Farrell has inherited a dilapidated old farmhouse in County Meath. Seizing the chance to escape her unhappy marriage she strikes out on her own for the first time, hoping the old building might also provide clues to her family's shadowy history. As she sets out to put the place – and herself – back to rights, she stumbles across a long-forgotten hiding place, with a clue to a secret that has lain buried for decades.

For fans of Kate Morton and Gill Paul comes an unforgettable novel about two women fighting for independence.

The Secret of the Château

Everything is about to change . . .

1789. Pierre and Catherine Aubert, the Comte and Comtesse de Verais, have fled the palace of Versailles for their château, deep in the French Alps. But as revolution spreads through the country, even hidden away the Auberts will not be safe for ever. Soon they must make a terrible decision in order to protect themselves, and their children, from harm.

Present day. When Lu's mother dies leaving her heart-broken, the chance to move to a château in the south of France with her husband and best friends seems an opportunity for a new beginning. But Lu can't resist digging into their new home's history, and when she stumbles across the unexplained disappearance of Catherine Aubert, the château begins to reveal its secrets – and a mystery unsolved for centuries is uncovered . . .

Unlock the secret of the château today. Perfect for fans of Kate Morton, Fiona Valpy and *The Forgotten Village*!

Author's Note

Gráinne, her family and Emmett are fictional but all other characters in the historical story are real people. I have used a novelist's licence to put Gráinne right in the middle of the action during the rebellion, but all events in the novel associated with the Easter Rising are as true to history as I could make them.

Some of the dialogue of major figures during the Rising is taken from articles and pamphlets they wrote at the time. To avoid having too many characters I have not mentioned all the leaders of the Rising – there are more than I can do justice to. As well as Pádraig Pearse, James Connolly and Joseph Plunkett, the Declaration of the Republic was signed by Thomas Clarke, Thomas MacDonagh, Seán MacDiarmada and Éamonn Ceannt, all of whom were executed in May 1916.

I was inspired to write about the wedding of Grace Gifford and Joseph Plunkett after hearing the song *Grace* written by Frank and Seán O'Meara in 1985. Many artists have covered this but my favourite version is sung by Jim McCann. Search it out on YouTube, but make sure you have some tissues handy.

Grace continued the fight for Irish independence, but never remarried. She died in 1955 and was buried in Glasnevin Cemetery.

Acknowledgements

Firstly, thank you so much to my editor, Abigail Fenton, for her brilliant insights into what needed to be done to turn my first attempt at this novel into something readable. It wasn't an easy book to write and I imagine it wasn't an easy one to edit either, but between us I think we got there!

Secondly, thanks as always to my husband, Ignatius. Being Irish and Republican, he was, of course, the perfect person to read an early draft of this novel and provide feedback. Not only that, but during the more than thirty years I've been with him, he's provided me with the education into Irish history that was so sorely lacking from my schooldays in England. I remember very clearly my first trip to Dublin when he took me to see the GPO in O'Connell Street. I couldn't understand why I was visiting a post office – I had no idea of the significance of that building to Irish history. Thanks also to all the other McGurls who've helped me understand the tricky relationship between Ireland and Britain, from the other side of the fence.

My son Fionn also provided feedback on an early version ('too much history, Mum!') and my son Connor was on hand to help me thrash out plot and character development.

319

He's now a writer himself so he gets what it takes. Thank you to both my fantastic sons.

Finally, thank you to all at HQ – cover designers, copy-editors and proofreaders, marketing department – you all do a fantastic job and I am proud to be part of the HQ family.

Dear Reader,

We hope you enjoyed reading this book. If you did, we'd be so appreciative if you left a review. It really helps us and the author to bring more books like this to you.

Here at HQ Digital we are dedicated to publishing fiction that will keep you turning the pages into the early hours. Don't want to miss a thing? To find out more about our books, promotions, discover exclusive content and enter competitions, you can keep in touch in the following ways:

JOIN OUR COMMUNITY:

Sign up to our new email newsletter:
http://smarturl.it/SignUpHQ

Read our new blog www.hqstories.co.uk

🐦 : https://twitter.com/HQStories

📘 : www.facebook.com/HQStories

BUDDING WRITER?

We're also looking for authors to join the HQ Digital family! Find out more here:

https://www.hqstories.co.uk/want-to-write-for-us/

Thanks for reading, from the HQ Digital team